AF172636

The Two Dianas
Vol. I

by

Alexandre Dumas

ABOUT THE AUTHOR

French author and playwright Alexandre Dumas is best known for his romantic novel La Dame aux Camélias (The Lady of the Camellias), published in 1848. Giuseppe Verdi adapted it into his opera La traviata (The Fallen Woman), which debuted in 1853. Other notable works by Dumas include a number of stage and film adaptations, which are usually titled Camille in English-language adaptations. The playwright Alexandre Dumas père ("father"), the author of classic works including The Three Musketeers and The Count of Monte Cristo, was the father of Dumas. Dumas received the Légion d'honneur (Legion of Honour) in 1894 after being accepted into the Académie française (French Academy) in 1874. The illegitimate child of tailor Marie-Laure-Catherine Labay (1794–1868) and novelist Alexandre Dumas, Dumas was born in Paris, France. His father gave him official recognition in 1831 and made sure the young Dumas attended the Collège Bourbon and the Institution Goubaux for the greatest education available. The elder Dumas was then permitted by law to remove the child from his mother. The younger Dumas was driven to write about sad female characters by her anguish.

CONTENTS

INTRODUCTORY NOTE

The claim of Alexandre Dumas to be considered first among historical romancists, past or present, can hardly be disputed; and his magic pen finds abundant, rich material for the historical setting of the tale told in the following pages. The period in which the action of "The Two Dianas" is supposed to take place, covers the later years of Henri II. and the brief and melancholy reign of his oldest son, François II., the ill-fated husband of Mary Stuart, whose later history has caused her brief occupancy of the throne of France to be lost sight of. This period saw the germination and early maturity, if not the actual sowing, of the spirit of the Reformation in France. It was during these years that the name of John Calvin acquired the celebrity which has never waned, and that his devoted followers, La Renaudie, Théodore de Bèze, Ambroise Paré, the famous surgeon, and the immortal Coligny began the crusade for freedom of worship which was steadily maintained, unchecked by Tumult of Amboise, or Massacre of St. Bartholomew, until Henri of Navarre put the crown upon their heroic labors, and gave them respite for a time with the famous "Edict of Nantes," made more famous still by its "Revocation" a century later under the auspices of Madame de Maintenon, at the instigation of her Jesuit allies. Those portions of the story which introduce us to the councils of the Reformers are none the less interesting because the characters introduced are actual historical personages, nor can it fail to add interest to the encounter between La Renaudie and Pardaillan to know that it really took place, and that the two men had previously been to each other almost nearer than brothers. It was but one of innumerable heart-rending incidents, inseparable from all civil and religious conflicts, but in which those presided over by the Florentine mother of three Valois kings of France were prolific beyond belief.

How closely the author has adhered to historical fact for the groundwork of his tale, will appear by comparing it with one of Balzac's Études Philosophiques, entitled "Sur Catherine de Médicis," the first part of which covers the same period as "The Two Dianas," and describes many of the same events; the variations are of the slightest.

The patient forbearance of Catherine de Médicis, under the neglect of her husband, and the arrogant presumption of Diane de Poitiers, abetted by the Constable de Montmorency; her swift and speedy vengeance upon them as soon as she was left a widow with her large brood of possible kings; her jealous fear of the influence of the Duc de Guise and his brother the Cardinal de Lorraine, which led her to desire the death of her eldest son, the unfortunate François, because his queen was the niece of the powerful and ambitious brothers, and which also led her to oppose their influence by a combination with two such incongruous elements as the Constable Montmorency and the Protestant Bourbon princes of Navarre, remaining all the while the bitterest foe that the reformed religion ever had,—all these, as described in the following pages, are strictly in conformity with historical fact So, too, is the story of the defence of St. Quentin in its main details, and of the siege of Calais, where the Duc de Guise did receive the terrible wound which caused the sobriquet of *Le Balafré* to be applied to him, and was cured by the skilful hand of Master Ambroise Paré. So of the Tumult of Amboise, and the painful scenes attending the execution of the victims; and so, finally, of the scene at the death-bed of François II., the controversy between the shrinking conservatism of the King's regular medical advisers, and the daring eclecticism of Paré, proposing to perform the "new operation" of trepanning. It may, perhaps, be said that the Chancellor de l'Hôpital is made to appear in too unfavorable a light; he certainly was something far above the mere bond-slave of Catherine de Médicis.

Dumas himself tells us what basis of truth there is for the sometimes amusing, sometimes serious, but always intensely interesting confusion between Martin-Guerre and his unscrupulous double.

Nowhere, it may be said, in history or romance, is there to be found so touching a glimpse as this of poor Mary Stuart. Here we see naught save the lovely and lovable side of the unfortunate queen, without a hint of the fatal weakness which, as it developed in the stormy later years of her life, made her marvellous beauty and charm the instruments of her ruin.

So much for those portions of "The Two Dianas" which rest upon a basis of fact. History records further that Henri II. was accidentally killed in friendly jousting by the Comte de Montgommery; but with that history ends and romance begins. The personage whom Monsieur Dumas presents to us under that title perhaps never existed; but let the reader be the judge, after reading of the pure and sacred but unhappy love of Gabriel de Montgommery and Diane de Castro, if a lovelier gem of fiction was ever enclosed in an historical setting.

CHAPTER I
A COUNT'S SON AND A KING'S DAUGHTER

It was the 5th of May, 1551. A young man of eighteen years, and a woman of forty, together leaving a house of unpretentious appearance, walked side by side through the main street of the village of Montgommery, in the province of Auge.

The young man was of the fine Norman type, with chestnut hair, blue eyes, white teeth, and red lips. He had the fresh, velvety complexion common to men of the North, which sometimes takes away a little manly strength from their beauty, by making it almost feminine in its quality; but his figure was superb, both in its proportions and its suppleness, partaking at once of the character of the oak and the reed. He was simply but handsomely dressed, in a doublet of rich purple cloth, with light silk embroidery of the same color. His breeches were of similar cloth, and trimmed in the same way as the doublet; long black leather boots, such as pages and varlets wore, extended above his knees; and a velvet cap, worn slightly on one side and adorned with a white plume, covered a brow on which could be read indications of a tranquil and steadfast mind.

His horse, whose rein was passed through his arm, followed him, raising his head from time to time, snorting and neighing with pleasure in the fresh air that was blowing.

The woman seemed to belong, if not to the lower orders of society, at least to a class somewhere between them and the bourgeoisie. Her dress was simple, but of such exquisite neatness that very quality seemed to give it elegance. More than once the young man offered her the support of his arm, but she persistently declined it, as if it would have been an honor above her condition.

As they walked through the village, and drew near the end of the street that led to the château, whose ponderous towers were in full sight, overlooking the humble settlement, it was very noticeable that not only the young people and the men, but even the gray heads bowed low as the young man passed, while he responded with a friendly nod of the head.

Each one seemed to recognize a superior and a master in this youth, who, as we shall soon see, did not know his own identity.

Leaving the village behind them, they followed the road, or rather the path, which, in its winding course up the slope of the mountain, was barely wide enough for two people to walk abreast. So, after some objections, and upon the young man's remarking to his companion that as he was obliged to lead his horse it would be dangerous for her to walk behind, the good woman was induced to go in advance.

The young man followed her without a word. One could see that his thoughtful brow was wrinkled beneath the weight of some engrossing preoccupation.

A fine and lordly château it was toward which our two pilgrims, so different in age and station, were thus wending their way. Four centuries and ten generations had hardly sufficed for that mass of rock to grow from foundation to battlements; and there it stood, itself a mountain towering above the mountain on which it was built.

Like all the structures of that age, the château of the counts of Montgommery was absolutely irregular in its formation. Fathers had bequeathed it to their sons, and each temporary proprietor had added to this stone colossus according to his fancy or his need. The square donjon, the principal fortification, had been built under the dukes of Normandy. Then the fanciful turrets on the battlements and the ornamented windows had been added to the frowning donjon, multiplying the chased and sculptured stonework as time went on, as if the years had been fruitful in this granite vegetation. At last, toward the end of the reign of Louis XII., and in the early days of François I., a long gallery with pointed windows had put the last touch to this secular agglomeration.

From this gallery, and still better from the summit of the donjon, could be had an extended view over several leagues of the rich, blooming plains of Normandy. For, as we have already said, the county of Montgommery was situated in the province of Auge, and its eight or ten baronies and its hundred and fifty fiefs were dependencies of the bailiwicks of Argentan, Caen, and Alençon.

At last they reached the great portal of the château.

Think of it! For more than fifteen years this magnificent and formidable donjon had been without a master. An old intendant still continued to collect the rents; and there were some of the servants, too, who had grown old in that solitude, and who continued to look after the château, whose doors they threw open every day, as if the master was to be expected at any moment, while they closed them again at evening, as if his coming were simply postponed till the next day.

The intendant received the two visitors with the same appearance of friendliness that every one seemed to show to the woman, and the same deference which all agreed in according to the young man.

"Master Elyot," said the woman, who was in advance, as we have seen, "do you mind letting us go into the château? I have something to say to Monsieur Gabriel" (pointing to the young man), "and I can only say it in the *salon d'honneur.*"

"Come in, Dame Aloyse," said Elyot, "and say what you have to say to young master here, wherever you choose. You know very well that unhappily there is no one here to interrupt you."

They passed through the *salle des gardes*. Formerly twelve men, raised upon the estates, used to be on guard without intermission in that apartment. During fifteen years seven of these men had died, and their places had not been filled. Five of them were left; and they still lived there, doing the same duty as in the count's time, and waiting till their turn to die should come.

They passed through the gallery and entered the *salon d'honneur.*

It was furnished just as it had been the day that the last count had left it. But this salon, where in former days all the Norman nobility had used to assemble, as in the salon of a lord paramount, not a soul had entered for fifteen years, save the servants whose duty it was to keep it in order, and a faithful dog, the last count's pet, who every time that he entered the room called for his master mournfully, and at last had refused to go out one day, and had stretched himself out at the foot of the dais, where they found him the next morning, dead.

It was not without emotion that Gabriel (such was the name that had been given to the young man by his companion) entered this salon, with its memories of other days. However, the impression made upon him by these gloomy walls, the majestic dais, and the windows cut so deep into the wall that although it was only ten in the morning, the daylight seemed to have stopped at the threshold,—the impression, we repeat, was not strong enough to divert his mind for a single moment from the purpose which had drawn him thither; and as soon as the door was closed behind him, he turned to his companion.

"Come, dear Aloyse, my good nurse," said he, "really, although you seem more moved than I, you have no longer the least excuse for refusing to tell me what you have promised. Now, Aloyse, you must speak without fear, and, above all, without delay. Haven't you hesitated long enough, my dear, kind nurse; and have I not, like an obedient son, waited long enough h When I asked you what name I had the right to bear, and to what family I belonged, and who my father was, you replied, 'Gabriel, I will tell you the whole story on the day that you are eighteen,—the age at which he who has the right to wear a sword attains his majority.' Now, to-day, this 5th of May, 1551, I have lived eighteen full years; so I called upon you this morning to keep your promise, but you replied with a solemn visage which almost terrified me, 'It is not here in the humble dwelling of a poor squire's widow that I should make you known to yourself, but in the château of the counts of Montgommery, and in the *salon d'honneur* in that château.' Now we have come up the mountain, good Aloyse, have crossed the threshold of the noble counts, and here we are in the *salon d'honneur*; so, speak!"

"Sit down, Gabriel, for you will allow me to call you by that name once more."

The young man took her hands with a most affectionate movement.

"Sit down," she repeated, "not on that chair, nor on that sofa."

"But where do you want me to sit, then, dear nurse?" interrupted the young man.

"Under this dais," said Aloyse, with an accent of deep solemnity.

The young man complied.

Aloyse nodded her head.

"Now, listen to me," said she.

"But do you be seated too," said Gabriel

"Will you permit me?"

"Are you laughing at me, nurse?"

The good woman took her place on the steps of the dais, at the feet of the young man, who was all attention, and devoured her with a gaze full of kindliness and curiosity.

"Gabriel," said the nurse, when she had at last made up her mind to speak, "you were scarcely six years old when you lost your father and I lost my husband. You had been my foster-child, for your mother died in giving birth to you. From that day, I, your mother's foster-sister, loved you as if you were my own child. The widow devoted her life to the orphan. As she had given you her breast, she gave you her heart too; and you will do me this justice, will you not, Gabriel, that in your belief, my thoughts, when you have been away from me, have never failed to be with you and watching over you?"

"Dear Aloyse," said the young man, "many real mothers would have done less than you have. I swear it; and not one, I swear again, could have done more."

"Every one, in fact, was as eager to serve you as I, who had been the first to show my zeal." continued the nurse. "Dom Jamet de Croisic, the worthy chaplain of this very château, and whom the Lord called to himself three months since, instructed you very carefully in letters and science, and according to what he said, you had nothing to learn from any one in the matter of reading and writing and knowledge of history, especially of the great families of France. Enguerrand Lorien, the intimate friend of my dead-and-gone husband, Perrot Travigny, and the old squire of our neighbors, the counts of Vimoutiers, taught you the science of arms, the management of the lance and sword, horsemanship, and in fact all the knightly accomplishments; and then the fêtes and tournaments which were held at Alençon at the time of the marriage and coronation of our Lord King Henri II., gave you an opportunity to prove, two years since, that you have taken advantage of Enguerrand's instructions. I, poor know nothing, could only love you and teach you to worship God. That is all that I have tried to do. The Holy Virgin has been my guide, and here you are to-day, at eighteen, a pious Christian man, a learned gentleman, and an accomplished knight; and I hope that with God's help, you will not fail to show yourself worthy of your ancestors, MONSIEUR GABRIEL, SEIGNEUR DE LORGES, COMTE DE MONTGOMMERY."

Gabriel involuntarily rose to his feet, as he cried, —

"Comte de Montgommery! I!" Then he went on, with a proud smile on his lips, —

"Oh, well, I hoped so, and I almost suspected it; in fact, Aloyse, in the days of my boyish dreams I said as much to my little Diane. But what are you doing to my feet, Aloyse, pray? Rise, and come to my arms, thou saintly creature! Don't you choose to acknowledge me as your child any more now that I am heir of the Montgommerys? Heir of the Montgommerys!" he repeated, as if in spite of himself, trembling with pride as he embraced the good old soul. "Heir of the Montgommerys! And I bear one of the oldest and most honorable names of France! Yes; Dom Jamet has taught me the history of my ancestors, reign by reign, and generation by generation. Of my ancestors! Embrace me again, Aloyse! I wonder what Diane will say to all this. Saint Godegrand, Bishop of Chartres, and Sainte Opportune, his sister, who lived in Charlemagne's day, were of our family. Roger de Montgommery commanded an army under William the Conqueror. Guillaume de Montgommery made a crusade at his own expense. We have been allied more than once to the royal families of Scotland and France; and the noblest lords of London and the most illustrious noblemen of Paris will call me cousin. My father, too—"

The young man stopped short, as if he had been struck; but he soon continued:—

"But, alas! for all this, Aloyse, I am alone in the world. This great lord is nothing but a poor orphan, and the descendant of so many royal ancestors has no father. My poor father! I can only weep just now, Aloyse. And my mother, too,—both dead! Oh, do tell me of them, so that I may know what they were like now that I know that I am their son! Come, begin with my father. How did he die? Tell me all about it."

Aloyse remained dumb. Gabriel looked at her in amazement.

"I ask you to tell me, nurse," he said again, "how my father died."

"Monseigneur, God alone can tell you!" said she. "One day Jacques de Montgommery left the hotel where he was then living, in the Rue des Jardins St. Paul in Paris. He never came back to it. His friends and his cousins sought for him, but to no purpose. He had disappeared, Monseigneur! King François I. ordered an inquiry, which came to nothing. His enemies, if he fell a victim to treachery, were either very cunning or very powerful. You have no father, Monseigneur; and yet the tomb of Jacques de Montgommery is missing in the chapel of your château, for he has never been found, living or dead!"

"That is because it was not his son who sought him!" cried Gabriel. "Ah, nurse, why have you kept quiet so long? Did you hide the secret of my birth from me because it would have been my duty either to save my father or to avenge him?"

"No; but because it was my duty to save yourself, Monseigneur. Listen! Do you know what the last words were that were uttered by my husband, brave Perrot Travigny, who had a religious devotion to your family? 'Wife,' said he, a few minutes before he breathed his last, 'don't even wait till I am buried; just close my eyes, and then leave Paris with the child as fast as ever you can. You will go to Montgommery; not to the château, but to the house which belongs to us, thanks to Monseigneur's bounty!

"'There do you bring up the descendant of our masters with no affectation of mystery, but without display. The good people of our country will respect him, and will not betray him. But, above all things, hide his origin from himself, or he will show himself and be his own destruction.

Let him know only that he is of gentle birth, and that will be enough to satisfy his dignity and your own conscience. Then, when years shall have brought him discretion and gravity, as his blood will make him brave and true,—when he is about eighteen, for instance,—tell him his name and his descent, Aloyse. Then he can judge for himself of his duty and his ability. But until then be very careful; for formidable enmities and invincible hatred will be on his track if he should be discovered, and those who have stricken and brought down the eagle will not spare the eaglet.' He said those words and died, Monseigneur; and I, in obedience to his commands, took you, poor orphan of six years, who had hardly seen your father, and I brought you with me to this village. The count's disappearance was already known here; and it was suspected that implacable foes were threatening any one who bore his name. You were seen and acknowledged without hesitation in the village, but by tacit agreement not a soul asked me a question or expressed any surprise at my silence. A short time after, my only son, your foster-brother, my poor Robert, was carried off by a fever. God seemed to will that I should have no excuse for not devoting myself entirely to you. May God's will be done! Everybody made a pretence of believing that it was my son that lived, and yet they all treated you with the deepest respect and a touching obedience. That was because you already strikingly resembled your father, both in face and in heart. The lion-like instinct showed itself in you: and it was easy to see that you were born to be a master and a leader of men. The children of the neighborhood soon got into the habit of forming themselves into a little company under your command. In all their games you marched at their head, and not one of them would have dared to refuse you his respect. You became a young king of the province; and it was the province which brought you up, and which has looked on in admiration to see you daily growing in pride and beauty. The quit-rent of the finest fruits, and the tithe of the harvest, were brought regularly to the house without my having to ask for anything. The finest horse in the pastures was always kept for you. Dom Jamet, Enguerrand, and all the varlets and retainers at the château offered you their services as naturally due to you; and you accepted them as your right. There was nothing about you that was not gallant and brave and large-hearted. In your slightest actions you showed to what race you belonged. They still tell by the village firesides in the evening how you once traded off my two cows for a falcon with one of the pages. But all these instincts and impulses only betrayed you to those who were to be trusted, and you remained hidden and unknown to the evil-disposed. The great excitement aroused by the wars in Italy, Spain, and Flanders against the Emperor Charles V. helped not a little, thank God! to protect you; and you have at last arrived safe and sound at that age when Perrot told me that I might trust to your good sense and your discretion. But you, who are ordinarily so sober and so cautious, behold! your first words are all for a rash outburst, vengeance, and exposure."

"Vengeance, yes; but exposure, no! Do you suppose, Aloyse, that my father's enemies are still living?"

"I don't know, Monseigneur; but it would be much safer to assume that some of them are. And suppose that you make your appearance at court, still unknown, but with your well-known name, which will attract universal attention to you,—brave but without experience, strong in your worthy ambition and in the justice of your case, but without friends or allies, or even any personal repute,—and what, pray, will happen then? Those who hate you will see you come, while you will not see them; they will attack you, and you will not know where the blow comes from, and not only will your father not be revenged, but you yourself, Monseigneur, will be destroyed."

"And that, Aloyse, is just the reason why I am so sorry that I have had no time to make friends for myself and win a little bit of renown. Ah, if I had been warned two years since, for instance! But never mind! It is only a little delay, and I will soon make up for lost time. And indeed for other reasons I am very glad that I have been at Montgommery these last two years; but I must be off so much the quicker now. I will go to Paris, Aloyse; and without concealing the fact that I am a Montgommery, I need not say that I am the son of Comte Jacques. Fiefs and titles are no less plentiful in our family than in the royal house of France, and our branches are sufficiently numerous in England and France for an unimportant scion to fail of recognition. I can take the name of Comte d'Exmès, Aloyse, and that will neither conceal nor reveal my identity. Then I shall find—whom shall I find at court? Thanks to Enguerrand, I am equally conversant with men and affairs. Shall I pay my addresses to the Constable de Montmorency, the hard-hearted mumbler of pater-nosters? No; and I quite agree with the face you made, Aloyse. To the Maréchal de Saint-André, then? He is neither young nor enterprising enough. Would not François de Guise be preferable? Yes; he is the man for me. Montmédy, St. Dizier, and Bologne have already shown what stuff he is made of. It is to him that I will go; and under his banners I will win my spurs. In the shadow of his name I will conquer a name for myself."

"Will Monseigneur allow me to remind him that the honest and faithful Elyot has had time to put by a handsome sum for the heir of his former masters. You may maintain a royal establishment, Monseigneur; and the young men, who are your tenants, and whom you have drilled in playing at war, are in duty bound and will be only too glad to follow you to battle in good earnest. It is your right to call them about you, as you well know, Monseigneur."

"And we will use this right, never fear, Aloyse; we will use it."

"Is Monseigneur really willing to receive all his domestics and retainers, and the tenants of all his fiefs and baronies, who are consumed with the desire to pay their respects to him?"

"Not yet, please, good Aloyse; but tell Martin-Guerre to saddle a horse and be ready to go with me. I must, first of all, take a ride about the neighborhood."

"Are you going in the direction of Vimoutiers?" said good Aloyse, smiling mischievously.

"Perhaps so. Don't I owe old Enguerrand a visit and my thanks?"

"And with Enguerrand's congratulations, Monseigneur will not find it at all amiss to receive those of a certain fair damsel called Diane. Am I not right?"

"But," said Gabriel, laughing, "that same fair damsel has been my wife and I her husband these three years; since I was fifteen, that is to say, and she nine."

Aloyse lost herself in thought.

"Monseigneur," said she, "if I did not know how sober-minded and open you are, notwithstanding your extreme youth, and that your every emotion is a serious and profound one, I should keep back the words which I am going to venture to say to you. But what is a joking matter to others is often a matter of serious importance to you. Remember, Monseigneur, that no one knows whose daughter Diane is. One day, the wife of Enguerrand, who had gone to Fontainebleau at that time, with his master, Comte de Vimoutiers, found, as she was going into her house, a child in a cradle at her door, and a heavy purse of gold on her table. In the purse was a considerable sum of money, half of an engraved ring, and a paper on which was this one word, 'Diane.' Berthe, Enguerrand's wife, had no child of her own, and she welcomed joyfully these other maternal duties which were asked at her hands. But on her return to Vimoutiers she died, just as my husband died, to whom your father intrusted you, Monseigneur; and as it was a woman who brought up the male orphan, so it was a man to whose care the female child fell. But Enguerrand and I, both intrusted with a like task, have exchanged our duties? and I have tried to make of Diane a good, pious woman, while Enguerrand has brought you up to be clever and wise. Naturally you have known Diane, and naturally, too, you have become attached to her. But you are the Comte de Montgommery, as can be proved by authentic documents and by public repute, while no one has yet appeared to lay claim to Diane, by producing the other half of the golden ring. Take care, Monseigneur!

I know well that Diane is now a mere child of scarcely twelve years, but she will grow, and will be exceedingly beautiful; and with such a nature as yours, I say again, everything is apt to be serious. Take care! It may be that she will always remain what she is now, — a foundling; and you are too great a nobleman to marry her, and too true a gentleman to lead her astray."

"But, nurse, when I am going away, to leave you, and to leave Diane—" said Gabriel, thoughtfully.

"That is all right, then. Forgive your old Aloyse for her uneasy foreboding; and if you choose, go and see that sweet and lovely child whom you call your little wife. But don't forget that you are being impatiently awaited here. You will soon be back, will you not, Monsieur le Comte?"

"Very soon; and kiss me again, Aloyse. Call me your child always, and accept my thanks a thousand times, dear old nurse."

"A thousand blessings on thee, my child and my lord!"

Master Martin-Guerre was waiting for Gabriel at the gate, and they both mounted, and left the château.

CHAPTER II
A BRIDE WHO PLAYS WITH DOLLS

Gabriel took a by-path well-known to him, so as to go more quickly; and yet he let his horse slacken his pace, so that it seemed almost as if he were allowing the handsome beast to adapt his gait to his own train of thought. Emotions of very different sorts succeeded one another in the young man's mind, by turns passionate and gloomy, haughty and subdued. When he remembered that he was the Comte de Montgommery, his eyes sparkled, and he drove his spurs into his horse as if drunken with the breeze which fanned his temples; and then he would say to himself, "My father has been murdered, and his death is not avenged!" and his rein would drop listlessly from his hand. But all at once he would reflect that he was going into the world to fight, to make a name for himself, formidable and dreaded, and to pay all his debts of honor and of blood; and he would start off at a mad gallop as if he were really on his way to fame at that moment, until the thought came to him that he would be obliged to leave his little Diane, so blithe and pretty, when he would relapse into gloom again, and would gradually slacken his pace to a walk; as if he could thus delay the cruel moment of separation. "But," thought he, "I will come back again, after I have found my father's enemies and Diane's relatives;" and Gabriel, spurring his steed on fiercely once more, flew as swiftly as his own hopes. His destination was at hand; and surely in that young heart thirsting for happiness, joy had driven away gloom.

Looking over the hedge which enclosed old Enguerrand's orchard, Gabriel spied Diane's white dress among the trees. To tie his horse to a willow-tree and leap the hedge at a bound was the work of but a moment; glowing with pride and triumph, he fell at the young girl's feet.

But Diane was weeping.

"What is it, my dear little wife," said Gabriel; "and whence this bitter sorrow? Has Enguerrand been scolding us because of a torn dress, or because we made a slip in saying our prayers; or has our pet bullfinch flown away? Tell me, Diane dear. See, your faithful knight has come to comfort you."

"Alas! Gabriel, you cannot be my knight any more," said Diane; "and that is just why I am sad and am crying."

Gabriel supposed that Diane had learned from Enguerrand her playfellow's name, and that perhaps she wished to test him. He replied, —

"What has happened, pray, Diane, lucky or unlucky, that can ever make me give up the dear title which you have allowed me to assume, and which I am so proud and happy to bear? See, here I am at your knees."

But Diane did not seem to understand; and she wept more bitterly than before, as she hid her face on Gabriel's breast, and sobbed, —

"Oh, Gabriel, Gabriel! We must not see each other any more."

"And who is to prevent us?" he rejoined quickly.

She raised her lovely fair head and her eyes swimming with tears; then with a little pout, altogether sober and solemn, she replied, sighing profoundly, —

"Duty."

Her sweet face assumed an expression that was so despairing and so comical at the same time that Gabriel, fascinated, and entering, as he supposed, fully into her thoughts, could not forbear a laugh; and taking the child's fair face in his hands, he kissed it over and over again; but she nervously drew away from him.

"No, my friend," said she, "no more of these little chats of ours. *Mon Dieu! mon Dieu!* they are forbidden us now."

"What stories has Enguerrand been telling her?" said Gabriel to himself, persisting in his error; and he added aloud, "Don't you love me any longer, then, dear Diane?"

"I! not love you any longer!" cried Diane. "How can you think and say such things, Gabriel? Are you not the friend of my childhood, and my brother for my whole life? Have you not always been as kind and loving as a mother to me? When I laughed, and when I wept, whom was I sure to find at my side, to share my joy or my sorrow? You, Gabriel! Who carried me when I was tired? Who helped me to learn my lessons? Who took the blame for my mistakes, and insisted on sharing my punishment when he couldn't succeed in having it all himself? You again! Who invented a thousand games for me? Who made sweet nosegays for me in the meadows? Who hunted out goldfinches' nests for me in the woods? You, always you! I have found you always, in every place and at all times, so kind and generous and devoted to me, Gabriel. I shall never forget you, Gabriel; and while my heart lives, you will live in my heart. I should have liked to give you my life and my soul, and I have never dreamed of happiness except when I have dreamed of you. But all this, alas! doesn't keep us from being obliged to part, never to see each other again, no doubt."

"And why not? Is it to punish you for mischievously letting your dog Phylax into the poultry-yard?" asked Gabriel.

"Ah, no, for something very different, believe me!"

"Well, what is it, then?"

She rose, and as she stood with her arms hanging by her side, and her head cast down, she said, —

"Because I am somebody else's wife."

Gabriel did not joke any more, and a vague dread pierced his heart; he replied with a trembling voice, —

"What do you mean by that, Diane?"

"I am no longer Diane," was the reply, "but Madame la Duchesse de Castro, since my husband's name is Horace Farnèse, Duc de Castro."

And the child could not help smiling a little through her tears as she said it. "My husband" indeed, and she a child of twelve! Oh, it was magnificent: "Madame la Duchesse!" But she speedily became sad again when she saw Gabriel's suffering.

The young man was standing before her, pale, and with a frightened look in his eyes.

"Is this a joke? Is it a dream?" said he.

"No, my poor friend, it is a sad truth," replied Diane. "Didn't you meet Enguerrand on the way? He started for Montgommery half an hour since."

"I came by the short cut. But go on and finish your story."

"Why is it, Gabriel, that you have been four days without coming here? Such a thing never happened before, and it made us unhappy, don't you see? Night before last I had very hard work to go to sleep. I hadn't seen you for two days, and was very uneasy, and I made Enguerrand promise that if you didn't come the next day we should go to Montgommery the day after that. And then, as if we had had a presentiment, Enguerrand and I fell to talking of the future, and then of the past, and of my relatives, who seemed, alas! to have forgotten me. It is a wretched tale that I have to tell you, and I should have been happier perhaps if they had really forgotten me. All this serious talk had naturally made me a little sad, and had wearied me; and I was, as

I said, a long while going to sleep, and that is why I awoke rather later than usual yesterday morning. I dressed myself in a great hurry, told my beads, and was just ready to go downstairs when I heard a great commotion under my window before the house door. There were magnificent cavaliers there, Gabriel, attended by squires, pages, and varlets, and behind the cavalcade was a gilded carriage, quite dazzling in its splendor. As I was looking curiously at this retinue, and marvelling that it should have stopped at our modest dwelling, Antoine came and knocked at my door, and gave me a message from Enguerrand that I should come down at once. I don't know why I was afraid to go, but I had to obey, and I obeyed. When I went into the great hall, it was filled with these superb seigneurs whom I had seen from my window. I then fell to blushing and trembling, more alarmed than ever; you can understand that, Gabriel, can't you?"

"Yes," said Gabriel, bitterly. "But go on, for the thing is becoming decidedly interesting."

"As I entered," continued Diane, "one of the most elaborately dressed of the gentlemen came to me, and offering me his gloved hand, led me up to another gentleman no less richly adorned than he, to whom he said, bowing low,—

"'Monseigneur le Duc de Castro, I have the honor to present to you your wife. 'Madame,' he added, turning to me, 'Monsieur Horace Farnèse, Duc de Castro, your husband.'

"The duke saluted me with a smile. But I, in my confusion and grief, threw myself into Enguerrand's arms, as I spied him standing in a corner.

"'Enguerrand! Enguerrand! this is not my husband, this prince; I have no husband but Gabriel. Enguerrand, tell these gentlemen so, I beg you.'

"The one who had presented me to the duke knitted his brows.

"'What is all this fol-de-rol?' he said to Enguerrand sternly.

"'Nothing, Monseigneur; mere childishness,' said Enguerrand, pale as a ghost. And he said to me in an undertone, 'Are you mad, Diane? What do you mean by being so rebellious?—refusing thus to obey your relatives, who have found you out, and come to claim you!'

"'Where are these relatives of mine?' said I, aloud. 'It is to them that I must speak.'

"'We come in their name, Mademoiselle,' replied the frowning gentleman. 'I am their representative. If you don't believe what I say, here is the order signed by Henri II., our Lord the King; read it.'

"He handed me a parchment sealed with a red seal, and I read at the top of the page, 'We, Henri, by the grace of God;' and at the foot the royal signature, 'Henri.' I was blinded and stunned and overwhelmed. I was dizzy and delirious. All that crowd of people with their eyes on me! And even Enguerrand abandoning me! The thought of my relatives! The name of the king! All this was too much for my poor little head. And you were not there, Gabriel!"

"But it seems as if my presence could have been of no use to you," was Gabriel's reply.

"Oh, yes, Gabriel, if you had been there, I would have continued to resist; while, as you were not there, when the gentleman who seemed to be managing the whole thing said to me, 'Come, there has been delay enough. Madame de Leviston, I leave Madame de Castro in your hands; we shall expect you presently in the chapel,' his tone was so sharp and imperious, and seemed to allow so little remonstrance, that I let myself be led away. Gabriel, forgive me; I was worn out and bewildered, and I hadn't an idea in my head."

"Go on! that is very easily understood," said Gabriel, with a bitter smile.

"They took me to my chamber," Diane resumed. "There, this Madame de Leviston, with the help of two or three women, took a fine dress of white silk from a great chest. Then, in spite of my shrinking, they undressed me and dressed me again. I scarcely dared to take a step in such fine clothes. Then they put pearls in my ears, and a string of pearls about my neck; my tears fell fast upon the pearls. But these ladies no doubt only laughed at my embarrassment, and at my grief too, perhaps. In half an hour I was ready, and they were so kind as to say that I was charming thus arrayed. I think it was true, Gabriel; but I cried away all the same. I at last convinced myself that I was going through a dazzling but dreadful dream. I stepped without any exertion of my own, and went back and forth like a machine. Meanwhile the horses were stamping at the door, and squires, pages, and varlets were standing in attendance. We descended the stairs. Again the gaze of the whole assemblage seemed to go right through me. The gentleman with the harsh voice offered me his hand again, and led me to a litter all of satin and gold, where I was to take my seat on cushions almost as beautiful as my dress. The Duc de Castro rode by the side of my litter, and so the procession slowly ascended to the chapel of the Château de Vimoutiers. The priest was already at the altar. I don't know what words were said over me or to me; but I felt suddenly, in the midst of this strange dream, that the duke placed a ring on my finger. Then, after twenty minutes or twenty years, I didn't know which, a fresher air seemed to be blowing on my face. We were leaving the chapel; they called me 'Madame la Duchesse.' I was married! Do you hear that, Gabriel? I was married!"

Gabriel replied only with a wild burst of laughter.

"Just think, Gabriel," continued Diane, "I was so entirely beside myself that it was not until just as I was going into the house again that it occurred to me for the first time, having recovered myself a little, to look at the husband whom all these strangers had come to force upon me. Until then I had not looked at him, Gabriel, although I had seen him. Oh, my poor dear Gabriel, he isn't half as handsome as you are! He is only moderately tall, and for all his fine clothes he looked much less distinguished than you in your plain brown doublet. And then he had an expression as impertinent and overbearing as yours is sweet and refined. Add to this hair and a long beard of a bright red. I have been sacrificed, Gabriel. After he had talked a while with the man who had passed himself off as the king's representative, the duke approached me and took my hand.

"'Madame la Duchesse,' said he, with a very cunning smile, 'I beg you will pardon the stern necessity which compels me to leave you so soon. But you may or may not know that we are in the midst of a war with Spain, and my men-at-arms demand my presence immediately. I hope to have the pleasure of seeing you again soon at court, where you will go to take up your abode near his Majesty the King, after this week. I trust you will deign to accept some trifling presents which I will leave here for you. *Au revoir*, Madame. Continue to be light-hearted and fascinating, as befits your age, and amuse yourself, and play with all your heart, while I am fighting.'

"With these words he kissed me familiarly on the forehead, and his long beard pricked me: it is not soft like yours, Gabriel. And then all these fine gentlemen and ladies saluted me, and away they went, Gabriel, one by one, leaving me at last alone with my father Enguerrand. He didn't understand this transaction much better than I. They had given him the parchment to read, wherein the king commanded me, so far as he could make it out, to marry the Duc de Castro. The gentleman who represented his Majesty was the Comte d'Humières; Enguerrand recognized him from having seen him formerly with Monsieur de Vimoutiers. All that Enguerrand knew more than I, was the melancholy fact that this Madame de Leviston, who had superintended my toilette, and who lives at Caen, would come one of these days to take me to court with her, and that I must be always ready. There is the whole of my strange and mournful story, Gabriel. Ah, no, I forgot. When I went back into my chamber I found a great box, and what do you suppose was in it? You could never guess. A superb doll, with a complete outfit of linen and three dresses,—white silk, red damask, and green brocade,—

all for the use of the doll. I was beside myself with rage, Gabriel, to think that these were my husband's presents! The idea of treating me like a little girl! The red dress is most becoming, to the doll, because her complexion is painted so naturally. The little shoes are lovely, too; but the whole affair is shameful, for it seems to me that I am no longer a child."

"Yes! you are a child, Diane," replied Gabriel, whose anger had insensibly changed to sadness; "nothing but a child! I have no grudge against you for being only twelve years old, for that would be unfair and absurd. But I see that I have done wrong to allow myself to feel so earnest and deep a sentiment for such a young and fickle creature; for my grief has taught me how dearly I loved you, Diane. I repeat that I wish you no ill, but if you had been stronger, and had mustered up sufficient force to resist such an unjust command, if you had only known how to obtain a little delay, Diane, we might have been very happy together, since you have found your relatives, and they seem to be of noble birth. I, too, Diane, have come to tell you a great secret which was not revealed to me till this very day. But what's the use now? It is too late. Your weakness has broken the thread of my destiny, which I thought I held in my hand at last. Can I ever fasten the ends together again? I foresee that my whole life will be filled with thoughts of you, Diane, and that my youthful love will always hold the first place in my heart. But you, Diane, in the lustre of the court, and in the continual whirl and excitement of parties and festival-making, will soon lose sight of him who has loved you so dearly in the time of your obscurity."

"Never!" cried Diane. "And see, Gabriel, now that you are on the spot, and can encourage and help me, do you want me to refuse to go when they come after me, and to say no to all their prayers and entreaties and commands, so that I may always stay with you?"

"Thank you, dear Diane, but don't you see that henceforth, in the sight of God and man, you belong to another? We must do our duty and abide our fate. We must, as the Duc de Castro said, go each to his place,—you to the dissipations of the court, and I to the battlefield. I only pray God that I may see you again some day!"

"Yes, Gabriel, I shall see you again, and I shall always love you!" cried poor Diane, throwing herself, sobbing, into her friend's arms.

But just at this moment Enguerrand appeared in a path close by, with Madame de Leviston at his heels.

"Here she is, Madame," said he, pointing to Diane. "Ah! is that you, Gabriel?" said he, as he saw the young count. "I was just on my way to Montgommery to see you when I met Madame de Leviston's carriage, and had to retrace my steps."

"Yes, Madame," said Madame de Leviston, addressing Diane, "the king has written to my husband that he is in haste to see you, and so I have anticipated the date of our departure. If you please, we will set out in an hour. Your preparations will not require much time, I fancy, will they?"

Diane looked at Gabriel.

"Courage!" said he, gravely.

"I am very happy to say," resumed Madame de Leviston, "that your good foster-father can and will go to Paris with us, and will overtake us to-morrow at Alençon, if agreeable to you."

"If it is agreeable to me!" cried Diane. "No one has yet named my relatives to me, but I shall always call Enguerrand Father."

And she held out her hand to Enguerrand, who covered it with kisses, so that she might have an opportunity to steal another glance undercover of her tears at Gabriel, who stood there thoughtful and sad, but none the less resigned and determined.

"Come, Madame," said Madame de Leviston, who was vexed a little perhaps by these leave-takings and delays, "remember that you must be at Caen before night."

Diane, almost suffocated with her sobs, rushed off without more ado to her chamber after signing to Gabriel to wait for her. Enguerrand and Madame de Leviston followed her, and Gabriel waited.

After an hour or so, during which the luggage that Diane was to carry with her was stowed away in the carriage, Diane appeared, all ready for the journey. She asked Madame de Leviston, who followed her about like a shadow, to allow her to take one last turn around the garden, where she had spent twelve years in careless, happy play. Gabriel and Enguerrand walked behind her while she made this visit to her old haunts. Diane stopped before a bush of white roses which Gabriel and she had planted the year before. She picked two roses, one of which she fastened in her dress, while she breathed a kiss upon the other and gave it to Gabriel. The young man felt that she slipped a paper in his hand at the same time, and he put it hastily into his doublet.

When Diane had said adieu to all the paths and all the groves and all the flowers, she had to make up her mind to take her departure. When she reached the carriage which was to take her away, she shook hands with each of the servants, and with the good folks from the village, who knew and loved her every one. She had not strength to say a word, poor child; she only gave each of them a kind nod of the head. Then she embraced Enguerrand,

and Gabriel last of all, with no signs of being embarrassed by Madame de Leviston's presence. In her friend's embrace she found her voice a moment, and when he said, "Adieu! adieu!" she replied, "No, *au revoir!*"

Then she entered the carriage that was waiting, and childhood, after all, seemed not quite to have lost its hold on her, for Gabriel heard her ask Madame de Leviston, with the little pout which became her so well, —

"Have they put my big doll up there somewhere?"

Away went the carriage at a gallop.

Gabriel opened the paper Diane had handed him; in it he found a lock of the fair yellow hair that he used to like so to kiss.

A month later, Gabriel, having arrived in Paris, presented himself to Duc François de Guise, at the Hôtel de Guise, under the name of Vicomte d'Exmès.

CHAPTER III
IN CAMP

"Yes, gentlemen," said the Duc de Guise, as he entered his tent, to the noblemen who were in attendance upon him; "yes, to-day, this 24th of April, 1557, in the evening, after having entered Neapolitan territory on the 15th, and taken Campli in four days, we are laying siege to Civitella. On the 1st of May, having made ourselves masters of Civitella, we will sit down before Aquila. On the 10th of May we shall be at Arpino, and on the 20th at Capua, where we will not be caught napping, as Hannibal was. On the 1st of June, gentlemen, I hope to show you Naples, please God."

"And how about the Pope, my dear brother?" said the Duc d'Aumale. "His Holiness, who was so very free with his promises of assisting us with the papal troops, has abandoned us so far to our own resources, so it seems to me; and our army is hardly strong enough to take such risks in a hostile country."

"Paul IV.," said François, "is too deeply interested in the success of our forces to leave us without assistance. What a beautifully clear, bright night it is, gentlemen! Biron, do you know whether the partisans, of whose expected rising in the Abruzzi the Caraffas told us, have begun to make any stir yet?"

"They don't budge, Monseigneur; I have late news that can be depended on."

"Well, our musketry will wake them up," said the Duc de Guise. "Monsieur le Marquis d'Elbœuf," he resumed, "have you heard aught from the convoys of provisions and ammunition which we should have met at Ascoli, and which surely ought to come up to us here, I should say?"

"Yes, I have heard from them, Monseigneur, but at Rome; and since then, alas—"

"Merely a little delay," the Duc de Guise broke in, —"surely it is nothing but a little delay; and after all, we are not altogether unprovided. The taking of Campli helped out our commissariat somewhat; and if I should enter the tent of any one of you gentlemen an hour from now, I'll warrant I should find a first-rate supper on the board, and seated at table with you some disconsolate widow or pretty orphan from Campli, whom you make it your duty to console. Nothing could be better, gentlemen. Besides, it is the bounden duty of the conqueror, and is what makes victory so sweet, is it not? Well, I will keep you no longer now from your pleasures. To-morrow, at daybreak, I will send for you to concert the means of cutting into this sugar-loaf of Civitella; till then, gentlemen, a good appetite, and good-night."

The duke smilingly escorted his generals to the door of his tent; but when the curtain which formed the door had fallen behind the last of them, and François de Guise was left alone, his manly features at once assumed a careworn expression, and seating himself at a table and leaning his head on his hands, he said beneath his breath with much anxiety,—

"Can it be that I should have done better to renounce all personal ambition, to content myself with being simply Henri II.'s general, and to limit my achievements to the recovery of Milan and the liberation of Sienna? Here am I in this kingdom of Naples of which in my dreams I have heard myself called the king; but I am without allies, and shall soon be without provisions; and all my officers, with my brother at their head, with not an energetic, capable mind among them, are already beginning to be disheartened, and to lose their courage, I can see plainly."

At this moment the duke heard a step behind him. He turned quickly, with an angry greeting on his lips for the bold intruder; but when he saw who it was, instead of reproving him, he held out his hand to him.

"You are not the man, Vicomte d'Exmès, are you," said he, "you are not the man, my dear Gabriel, ever to think twice about going on with an undertaking, because bread is scarce and the enemy plenty?—you, who were the last to go out of Metz, and the first to enter Valenza and Campli. But have you come to tell me anything new, my friend?"

"Yes, Monseigneur, a courier has arrived from France," Gabriel replied. "He is, I think, the bearer of letters from your illustrious brother, Monseigneur le Cardinal de Lorraine. Shall I have him brought before you?"

"No, but let him hand you the despatches that he has, Viscount, and do you bring them to me yourself, please."

Gabriel bowed, left the tent, and came back almost immediately, bringing a letter sealed with the arms of the house of Lorraine.

The six years that had passed since our story opened had scarcely changed our old friend Gabriel, except that his features had taken on a more manly and determined expression. He would at once have been picked out as a man who had put his own worth to the proof and knew it well. But he had always the same calm and serious brow, the same true and open look, and, let us say at once, the same heart full of the hopes and illusions of youth; and well it might be so, for he was only twenty-four even now.

The Duc de Guise was thirty-seven; and although his was a noble and generous nature, his mind had already returned from many places where Gabriel's had never yet been; and more than one disappointed ambition, more than one burnt-out passion, more than one fruitless contest, had sunk his eye deep in his head, and worn the hair from his temples. Yet he none the less understood and loved the chivalrous and devoted character of Gabriel; and an irresistible attraction drew the man of years and experience toward the trustful youth.

He took his brother's letter from Gabriel's hands, and said to him before opening it,—

"Listen, Vicomte d'Exmès: my secretary, Hervé de Thelen, whom you knew, died under the walls of Valenza; my brother D'Aumale is only a soldier, gallant but without ability; I need a right arm, Gabriel, a confidential friend and assistant. Now, since you came to me at my hotel at Paris, some five or six years since, I should say, I have become convinced that you have a mind above the ordinary, and better still, a faithful heart. I know nothing of you but your name,—and there never lived a Montgommery who wasn't brave; but you came to me without a word of recommendation from any one, and notwithstanding, I was attracted by you at once! I took you with me to the defence of Metz; and if that defence is to furnish one of the fairest pages of my life's story, if after sixty-five days of assault we succeeded in driving from before the walls of Metz an army of a hundred thousand men and a general who was called Charles V., I must remember that your gallantry, conspicuous at every turn, and your keen mind, always on the watch, had no inconsiderable share in that glorious result. The following year you were still with me when I won the battle of Renty; and if that ass Montmorency, well christened the—but I must not insult my foe, I must rather praise my friend and my brave companion,—Gabriel, Vicomte d'Exmès, the worthy relative of the worthy Montgommerys. I must say to you, Gabriel, that on every occasion, and more than ever since we came into Italy, I have found your assistance, your advice, and your affection of advantage to me, and have absolutely only one fault to find with you, and that is being too reserved and discreet with your general. Yes, I am sure that there is, somewhere or other in your life, a sentiment or a thought that you are hiding from me, Gabriel. But what of that? Some day you will confide it to me, and the important thing is to know that there is something for you to do. *Pardieu!* I also have something to do,—I, Gabriel; and if you say the word, we will join our fortunes, and you will help me, and I you. When I have an important and difficult undertaking to intrust to another, I will call upon you. When a powerful patron becomes essential to the furtherance of your plans, I will be on hand. Is it a bargain?"

"Oh, Monseigneur," Gabriel replied, "I am yours, body and soul! What I desired, first of all, was to be able to trust in myself and induce others to trust in me. Now I have succeeded in acquiring a little self-confidence, and you condescend to have some regard for me; so I have succeeded in my ambition up to the present time. But that a different ambition may hereafter summon me to fresh exertions, I do not deny; and when that time comes, Monseigneur,—since you have been kind enough to allow me to take such a step,—I will surely have recourse to you, just as you may count upon me in life or in death."

"Well said, *per Bacco!* as these drunken dogs of cardinals say. And do you be quite easy in your mind, Gabriel, for François de Lorraine, Duc de Guise, will spare no warmth to serve you in love or in hatred; for one or the other of these passions is at work in us, is it not, my master?"

"Both, perhaps, Monseigneur."

"Ah! so? And when your heart is so full, how can you resist letting it overflow into the heart of a friend?"

"Alas, Monseigneur, because I scarcely know whom I love, and have no idea at all whom I hate!"

"Indeed! Just suppose, then, Gabriel, since your enemies are to be mine henceforth,—just suppose that old rake Montmorency should happen to be among them!"

"It may very well be so, Monseigneur; and if my suspicions have any foundation—But we must not bother about my affairs at this crisis; it is with you and your far-reaching plans that we have to do. How can I be of service to you, Monseigneur?"

"In the first place, read me this letter from my brother, the Cardinal de Lorraine, Gabriel."

Gabriel broke the seal and unfolded the letter, and after having cast a glance at it, handed it back to the duke, saying, as he did so,—

"Pardon, Monseigneur, but this letter is written in peculiar characters, and I cannot read it."

"Ah!" said the duke, "was it Jean Panquet's courier who brought it, then? It must be a confidential communication, I see,—a grated letter, so to speak. Wait a moment, Gabriel!"

He opened a casket of chased iron and took from it a paper with pieces cut out at regular intervals, which he laid carefully upon the cardinal's letter. "There," said he, handing it to Gabriel, "read it now!"

Gabriel seemed to have some hesitation about doing as he was bid; but François took his hand and pressed it, and said again, with a look of perfect confidence and good faith, "Come, read it; there's a good fellow!"

So the Vicomte d'Exmès read as follows:—

> "Monsieur, my most honored and illustrious brother (ah, when shall I be able to call you by that one little word of four letters,—*Sire!*)—"

Gabriel stopped again; and the duke said, smiling,—

"You are astonished, Gabriel, and no wonder; but I trust that you have no suspicions of me. The Duc de Guise is not another Constable de Bourbon, my friend; and may God keep Henri's crown on his head, and grant him long life! But is there no other throne in the world save the throne of France? Since chance has placed me on an absolutely confidential footing with you, Gabriel, I do not wish to hide anything from you; but I am anxious to make known to you all my plans, and all my dreams, which are not, I think, such as could spring from a commonplace soul."

The duke rose and strode up and down the tent.

"Our family, which is allied to so many royal houses, may well, in my mind, Gabriel, aspire to any height of greatness. But the mere aspiration is nothing; attainment is my ambition. Our sister is Queen of Scotland; our niece, Mary Stuart, is betrothed to the Dauphin François; our grand-nephew, the Duc de Lorraine, is the chosen son-in-law of the king. And that is not all: in addition, we claim to represent the second house of Anjou, from which we are descended in the female line. Thence we derive our claims or rights—it's all the same thing—to Provence and Naples. Let us be content with Naples for the moment. Would not that crown look better on a Frenchman's head than on a Spaniard's? Now, what was my purpose in coming to Italy? To seize that crown. We are in alliance with the Duc de Ferrara, and closely bound to the Pope's nephews, the Caraffas. Paul IV. is an old man, and my brother, the Cardinal de Lorraine, will succeed him. The throne of Naples is tottering, and I will mount it; and that is why, *mon Dieu!* I left Sienna and the Milanais behind me to pounce upon the Abruzzi. It was a glorious dream; but I fear greatly that it will never be more than a dream. For just consider, Gabriel, that I had less than twelve thousand men when I crossed the Alps! The Duc de Ferrara had promised me seven thousand; but he kept them on his own territory. Paul and the Caraffas had boasted how they would stir up a powerful faction in my interest in the kingdom of Naples, and agreed to furnish me with troops and money and supplies; but they have not sent me a man or a wagon or a sou. My officers are beginning to draw back, and my troops are murmuring. But it makes no difference; I will go on to the bitter end. I will not leave this promised land which my foot is now upon except at the last gasp; and if I do leave it, I will return! I will return!"

The duke stamped on the ground as if to take possession of it; his eyes shone; and he was noble and beautiful to look upon.

"Monseigneur," cried Gabriel, "how proud am I that I may be allowed to be your companion, to have such a trifling part as I may in such a glorious ambition!"

"And now," the duke said, smiling, "that I have given you the key to my brother's letter twice over, I fancy that you will be able to read and understand it So go on with it, while I listen."

"'Sire!' That is where I left off," said Gabriel.

> "I have to inform you of two items of bad tidings and one of good. The good news is that the nuptials of our niece, Mary Stuart, are finally fixed for the 20th of next month, and are to be celebrated in due form at Paris on that day. One of the other pieces of news, of an evil tenor, comes from England. Philip II. of Spain has landed there, and is urging every

day upon Queen Mary Tudor, his wife, who is passionately devoted to him, a declaration of war against France. No one has any doubt that he will succeed, although his wishes are directly opposed to the interest and the desire of the English people. There is talk already of an army to be assembled on the frontiers of the Low Countries, under the command of Philibert Emmanuel of Savoy. In that event, my dearest brother, we are suffering so from scarcity of troops here at home that Henri will be forced to recall you from Italy, so that our plans in that direction will at least have to be postponed. And consider, François, how much better it would be to delay their execution for a while than to compromise them; let there be no headstrong recklessness. It will be in vain for our sister, the Queen Regent of Scotland, to threaten to break with England, for you may believe that Mary of England, altogether infatuated with her young husband, will pay no attention to it; so take your measures accordingly."

"By Heaven!" broke in the Duc de Guise, bringing his fist down violently on the table, "you say only too well, my brother; and it takes a sly fox to smell the hounds. Yes, Mary the prude will surely allow herself to be led astray by her lawful husband; and no, of course I cannot openly disobey the king when he calls upon me to send his soldiers to him at so serious a crisis; and I would rather hold my hand from all the kingdoms on earth. Well, then, one obstacle the more in the way of this accursed expedition; for I leave it to you to say if it is not accursed, Gabriel, in spite of the Holy Father's blessing! Come, Gabriel, tell me frankly, for my ear alone, you do look upon it as hopeless, don't you?"

"I should not like, Monseigneur," said Gabriel, "to have you class me with those who easily lose their courage; and yet, since you ask my opinion in all sincerity—"

"Enough, Gabriel! I understand you and agree with you. I foresee that it is not at this time that we are fated to accomplish together the great things that we were planning just now; but I swear to you that this is only a postponement, and to strike a blow at Philip II. in any part of his dominions will always be equivalent to attacking him here at Naples. But go on, Gabriel, for if I remember aright we have other evil tidings still to hear."

Gabriel resumed his reading.

"The other troublesome affair that I have to tell you of will be of no less serious moment, because it concerns our family's private matters; but there is no doubt still time to avert it, and so I make haste to give you notice of it. It is necessary that you should know that since your departure Monsieur le Connétable de Montmorency has shown, and quite naturally, the same ugly and bitter spirit toward us, and has never ceased to be envious of us, and to fume and swear, as has always been his custom whenever the king showed any favor to our family. The approaching celebration of our dear niece Mary's nuptials with the dauphin is not calculated to put him in a good humor. The balance which it is to the king's interest to preserve between the two houses of Guise and Montmorency is depressed considerably in our favor by this event; and the old constable is making a terrible clamor and outcry for something to counterbalance it. He has found this counterpoise, my dear brother, in a match between his son François, the prisoner of Thérouanne, and—"

The young count did not finish the sentence. His voice faltered, and every drop of blood left his face.

"Well, what's the matter, Gabriel?" asked the duke. "How pale you are and how discomposed! Did you have a sudden attack of pain?"

"Nothing, Monseigneur, absolutely nothing, except possibly a little over-fatigue and a slight dizziness; but I am all right again now, and will go on if you please. Let me see, where was I? The cardinal was saying, I think, that there was a remedy. Oh, no, farther along. Here's the place:—"

"In a match between his son François and Madame Diane de Castro, the legitimatized daughter of the king and Madame Diane de Poitiers. You will remember, brother, that Madame de Castro, who was left a widow at the age of thirteen, her husband, Horace Farnèse, having been killed at the siege of Hesdin six months after the wedding, remained for five years at the convent of the Filles-Dieu at Paris. The king, at the constable's solicitation, sent for her to return to court. She is a perfect pearl of beauty, my brother, and you know that I am a competent judge. Her charms made a conquest of all hearts at first sight, and of the father's heart more than all the rest. The king, who had already endowed her with the duchy of Chatellerault, has added the duchy of Angoulême to her possessions. She has been here only two weeks, and yet her supreme influence over the king is already an admitted fact. Her fascination and her sweet disposition are, no doubt, the moving causes of his very great fondness for her. At last things have got to such a point that Madame de Valentinois, who for some unknown reason has thought fit to invent another mother for Madame de Castro, seems to me just at present to be very jealous of this newly risen power. So it will be a very good thing for the constable if he succeeds in getting such a potent ally into his household. Between ourselves, you know that Diane de Poitiers never can refuse much of anything to the old villain; and although our brother D'Aumale is her son-in-law, Anne de Montmorency is still more closely connected with her. The king, moreover, is inclined to make some amends for the preponderating force which he sees that we are beginning to wield in his council and his armies. And this infernal marriage is very likely to be brought about."

"Again your voice falters, Gabriel," the duke interposed; "rest a bit, my boy, and let me finish the letter myself, for it interests me exceedingly. For, to tell the truth, that will give the constable a dangerous advantage over us. But I thought that great gaby of a François was already married to a De Fiennes. Come, give me the letter, Gabriel."

"But I am all right, upon my word, Monseigneur," said Gabriel, who had been reading a few lines ahead, "and I am perfectly well able to read the few lines that remain."

"This infernal marriage is very likely to be brought about. There is only one thing in our favor. François de Montmorency is bound by a secret marriage to Mademoiselle de Fiennes; and so a divorce is a necessary preliminary. But for that, the Pope's assent must be obtained; and François is just setting out for Rome to obtain it. So make it your business, my dear brother, to anticipate him with his Holiness, and through our friends the Caraffas and your own influence to induce him to reject the petition for a divorce, which will be supported, let me warn you, by a letter from the king. But the threatened position is of sufficient importance to call forth your best energies to defend it, as you defended St. Dizier and Metz. I will act with you to the best of my ability, for it will need all we both can do. And with this, my dear brother, I pray God to grant you a long and happy life."

"Well, nothing is lost yet," said the Duc de Guise, when Gabriel had finished reading the cardinal's letter; "and the Pope, who refuses to supply me with soldiers, might at least be willing to make me a present of a bull."

"So, then," said Gabriel, trembling with emotion, "you have some hope that his Holiness will refuse to ratify this divorce from Jeanne de Fiennes, and will be opposed to this marriage of François de Montmorency?"

"Yes, yes! indeed, I have hopes of it. But how deeply moved you are, my friend! Dear Gabriel! he does enter passionately into our interests! I am quite as heartily at your service, Gabriel, be sure of that. And come now, let us talk about your affairs a little; and since, in this undertaking, of which I can foresee the issue only too plainly, you will scarcely have an opportunity, I imagine, to swell the list of noteworthy services for which I am in your debt, by any fresh exploits, suppose I make a beginning of paying my debt to you? I don't choose to be too heavily in arrear, my good fellow. Can I be of help or assistance to you in any way whatever? Tell me now; come, tell me frankly."

"Oh, Monseigneur is too kind," replied Gabriel; "and I do not see—"

"For these last five years, when you have been continually fighting under me," said the duke, "you have never accepted a sou from me. You must be in need of money; why, God bless me, everybody needs money. It is not a gift or a loan that I offer you, but payment of a debt. So let's have no empty scruples; and although we are, as you know, rather pressed for money, still—"

"Yes, I do know very well, Monseigneur, that the want of a little means sometimes causes your grandest schemes to fall through; and I am so far from being in need myself that I was going to offer you some thousands of crowns, which would come in very handily for the army, and are quite useless to me, really."

"And which I will gladly accept, for they come at a very good time, I confess; and so one can do absolutely nothing for you, O young man without a wish! But stay," he added in a lower tone, "that rascal Thibault, my body-servant, you know, at the sack of Campli, day before yesterday, put aside for me the young wife of the *procureur* of the town, the beauty of the neighborhood, judging from what I hear, always excepting the governor's wife, on whom no one can lay his hand. But as for me, upon my word, I have too many other cares in my head, and my hair is getting grizzly. Come, Gabriel, what would you say to my prize? *Sang-Dieu!* but you are built just right to make amends for the loss of a *procureur*! What do you say to it?"

"I say, Monseigneur, with regard to the governor's wife, of whom you speak, and upon whom no hand has been laid, that it was I who fell in with her in the confusion, and carried her away, not to abuse my rights, as you might think. On the contrary, my object was to shield a noble and beautiful woman from the violence of a licentious soldiery. But I have since discovered that the fair creature would have no objection to adopting the cause of the victors, and would be very glad to shout, like the soldier of Gaul: 'Væ victis!' But since I am now, alas! less inclined than ever to echo her sentiments, I can, if you desire, Monseigneur, have her brought here to one who can appreciate better than I, and more worthily, her charms and her rank."

"Oh, oh!" cried the duke, laughing heartily. "Such extraordinary morality almost savors of the Huguenot, Gabriel. Can it be that you have a secret leaning toward those of the religion? Ah, take heed, my friend! I am by conviction, and by policy, which is worse, an ardent Catholic, and I will have you burned without pity. But come, joking apart, why the deuce are you so strait-laced?"

"Because I am in love, perhaps," said Gabriel.

"Oh, yes, I remember, a hate and a love. Well, then, can't I show my good-will to you by putting you in a way to meet your foes or your love? Are you in want of a title, for example?"

"Thanks, Monseigneur; I am no longer in need of that, and as I said to you in the first place, my ambition is not for vague and empty honors, but for a little personal renown. Therefore, since you conclude that there is nothing more of importance to be done here, and I am not likely to be of much use to you, it would be a very great gratification to me to be commissioned by you to carry to Paris, for the marriage of your royal niece, for instance, the flags you have won in Lombardy and in the Abruzzi. My happiness would leave nothing to be desired if you would deign to give me a letter to his Majesty, which should bear witness to him and to the whole court that some of these flags have been taken by my own hand, not altogether without danger to myself."

"Indeed, I will! That is very easily done; and more than that, it is quite right too," said the Duc de Guise. "I shall be very sorry to part with you; but in all probability it will only be for a short time, if war breaks out on the Flemish frontier, as everything seems to indicate, and we will meet again there, will we not, Gabriel? Your place is always where there is fighting to be done; and that is why you are so anxious to get away from here, where there is nothing to be had now but weariness and ennui, by Heaven! But we will have better sport in the Low Countries, Gabriel, and I trust that we shall enjoy it together there."

"I shall be only too glad to follow you, Monseigneur."

"Meanwhile, how soon would you like to be off, Gabriel, to carry to the king this wedding gift, of which your brain conceived the idea?"

"The sooner the better, I should say, Monseigneur, if the marriage is to take place on the 20th of May, as Monseigneur le Cardinal de Lorraine informs you."

"Very true. Well, then, you shall go to-morrow, Gabriel; and you will have none too much time either. So go and get some rest, my friend, while I write the letter which will commend you to the king's notice, as well as the reply to my brother's, of which you will kindly take charge; and say to him besides, that I hope for a favorable result to the matter in which the Pope is concerned."

"And perhaps, Monseigneur," said Gabriel, "my presence at Paris may help along the result you desire to that matter, and so my absence may be of some service to you."

"Always mysterious, Vicomte d'Exmès! but I am used to it from you. Adieu, then; and may the last night that you pass near me be a pleasant one!"

"I will return in the morning to get my letters and your blessing, Monseigneur. Ah! I leave with you my retainers, who have followed me in all my campaigns. I ask your permission to take with me only two of them and my squire, Martin-Guerre; he will answer all my needs; he is devoted to me, and is afraid of only two things in the whole world,—his wife and his shadow."

"How is that?" said the duke, laughing.

"Monseigneur, Martin-Guerre fled from his native place, Artigues, near Rieux, to get away from his wife Bertrande, whom he adored, but who used to beat him. He entered my service after Metz; but either the Devil or his wife, to torment him or punish him for his sins, kept appearing to him from time to time in his own image. Yes, all of a sudden, he would see by his side another Martin-Guerre, a striking likeness of himself, as like as if it were his reflection in a mirror; and by our Lady! that frightened him. But for all that he has an utter contempt for bullets, and would carry a redoubt single-handed. At Renty and at Valenza he twice saved my life."

"Take this valiant coward with you by all means, Gabriel. Give me your hand again, my dear friend, and be ready in the morning. My letters will be waiting for you."

Gabriel was ready to start bright and early the next day; he passed the night dreaming without closing his eyes. He waited on the Duc de Guise to receive his last instructions, and pay his parting respects, and on the 26th of April, at six in the morning, he set out for Rome, and thence for Paris, attended by Martin-Guerre and two of his followers.

CHAPTER IV
A KING'S MISTRESS

It is the 20th of May, and we ask our readers to go with us to the Louvre at Paris, and to the apartments of the wife of the Great Seneschal, Madame de Brézé, Duchesse de Valentinois, commonly called Diane de Poitiers. Nine o'clock in the morning has just struck on the great clock of the château. Madame Diane, all in white, in a decidedly coquettish *negligé*, is leaning or half reclining on a bed covered with black velvet. King Henri, already dressed in a magnificent costume, is sitting on a chair at her side.

Let us glance a moment at the scene and the *dramatis personæ*.

The apartment of Diane de Poitiers was resplendent with all the magnificence and taste which that fair dawning of art called the Renaissance had had the skill to lavish upon a king's chamber. Paintings signed "Le Primatice" represented various incidents of the hunting field, wherein the Huntress Diane, goddess of woods and forests, naturally figured as the principal heroine. The gilded and colored medallions and panels repeated on all sides the intertwined armorial bearings of François I. and Henri II. In like manner were memories of father and son intertwined in the heart of the fair Diane. The emblems were no less historical and full of meaning, and in twenty places was to be seen the crescent of Phœbus-Diane, between the Salamander of the conqueror of Marignan, and Bellerophon overthrowing the Chimæra, a device adopted by Henri II. after the taking of Boulogne from the English. This fickle crescent appeared in a thousand different forms and combinations which did great credit to the decorators of the time: here the royal crown was placed above it, and there four H's, four *fleurs de lis,* and four crowns together made a superb setting for it; again it was threefold, and then shaped like a star. The mottoes were no less varied, and most of them were written in Latin. "Diana regum venatrix" (Diana, huntress of kings),—was that a piece of impertinence or of flattery? "Donec totum impleat orbem" can be translated in two ways,—"The crescent is to become a full moon," or "The king's glory will fill the whole world." "Cum plena est, fit æmula solis," can be freely translated, "Beauty and royalty are sisters." And the lovely arabesques which enclosed devices and mottoes, and the superb furnishings on which they were reproduced,—all these, if we should attempt to describe them, would not only put our magnificence of the present day to the blush, but would lose too much in the description.

Now let us cast our eyes upon the king.

History tells us that he was tall, supple, and strong. He had to resort to regular diet and daily exercise to combat a certain tendency to stoutness; and yet in the chase he left the swiftest far behind, and carried away the palm from the strongest at the jousts and tourneys. His hair and beard were black, and his complexion very dark, which gave him so much more animation, if we may believe contemporary memoirs. He wore, at the time we make his acquaintance, as indeed he always did, the colors of the Duchesse de Valentinois,—a coat of green satin slashed with white, glistening with pearls and diamonds; a double chain of gold, to which was suspended the medal of the order of Saint Michael; a sword chased by Benvenuto; a collar of white point de Venise; a velvet cloak dotted with golden lilies hung gracefully from his shoulders. It was a costume of singular richness, and suitable to a cavalier of exquisite elegance.

We have said in brief that Diane was clad in a simple white peignoir of a singularly thin and transparent stuff. To paint her divine loveliness would not be so easy a matter; and it would be hard to say whether the black velvet cushion on which her head lay, or the dress, startling in its purity, by which her form was enveloped, served best to set off the snows and lilies of her complexion. And surely it was such a perfect combination of delicate outlines as to drive Jean Goujon himself to despair. There is no more perfect piece of antique statuary; and this statue was alive, and very much alive too, if common report is to be believed. As for the graceful motion with which these lovely limbs were instinct, we must not attempt to describe it. It can no more be reproduced than can a ray of sunlight. As for age, she had none. In this point, as in so many others, she was like the immortals; but by her side the youngest and most blooming seemed old and wrinkled. The Protestants babbled about philters and potions, to which they said that she had recourse to enable her to remain always sixteen. The Catholics replied that all she did was to take a cold bath every day, and wash her face in ice water even in winter. Her prescription has been preserved; but if it be true that Jean Goujon's "Diane au Cerf" was carved from this royal model, that prescription has no longer the same effect.

A King's Mistress.

Thus was she a worthy object of the affection of the two kings whom one after the other her beauty had dazzled. For if the story of the favor obtained by Monsieur Saint-Vallier, thanks to his fine brown eyes, seems apocryphal, it is almost conclusively proved that Diane was François's mistress before she became Henri's.

"It is said," chronicles Le Laboureur, "that King François, who was the first lover of Diane de Poitiers, having expressed to her one day, after the death of François the dauphin, some dissatisfaction at the lack of animation exhibited by Prince Henri, she told him that he needed to have a love affair, and that she would make him fall in love with her."

What woman wills, God wills; and Diane was for twenty years the dearly and only beloved of Henri.

But now that we have examined the king and the favorite, is it not time to hear what they are saying?

Henri, holding a parchment in his hand, was reading aloud the following verses, not without some interruptions and by-play which we cannot set down here, because they were part of the setting of the piece.

> Douce et belle bouchelette,
> Plus fraîche, et plus vermeillette
> Que le bouton églantine,
> Au matin!
> Plus suave et mieux fleurante
> Que l'immortelle amarante,
> Et plus mignarde cent fois
> Que n'est la douce rosée
> Dont la terre est arrosée
> Goutte à goutte au plus doux mois!
> Baise-moi, ma douce amie,
> Baise-moi, chère vie,
> Baise-moi, mignonnement,
> Serrement,
> Jusques à tant que je die:
> Las! je n'en puis plus, ma mie;
> Las! mon Dieu, je n'en puis plus.
> Lors ta bouchette retire,
> Afin que mort, je soupire,
> Puis, me donne le surplus.
> Ainsi ma douce guerrière,
> Mon cœur, mon tout, ma lumière,
> Vivons ensemble, vivons,
> Et suivons
> Les doux soutiens de jeunesse,
> Aussi bien une vieillesse
> Nous menace sur le port,
> Qui, toute courbe et tremblante,
> Nous attraîne, chancelante,
> La maladie et la mort.[1]

"And what might be the name of this polite versifier who tells us so well what we are doing?" asked Henri when he had finished his reading.

"He is called Remy Belleau, Sire, and promises to rival Ronsard, it seems to me. Oh, well!" continued the duchess, "do you put the value of this lover's poem at five hundred crowns, as I do?"

"He shall have them, this protégé of yours, my beautiful Diane."

"But we must not allow this to make us forget the earlier ones, Sire. Have you signed the warrant for the pension that I promised in your name to Ronsard, the prince of poets? You have, haven't you? Well, then, I have only one favor more to ask at your hands, and that is the vacant abbey of Recouls for your librarian, Mellin de Saint-Gelais, our French Ovid."

"Ovid shall have his abbey, never fear, my fair Maecenas," said the king.

"Ah, how fortunate are you, Sire, to have the power of disposing of so many benefices and offices at your pleasure! If I could only have your power just for one short hour!"

"Haven't you it always, ingrate?"

"Really, have I, my Lord? But you haven't given me a kiss for two whole minutes! That's right, dear. So you say that your power is always at my command? Don't tempt me, Sire! I warn you that I shall avail myself of it to pay the enormous claim which Philibert Delorme has presented to me, on the ground that my Château d'Anet is finished. It will be the glory of your reign; but how dear it is! Just one kiss, my Henri!"

"And for this kiss, Diane, take for your Delorme the sum produced by the sale of the governorship of Picardy."

"Sire, do you think that I sell my kisses? I give them to you, Henri. This Picardy governorship is worth two hundred thousand livres, I should think, is it not? And then I can take the pearl necklace which has been offered me, and which I was very anxious to wear to-day at the wedding of your dear son François. A hundred thousand livres to Philibert, and a hundred thousand for the necklace; this Picardy matter will do very well."

"Especially as you estimate it at quite double its real worth, Diane."

"What! is it worth only one hundred thousand livres? Well, then, it's a very simple matter for me to let the necklace go."

"Nonsense!" said the king, laughing; "there are three or four vacant companies somewhere which will pay for the necklace, Diane."

"Oh, Sire, you are the most generous of kings, as you are the best beloved of lovers."

"Yes, you do really love me as I love you, do you not, Diane?"

"He really has the face to ask such a question!"

"But I, you see, dear, I adore you more and more every day, because you are every day more beautiful. Ah, what a lovely smile you have, sweetheart, and what a sweet expression! Let me kneel here at your feet. Put your fair hands on my shoulders. Oh, Diane, how lovely you are, and how dearly I love you! I could stay here and just gaze at you for hours, nay, for years. I would forget France, I would forget the whole world."

"And even this formal celebration of Monseigneur the Dauphin's marriage?" said Diane, smiling; "and yet it is to be solemnized this very day and in two hours' time. And even if you are all ready in your magnificence, Sire, I am not ready at all, you see. So go, my dear Lord, for it is time for me to call my women. Ten o'clock will strike in a moment."

"Ten o'clock," said Henri; "and upon my word, I have an appointment at that hour."

"An appointment, Sire? With a lady, perhaps?"

"With a lady."

"Pretty, no doubt?"

"Yes, Diane, very pretty."

"Then it can't be the queen."

"Oh, you wretch! Catherine de Médicis has a certain sort of beauty of her own, a stern and cold style of beauty, but undeniable. However, it is not the queen whom I expect. Can you guess who it is?"

"No, I really cannot, Sire."

"It is another Diane, dear,—the living memento of our young affections, our daughter, our darling daughter."

"You said that too loud and too often, Sire," said Diane, frowning, and in a somewhat embarrassed tone. "It was agreed that Madame de Castro should pass for the child of another than myself. I was born to have legitimate children by you. I have been your mistress because I loved you; but I will not put up with your openly declaring me your concubine."

"That shall be as your pride dictates, Diane," was the king's reply; "but you love our child dearly, do you not?"

"I like to have you love her."

"Oh, yes! I love her very much. She is so fascinating, so clever, so sweet! And then, Diane, she reminds me so of my younger days and of the time when I loved you—ah! no more passionately than to-day, God knows, but when I loved you so that I was willing to commit a crime."

The king, who had suddenly fallen into gloomy reflection, raised his head.

"This Montgommery! You didn't care for him, did you, Diane? You didn't care for him?"

"What a foolish question!" said the favorite, with a disdainful smile. "Still so jealous after twenty years!"

"Yes, I am jealous; I am, and shall always be jealous of you, Diane. Surely you didn't love him; but he loved you, the villain,—he dared to love you!"

"*Mon Dieu*! Sire, you have always lent too willing an ear to the slanders with which these Protestants are always pursuing me. That is not the part of a Catholic king. In any event, whether the man loved me or not, what does it matter, if my heart never for an instant ceased to be wholly yours, for the Comte de Montgommery has been dead many years?"

"Yes, dead!" said the king, in a hollow voice.

"Come, let us not grow mournful over these reminiscences on a day which ought to be a day of rejoicing," said Diane. "Have you seen François and Marie yet? Are they always so lovelorn, these children? Well their terrible impatience will soon be at an end. Think, in two hours they will be made one, and so glad and happy, but still not so delighted as the Guises, whose wishes are fully satisfied by this marriage."

"Yes, but who is in a fury about it?" said the king. "My old Montmorency; and the constable has so much the more reason to lose his head, because I greatly fear that our Diane is not destined for his son."

"But, Sire, didn't you promise him this marriage by way of amends?"

"Certainly I did; but it seems that Madame de Castro has objections—"

"A child of eighteen just out of a convent! What objections can she possibly have?"

"It is to confide them to me that she is probably waiting in my apartments at this very moment."

"Go to her, then, Sire, while I proceed to beautify myself to please you."

"And after the ceremony I shall see you again at the tilting match. I am going to break a lance in your honor once more to-day, and I propose to make you queen of the lists."

"The queen? And who is the other?"

"There is only one, Diane, and you know it very well. *Au revoir*."

"*Au revoir*, Sire, and pray don't be rash and careless in this tilting; you make me shudder sometimes."

"There is no danger there, I'm sorry to say; for I could wish that there might be, so that I might seem a little more deserving in your eyes. But time is passing, and my two Dianes are both impatient. Tell me just once more that you love me."

"Sire, I love you as I always have loved you, and as I shall love you forever."

The king, before letting the curtain fall behind him, threw her a last kiss with his hand. "Adieu, my dearly loving and dearly loved Diane," said he. And he left her.

Then a panel hidden by hangings in the opposite wall opened.

"For the love of heaven, have you done enough chattering for to-day?" said the Constable de Montmorency, roughly, as he came into the room.

"My friend," said Diane, rising, "you must have seen that even before ten o'clock, which was the hour of my appointment with you, I did everything I could to send him away. I was quite as uncomfortable as you were, believe me."

"As uncomfortable as I! *Pasques-Dieu*! no, my dear; and if you flatter yourself that your discourse was either instructive or entertaining—In the first place, what is this new crotchet, of refusing your daughter Diane's hand to my son François, after having solemnly promised it? By the crown of thorns! would one not say that the bastard was conferring a great honor on the Montmorency family by condescending to enter it? The marriage must take place; do you understand, Diane? And you must take measures to see that it does. It is the only means left of restoring the balance between us and the Guises, whom the deuce take! So, Diane, in spite of the king, in spite of the Pope, in spite of everything, I wish that this should come to pass."

"But, my friend—"

"Ah!" cried the constable, "and when I tell you that I wish it so, *Pater noster*!"

"It shall be as you say, my friend," Diane in her fear of him made haste to say.

[1] Sweet and lovely little mouth,
Fresher and ruddier than bud of eglantine
At morn!
Sweeter and more fragrant than the immortal amaranth,
And a hundred times dearer

Than the gentle dew which waters the earth,
Drop by drop, in the sweetest month!
Kiss me, sweet friend; kiss me, dear life.
Kiss me lovingly, closely, until I say:
Alas, my love, I can bear no more!
Alas, my God, I can bear no more!
Then take away thy little mouth, till dead I sigh;
Then bestow on me the rest.
Thus, sweet warrior, my heart, my light, my all,
Let us live together; let us live
And follow the sweet delights of youth,
Since near the haven old age threatens us,
Which, bowed and trembling, tottering, brings usSickness
and death.

CHAPTER V
IN THE APARTMENTS OF THE ROYAL CHILDREN

The king, on returning to his own apartments, did not find his daughter there; but the usher who was in attendance told him that after waiting for him a long while Madame Diane had gone to the rooms set apart for the king's children, leaving word that she should be informed as soon as his Majesty returned.

"Very well," said Henri, "I will join her there. Leave me, for I will go alone."

He passed through a large hall, then a long corridor, at the end of which he softly opened a door, and stood looking behind a long half-drawn curtain. The children's cries and shouts of laughter had drowned the noise of his steps; and he was able, himself unseen, to watch a most delightful and graceful picture.

Standing at the window, Mary Stuart, the beautiful young bride, had gathered around her Diane de Castro, and Elisabeth and Marguerite de France, all three very assiduous to help her, and chattering away for dear life, smoothing out a fold in her dress or fixing a lock of hair that had escaped from its fastening,—in short, giving that finishing touch to her lovely toilette which only women know how to give. At the other end of the room, the brothers, Charles, Henri, and François, the youngest of all, laughing and shouting at the top of their voices, were pushing with all their strength against a door which François the dauphin, the young bridegroom, was trying in vain to open, while the little rogues were determined to prevent him from having a sight of his wife till the last moment.

Jacques Amyot, the preceptor of the princes, was talking seriously in a corner with Madame de Coni and Lady Lennox, the governesses of the princesses.

There in one apartment, within a space that could be covered by one glance, was assembled a large part of the history of the future, its woes, its passions, and its glory. There were the dauphin, who became François

II.; Élisabeth, who married Philip II., and became Queen of Spain; Charles, who was Charles IX.; Henri, who was Henri III.; Marguerite de Valois, who married Henri IV., and was Queen of Navarre; François, who was successively Duc d'Alençon, d'Anjou, and de Brabant; and Mary Stuart, who was twice a queen, and a martyr too.

The illustrious translator of Plutarch watched with a gaze at once sad and absorbed the sports of these children and the future destinies of France.

"No, no, François, you shall not come in!" cried rather harshly the brutal Charles Maximilien, who was in after years to give the word for the fearful slaughter of Saint Bartholomew.

And with his brothers' help he succeeded in pushing the bolt, and thus made an entrance out of the question for poor François, who was too frail in any event to have made his way in, even against these children, and who could only stamp in his vexation, and beg from the other side of the door.

"Dear François, how they do torment him!" said Mary Stuart to his sisters.

"Keep quiet, do, Madame la Dauphine, at least until I put in this pin," laughed little Marguerite. "What a fine invention these pins are, and what a great man the one who thought of them last year ought to become!" said she.

"And now that the pin is in place," said gentle Élisabeth, "I am going to open the door for poor François, in spite of these young fiends; for it makes me sad to see him so sad."

"Oh, yes, you know all about that, you do, Élisabeth," said Mary Stuart, sighing; "and you are thinking of your courtly Spaniard, Don Carlos, son of the King of Spain, who fêted us and amused us so at St. Germain."

"See how Elisabeth is blushing," cried little Marguerite, clapping her hands mischievously. "The fact is that he was very fine and gallant, this Castilian of hers."

"Come, come," said Diane de Castro, the eldest of the sisters, in a motherly sort of way, "it isn't right to jest so among sisters, Marguerite."

Nothing could have been more fascinating than the sight of these four lovely maidens, each so different from the others, and each so perfect in herself. Beautiful flowers just opening their buds: Diane, all purity and sweetness; Élisabeth, serious and affectionate; Mary Stuart, all captivating languor; and Marguerite a sparkling madcap. Henri, moved and fascinated, could not feast his eyes enough with the charming picture.

However, he had to make up his mind to go in. "The king!" they cried with one breath; and all, boys and girls together, rushed to meet their king and father. Only Mary Stuart held back a little, and went softly and drew the bolt which was keeping François prisoner. The dauphin lost no time in coming in, and the young family was complete.

"Good-morning, my dears," said the king. "I am very glad to find you all so well and happy. Were they keeping you out, François, my poor boy? But you are going to have time enough now to see your betrothed sweetheart often and always. Are you very fond of one another, my children?"

"Oh, yes, Sire, I do love Mary!" and the passionate boy pressed a burning kiss on the hand of her who was to be his wife.

"Monseigneur," said Lady Lennox, sharply and rather sternly, "one does not kiss a lady's hand in public in that way, especially in his Majesty's presence. What will he think of Madame Mary and her governess?"

"But isn't this hand mine?" said the dauphin.

"Not yet, Monseigneur," said the duenna; "and I propose to fulfil my duty till the last minute."

"Don't be afraid," said Mary, in an undertone to her young husband, who was beginning to sulk; "when she isn't looking, I will give it you again."

The king laughed beneath his beard.

"You are very strict, my Lady; but then you are quite right," he added, checking himself. "And you, Messire Amyot, you are not dissatisfied with your pupils, I trust. Pay great regard to the words of your learned preceptor, young gentlemen, for he is on intimate terms with the great heroes of antiquity. Messire Amyot, is it long since you have heard from Pierre Danot, who was our old master, and from Henri Étienne, our fellow-pupil?"

"The old man and the young one are both well, Sire, and will be very proud and happy to know that your Majesty has deigned to remember them."

"Well, children," said the king, "I wanted to see you before the ceremony, and am very glad that I have seen you. Now, Diane, I am at your service, my dear, so come with me."

Diane bowed low and followed the king from the room.

CHAPTER VI
DIANE DE CASTRO

Diane de Castro, whose acquaintance we made when she was yet a mere child, was now almost eighteen years old. Her beauty had fulfilled all its promise, and had developed in regularity and charm at the same time; the predominant expression of her sweet and lovely face was one of childlike openness and honesty. Diane de Castro in character and in mind was still the child whom we first knew. She was not yet thirteen when the Duc de Castro, whom she had never seen since the day she was married to him, had been killed at the siege of Hesdin. The king had sent the child-widow to pass her mourning period at the convent of the Filles-Dieu at Paris; and Diane had found such warm affection and such pleasant customs there that she had asked her father's permission to remain with the kind sisters and her companions until he should be ready to make some other disposition of her. One could but respect such a devout request; and Henri had not taken Diane from the convent until about a month before, when the Constable de Montmorency, jealous of the preponderance acquired by the Guises in the government, had solicited and obtained for his son the hand of the daughter of the king and his favorite.

During the mouth she had passed at court, Diane had not failed at once to attract universal respect and admiration. "For," says Brantôme, in his work on famous women, "she was very kind, and did nothing to offend anybody; and yet her spirit was very noble and high, and she was very obliging and discreet, and most virtuous." But her virtue, which shone forth so pure and lovely amid the general wickedness of the time, was entirely free from any touch of austerity or harshness. One day some man remarked in her hearing that a daughter of France ought to be valiant and strong, and that her shyness smacked somewhat of the cloister, whereupon she learned to ride in a very few days, and there was no cavalier who was so fearless and dashing a rider as she. After that she always went with the king to the chase; and Henri yielded more and more to her charming way of seeking, without the least pretence for any occasion, however trifling, of anticipating his wishes and making herself agreeable to him. So Diane was granted the privilege of entering her father's apartments whenever she chose, and she was always sure of a welcome. Her touching grace, her modest ways, and the odor of sweet maidenliness and innocence which one seemed to breathe when she was near, even to her smile, which was the least bit sad, combined to make her perhaps the most exquisite and ravishing figure of that whole court, which could boast of so many dazzling beauties.

"Well, my darling," said Henri, "now I am ready to hear what you have to tell me. There's eleven o'clock striking. The marriage ceremony at St. Germain l'Auxerrois is not to be performed till noon, so that I have half an hour to give you, and no more. These are the pleasant moments of my life that I pass with you."

"Sire, what a kind and indulgent father you are!"

"Oh, no, but I love you dearly, my precious child; and I desire with all my heart to do something that will gratify you, so long as I do not thereby prove false to the grave interests of state which a king must always consider before any natural ties. And now, Diane, to prove it to you, I will first of all give you my answer to the two requests you made of me. Good Sister Monique, who loved you and watched over you at your convent of the Filles-Dieu, has been appointed at your recommendation Lady Abbess of the convent of Origny at St. Quentin."

"Oh, how grateful I am, Sire!"

"As for brave Antoine, your favorite servant at Vimoutiers, he will draw a handsome pension from our treasury for life. I am very sorry, Diane, that Enguerrand is no longer alive. We should have liked to show our gratitude in kingly style to the worthy squire who brought up our dear daughter Diane so happily; but you lost him last year, I think, and he has not even left an heir."

"Sire, you are too generous and kind really."

"And more than that, Diane, here are the letters-patent which make you Duchesse d'Angoulême. And this is not a fourth part of what I should like to do for you; for I see that you are sometimes thoughtful and sad, and that is why I was in haste to talk with you, because I longed to comfort you, or to cure your sorrow. What is it, my dear? Aren't you happy?"

"Ah, Sire," replied Diane, "how can I help being happy, being thus surrounded by your love and your continual kindness? I only long for one thing, and that is that the present, so full of happiness, may continue. The future, fine and glorious as it may be, will never equal it."

"Diane," said Henri, in a grave voice, "you know that I took you from the convent to give your hand to François de Montmorency. It would be a grand match, Diane; and yet this alliance, which, I don't conceal from you, would have been of great advantage to the interests of my crown, seems to be very distasteful to you. You owe me at least your reasons for this refusal, which troubles me so, Diane."

"Surely I will not hide them from you, my Father. And in the first place," said Diane, with some embarrassment, "I have been told that François de Montmorency has already been secretly married to Mademoiselle de Fiennes, one of the queen's ladies."

"It is true," replied the king; "but this marriage, contracted clandestinely, without the constable's consent and mine, is rightfully void; and if the Pope decrees a divorce, you certainly, Diane, will not show yourself more exacting than his Holiness. So if this is your only reason—"

"But there is another, dear Father."

"And what is it, pray? How can an alliance which would be esteemed an honor by the highest-born and wealthiest heiresses in France work ill to you?"

"Why, Father, because—because I love some one else," cried Diane, throwing herself, confused and weeping, into her father's arms.

"You love some one, Diane?" repeated Henri, amazed; "and what might be the name of this favored individual?"

"Gabriel, Sire."

"Gabriel what?" asked the king, smiling at her.

"I have no idea, Father."

"How can that be, Diane? In Heaven's name, explain yourself!"

"I will tell you everything, Sire. It is an attachment of my childhood's days. I used to see Gabriel every day He was so courteous and obliging and gallant and handsome and clever and affectionate! He used to call me his little wife. Ah, Sire, do not laugh; it was a very serious and holy sentiment, and the first that ever made its impression on my heart. Other attachments may take their places beside it, but can never destroy it. And yet I allowed myself to be married to the Duc Farnèse, Sire, but it was because I knew not what I did; because I was forced into it, and obeyed blindly like the little girl that I was. Since then I have lived and learned, and have come to understand of what treachery I was guilty to Gabriel. Poor Gabriel! when he left me he didn't shed a tear, but what unutterable sadness there was in the look he gave me! All this has come back to me with the happy memories of my childhood during the lonely years that I passed at the convent. And thus I have lived each of the years that I was with Gabriel twice over, — in fact and in fancy, in reality and in my dreams. And since I have returned to court here, Sire, I have seen among the accomplished gentlemen who surround you like another crown not one who can compare with Gabriel; and François, the obsequious son of the haughty constable, will never make me forget the proud and gentle companion of my young days. And so, dear Father, now that I realize what I did and its effect, I shall remain true to Gabriel so long as you leave me free."

"Have you ever seen him since you left Vimoutiers, Diane?"

"Alas, no, Father!"

"But you must have heard from him at least?"

"Not a word. I simply know from Enguerrand that he left the province after my departure; he told Aloyse, his nurse, that he would never come back until he had made himself an honorable and dreaded name, and that she need not be anxious about him. And with that he left her, Sire."

"And have his family never heard aught of him?" asked the king.

"His family?" repeated Diane. "I never knew of his having any other family than Aloyse, Father; and I never saw any relatives of his when I went with Enguerrand to pay a visit at Montgommery."

"At Montgommery!" cried Henri, while the color fled from his face. "Diane, Diane, I trust he is not a Montgommery! Tell me, for Heaven's sake, that he is not a Montgommery!"

"Oh, no, indeed, Sire for if he had been, he surely would have lived at the château, whereas he lived with Aloyse, his nurse, in her modest dwelling. But what have the counts of Montgommery ever done to you, Sire, to move you to such an extent? Are they enemies of yours? In their province they are mentioned only with the deepest respect."

"Of course, that is true!" said the king, with a nervous, disdainful laugh; "and they have done nothing to me, nothing at all, Diane! What could a

Montgommery do to a Valois, pray? But to return to this Gabriel of yours. Was it not Gabriel that you called him?"

"Yes."

"And he had no other name?"

"No other that I know of, Sire; he was an orphan like me, and no one ever mentioned his father in my presence."

"And you have no other objection to make, Diane, to this projected alliance with Montmorency, except your former affection for this young man? No other at all, have you?"

"That one is enough; so my heart tells me, Sire."

"Very true, Diane; and perhaps I should not undertake to overcome your scruples if your friend were on the spot, where we could know and appreciate him, and although he may be, I can guess, of uncertain parentage—"

"But is there not a bar on my escutcheon too, your Majesty?"

"Yes, but at least you have an escutcheon, Madame; and you will be good enough to bear in mind that the Montmorencys no less than the Castros consider it an honor to receive into their family a legitimatized daughter of mine. Your Gabriel, on the other hand—but then, that is not the question now. The important fact in my mind is that he has not turned up in six years, and that he has probably forgotten you, Diane, and has, it is more than likely, given his heart to another."

"Sire, you do not know Gabriel: his is an untutored and faithful heart, which will burn itself out in love for me."

"Very well, Diane. To you no doubt it seems improbable that he would be unfaithful to you; and you are quite right to deny it. But everything leads you to suppose that this young man went to the wars. And if so, is it not probable that he has died there? I afflict you, my dear child, for your fair brow has grown pale, and your eyes are swimming in tears. Yes, I can see that your feeling for him is a very deeply rooted one; and although it has seldom been my lot to meet with such, and I have got into the habit of being incredulous about these great passions, I have no inclination to laugh at this of yours, but I respect it. But just see, my darling, in what an embarrassing position you place me by your refusal, and all on account of a childish attachment whose object is nothing more than a mere memory and a shadow. The constable, if I insult him by withdrawing my pledged word, will be angry, and not unjustly, my child, and will very probably leave my service; and then it will be no longer I, but the Duc de Guise, who will be king. Think for a moment, Diane, of the six brothers of that family: the Duc de Guise has at his command the whole military power of France; the cardinal all the finances; a third controls my Marseilles fleet; a fourth commands in Scotland; and a fifth is about to take Brissac's place in Piedmont. So that from one extremity of my realm to the other, I, the king, cannot dispose of a soldier or a crown without their assent. I speak gently to you, Diane, and explain these matters to you; I stoop to implore where I might command. But I think it much better to let you judge for yourself, and that it should be the father and not the king who obtains his daughter's consent to his plans. And I shall obtain it, for you are a good and obedient child. This marriage will be my salvation, my dear child; it will give to the Montmorencys that measure of influence which it will withdraw from the Guises. It will equalize the two arms of the balance of which my royal power is the beam. Guise will become less overbearing, and Montmorency more at my devotion. What! you do not answer, dear. Do you remain deaf to the prayer of your father, who does not storm at you or use harsh words, but who, on the contrary, enters into all your thoughts, and asks of you only that you will not deny him the first service which you can do him in return for what he has done, and all that he wishes still to do for your happiness and honor? Come, Diane, my dear daughter, you will consent, won't you?"

"Sire," replied Diane, "you are a thousand times more powerful when your voice sues for something that it might command. I am ready to sacrifice myself to your interests, but only on one condition, Sire."

"And what is that, you spoiled child?"

"That this marriage shall not take place for three months, and meanwhile I will send to Aloyse for news of Gabriel, and will resort to every other possible source of information, so that if he is no more, I may know it; and if he is still living, I may at least ask him to return me my plighted word."

"Granted with all my heart," said Henri, overjoyed beyond measure; "and I will say in addition that wiser words never fell from a child's lips. So you shall search for your Gabriel, and I will help you as you have need of me; and in three months you shall marry François, whatever be the result of our investigations, and whether your young friend be living or dead."

"And now," said Diane, sadly shaking her head, "I don't know whether I ought to pray most earnestly for his death or his life."

The king opened his lips, and was on the point of giving utterance to a suggestion not very paternal in character, and of rather doubtful consoling power. But he had only to look at Diane's frank expression and lovely face, to stop the words before they came; and he betrayed his thought only by a smile.

"For good or for ill, she will conform to the customs of the court," he said to himself.

And then aloud,—

"The time has come to go to the Church, Diane; allow me to escort you to the great gallery, Madame, and then I will see you again at the tilting, and at the games in the afternoon. And if you are not too much incensed with me for my tyrannical conduct, perhaps you will condescend to applaud my strokes with the lance, and my passades, my fair umpire."

CHAPTER VII
HOW THE CONSTABLE SAID
HIS PATER NOSTER

That same day, in the afternoon, while the jousting and holiday-making was in progress at Tournelles, the Constable de Montmorency was completing his examination, in Diane de Poitiers's closet at the Louvre, of one of his secret agents.

The spy was of medium height and swarthy complexion; he had black hair and eyes, an aquiline nose, a forked chin, and projecting lower lip, and his back was slightly crooked. He bore a most striking resemblance to Martin-Guerre, Gabriel's faithful squire. Any one seeing them separately might well have mistaken either for the other; and he who saw them standing side by side would have taken them for twin brothers, so exactly alike were they in every respect. They had the same features and the same figure, and were apparently of the same age.

"And the courier, what did you do with him, Master Arnauld?" asked the constable.

"Monseigneur, I put him out of the way. It had to be done; but it was in the night and in the forest of Fontainebleau. The murder was laid at the door of robbers. I am very careful."

"Never mind, Master Arnauld; it is a very serious matter, and I blame you for being so ready to play with your knife."

"I shrink at nothing when Monseigneur's service is at stake."

"That's all very well; but once for all, Master Arnauld, remember that if you allow yourself to steal, I will allow you to hang," said the constable, dryly and rather contemptuously.

"Never fear, Monseigneur; I am a man of discretion and foresight."

"Now let's see the letter."

"Here it is, Monseigneur."

"Very well! unseal it without breaking the seal, and read it. For Heaven's sake, do you suppose for a moment that I am going to read it?"

Master Arnauld du Thill took from his pocket a sharp little chisel, and cut carefully around the seal, and unfolded the letter. He turned at once to the signature.

"Monseigneur sees that I was not mistaken. The letter addressed to the Cardinal de Guise is from Cardinal de Caraffa, as that wretched courier was simpleton enough to tell me."

"Read it, then, by the crown of thorns!" cried Anne de Montmorency.

Master Arnauld read as follows, —

> "MONSEIGNEUR AND DEAR FRIEND, — Just three words of importance. In the first place, in accordance with your request, the Pope will let the affair of the divorce drag slowly along, and will put François de Montmorency off from consistory to consistory (he arrived at Rome yesterday) before finally refusing the dispensation that he solicits."

"*Pater noster!*" growled the constable. "May the Devil take them, all these red hats!"

Arnauld continued his reading: —

> "In the second place, Monsieur de Guise, your illustrious brother, after having taken Campli, is holding Civitella in check. But before we resolve to send him the men and supplies that he asks, and which we can only give him at a great sacrifice, we must at least be assured that you will not call him away to serve in Flanders, as the report goes is likely to be the case. Just see that he remains with us, and his Holiness will make up his mind to an extensive issue of indulgences, hard though the times may be, to assist Monsieur François de Guise in soundly whipping the Duke of Alva and his haughty master."

"*Adveniat tuum regnum,*" growled Montmorency. "We will remember that, body and blood! We will remember that, even if we have to call the English into France. Go on, Arnauld, go on, by the Mass!"

The spy resumed: —

> "In the third place, I have to announce to you, Monseigneur, to encourage you and support you in your endeavors, the speedy arrival at Paris of a messenger from your brother,

Vicomte d'Exmès, who is bringing to Henri the flags conquered in this Italian campaign. He is about to set out, and will arrive no doubt at the same time that my letter does, which, however, I have chosen to intrust to our regular courier; his presence, and the glorious trophies which he will offer to the king, will assuredly be of great service to you in conducting your negotiations in every direction."

"*Fiat voluntas tua*," cried the constable, in a perfect fury of rage. "We will give this ambassador from hell a fine reception. I commend him to you, Arnauld. Is that the end of that cursed letter?"

"Yes, Monseigneur, all but the usual complimentary words, and the signature."

"Good! you see that there is some work cut out for you, my fine fellow."

"I ask for nothing better, Monseigneur, with a little money thrown in to assist in obtaining good results."

"Here are a hundred ducats, knave. You must always feel the money in your hand."

"But I spend so much in Monseigneur's service."

"Your vices cost you more than my service does, you scoundrel."

"Oh, how mistaken Monseigneur is in me! I dream only of leading a quiet life, in happiness and affluence, somewhere in the country, with my wife and children about me, and passing the rest of my days in peace, like an honest father and husband."

"A most charmingly virtuous and bucolic picture, to be sure! Oh, well, then, mend your ways, put by a few doubloons, and marry, and you will be in a fair way to realize these dreams of domestic felicity. What prevents you?"

"Ah, Monseigneur, my fiery spirit! And then what woman would ever have me?"

"Meanwhile, and pending your hymeneal plans, suppose you seal that letter again very carefully, and carry it to the cardinal. You must disguise yourself, you understand, and say that your dying comrade enjoined upon you—"

"You may trust me, Monseigneur. The resealed letter and the substituted courier will seem more authentic than the real articles."

"The deuce take it!" said Montmorency; "we forgot to take down the name of this plenipotentiary whose coming is announced. What is he called?"

"Vicomte d'Exmès, Monseigneur."

"Ah, yes, that was it, villain. Now see that you remember the name. Well! who dares to interrupt me again?"

"Pardon, Monseigneur," said the constable's fourrier, entering. "A gentleman arrived from Italy is asking to see the king on behalf of the Duc de Guise; and I thought I ought to advise you of it, especially since he was very anxious to speak with the Cardinal de Lorraine. He calls himself Vicomte d'Exmès."

"That was very proper of you, Guillaume," said the constable. "Show the gentleman in here. And do you, Master Arnauld, take your place there behind that hanging, and don't let slip this opportunity of having a good look at the man with whom no doubt you will have some business to transact. It is for your benefit that I receive him, so keep your eyes and ears open."

"I am quite sure, Monseigneur," replied Arnauld, "that I have already come across him in my travels. But no matter! It is just as well to be certain of it. Vicomte d'Exmès, is it?"

The spy slipped behind the hangings, as Guillaume appeared, ushering Gabriel into the room.

"Pardon me," said the young man, politely saluting the old constable; "but to whom have I the honor of addressing myself?"

"I am the Constable de Montmorency, Monsieur; what is your will?"

"Pardon me again," said Gabriel; "but what I have to say I must say to the king."

"But you know that his Majesty is not at the Louvre, do you not? and in his absence—"

"I will follow his Majesty or await his return," Gabriel interposed.

"His Majesty is at the fêtes at the Tournelles, and will not return before evening. Don't you know that the marriage of Monseigneur le Dauphin is being celebrated to-day?"

"No, Monseigneur; I only learned of it on my way hither. But I came by way of the Rue de l'Université and the Pont au Change, and did not pass through the Rue St. Antoine."

"Then you ought to have followed the crowd. That would have shown you the way to the king."

"But I have not yet had the honor of being presented to his Majesty. I am an entire stranger at court. I hoped to find Monseigneur le Cardinal de Lorraine at the Louvre. It was his Eminence for whom I inquired, and I can't imagine why I have been conducted to you, Monseigneur."

"Monsieur de Lorraine," said the constable, "loves these sham fights, being a churchman; but I, who am a man of the sword,—I care only for real fighting, and that is why I am at the Louvre, while Monsieur de Lorraine is at the Tournelles."

"If you please, Monseigneur, I will go and seek him there, then."

"But, *mon Dieu*, stay and rest a bit, Monsieur; for you seem to have arrived from a distance,—from Italy, no doubt, since you entered the city by the Rue de l'Université."

"From Italy, in truth, Monseigneur. I have no reason to conceal the fact."

"You come from the Duc de Guise, perhaps? Well, what is he about down there?"

"Permit me, Monseigneur, to inform his Majesty in the first instance, and to take my leave to the end that I may fulfil that duty."

"So be it, Monsieur, since you are in such haste. No doubt," he added with an assumed air of pleasantry, "you are in a hurry to renew your acquaintance with some fair lady or other. I'll warrant that you are in haste and fear at the same time. Come, now, isn't that so, my young sir?"

But Gabriel put on his coldest and most serious expression, and replied only with a low bow, as he left the apartment.

"*Pater noster qui es in cœlis*" snarled the constable, when the door had closed behind Gabriel. "Does this cursed fop imagine that I wanted to make advances to him, to win him over to my side, perchance, or to corrupt him possibly? As if I didn't know perfectly well what he is going to say to the king! No matter! if I fall in with him again, he shall pay me dear for his unsociable airs and his defiant insolence! Ho, there, Master Arnauld! Come, come! Where is the blackguard? Vanished too, by the cross! Everybody seems to have taken on a fit of stupidity to-day. The Devil seize them! *Pater noster!*"

While the constable was thus venting his ill-humor in curses and *Pater nosters*, as his wont was, Gabriel, on his way out of the Louvre, was passing through a rather dark gallery, when to his great amazement he saw his squire, Martin-Guerre, standing near the door, although he had ordered him to await him in the courtyard.

"Is it you, Master Martin?" said he. "So you have come to meet me! Very well! Go you ahead with Jérôme, and wait for me with the flags well wrapped up at the corner of the Rue St. Catherine on the Rue St. Antoine. Perhaps Monseigneur le Cardinal would prefer that we should present the flags to the king on the spot, and in the presence of the whole court assembled at the jousting. Christopher will hold my horse and bear me company. Go on! you understand me, don't you?"

"Yes, Monseigneur, I know what I wanted to know," replied Martin-Guerre.

And he started down the staircase ahead of Gabriel with an alacrity which augured well for the speedy execution of his commission. Imagine Gabriel's extreme surprise, when he came out more slowly and like one who dreamed, to find his squire still in the court, and now apparently terrified and pale as a ghost.

"Well, Martin, what is it, and what is the matter with you?" he asked him.

"Ah, Monseigneur, I have just seen him; he passed right near me this very moment, and spoke to me."

"Who, pray?"

"Who? Why, who but the devil, the ghost, the phantom, the monster, the other Martin-Guerre?"

"Still this madness. Martin! Are you dreaming as you stand there?"

"No, no, indeed I was not dreaming. He spoke to me, Monseigneur, I tell you; he stopped in front of me, turned me to stone with his wizard's look, and said to me, laughing his infernal laugh, 'So we are still in Vicomte d'Exmès's service, are we?' Note the plural, 'we are,' Monseigneur; 'and we have brought from Italy the flags taken in the field by Monsieur de Guise?' I said yes, in spite of myself, for he fascinated me. How does he know all this, Monseigneur? And he went on: 'Let us not be afraid, for are we not friends and brothers?' And then he heard your footsteps approaching, Monseigneur, and he added, with a diabolical irony which made my hair stand on end, just these words: 'We shall meet again, Martin-Guerre; we shall meet again.' And he disappeared through that little wicket, perhaps, or more likely into the wall."

"You poor fool!" said Gabriel. "How could he have had the necessary time to say and do all this since you left me up there in the gallery?"

"I, Monseigneur! I haven't stirred from this spot, where you ordered me to await you."

"It must have been another, then; and if not to you to whom have I just been speaking?"

"Most certainly to the other. Monseigneur; to my double, my ghost."

"Poor Martin!" said Gabriel, compassionately, "are you in pain? Doesn't your head ache? Perhaps we have walked too far in the hot sun."

"Oh, yes!" said Martin-Guerre, "I see that you fancy that I am wandering, do you not? But a sure proof that I am not mistaken, Monseigneur, is that I don't know a single word of the orders that you think you gave me."

"You must have forgotten them, Martin," said Gabriel, gently. "Well, then, I will repeat them, my good fellow. I told you to go and wait for me with the flags in the Rue St. Antoine at the corner of the Rue St. Catherine. Jérôme will accompany you, and I will keep Christopher with me; don't you remember now?"

"Pardon, Monseigneur; but how can you expect me to remember what I never knew?"

"At all events, you know it now, Martin," said Gabriel. "Come, let us take our horses again at the gates, where our people ought to be waiting with them, and then be off at once. To the Tournelles!"

"I obey, Monseigneur. The amount of it is that you have two squires; but I am very glad at least that I have not two masters."

The lists for the formal celebration had been laid out across the Rue St. Antoine from the Tournelles to the royal stables. They were in the form of a large square, bordered on each side by scaffolding filled with spectators. At one end were the queen and the court; at the other end was the entrance to the lists where the participants in the games were waiting; the general public filled the two remaining galleries.

When, after the marriage ceremony and the banquet which immediately succeeded it were at an end, the queen and court, about three in the afternoon, took their places on the seats reserved for them, vivas and shouts of joy resounded on all sides.

But this noisy jubilation caused the fête to be marred by an accident at its very beginning. The horse of Monsieur d'Avallon, one of the captains of the Guards, terrified by the uproar, reared and leaped into the arena, and his rider, unhorsed by the shock, hit his head a terrible blow against one of the wooden barriers which made the enclosure, and he was taken up half dead, and given over to the care of the surgeons in an almost hopeless condition.

The king was much moved by this sad casualty; but his passion for games and jousting soon got the better of his sorrow.

"Poor Monsieur d'Avallon," said he, "and such a devoted subject! Let us hope at least that he will be well looked after."

And then he added, —

"Come! the races for the ring can begin at any time."

The game of the ring of that epoch was much more complicated and difficult than the one that we know. The crutch from which the ring was suspended was placed almost two thirds of the way down the lists. It was necessary to ride at a hand gallop the first third, and at a full gallop the second third, and while going at this high rate of speed to carry off the ring on the end of the lance. But the lance must not be allowed to touch the body anywhere; it must be held horizontally with the elbow, high above the head. The game was ended by riding around the arena at a trot. The prize was a diamond ring offered by the queen.

Henri II., on his white steed, magnificently caparisoned in gold and velvet, was the most superb and most graceful cavalier of all. He carried and handled his lance with admirable grace and precision, and hardly ever missed the ring. But Monsieur de Vieilleville pressed him close; and there was a moment when it seemed as if the prize would go to him. He had two rings more than the king, and but three remained to be taken; but Monsieur de Vieilleville, like an accomplished courtier, missed them all three by extraordinary ill luck, and the prize was awarded to the king.

As he received the ring, he hesitated a moment, and his look turned regretfully toward Diane de Poitiers; but the gift was offered by the queen, and it was his bounden duty to present it to the new dauphine, Mary Stuart, the bride of the day.

"Well!" he asked, in the interval which followed this first contest, "are there any hopes of saving Monsieur d'Avallon's life?"

"He still breathes, Sire," was the reply; "but there is almost no chance that he will ever regain consciousness."

"Alas!" said the king, "let us have the gladiators' contest now."

This gladiators' contest was a mock combat with passades and manœuvring, quite new, and a great curiosity in those days; but which would have no special interest, probably, for the imagination of the spectator of our time, or of the readers of this book. We beg to refer to the pages of

Brantôme those who are curious to read about the marches and counter-marches of these twelve gladiators, "of whom six were clad in white satin, and six in crimson satin, made up according to the style in vogue in ancient Rome." All of which should be of great historical interest in an age when local coloring had not been invented.

This fine contest came to an end amid general applause, and the necessary preparations were made for beginning the stake-race.

At the court end of the lists several stakes five or six feet long were stuck into the earth at regular intervals. The rules required that the contestants should ride at a hand-gallop in and out among these improvised trees in every direction, without missing or omitting a single one. The prize was a bracelet of marvellous workmanship.

Out of eight courses that were run, the honors remained with the king in three and with Monsieur le Colonel-Général de Bonnivet in a like number. The ninth and last was to be the decisive one; but Monsieur de Bonnivet was no less respectful than Monsieur de Vieilleville had been; and notwithstanding the very willing disposition of his horse, he came in third, and again Henri won the prize.

This time the king sat down beside Diane de Poitiers, and put upon her arm without concealment the bracelet he had received.

The queen turned pale with rage.

Gaspard de Tavannes, who was just behind her, leaned forward and whispered in Catherine de Médicis's ear, —

"Madame, follow me with your eyes, and see what I am going to do."

"And what is it that you are going to do, my good Gaspard?" said the queen.

"To cut off Madame de Valentinois's nose," replied Tavannes, with the utmost gravity and seriousness.

He was just about to leave her, when Catherine, half terrified and half delighted, held him back.

"But, Gaspard, do you realize that it will be your destruction?"

"I do, Madame; but I will save the king and France!"

"Thanks, Gaspard," replied Catherine; "you are a valiant friend no less than a rough soldier. But I command you to be still, Gaspard, and have patience."

"Patience." In truth, that was the watchword by which Catherine de Médicis seemed to have ordered her life up to that time. She, who subsequently was so forward to take her place in the very first rank, had not yet appeared to have any ambition to emerge from the obscurity of the second. She bided her time. And yet she was at this time in the full bloom of a beauty of which Sieur de Bourdeille has left us most minute details; but she sedulously avoided all parade, and it is probably to this modesty that she owed the utter absence of slander in relation to her during her husband's lifetime. There was no one but the brute of a constable who would have dared to call the king's attention to the fact that the ten children that Catherine de Médicis had bestowed on France after ten years of sterility were very little like their father. No other person would have been bold enough to breathe a word against the queen.

It was always Catherine's custom to appear, as she did on this day, not even to notice the attentions which the king lavished on Diane de Poitiers in the sight and bearing of the whole court. After she had soothed the fiery indignation of the marshal she went on talking with her ladies of the races that had taken place, and of the address displayed by Henri.

CHAPTER VIII
A FORTUNATE TOURNEY

The tournaments proper were not to take place until the next and following days; but several gentlemen attached to the court asked the king's leave, as it was still quite early, to break a lance or two in honor of the ladies and for their entertainment.

"So be it, gentlemen," the king replied as a matter of course. "I give you leave with all my heart, especially as it is likely to bother Monsieur le Cardinal de Lorraine, who has never had to deal with so numerous a correspondence, I fancy, as during the two hours that we have been here. There are two messages that he has received one right after the other, and he seems much preoccupied with them. But never mind! we shall know by and by what the matter is, and meanwhile you may break a lance or two. And here is a prize for the victor," added Henri, taking from his neck the gold necklace that he wore. "Do your best, gentlemen, and remember that if the contest grows warm, I shall be very likely to take a hand in it, and try to win back what I am offering you, especially as I owe something to Madame de Castro. Take notice, too, that at precisely six o'clock the contest will be declared at an end, and the victor, whoever he may be, will receive his crown. Come, you have an hour in which to show off your fine strokes. Be always careful that no harm comes to any one. And, apropos, how does Monsieur d'Avallon?"

"Alas, Sire, he is just at the point of death."

"God rest his soul!" said Henri. "Of all the captains of my Guards he was the most devoted to my service and the bravest. Who is there to take his place? But the ladies are waiting, gentlemen; and the lists are open. How, who shall receive the necklace from the hands of the queen?"

The Comte de Pommerive was the first challenger, and he had to yield to Monsieur de Burie, from whom Monsieur le Maréchal d'Amville soon wrested the field; but the marshal, who was very strong and skilful as well, held his ground against five challengers one after the other.

The king could not contain himself.

"I propose to find out, Monsieur d'Amville, if you are riveted there for all time," he said to the marshal.

He put on his armor, and at the very first onset Monsieur d'Amville lost his stirrups. It was Monsieur d'Aussun's turn next; but after him no other combatant appeared.

"How's this, gentlemen?" said Henri. "What! No one else wishes to tilt against me. Can it possibly be that you are humoring me?" he continued, with a gathering frown. "Ah, *mordieu*! if I thought so! There is no king here but the victor, and no privileges save those of knightly skill. Come, attack me, gentlemen, boldly."

But no one ventured to try a pass with the king; for they dreaded equally to vanquish him and to be vanquished.

But the king was much annoyed. He began to suspect that perhaps in former tourneys his opponents had not put forth all their science against him; and this thought, which made his prowess seem small in his own eyes, filled him with anger.

At last a new champion passed the barrier. Henri, without a single glance to see who it was, set his horse in motion and rushed at him. The two lances were shattered; but the king, throwing away the fragment, reeled in his saddle, and was forced to cling to the saddlebow to save himself. At that instant six o'clock struck. Henri was beaten.

He leaped quickly and joyously to the ground, threw his reins to a squire, and rushed to seize the hand of his vanquisher to escort him to the queen himself. To his vast surprise he saw a face which was absolutely unfamiliar to him. Moreover, he was a cavalier of fine presence and noble bearing; and the queen, as she passed the necklace around the young man's neck, while he knelt before her, could not forbear remarking it, and smiling upon him.

But he, after bowing to the ground, rose, took a few steps toward the platform appropriated to the court, stopped before Madame de Castro, and offered her the necklace, the prize of victory.

The trumpets were still sounding, so that no one heard the two cries which issued at the same moment from two mouths.

"Gabriel!"

"Diane!"

Diane, pale, and trembling with joy and wonder, took the necklace with a shaking hand. Every one supposed that the unknown knight had heard the king promise the necklace to Madame de Castro; and that he did not wish to disappoint so fair a damsel. It was agreed that his proceeding was very courteous, and bore the stamp of a true gentleman. The king himself put no other construction on the incident.

"I am touched by such extreme gallantry," said he; "but I, who am supposed to be able to call all my nobles by name, I confess that I cannot recall, Monsieur, where or when I have seen you before, and I shall be more than delighted to know to whom I am indebted for the sturdy blow just now which would have unsaddled me, I believe, if, thank God! I had not had such strong legs."

"Sire," replied Gabriel, "this is the first time that I have had the honor of appearing before your Majesty. I have been hitherto with the army, and have only just arrived from Italy. I am called Vicomte d'Exmès."

"Vicomte d'Exmès!" echoed the king. "I shall remember the name of my vanquisher, never fear."

"Sire," said Gabriel, "there can be no vanquisher where you are concerned, and I bring a glorious proof of it to your Majesty."

He made a sign; and Martin-Guerre and the two men-at-arms entered the lists with the Italian flags, which they laid at the king's feet.

"Sire," Gabriel continued, "these are the flags conquered in Italy by your army, and sent to your Majesty by Monseigneur le Duc de Guise. His Eminence, Monseigneur le Cardinal de Lorraine, assures me that your Majesty will not take it ill of me to deliver these trophies to you thus unexpectedly, and in the presence of your court and the French people, who are the deeply interested witnesses of your greatness and glory. Sire, I have also the honor to hand you these letters from Monsieur le Duc de Guise."

"Thanks, Monsieur d'Exmès," said the king. "So this is the secret of all Monsieur le Cardinal's correspondence. These letters are your credentials to our favor, Viscount. But you have a very striking and triumphant way of presenting yourself. But what do I read here? That you have yourself taken four of these flags? Our cousin Guise rates you as one of his most gallant captains. Monsieur d'Exmès, ask of me what you choose; and I swear by all that is holy that you shall have it on the spot!"

"Sire, you overwhelm me; and I put myself entirely at the disposition of your Majesty's favor."

"You were a captain under Monsieur de Guise, Monsieur," said the king. "Would it suit you to hold the same rank in our Guards? I was perplexed as to how I should fill the place of Monsieur d'Avallon, who met such a sad fate here to-day; but I see that in you he will have a worthy successor."

"Your Majesty—"

"Do you accept? Then it's done. You will begin your duties to-morrow. Now we are about to return to the Louvre. You will tell me more at length of the particulars of this Italian war at some future time."

Gabriel saluted him.

Henri gave the word for departure. The crowd dispersed amid shouts of *Vive le roi*! Diane, as if by magic, found herself at Gabriel's side for an instant.

"To-morrow at the queen's levee," said she in a low voice.

She disappeared under her escort's wing, but leaving hope divine to blossom in the heart of her old-time friend.

CHAPTER IX
HOW ONE MAY PASS CLOSE BY HIS DESTINY WITHOUT KNOWING IT

When the queen held a levee, it was generally in the evening after supper; so much Gabriel learned, and was told also that his new post of captain of the Guards not only allowed but required him to show himself there. He had no desire to shirk that duty, and his only regret was that he had to wait twenty-four hours before fulfilling it. We can see that in zeal and gallantry Monsieur d'Avallon's place was likely to be worthily filled.

But he had to think about killing those twenty-four hours, one after the other,—those everlasting hours which separated him from the eagerly desired moment. This young man, whose joy made him forget his weariness, and who had as yet hardly seen Paris except on his way from one camp to another, started to scour the city with Martin-Guerre in search of a suitable lodging. He had the good luck, for he was in luck that day, to find vacant the very apartments which had formerly been occupied by his father, the Comte de Montgommery. He hired them, although they were somewhat over-fine for a mere captain of the Guards; but he could make himself easy in that regard by simply writing to his faithful Elyot to send him some money from Montgommery. He also wrote to his good nurse Aloyse to come and join him there.

Gabriel's first purpose was thus attained. He was a child no longer now, but a man who had already proved his manhood, and with whom there must be a reckoning; to the honorable qualities which he had inherited from his ancestors he had been able to add some personal renown. Alone and with no other support than his sword, and no recommendation but his gallant behavior, he had reached high rank at twenty-four. At last he might proudly show himself to her whom he loved, as well as to those whom it was his duty to hate. The latter Aloyse could help him to find; the former had found him.

Gabriel went to sleep with his heart at rest, and slept long and well.

The next day he had to present himself to Monsieur de Boissy, Grand Equerry of France, to furnish his proofs of nobility. Monsieur de Boissy, a man of honor, had been the Comte de Montgommery's friend. He understood Gabriel's motives for concealing his true title, and gave him his word that he would keep his secret. In the next place, Monsieur le Maréchal d'Amville presented Gabriel to his company. Then Gabriel at once began his duties by visiting and inspecting the State prisons in Paris, — a painful necessity which it was a part of his functions to yield to once a month.

He began with the Bastille, and ended with the Châtelet.

The governor handed him his list of prisoners, told him which ones had died or been transferred or set free, and which were sick, and finally made them pass in review before him, — a sad review, a mournful spectacle. He thought his duties were done, when the governor of the Châtelet called his attention to a page in his register which was almost blank, and bore only this extraordinary memorandum, which impressed Gabriel more than all the rest: —

"No. 21, X. — Secret prisoner. If during the visit of the governor or the captain of the Guards he makes the least attempt to speak, have him removed to a deeper and harsher dungeon."

"Who is this prisoner of such importance? May I know?" Gabriel asked Monsieur de Salvoison, governor of the Châtelet.

"No one knows who he is," was the reply. "I received him from my predecessor as he had received him from his. You notice that the date of his imprisonment is left blank. It must have been during the reign of François I. that he was brought here. He has undertaken to speak two or three times, so I am told; but at his first word the governor is bound, under the severest penalties, to close the door of his cell, and to remove him at once to a more rigorous dungeon; and this has always been done. There is now only one dungeon left more severe than that he occupies, and confinement in that means death. No doubt they desire that he should finally come to that; but just now the prisoner makes no attempt to speak. He must be some very dangerous criminal. He is always in shackles; and his jailer, to guard against any possibility of an escape, is in and out of his cell every minute."

"But suppose he speaks to the jailer?" said Gabriel.

"Oh, he is a deaf mute, born in the Châtelet, who has never been outside the walls."

Gabriel shuddered. This man, so completely isolated from the world of the living, and who yet lived and thought, inspired in his breast a feeling of compassion mingled with an undefinable dread. What resolution or compunction, what fear of hell or trust in heaven, could prevent so wretched a being from dashing out his brain against the walls of his dungeon? Could it be the thirst for revenge, or some hope of deliverance that enabled him to retain his hold on life!

Gabriel felt a sort of anxious eagerness to see this man; his heart beat faster than it had ever done before except when he was on his way to see Diane. He had visited a hundred other prisoners with no other emotion than a sort of general compassion for their lot; but the thought of this poor wretch appealed to him and moved him more than all the others, and his heart was filled with sorrow when he thought of his tomb-like existence.

"Let us go to Number 21," he said to the governor with a choking voice.

They went down several damp, black stairways, passed under several arches which resembled the horrible spirals of Dante's Inferno; at last the governor said, stopping before an iron door, —

"This is the place. I am not his jailer; he is in the cell, no doubt. But I have duplicate keys; let us go in."

He opened the door, and they went in, with no light but a lantern, held by a turnkey. Then Gabriel saw before him a mute and frightful picture, such as one hardly sees except in the nightmare of delirium.

For walls, nothing but solid rock, black, moss-grown, and noisome; for this gloomy hole was excavated below the bed of the Seine, and the water, in times of freshet, filled it half full. On these loathsome walls were crawling slimy things; and the icy air was broken by no sound except that made by the regular, dull falling of a drop of water from the hideous arch. A little less alive than the drop of water, a little more alive than the almost motionless slugs, two beings that had been human were dragging out their existence there, one guarding the other, both dumb and awe-inspiring.

The jailer, a sort of idiot, a dull-eyed giant, with a face of deathlike pallor, was standing in the shadow, gazing stupidly at the prisoner, who was lying in the corner on a pallet of straw, shackled hand and foot to a chain riveted to the wall. He was an old man, with a long white beard and white hair. When they entered he seemed to be sleeping, and did not stir; he might have been taken for a corpse or a statue.

But suddenly he sat up and opened his eyes, and his gaze met Gabriel's.

He was forbidden to speak; but this terrible and piercing gaze spoke for him. Gabriel was fascinated by it, and could not remove his eyes. The governor and turnkey overhauled all the corners of the dungeon. He,

Gabriel, rooted to the spot, neither moved forward nor back, but stood there transfixed by those blazing eyes; he could not get away from them, and at the same time a thousand confused and unutterable thoughts were whirling through his brain.

The prisoner seemed no longer to view his visitor with mere indifference, and there was a moment when he made a motion and opened his lips as if to speak; but the governor having turned back toward them, he remembered in time the rule laid down for him, and his lips spoke only by a bitter smile. He closed his eyes once more, and relapsed into his corpse-like immobility.

"Oh, let us go out!" said Gabriel to the governor. "For God's sake, let us go out! I must have fresh air and see the sunlight again."

He did not recover his tranquillity and his life, so to speak, until he found himself once more in the throng and tumult of the street. And even then the gloomy vision he had seen remained in his mind and pursued him the livelong day, as he walked thoughtfully hither and thither through the streets.

Something seemed to tell him that the fate of this wretched captive was connected with his own, and that a great crisis in his life was impending. Worn out at last by these mysteriously recurring presentiments, he directed his steps as the day drew to its close toward the lists of the Tournelles. The day's jousting, in which Gabriel had not cared to take part, was just coming to an end. Gabriel could see Diane, and she saw him; and this interchange of glances at once put his gloomy thoughts to flight as the rays of the sun disperse the clouds. Gabriel forgot the unfortunate prisoner whom he had seen that day, to give himself up entirely to thoughts of the lovely maiden he was to see again in the evening.

CHAPTER X
AN ELEGY DURING THE
PROGRESS OF A COMEDY

If was a custom handed down from the reign of François I. At least three times a week, the king, the nobles, and all the ladies of the court assembled in the evening in the queen's apartments. There they would chat about the gossip of the day with perfect freedom, and sometimes with a good deal of license. Private tête-à-têtes would often take place amid the general conversation; and, says Brantôme, "as a throng of earthly goddesses were assembled there, every nobleman and gentleman talked with her whom he loved the best." Frequently there was dancing too, or a play.

It was a party of this description that our friend Gabriel was to attend on the evening in question; and contrary to his custom, he arrayed and perfumed himself with considerable solicitude, so that he might not appear to disadvantage in the eyes of her "whom he loved the best," to quote Brantôme once more.

But Gabriel's delight was not altogether unalloyed by a feeling of uneasiness; and certain vague and offensive words which had been whispered in his hearing concerning Diane's approaching marriage had not failed to cause him some inward anxiety. Thanks to the joy he had felt in seeing Diane again, and in believing that he could distinguish in her expression signs of her former affection for him, he had almost forgotten that letter from the Cardinal de Lorraine which had been the cause of his taking his departure so hurriedly; but the rumors which were flying around, and the continual coupling of the names of Diane de Castro and François de Montmorency, which came to his ears only too plainly, brought back memory to his passionate heart. Was Diane reconciled, then, to that hateful marriage? Did she love this François? Distracting doubts which the evening's interview might not avail to solve satisfactorily.

Gabriel resolved therefore to question Martin-Guerre on the subject, for he had already made more than one acquaintance, and like most squires, was likely to have a much more extended knowledge in such matters than his master; for it is a fact of common observation in acoustics that reports of all sorts sound much louder on low ground, and that echoes are seldom heard except in valleys. This resolution came at a so much more fortunate time, because Martin-Guerre had also made up his mind to question his master, whose preoccupation had not escaped his notice, but who had not, in all conscience, any right to conceal his actions or his thoughts from a faithful retainer of five years' standing, and even more than that,—one who had saved his life.

From this mutual determination, and the conversation which ensued, Gabriel came to the conclusion that Diane de Castro did not love François de Montmorency, and Martin-Guerre that Gabriel did love Diane de Castro.

This twofold conclusion was so satisfactory to both parties that Gabriel arrived at the Louvre fully an hour before the gates were opened; and Martin-Guerre, as a mark of respect to the viscount's royal sweetheart, went off to the court tailor to buy a brown cloth jerkin and small-clothes of yellow tricot. He paid cash for the whole costume, and immediately arrayed himself in it so as to exhibit it in the evening in the antechambers of the Louvre, where he was to go in attendance on his master.

Imagine the tailor's amazement half an hour later to see Martin-Guerre appear again in other clothes. He commented on the fact. Martin-Guerre replied that the evening had seemed a bit cool to him, and that he had thought best to clothe himself a little more warmly. However, he was so very well pleased with the jerkin and the small-clothes that he had come to beg the tailor to sell him or make him another jerkin of the same material and like cut. To no purpose did the man of the yardstick remind Martin-Guerre that he would seem to have only one suit of clothes, and that he would do much better to order a different costume; for instance, a yellow jerkin and brown small-clothes, since he seemed to have a weakness for those particular colors. Martin-Guerre would not recede from his idea, and the tailor had to agree not to make a shade of difference in the garments, which he was to make for him at once, since he had none ready-made; but on this second order Martin-Guerre asked for some credit. He had paid cash handsomely for the first; he was the squire of Vicomte d'Exmès, captain of the king's Guards. The tailor had that monumental trust in human nature which has been from time immemorial the traditional propensity of his craft; so he consented, and promised to deliver the second costume complete the next day.

Meanwhile the hour during which Gabriel had had to gnash his teeth outside the gates of his paradise had passed away, and with a number of others, gentlemen and ladies, he had succeeded in making his way to the queen's apartments.

At the first glance Gabriel saw Diane; she was seated beside the Queen-Dauphine, as Mary Stuart was henceforth called.

To approach her at once would have been very presumptuous for a new-comer, and very imprudent too, no doubt. Gabriel resigned himself to await a favorable opportunity when the conversation should become animated and the attention of those who were near be called to other objects. Meanwhile he entered into conversation with a young nobleman of unhealthy pallor and delicate appearance, near whom he chanced to be standing. But after some little talk on matters as insignificant as his person seemed to be, the young cavalier asked of Gabriel, —

"To whom have I the honor of speaking, Monsieur?"

Gabriel replied, "I am Vicomte d'Exmès. And may I venture to ask you the same question, Monsieur?" he added.

The young man looked at him in amazement as he replied, —

"I am François de Montmorency."

He might as well have said, "I am the Devil!" and Gabriel would have shown less alarmed haste in leaving him. François, whose mind did not work very quickly, was entirely dumfounded; but as he was not fond of using his brain, he soon gave up the riddle, and sought elsewhere for auditors who should be somewhat less unceremonious.

Gabriel had taken care to direct his flight toward Diane de Castro; but his progress was arrested by a great commotion about the king. Henri was just announcing that as he desired to close the day by treating the ladies to a surprise, he had caused a stage to be arranged in the gallery, and that a five-act comedy in verse by Monsieur Jean Antoine de Baïf, entitled "Le Brave," would be performed there. This intelligence was naturally greeted with general gratitude and applause. The gentlemen gave their hands to the ladies to escort them into the neighboring *salle*, where the stage had been erected; but Gabriel was too late to escort Diane, and could do no better than take his place at a short distance from her behind the queen.

Catherine de Médicis perceived him and called him, and he had no choice but to present himself before her.

"Monsieur d'Exmès," said she, "how is it that we didn't see you at the tournament to-day?"

"Madame," replied Gabriel, "the duties of the office which his Majesty has done me the honor to bestow upon me, prevented."

"So much the worse," said Catherine, with a sweet smile, "for you are surely one of our most daring and skilful cavaliers. You made the king reel yesterday, and that is a very rare thing. I should have been glad to be a witness again of your prowess."

Gabriel bowed, feeling decidedly ill at ease under this shower of compliments, to which he knew not how to reply.

"Do you know the play that they are going to give us?" pursued Catherine, evidently very favorably inclined toward the handsome and modest youth.

"I know it only in Latin," was his reply; "for I am told that it is nothing more than an imitation of one of Terence's plays."

"I see that you are as learned as you are valiant," said the queen, "as well versed in literary matters as you are skilful with thrusts of the lance."

All this was said in an undertone, and accompanied by glances which were not exactly cruel. To be sure, Catherine's heart was empty for the moment. But Gabriel, uncouth as Euripides' Hippolyte, received the Italian's advances with an air of constraint and a frowning brow. Ungrateful wretch! when he was to owe to this kindly disposition, at which he turned up his nose, not only the place which he had so longed for at Diane's side, but the most fascinating pouting by which the love of a jealous sweetheart can betray itself.

In fact, when the prologue began, according to custom, to appeal to the indulgence of the spectators, Catherine said to Gabriel, —

"Go and sit there behind me among these ladies, my literary friend, so that I may at need resort to your fund of information."

Madame de Castro had selected her seat at the end of a row, so that there was only the passage-way beyond her. Gabriel, having paid his respects to the queen, took a stool and modestly seated himself in the passage-way by Diane's side, so as to discommode no one.

The play began.

It was, as Gabriel had told the queen, an imitation of the "Eunuchus" of Terence, written in lines of eight syllables, and translated with all the pedantic simplicity of the time. We will abstain from criticising the play. It would be, moreover, an anachronism, for criticism had not yet been invented at that barbarous epoch. It will suffice for us to remind our readers that the principal character is a braggart, a swaggering soldier who allows himself to be duped and bullied by a sycophant.

Now, from the very beginning of the play, the many partisans of the Guises who were in the hall could see in the absurd old bully only the Constable de Montmorency, while the Montmorency faction chose to recognize the ambitious views of the Duc de Guise in the bluster of the swaggering soldier. And so every scene was a piece of satire, and every sally a pointed hit. The two factions laughed uproariously, and pointed at one another with their fingers; and, truth to tell, this comedy which was being enacted in the hall was no less entertaining than that which the actors were performing on the platform.

Our lovers took advantage of the interest which the two rival camps took in the performance to speak quietly and calmly of their love amid the shouts and laughter. In the first place, each pronounced the other's name in a low voice. It was the sacred invocation.

"Diane!"

"Gabriel!"

"Are you really going to marry François de Montmorency?"

"You have made rapid strides in the queen's good graces, haven't you?"

"But you heard her call me."

"And you know that the king wishes this marriage."

"But have you not consented to it, Diane?"

"But haven't you listened to Catherine, Gabriel?"

"One word, just one!" replied Gabriel. "But you still feel some interest, do you, in the feeling which may be aroused in me by another than yourself? Then you must care something for what is passing in my heart."

"I care as much for it," said Madame de Castro, "as you do for what is passing in mine."

"Oh! then let me tell you, Diane, that if you are like me, you are jealous; if you are like me, you love me to distraction."

"Monsieur d'Exmès," said Diane, who tried for an instant to be severe, poor child!—"Monsieur d'Exmès, I am called Madame de Castro."

"But are you not a widow, Madame? Are you not free?"

"Free, alas!"

"Oh, Diane, you sigh. Tell me, Diane, that your childish affection, which made our early years so sweet, has left some trace in the maiden's heart. Oh, tell me, Diane, that you still love me a little! Don't fear that any one will hear you, for everybody near us is taken up with the jokes of that sycophant; they have no tender words to listen to, so they are laughing. Oh, Diane, smile upon me and answer me; do you love me, Diane?"

"Hush! Don't you see that the act is coming to an end?" said the roguish damsel. "Wait at least till the play begins again."

The *entr'acte* lasted ten minutes,—ten centuries, rather! Fortunately, Catherine, talking busily with Mary Stuart, did not call Gabriel to her side. He would have been quite capable of declining to go, even if it had been his everlasting ruin.

When the comedy began again amid shouts of laughter and noisy applause,—

"Well?" Gabriel inquired.

"Well, what?" replied Diane, feigning an indifference that she was very far from feeling. "Oh, yes, you were asking me, I believe, if I love you. Well, then! Didn't I answer you just now, thus: 'I love you as much as you love me'?"

"Ah!" cried Gabriel, "do you realize what you are saying, Diane? Do you know the extent of this love of mine to which you say that yours is equal?"

"But," said the little dissembler, "if you want me to know about it, the least you can do is to tell me."

"Listen to me, then, Diane, and you will see that since I left you six years ago every action of every hour of my life has tended to bring me nearer to you. It was only on my arrival at Paris a month after your departure from Vimoutiers, that I learned who you were: the daughter of the king and Madame de Valentinois. But it was not your title as a daughter of France that terrified me; it was your title as wife of the Duc de Castro, and yet something said to me: 'No matter! raise yourself to her level; win some renown for yourself, so that some day she may hear your name at least, and may admire you as others fear you.' Such were my thoughts, Diane; and I entered the service of the Duc de Guise, as the one who seemed most likely to put me in a way to win the honorable name at which my ambition pointed, speedily and well. In brief, I was shut up with him within the walls of Metz in the following year, and did my best to bring about the almost-despaired-of result, the raising of the siege. It was at Metz, where I remained to restore the fortification and repair all the damage inflicted in sixty-five days of assault, that I heard of the taking of Hesdin by the imperial troops and the death of the Duc de Castro, your husband. He had never even seen you again, Diane! Oh, I pitied him, but how I did fight at Renty! Ask Monsieur de Guise about it. I was also at Abbeville, Dinant, Bavay, and Cateau-Cambrésis. I was everywhere where the fire of musketry was to be heard; and I can fairly say that there has been no glorious action during this reign in which I have not had some little share.

"After the truce of Vaucelles," said Gabriel, continuing his narrative, "I came to Paris, but you were still at the convent, Diane; and my enforced repose was becoming very wearisome when, by good luck, the truce was broken. The Duc de Guise, who was anxious to give me some token of his good-will, asked me if I would follow him to Italy. If I would! Crossing the Alps in the depths of winter, we made our way through the Milanais, carried Valenza by storm, were allowed free passage through the duchies of Parma and Plaisance, and after a triumphal progress through Tuscany and the States of the Church, we arrived at the Abruzzi. Meanwhile Monsieur de Guise lacked money and troops; yet he took Campli, and laid siege to Civitella; but the army was demoralized, and the success of the expedition compromised. It was at Civitella, Diane, that I learned from a letter from his Eminence, the Cardinal de Lorraine, to his brother of your approaching marriage to François de Montmorency.

"There was nothing more for me to do on that side of the Alps. Monsieur de Guise himself agreed to that, and I obtained from his kindness permission to return to France, fortified with his weighty recommendation, and to bring to the king the flags we had conquered. But my only ambition and desire was to see you, Diane, to speak with you, and to learn from your own lips if you were entering into this new contract of your own free will; and finally, after having told you, as I have just done, of all my struggles and endeavors for these six years, to ask you what I now ask you once more: 'Tell me, Diane, do you love me as I love you?'"

"Dear friend," said Madame de Castro, softly, "I will now respond by telling you of my life in return for yours. When I came to court, a mere child of twelve, after the first moments of wonder and childish curiosity, I grew weary of it all; the gilded chains of my life here weighed heavily upon me, and I bitterly regretted our dear woods and fields at Vimoutiers and Montgommery, Gabriel! Every night I cried myself to sleep. But the king my father was very kind to me, and I tried to give him my love in return for his tenderness. But where was my freedom? Where was Aloyse? And, oh, where were you, Gabriel? I didn't see the king every day. Madame de Valentinois was very cold and constrained with me, and seemed almost to avoid me; and I, Gabriel, I had always need of being loved, as you must remember. Oh, I suffered bitterly that first year, dear."

"Poor dear Diane!" said Gabriel, much moved.

"And so," Diane resumed, "while you were fighting, I was pining away. Man acts, and woman waits,—such is destiny. But it is sometimes much harder to wait than to act. After the first year of my loneliness, the death of the Duc de Castro left me a widow, and the king sent me to pass my period of mourning at the convent of the Filles-Dieu. But the tranquil and peaceful life which we led at the convent suited my nature much better than the everlasting intriguing and excitement of the court; so when my mourning was at an end, I sought and obtained the king's leave to remain at the convent. At least, they loved me there,—good Sister Monique above all, who reminded me of Aloyse. I tell you her name, Gabriel, so that you may love her too. And then, not only did all the sisters love me, but I could still dream, Gabriel; I had the time to do it and the right. I was free; and who was the central figure of all my dreams, of the past as well as of the future? Dear friend, you can guess, can you not?"

Gabriel, reassured and enraptured, answered only by a look of passionate affection. Luckily the comedy had become very engrossing. The braggart was being well scoffed at; and the Guise and Montmorency factions were howling themselves hoarse with delight. The lovers might as well have been alone in a desert.

"Five tranquil and hopeful years passed away," continued Diane. "I had had only one misfortune, in the death of Enguerrand, my foster-father. But a second one was not long in coming. The king recalled me to court, and informed me that I was the destined bride of François de Montmorency. I resisted this time, Gabriel, for I was no longer a child, who did not know what she was doing. I resisted. Then my father went on his knees to me, and pointed out to me how deeply this marriage concerned the well-being of the realm. You had forgotten me, no doubt. It was the king who said that, Gabriel. And then where were you, and who were you? In short, the king persisted so, and begged me so appealingly—it was yesterday, yes, only yesterday—that I promised what he wished, Gabriel, but only on condition that, in the first place, my sacrifice should be delayed for three months; and in the second place, I should find out what had become of you."

"But you did promise?" said Gabriel, turning pale.

"I did, but I had not then seen you, dear; and I had no idea that the very same day your unlooked-for appearance was to stir again in my heart both joyful and sad emotions as soon as I recognized you. Ah, Gabriel, handsomer and prouder than of old, but still the same! I knew all at once that my promise to the king was of no effect, and this marriage impossible; that my life belongs to you, and that, if you still loved me, I would love you forever. Well, now, don't you agree that I am no longer in debt to you, and that your life has no reproach to make to mine?"

"Oh, you are an angel, Diane! And all that I have done to deserve your love is nothing."

"And now, Gabriel, since fate has brought us together for a little, let us consider the obstacles which still keep us asunder. The king is ambitious for his daughters; and the Castros and the Montmorencys between them have made him hard to manage, alas!"

"Make your mind easy on that score, Diane, for the family to which I belong has nothing to ask from either of them, and it will not be the first time either that it has been allied with the royal family of France."

"Really, Gabriel! you fill my cup of joy to the full, in telling me that. I am, as you know, very ignorant in heraldic matters; I do not know the Exmès. Down at Vimoutiers I called you Gabriel; and my heart had no need of a sweeter name than that. That is the name that I love; and if you think that your other name will satisfy the king, why, all is well, and I am happy indeed. Whether you are Exmès or Guise or Montmorency, as long as you are not called Montgommery, all is well."

"And why, then, must I not be a Montgommery?" asked Gabriel, beginning to be alarmed.

"Oh, the Montgommerys, our neighbors down yonder, have apparently done the king some injury, for he hates them bitterly."

"Indeed!" said Gabriel, who began to feel a choking sensation in his throat; "but is it the Montgommerys who have injured the king, or is it rather the king who has injured the Montgommerys?"

"My father is too kind-hearted to have ever been unjust, Gabriel."

"Kind to his daughter, yes," said Gabriel; "but where his enemies are concerned —"

"He may be terrible," replied Diane, "as you are against the enemies of France and the king. But what does it matter, and what have the Montgommerys to do with us, Gabriel?"

"But if I were a Montgommery, Diane?"

"Oh, do not say that, dear."

"But if it should be so?"

"In that case," said Diane, "if I found myself thus obliged to choose between my father and you, I would throw myself at the feet of the injured party, whichever it might be, and I would beg my father to forgive you for my sake, or I would beg you to forgive my father for my sake."

"And your voice is so powerful, dear Diane, that the injured one would surely yield to your prayers, if there had never been blood shed; for blood can only be washed out by blood."

"Oh, you frighten me, Gabriel! Come, this is far enough to carry this test of my love; for it was nothing but a test, was it?"

"No, Diane, nothing but a test. God grant that it may prove to be nothing more!" he murmured under his breath.

"And there is not, there cannot be any bad blood between my father and you?"

"I hope not, Diane, I hope not; I should suffer too bitterly in making you suffer."

"That's right, Gabriel. And if you hope not, Gabriel," she added with her lovely smile, "I hope, for my part, to induce my father to give up this marriage which would be my death-warrant. Such a mighty king as he ought to have enough ways of making it up to the Montmorencys."

"No, Diane; and all his treasures and all his power could not make up to them for losing you."

"Ah, that's your way of looking at it. But you did frighten me, Gabriel. But never fear, dear; François de Montmorency doesn't think as you do on this subject, thank God! and he would much prefer the bâton which will make a marshal of him, to your poor Diane. But I, having accepted this happy exchange, will prepare the king for it very gently. I will remind him of the royal alliances of the D'Exmès family, and of your own personal exploits, Gabriel."

She interrupted herself.

"Ah, *mon Dieu*! see, the play seems to be finished."

"Five acts, how short it has been!" said Gabriel. "But you are right, Diane; and the epilogue is just pointing the moral of the piece."

"Luckily," said Diane, "we have said almost all that we had to say to each other."

"I haven't said one thousandth part of it," said Gabriel.

"No, nor I really," said Diane; "and the queen's advances to you."

"Oh, you wretch!" said Gabriel.

"Oh, no, the wretch is she who smiles at you, and not I who grumble at you, do you hear? Don't speak to her again this evening, will you, dear, just to please me?"

"Just to please you! How good you are! No, I will not speak to her again. But, see, the epilogue is also finished, alas! Adieu! but only for a little while, is it, Diane? Say one last word to me to sustain and comfort me, dear Diane."

"To meet soon again, and forever, Gabriel, my little *husband*," whispered the beaming maiden in the ear of the delighted Gabriel.

And she disappeared in the pushing, noisy crowd. Gabriel slunk away so as to fulfil his promise of avoiding a meeting with the queen. Such touching fidelity to his oath! And he left the Louvre, convinced that Antoine de Baïf was a very great man, and that he had never been present at a performance which had given him so much pleasure.

As he passed into the vestibule, he picked up Martin-Guerre, who was awaiting him, all radiant in his new clothes.

"Well, Monseigneur, did you see Madame d'Angoulême?" the squire asked his master when they were in the street.

"I did see her," replied Gabriel, dreamily.

"And does Madame d'Angoulême still love Monsieur le Vicomte?" continued Martin-Guerre, who saw that Gabriel was in a good humor.

"Rascal!" cried Gabriel, "who told you that? Where did you learn that Madame de Castro loved me, or that I loved Madame de Castro alone? Be good enough to hold your tongue, villain!"

"Oh, well," muttered Master Martin, "Monseigneur must be beloved, else he would have sighed and would not have insulted me; and Monseigneur must be in love or he would have noticed my new cape and breeches."

"Why do you prate to me of breeches and cape? But really, you didn't have that doublet a short time ago, did you?"

"No, Monseigneur, I bought it this very evening to do honor to my master and his mistress, and I paid cash for it too,—for my wife Bertrande did teach me order and economy, as she taught me temperance and chastity and all the virtues. I must do her that much justice; and if I had only been able to instil a little mildness of temper into her, we should have made the happiest couple in the world."

"It was well done of you, chatterbox, and I will repay your outlay, since it was for me that you incurred it."

"Oh, how generous, Monseigneur! But if Monseigneur wishes me to hold my peace about his secret, he should not give me this new proof that he is loved as dearly as he loves. One never empties one's purse so readily, when the heart is not overflowing. Besides, Monsieur le Vicomte knows Martin-Guerre, and that he is to be trusted. Faithful and dumb as the sword that he wears!"

"Very true; but no more of this, Master Martin."

"I leave Monseigneur to his dreams."

Gabriel was dreaming to such an extent that when he reached his chambers he felt an absolute need of pouring his dreams into a sympathetic ear: and he wrote that same night to Aloyse,—

> MY DEAR ALOYSE,—Diane loves me! But no, that is not what I ought to say to you first of all. My dear Aloyse, come and join me here; after six years of separation, I must embrace you once more. The main points of my life are now fixed. I am captain of the king's Guards,—one of the most eagerly sought of all ranks in the army; and the name I have made for myself will help me to reinstate in honor and

renown that which I inherit from my ancestors. And I have need of you for this latter task too, Aloyse. And then I need you because I am so happy, because, I repeat it, Diane loves me,—yes, the Diane of former days, my child sister, who has never forgotten her good Aloyse, although she calls the king her father. And then, Aloyse, this daughter of the king and Madame de Valentinois, this widow of the Duc de Castro, has never forgotten, and still loves with her whole dear soul her obscure Vimoutiers playmate. She has told me so within the hour, and her sweet voice still echoes in my heart.

So come, Aloyse, for I really am too happy to be alone in my happiness.

CHAPTER XI
PEACE OR WAR?

On the 7th of June there was a sitting of the king's council, and there was a very full attendance of members of the council of state. About Henri II. and the princes of the blood were this day assembled Anne de Montmorency, the Cardinal de Lorraine and his brother Charles de Guise, Archbishop of Reims, the chancellor Olivier de Lenville, President Bertrand, Comte d'Aumale, Sedan, Humières, and Saint-André and his son.

Vicomte d'Exmès, in his capacity of captain of the Guards, stood near the door, with bared sword.

All the interest of the session was, as usual, centred in the contentions between the rival ambitions of the houses of Montmorency and Lorraine, represented on this occasion in the council by the constable himself and the cardinal.

"Sire," said the Cardinal de Lorraine, "the danger is imminent, and the enemy at our gates. A formidable army is being assembled in Flanders; and Philip II. may invade our territory to-morrow, and Mary of England declare war against you. Sire, you have a crying need for the presence of a gallant leader, young and vigorous, who is not afraid to act boldly, and whose very name would incite terror in the Spaniard by reminding him of recent defeats."

"Like the name of your brother, Monsieur de Guise, for example," said De Montmorency, sarcastically.

"Like the name of my brother, to be sure," replied the cardinal, valiantly; "like the name of the victor of Metz, of Renty, and of Valenza. Yes, Sire, the Duc de Guise is the man whom you should summon home at once from Italy, where men and supplies are lacking, where he is like to be compelled to raise the siege of Civitella, and where his presence and that of his army, which might be so useful against the threatened invasion here, can be of no further use."

The king turned carelessly toward Monsieur de Montmorency, as if to say, "Now it is your turn."

"Sire," the constable replied to his glance, "recall the army, by all means; and this absurd conquest of Italy, about which there has been so much braggadocio, will end, as I have always said, in ridicule. But what need have you of the general? Look at the latest intelligence from the North: the Flemish frontier is quiet; Philip II. is quaking in his shoes; and Mary of England hasn't a word to say. You may still renew the truce, Sire, or dictate terms of peace, as you choose. It is no adventurous captain of whom you now have need, but a shrewd and experienced minister, who is not blinded by the rash impetuosity of youth, and in whose eyes war is not the mere plaything of an insatiable ambition, but who can lay the foundations of an honorable peace on terms consistent with the glory and dignity of France—"

"Like yourself, for instance, Monsieur le Connétable," interrupted the Cardinal de Lorraine, bitterly.

"Like myself," was Anne de Montmorency's proud reply; "and I frankly advise the king not to trouble himself further about the chances of a war which can take place only if he chooses, and when he chooses. Interior affairs, the condition of the treasury, and religious interests have a much stronger claim upon our attention; and a prudent administrator to-day will be worth a thousand times more than the most enterprising general."

"And will have a thousand times greater claim upon his Majesty's favor, eh?" was the cardinal's sharp retort.

"His Eminence has rounded out my reflection for me," continued Montmorency, coolly; "and since he has put the question on that ground, I will venture to ask his Majesty for a proof that my services in behalf of peaceful measures are gratifying to him."

"What proof is that?" said the king, sighing.

"Sire, I beg your Majesty to make a public declaration of the honor which you condescend to do my house by bestowing upon my son the hand of Madame d'Angoulême. I must have this official demonstration and solemn promise, so that I may steadfastly pursue my present course, without having to combat the suspicions of my friends and the clamor of my enemies."

This bold request was received, despite the king's presence, with signs of applause or displeasure, according as the councillors belonged to one or the other faction.

Gabriel turned pale and shuddered; but he recovered his courage somewhat when he heard the Cardinal de Lorraine reply with spirit,—

"The Holy Father's bull, annulling the marriage of François de Montmorency and Jeanne de Fiennes, has not yet arrived, so far as I know, and may not arrive at all."

"Then we must get along without it," said the constable; "secret marriages may be annulled by royal decree."

"But a decree cannot be made retroactive," was the cardinal's retort.

"But such an effect may be given to it, may it not, Sire? Say it aloud, I conjure you, that those who attack me, as well as I myself, may have a certain demonstration of your approbation of my views! Tell them that your royal favor will go so far as to give a retroactive effect to this just decree!"

"No doubt I can do it," said the king, whose feeble indecision seemed to be yielding to this firm and steady language.

Gabriel had to lean heavily upon his sword to save himself from falling.

The constable's eyes shone with delight. The peace party seemed to be on the verge of a decided triumph, thanks to his daring.

But at this moment the sound of trumpets was heard in the courtyard. The air they were playing was an unfamiliar one, and the members of the council looked wonderingly at one another. The usher came in almost immediately, and bowing to the ground, announced, —

"Sir Edward Fleming, herald of England, begs the honor of being admitted to your Majesty's presence."

"Let the herald of England enter," said the king, marvelling, but outwardly calm.

He made a sign, and the dauphin and the princes came and stood about him, while the other members of the council took their places outside the royal circle. The herald, accompanied only by two armed attendants, was ushered in. He saluted the king, who nodded his head slightly from the sofa on which he remained seated.

Then said the herald, —

"Mary, Queen of England and France, to Henri, King of France: For having maintained friendly relations with the English Protestants, enemies of our religion and our State, and for having tendered and promised them aid and protection against the just and deserved penalties incurred by them, we, Mary of England, do declare war by land and by sea against Henri of France. And as a gage of this defiance, I, Edward Fleming, herald of England, do here fling down my gauntlet of battle."

At a sign from the king the Vicomte d'Exmès stepped forward and picked up Sir Edward's glove. Then Henri said coolly to the herald the one word, —

"Thanks!"

Thereupon he took off the magnificent necklace which he wore, and gave it to Gabriel to hand to the herald, and said, inclining his head once more, —

"You may now withdraw."

The herald bowed low and left the hall. A moment later the blare of the English trumpets was heard once more, whereupon the king broke the silence.

"Well, my Cousin de Montmorency," said he to the constable, "you seem to have been a little too hasty in promising peace, and in answering for the good intentions of Queen Mary. This alleged patronage of the English Protestants is a mere pious pretext to conceal the love of our sister of England for her young husband Philip II. War with the husband and wife both! Well, so be it! A king of France need not fear all Europe; and if the Flemish frontier will only give us a little time to look around— Well, Florimond, again? What is it now?"

"Sire," said the usher, re-entering, "a special courier with important despatches from Monsieur le Gouverneur de Picardie."

"Go and see what it is, I beg, Monsieur le Cardinal de Lorraine," said the king, graciously.

The cardinal returned with the despatches, which he handed to the king.

"Ah, ah, gentlemen," said the king, casting his eye upon them, "a different sort of news this. The forces of Philip II. are assembling at Givet, and Monsieur Gaspard de Coligny advises us that the Duke of Savoy is at their head. A worthy foe! Your nephew, Monsieur le Connétable, thinks that the Spanish troops are about to attack Mezières and Rocroy, so as to cut off Marienbourg. He asks for speedy reinforcements, to enable him to strengthen these places, and hold his own in case he is attacked."

The whole assemblage was in a state of great emotion and excitement.

"Monsieur de Montmorency," said Henri, smiling calmly, "you are not happy in your predictions to-day. 'Mary of England,' said you, 'has not a word to say;' and we have only just been hearing her trumpets sounding. 'Philip II. is afraid, and the Low Country quiet,' you added. Now, the King of Spain seems to be no more afraid than ourselves, while the Flemish are very far from quiet. I must say that I am convinced that the prudent administrator will have to make way for the gallant soldier."

"Sire," said Anne de Montmorency, "I am Constable of France, and war knows even more of me than peace."

"Very true, my good cousin, and I am glad to see that you remember Bicocque and Marignan, and that warlike impulses are coming back to you again. Draw your sword from the scabbard, then, and I shall rejoice. All that I wish to say is that we must think now of nothing but war, and of honorable and glorious war. Monsieur le Cardinal de Lorraine, be good enough to write to your brother, Monsieur de Guise, to return immediately. As for internal affairs and family matters, they must be postponed; and I think we shall have to wait for the Pope's dispensation, Monsieur de Montmorency, before considering farther the proposed marriage of Madame d'Angoulême."

The constable made a wry face, while the cardinal smiled, and Gabriel breathed again.

"Come, gentlemen," added the king, who seemed to have shaken off his indifference all at once, "come, we must collect our thoughts now with so many serious matters to consider. The session is at an end for this morning, but the council will meet again this evening. Till evening, then, and God protect France!"

"*Vive le roi!*" cried the members of the council with one voice.

And the assemblage dispersed.

CHAPTER XII
A TWOFOLD KNAVE

The constable left the king's presence buried in thought. Master Arnauld du Thill put himself in his way, and accosted him in a low voice.

This took place in the grand gallery of the Louvre,

"Monseigneur, one word—"

"Who is it?" said the constable. "Ah, you, Arnauld? What do you want with me? I am hardly in trim to listen to you to-day."

"Yes, I imagined," said Arnauld, "that Monseigneur was vexed by the turn which the marriage project concerning Madame Diane and Monseigneur François has taken."

"How did you know that, you rascal? But after all, what does it matter who knows it? The wind is from a stormy quarter, and favors the Guises, that is sure."

"But to-morrow it may be a fair wind for the Montmorencys," said the spy; "and if there is none but the king against this marriage to-day, why, he will be for it to-morrow. No, the fresh obstacle which bars our way, Monseigneur, is a more serious one, and comes from another quarter."

"And whence can come a more serious obstacle than the disapprobation or even lukewarmness of the king?"

"From Madame d'Angoulême herself, for instance," replied Arnauld.

"You have scented something in that quarter, have you, my keen hound?" said the constable, drawing nearer to him, and evidently becoming interested.

"And how did Monseigneur suppose that I had passed the fortnight that has elapsed?"

"True, it is a long while since I have heard a word of you."

"Neither directly nor indirectly, Monseigneur," replied Arnauld, proudly; "and you, who used to reproach me for being mentioned rather too often in the police-patrol reports, must confess, I think, that for two weeks I have worked shrewdly and quietly."

"True again," said the constable; "and I have been surprised that I haven't had to intervene to get you out of trouble, you varlet, who are always drinking when you're not gambling, and rioting when you're not fighting."

"And the troublesome hero of the last fifteen days has been not I, Monseigneur, but a certain squire of the new captain of the Guards, Vicomte d'Exmès, one Martin-Guerre."

"Yes, I remember now that Martin-Guerre's name has taken Arnauld du Thill's place in the report that I have to examine every evening."

"For instance, who was picked up drunk by the watch the other night?" asked Arnauld.

"Martin-Guerre."

"And who, after a quarrel at the gaming-table on account of dice found to be cogged, struck with his sword the finest of the king's gendarmes?"

"Martin-Guerre again."

"And who only yesterday was taken in the act of trying to carry off the wife of Master Gorju, the ironmonger?"

"Always this same Martin-Guerre," said the constable. "An abominable rascal, to be sure. And his master, this Vicomte d'Exmès, whom I instructed you to keep a sharp watch on, is not likely to be of much more worth than he; for he upholds and defends him, and vows that his squire is the mildest and most sedate of men."

"That is what you used to have the goodness to say of me, Monseigneur. Martin-Guerre believes that he is possessed by the Devil, whereas in truth it is I who possess him."

"What! What do you mean? You are not Satan, are you?" cried the constable, crossing himself in his terror, for he was as ignorant as a fool, and as superstitious as a monk.

Master Arnauld replied only with an infernal leer; but when he thought he had alarmed Montmorency sufficiently, he said, —

"Oh, no, I am not the Devil, Monseigneur. To prove it to you and to reassure you, I ask you to give me fifty pistoles. Now, if I were the Devil, should I have any need of money, and couldn't I draw myself out of all my scrapes with my tail?"

"That's true," said the constable; "and here are your fifty pistoles."

"Which I have well earned, Monseigneur, by gaining the confidence of Vicomte d'Exmès; for although I am not the Devil, I am a bit of a sorcerer, and have only to don a certain brown doublet, and draw on certain yellow breeches, to make Vicomte d'Exmès speak to me as if I were an old friend and a tried confidant."

"Hm! all this has a smack of the gallows," said the constable.

"Master Nostradamus, just from seeing me pass in the street, predicted for me, after one glance at my face, that I should die between heaven and earth. So I resign myself to my destiny, and devote it to your interests, Monseigneur. To know that one is to be hung is a priceless advantage. A man who is sure of meeting his end on the gallows, fears nothing, not even the gallows themselves. To begin with, I have made myself the double of Vicomte d'Exmès's squire. I told you that I would accomplish miracles! Now, do you know, or can you guess, who this viscount is?"

"*Parbleu*! a lawless partisan of the Guises."

"Better than that. The accepted lover of Madame de Castro."

"What's that you say, villain? How do you know that?"

"I am the viscount's confidant, as I told you. It is I who generally carry his notes to the fair one, and bring back the reply. I am on the best of terms with the lady's maid, who is astonished only to have so changeable a lover, — bold as a page one day, and the next day as shy as a nun. The viscount and Madame de Castro meet at the queen's levees three times a week, and write every day. However, you may believe me or not, their affection is absolutely pure. Upon my word, I should be interested for them, if I were not interested for myself. They love each other like cherubs, and have from childhood, so far as I can make out. I have opened their letters now and then, and they have really moved me. Madame Diane is jealous; and of whom, do you suppose, Monseigneur? Of the queen! But she is altogether wrong, poor child. It may be that the queen thinks about Monsieur d'Exmès—"

"Arnauld," the constable interposed, "you are a slanderer!"

"And that smile of yours is quite as slanderous as my words," replied the blackguard. "I was saying that while it might well be that the queen was thinking about the viscount, it is perfectly certain that the viscount is not thinking about the queen. Their young loves are Arcadian in their simplicity and perfectly irreproachable, and move me like a gentle pastoral of ancient Rome or of the days of chivalry; and yet it doesn't prevent me, God help me, from betraying them for fifty pistoles, the poor little turtle-doves! But confess, Monseigneur, that I was right in saying, as I did at first, that I have well earned those same fifty pistoles."

"Indeed you have," said the constable; "but once more I ask you how you have come to be so well informed?"

"Ah, Monseigneur, pardon me; that is my secret, which you may try to guess if you choose, but which I certainly shall not disclose. Besides, my means of information are of little consequence to you (for I alone am responsible for them, after all) provided you attain your end. Now, your end is to be informed as to all proceedings and plans which may tend to injure you; and it seems to me that my revelation of to-day is not unimportant, and may be of great use to you, Monseigneur."

"You are quite right, you rascal; but you must continue to play the spy on this damned viscount."

"I will, Monseigneur; I am as devoted to you as I am to vice. You will give me pistoles, and I will give you words, and we shall both be content. Ah, there's some one coming into the gallery. A woman! The devil! I must bid you adieu, Monseigneur."

"Who is it, pray?" asked the constable, whose sight was beginning to fail.

"Good Lord! it's Madame de Castro herself, who is going to the king, no doubt; and it is very important that she should not see me with you, Monseigneur, although she wouldn't know me in this dress. She is coming this way, and I must avoid her."

And he made his escape in the opposite direction from that in which Diane was coming.

The constable hesitated a moment; then, making up his mind to satisfy himself of the accuracy of Arnauld's report, he advanced boldly to meet Madame d'Angoulême.

"Were you going to the king's closet, Madame?" said he.

"I was, Monsieur le Connétable."

"I am much afraid that you will not find his Majesty disposed to listen to you, Madame," replied Montmorency, naturally alarmed at this step; "and the serious news he has received —"

"Make this just the very most opportune moment for me, Monsieur."

"And against me, Madame, am I not right? For you have bitter enmity for us."

"Alas, Monsieur le Connétable, I have no enmity against anybody in the world."

"Have you really nothing in your heart but love?" asked De Montmorency, in so meaning a tone that Diane blushed and lowered her eyes. "And it is on account of that love, no doubt, that you oppose the king's wishes and the hopes of my son?"

Diane in her embarrassment held her peace.

"Arnauld has told me the truth," thought the constable; "and she does love this handsome triumphal messenger of Monsieur de Guise."

"Monsieur le Connétable," Diane found strength to say at last, "my duty calls upon me to yield obedience to the king, but I have the right to implore my father."

"And so," said the constable, "you persist in going to find the king."

"Indeed I do."

"Oh, well! then I shall go and see Madame de Valentinois, Madame."

"As you please, Monsieur."

They bowed, and left the gallery by opposite doors; and as Diane entered the king's closet, old Montmorency was ushered into the favorite's apartments.

CHAPTER XIII
THE ACME OF HAPPINESS

"Here, Master Martin," said Gabriel to his squire on the same day and almost at the same hour, "I must go and make my rounds, and shall not return to the house within two hours. Do you, Martin, in one hour go to the usual place and wait there for a letter, an important letter, which Jacinthe will hand you as usual. Don't lose a moment, but make haste to bring it to me. If I have finished my rounds, I shall be before you, otherwise await me here. Do you understand?"

"I understand, Monseigneur, but I have a favor to ask of you."

"What is it?"

"Let me have one of the Guards to keep me company, Monseigneur, I implore you."

"A guard to keep you company. What is this new madness? What are you afraid of?"

"I am afraid of myself," replied Martin, piteously. "It seems, Monseigneur, that I outdid myself last night! Up to then I had exhibited myself only as a drunkard and a gambler and a bully; but now I have become a rake! I whom all Artigues respected for the purity of my morals and my ingenuous mind! Would you believe, Monseigneur, that I have sunk so low as to have made an attempt at abduction last night? Yes, at abduction! I tried by main force to carry off the wife of Gorju, the iron-monger,—a very lovely woman, so they say. Unfortunately, or fortunately rather, I was arrested; and if I had not been still in your employ, and recommended by you, I should have passed the night in prison. It's infamous!"

"Well, Martin, were you dreaming when you committed this last prank?"

"Dreaming! Monseigneur, here is the report. When I read it, I blushed up to my ears. Yes, there was a time when I believed that all these infernal performances were frightful nightmares, or that the Devil amused himself by taking on my form for the purposes of his horrible nightly deeds. But you undeceived me; and besides, I never see now the one that I used to take for my shadow. The holy priest in whose hands I have placed the guidance of my conscience has also undeceived me; and he who so persistently violates all divine and human laws, the guilty one, the wretch, the villain, is no doubt myself, judging from what is told me. So that is what I shall believe henceforth. Like a hen who hatches out ducklings, my soul has given birth to honest thoughts, which have resulted in wicked deeds. I should not dare to say except to you that I am possessed, Monseigneur, because if I did I should be burned alive at short notice; but it must be, as you can see, that at certain times I really do have, as they say, the Devil in me."

"No, no, my poor Martin," said Gabriel, laughing; "but you have been indulging rather too freely in strong drink for some time, I fancy, and when you are drunk, why, deuce take it! you see double."

"But I never drink anything but water, Monseigneur, nothing but water! Surely this water from the Seine doesn't go to the head—"

"But, Martin, how about the evening when you were laid under the porch dead-drunk?"

"Well, Monseigneur, that evening I went to bed and to sleep, commending my soul to God; I rose also as virtuous as when I went to bed; and it was from you and you only that I learned what I had been doing. It was the same way the night when I wounded that magnificent gendarme, and the other night of this most shameful assault. And yet I get Jérôme to shut my door and lock me into my room, and I close the shutters and fasten them with triple chains; but, *basta!* nothing is of any use. I must believe that I get up, and that my vicious night-walking existence begins. In the morning when I wake I ask myself. 'What have I been doing, I wonder, during my absence last night?' I go down to find out from you, Monseigneur, or from the district reports, and at once go to relieve my conscience of these new crimes at the confessional, where I can no longer obtain absolution, which is rendered impossible by my everlasting backsliding. My only consolation is to fast and mortify the flesh part of every day by severe scourging. But I shall die, I foresee it, in final impenitence."

"Rather believe, Martin, that this evil spirit will be appeased, and that you will become once more the discreet and sober Martin of other days. Meanwhile, obey your master, and faithfully discharge the commission with which he intrusts you. But how can you ask me to allow you to have any one with you? You know very well that all this business must be kept secret, and that you alone are in my confidence."

"Be sure, Monseigneur, that I will do my utmost to satisfy you. But I cannot answer for myself, I warn you beforehand."

"Oh, this is too much, Martin! Why do you say so?"

"Don't be impatient on account of my absence, Monseigneur. I think that I am there, and I am here; that I will do this, and I do that. The other day, having thirty *Paters* and thirty *Aves* to say for penance, I determined to triple the dose so as to mortify my spirit by tiring myself beyond endurance; and I remained or thought that I remained in the church of St. Gervais telling my beads for two hours and more. Oh, well! when I got back here I learned that you had sent me to carry a letter, and that in proof of it I had brought back a reply; and the next day Dame Jacinthe—another fine woman, alas!— complained of me for having been rather free with her the day before. And that has happened three times, Monseigneur; and you wish me to be sure of myself after my imagination has played me such tricks as that? No, no, I am not sufficiently master of myself for that; and although the blessed water does not burn my fingers, still there are times when there is somebody else than Master Martin in my skin."

"Well, I will run the risk," said Gabriel, losing his patience; "and since you have, at all events up to now, whether you have been at church or in the Rue Froid-Manteau, skilfully and faithfully acquitted yourself of the trust I have imposed upon you, you will do the same to-day; and let me tell you, if you need such a stimulus to your zeal, that in this letter you will bring me my happiness or my despair."

"Oh, Monseigneur, my devotion to you doesn't need to be worked upon, I assure you; and if it wasn't for these devilish substitutions—"

"What! are you going to begin again?" Gabriel interrupted. "I must go; and do you start too in about an hour, and don't forget a single point of my instructions. One word more: you know that for several days past I have been anxiously expecting my nurse Aloyse out of Normandy; and you understand that if she comes while I am away, you must give her the room adjoining mine, and make her as welcome as if she were in her own house. You will remember?"

"Yes, Monseigneur."

"Come, then, Martin, we must be prompt to act, and discreet, and, above all, not lose our presence of mind."

Martin replied only with a repressed sigh; and Gabriel left his house in the Rue des Jardins.

He came back two hours later, as he had said, absorbed and preoccupied. As he entered, he saw only Martin, rushed up to him, seized the letter which he had expected with so much impatience, made a gesture of dismissal, and read:—

"Let us thank God, Gabriel," said this letter; "the king has yielded, and our happiness is assured. You must have learned of the arrival of the herald from England, bearing a declaration of war in the name of Queen Mary, and of the great preparations in Flanders. These events, threatening for France, perhaps, are favorable to our love, Gabriel, since they add to the influence of the young Duc de Guise, and tend to lower that of old Montmorency. The king, however, still hesitated; but I implored him, Gabriel: I said that I had found you again, and that you were noble and valiant; and I told him your name—so much the worse! The king, without promising anything, said that he would reflect; that after all, when the affairs of State became less urgent, it would be cruel in him to compromise my happiness; and that he could make some amends to François de Montmorency with which he would have to be content. He has promised nothing, but he will do everything, Gabriel. Oh, you will learn to love him, as I do, this kind father of mine, who is going to bring to pass all the dreams we have dreamed these last six years! I have so much to say to you, and these written words are so cold! Listen, my friend, come to-night at six o'clock during the council. Jacinthe will bring you to me, and we will have a good long hour to talk of the bright future which is opening before us. But I can foresee that this Flanders campaign will claim you, and that you must make it, alas! to serve the king and to deserve my hand,—mine, who love you so dearly. For I do love you, *mon Dieu*, I do! Why should I try now to conceal it from you? Come to me, then, so that I may see if you are as happy as your Diane."

"Oh, yes, indeed I am happy!" cried Gabriel, aloud, when he had finished the letter; "and what is lacking to my happiness now?"

"The presence of your old nurse, no doubt," unexpectedly replied Aloyse, who had been sitting motionless and silent in the shadow.

"Aloyse!" cried Gabriel, rushing to her and embracing her: "oh, Aloyse, my dear old nurse, if you only knew how I wanted you! How are you? You have not changed a bit. Kiss me again. I have not changed any more than you, in heart at least,—the heart that loves you so. I was worried to death at your delay: ask Martin. And why have you kept me waiting so long?"

"The recent storms, Monseigneur, have washed away the roads; and if I had not been in so great a state of excitement over your letter that it made me brave enough to venture in spite of obstacles of every sort, I should not have been here yet."

"Oh, you did very well to make such haste, Aloyse, you did very well; for really what good is it to be so happy all by one's self? Do you see this letter I have just received? It is from Diane, your other child, and she tells me—do you know what she tells me?—that the obstacles which stood in the way of our love may be removed; that the king will no longer require her to marry François de Montmorency; and last and best of all, that Diane loves me,—yes, that she loves me! And you are at hand to hear all this, Aloyse; so tell me, am I not really at the very acme of happiness?"

"But suppose, Monseigneur," said Aloyse, maintaining the grave and melancholy tone she had assumed at first, "suppose that you had to give up Madame de Castro?"

"Impossible, Aloyse! and just when these difficulties have smoothed themselves all out!"

"Difficulties created by man may always be overcome," said the nurse; "but not so with those which God interposes, Monseigneur. You know whether I love you, and whether I would not give my life to spare yours the mere shadow of trouble; well, then, suppose I say to you: 'Without asking for the reason, Monseigneur, give up all thoughts of Madame de Castro, cease to see her, and crush out this passion for her by every means in your power. A fearful secret, which in your own interest I implore you not to ask me to disclose, lies between you two, to keep you apart.' Suppose I should say this to you, begging you on my knees to do as I asked, what would your reply be, Monseigneur?"

"If it were my life which you asked me to destroy, Aloyse, without asking for the reason, I would gratify you. But my love is a matter outside my own will, nurse, for it also comes from God."

"Oh, good Lord!" cried the nurse, joining her hands, "he blasphemes. But you see that he knows not what he does, so pardon him, good Lord!"

"But you terrify me; don't keep me so long in this deathly anguish, Aloyse, but whatever you would or ought to tell me, speak, speak, I implore you!"

"Do you wish it, Monseigneur? Must I really reveal to you the secret which I have sworn before God to keep, but which God Himself to-day bids me keep no longer? Well, then, Monseigneur, you are deceived; you must be, do you hear, it is absolutely necessary that you should be deceived as to the nature of the sentiment which Diane inspires in you. It is not desire and passion (oh, no! be sure that it is not), but it is a serious and devoted affection, due to her need of the protecting hand of a friend and brother,— nothing more tender or more absorbing than that, Monseigneur."

"But you are wrong, Aloyse; the fascinating beauty of Diane—"

"I am not wrong," Aloyse made haste to say, "and you will soon agree with me; for the proof of what I say will soon be as clear to you as to myself. Know, then, that in all human probability Madame de Castro—courage, my dear boy!—Madame de Castro is your sister!"

"My sister!" cried Gabriel, leaping from his chair as if he were on springs. "My sister!" he repeated, almost beside himself. "How can it be that the daughter of the king and Madame de Valentinois should be my sister?"

"Monseigneur, Diane de Castro was born in May, 1539, was she not? Comte Jacques de Montgommery, your father, disappeared in January of the same year; and do you know of what he was suspected? Do you know what the accusation was against him, your father? That he was the favored lover of Madame Diane de Poitiers, and the successful rival of the dauphin, who is to-day King of France. Now, compare the dates, Monseigneur."

"Heavens and earth!" cried Gabriel. "But let us see, let us see," he went on, making a supreme effort to collect his senses; "my father was accused, but who proved that the accusation had any basis in fact? Diane was born five months after my fathers death; but how does that prove that she is not the daughter of the king, who loves her as his own child?"

"The king may be mistaken, just as I too may be mistaken, Monseigneur; remember that I didn't say, 'Diane is your sister!' But it is probable that she is; or if you choose, it is possible that she may be. Is it any less my duty, my horribly painful duty, to give you this information, Gabriel? I am right to do it, am I not? for you wouldn't give her up without it. Now let your conscience decide as to your love; and may God guide your conscience!"

"Oh, but this uncertainty is a million times more horrible than the calamity itself," said Gabriel. "*Mon Dieu*! who can solve this doubt for me?"

"The secret has been known to only two persons on earth, Monseigneur," said Aloyse; "and there have been but two human beings who could have answered you: your father, who is buried in an unknown tomb, and Madame de Valentinois, who will not be likely to confess, I imagine, that she has deceived the king, and that her daughter is not his."

"Yes; and in any event, if I do not love my own father's daughter," said Gabriel, "I love the daughter of my father's murderer! For it is the king, it is Henri II., on whom I must wreak vengeance for the death of my father, is it not, Aloyse?"

"Who knows but God?" replied the nurse.

"Confusion and darkness, doubt and terror everywhere!" cried Gabriel. "Oh, I shall go mad, nurse! But no," continued the brave youth, "I must not go mad yet; I must not! I will in the first place exhaust every possible means of learning the truth. I will go to Madame de Valentinois, and will demand from her the secret, which I will sacredly keep. She is a good and devout Catholic, and I will obtain from her an oath which will make me sure of her sincerity. I will go to Catherine de Médicis, who may perhaps know something. I will go to Diane, too, and with my hand on my heart will ask the question of my heart-beats. I would go to my father's tomb, if I but knew where it lies, Aloyse, and I would call upon him with a voice so potent that he would rise from the dead to reply to me."

"Poor dear child!" whispered Aloyse, "so brave and strong, even after this fearful blow; and showing such a bold front to such a cruel fate!"

"And I will not lose a moment about going to work," said Gabriel, rising with a sort of feverish animation. "It is now four o'clock; in half an hour I shall be with Madame la Sénéchale; an hour later with the queen; and at six at the rendezvous where Diane awaits me; and when I see you again this evening, Aloyse, I may perhaps have lifted a corner of this gloomy veil in which my destiny is now shrouded. Farewell till evening."

"And I, Monseigneur, can I do nothing to help you in this formidable undertaking?"

"You can pray to God for me, Aloyse."

"For you and Diane, yes, Monseigneur."

"Pray for the king, too, Aloyse," said Gabriel, darkly, and he left the room precipitately.

CHAPTER XIV
DIANE DE POITIERS

The Constable de Montmorency was still with Diane de Poitiers, and was addressing her in a loud voice, as rough and imperious with her as she had shown herself sweet and gentle with him.

"Well, after all, she is your daughter, isn't she?" he was saying; "and you have the same rights and the same authority over her as the king has. Demand that this marriage take place!"

"But you must remember, my good friend, that having hitherto shown her very little of a mother's affection I can hardly hope to exert a mother's authority over her, and to chastise where I have never caressed. We are, as you know, Madame d'Angoulême and myself, on very cool terms with each other; and in spite of her advances at first, we have only met at very long intervals. Besides, she has succeeded in gaining a very great personal influence over the king's mind; and in truth, I should find it hard to say which of us two is the more powerful at this moment. What you ask me to do, my friend, is very difficult, not to say impossible. Lay aside all thought of this marriage, and let us replace it by a still more brilliant alliance. The king has betrothed his little Jeanne to Charles de Mayenne; we will induce him to bestow little Marguerite's hand on your son."

"My son sleeps in a bed and not in a cradle," replied the constable; "and how, I should like to know, could a young girl, just learning to talk, add to the fortunes of my family? Madame de Castro, on the other hand, has, as you have just reminded me most opportunely, a vast personal influence over the king; and that is why I wish her for my daughter-in-law. *Mon Dieu!* it is a most extraordinary thing that when a gentleman who bears the name of the foremost noble in Christendom stoops to wed a bastard, he should meet with so many obstructions in carrying out the *mésalliance*. Madame, you are no more the king's favorite for nothing than I am your lover for nothing. In spite of Madame de Castro, in spite of this fop who adores her, in spite of the king himself, I insist that this marriage shall take place,—I insist upon it."

"Oh, very well, my friend," replied Diane de Poitiers, meekly, "I agree to do the possible and impossible to help you to attain your ends. What more do you want me to say? But at least tell me that you will be kinder to me, and will not rage and storm at me so, cruel one!"

And with her lovely red lips the beautiful duchess lightly touched old Anne's rough grizzled beard, while he grumblingly submitted to the caress.

For such was this singular passion, inexplicable except on the theory of extraordinary depravity, which was nourished by the idolized favorite of a handsome young monarch for an old graybeard who abused her. Montmorency's rough brutality made amends to her for Henri's love-making; and she took more delight in being ill-treated by the one than in being petted and caressed by the other. Prodigious caprice of the feminine heart! Anne de Montmorency was neither clever nor brilliant; and he was, on very good grounds, reputed to be covetous and stingy. The inhuman punishments he had inflicted upon the rebellious population of Bordeaux had of themselves attached a sort of hateful notoriety to his name. He was brave, it is true; but that quality is common in France, and he had up to this time hardly ever been fortunate in the battles in which he had taken part. At the victories of Ravenna and Marignan, where he had held no command, he had not made himself conspicuous above the common herd; at Bicocque, where he was colonel of the Swiss Guards, he had let his regiment be almost cut to pieces; and at Pavia he was taken prisoner. His military celebrity had not since been increased, and St. Laurent had made a pitiable ending to it. Without the favor of Henri II., inspired, no doubt, by Diane de Poitiers, he would not have risen above the second place in the king's council any more than in the army; and yet Diane loved him, coddled him, and obeyed him in everything, being at once the favorite of a manly, handsome young monarch and the slave of a ridiculous old veteran.

Just at this moment there was a discreet knock at the door; and a page, entering at Madame de Valentinois's summons, announced that Vicomte d'Exmès earnestly begged to be allowed a very brief audience of the duchess on a most serious matter.

"The lover himself!" cried the constable. "What can he want of you, Diane? Can he possibly have come to ask you for your daughter's hand?"

"Shall I allow him to come in?" meekly asked the favorite.

"Of course, of course; this incident may help us. But let him wait a moment. Just one word more between ourselves."

Diane de Poitiers gave orders accordingly to the page, who left the room.

"If Vicomte d'Exmès comes to you, Diane," the constable went on, "it must be because some unexpected difficulties have arisen; and it must be a very desperate emergency to drive him to resort to so desperate a remedy. Now, listen carefully to what I say; and if you follow my instructions to the letter, I will answer for it that your hazardous interference with the king in this matter will be quite unnecessary. Diane, whatever the viscount asks at your hands, refuse it. If he asks what path he shall take, send him in the opposite direction to that in which he wishes to go. If he wants you to say 'yes,' say 'no;' but say 'yes' if he hopes for a negative answer. Be contemptuous with him, and haughty and ill-tempered, the worthy daughter of the fairy Mélusine, from whom you of the family of Poitiers are said to have descended. Do you understand me, Diane, and will you do as I say?"

"In every respect, my dear Constable."

"Then my fine fellow's threads will be considerably tangled, I fancy. The poor fool, thus to walk right into the jaws of the—" he started to say "she-wolf," but caught himself—"into the jaws of the waives. I leave him to you, Diane; and you must give me a good account of this handsome claimant. Till this evening!"

He condescended to kiss Diane's brow, and went out. Vicomte d'Exmès was ushered in by another door.

Gabriel saluted Diane most respectfully, while she responded with an impertinent nod. But Gabriel, buckling on his armor for this unequal combat of burning passion against frigid vanity, began calmly enough:—

"Madame," said he, "the step which I have ventured to take with reference to you is a bold one, no doubt, and may seem mad. But sometimes in one's life circumstances come to light of such serious moment as to lift us above the ordinary conventions and every day scruples. Now, I am involved in one of these terrible crises of my destiny, Madame. I, who speak to you, have come to put my life in your hands; and if you let it fall, it will be broken forever."

Madame de Valentinois made not the least sign of encouragement. With her body bent forward, resting her chin on her hand, and her elbow on her knee, she gazed at Gabriel with a look of wonder mingled with weariness.

"Madame," he resumed, trying to shake off the gloomy effect of this feigned indifference, "you either know or do not know that I love Madame de Castro. I love her, Madame, with a deep, ardent, overpowering love."

"What is that to me?" seemed to say Diane de Poitiers's careless smile.

"I speak to you of this love which fills my whole soul, Madame, to explain my saying that I ought to understand and excuse, yes, even admire, the blind fatalities and insatiable demands of an engrossing passion. So far from blaming it, as the common people do, or of pulling it to pieces like the philosophers, or of condemning it like the priests, I kneel before it and adore it as a blessing from the Most High. It makes the heart into which it enters purer and more noble and divine; and did not Jesus Himself consecrate it when He said to Mary Magdalene that she was blessed above all other women for having loved so well?"

Diane de Poitiers changed her position, and with eyes half closed stretched herself out carelessly on her couch.

"I wonder how much longer his sermon is going to last," she was thinking.

"Thus you see, Madame," continued Gabriel, "that love is in my eyes a holy thing, and more than that, it is omnipotent. If the husband of Madame de Castro were living still, I should love her just the same, and should not even try to overcome the irresistible impulse. It is only a false love which can be subdued; and true love no more flees from itself than it commands its own beginning. So, Madame, you yourself, chosen and beloved by the greatest king in the world,—you ought not to be, on that account, out of all danger of contracting a sincere passion; and if you had been unable to resist it, I should pity you and envy you, but I would not condemn you."

Still unbroken silence on the part of the Duchesse de Valentinois. Amused astonishment was the only emotion expressed upon her face. Gabriel went on with still more warmth, as if to melt this brazen heart with the flames that were seething in his own.

"A king falls in love with your adorable beauty, as may well be imagined. You are touched by his affection; but may it not be that your heart does not respond to it, much as it would like to do so? Alas! yes. But standing near the king, a handsome gentleman, gallant and devoted, sees you and loves you; and this more obscure but not less powerful passion meets a response in your heart, which has not opened to admit the thought of a king. But are you not a queen too, a queen of beauty, just as the king who loves you is king in power? Are you not as independent and free as he? Is it titles which win hearts? Who could prevent you from having for one day, for one hour even, in your kind and loving heart, preferred the subject to the master? It is not I, at all events, who would have so little sympathy with lofty sentiments as to esteem it a crime in Diane de Poitiers that being beloved of Henri II., she had loved the Comte de Montgommery."

Diane, at this home-thrust, made a sudden movement and half rose from her seat, opening her great bright eyes to their fullest extent. Too few persons at court knew her secret for her not to have felt a shock at these words of Gabriel.

"Have you any substantial proof of this love that you prate of?" she asked, not without a shade of anxiety in her tone.

"I have nothing but moral certainty of it, Madame," replied Gabriel; "but I have that."

"Ah!" said she, resuming her insolent pouting. "Well, then, it is all the same to me if I confess the truth to you. Yes, I did love the Comte de Montgommery. And what next?"

But next, Gabriel had no more positive knowledge, and could only stumble about in the darkness of conjecture. However, he continued:—

"You loved Jacques de Montgommery, Madame, and I venture to say that you still love his memory; for if he disappeared from the face of the earth, it was on your account and for your sake. Very well! it is in his name that I come to beg your indulgence, and to ask you a question which will seem to you, I say again, very presumptuous; but I also repeat that your reply, if you are good enough to reply, will arouse only gratitude and worship in my heart, for upon your reply my life hangs. Again I repeat that if you do not refuse to answer me, I will be henceforward at your service, body and soul; and the most firmly established power in the world may sometime be in need of a devoted heart and hand, Madame."

"Go on, Monsieur," said the duchess, "and let us get at this terrible question."

"I ought to ask it of you on my knees, Madame," said Gabriel, suiting the action to the word.

And then he resumed with beating heart and faltering voice,—

"Madame, it was in the course of the year 1538 that you loved the Comte de Montgommery, was it not?"

"Possibly," said Diane; "and then?"

"It was in January, 1539, that the Comte de Montgommery disappeared, and in May, 1539, that Madame Diane de Castro was born?"

"Well?" asked Diane.

"Well, Madame!" said Gabriel, so low that she could hardly hear him, "there lies the secret which at your feet I implore you to divulge to me,— the secret on which my fate depends, and which shall die with me, believe me, if you will deign to reveal it to me. On the crucifix which hangs above your head, I swear it, Madame; I will yield up my life rather than your confidence. And besides, you will always be able to prove me a liar, for your word would be believed before mine; and I ask you for no proof, but for your word alone. Madame, Madame, was Jacques de Montgommery the father of Diane de Castro?"

"Oho!" said Diane, with a contemptuous laugh, "that is rather a bold question; and you were quite right to precede it with such a lengthy preamble. But never fear, Monsieur, I bear you no ill-will for it. You have interested me like a riddle, and now you interest me still more; for what is it to you, pray, Monsieur d'Exmès, whether Madame d'Angoulême be the child of the king or the count? The king is supposed to be her father, and that should satisfy your ambition, if you are ambitious. Why do you draw me into it; and what claim have you to thus question me about the past to no purpose? You have a reason, no doubt; but what is the reason?"

"I have a reason indeed, Madame," said Gabriel; "but I conjure you not to ask it of me for mercy's sake!"

"Oh, yes," said Diane, "you want to know my secrets and to keep yours to yourself. That would be a very advantageous thing for you, no doubt!"

Gabriel detached the ivory crucifix which surmounted the carved oak *prie-Dieu* behind Diane's couch.

"By your everlasting salvation, Madame," said he, "swear to keep silent as to what I tell you, and to make no use of it to my disadvantage!"

"Such an oath as that!" said Diane.

"Yes, Madame, for I know you to be a zealous and devout Catholic: and if you swear by your everlasting salvation, I will believe you."

"And suppose I decline to swear?"

"I shall hold my peace, Madame, and you will have refused to save my life."

"Do you know, Monsieur," replied Diane, "that you have strangely aroused my woman's curiosity'? Yes, the mystery with which you so tragically surround yourself attracts me and tempts me, I confess. You have triumphed over my imagination to that extent, I tell you frankly; and I did not suppose that any one could so pique my curiosity. If I swear, it is, I give you fair warning, so that I may learn more about you. From curiosity, pure and simple, I agree to do it."

"And I too, Madame," said Gabriel, "I implore you thus, so that I may learn more; but my curiosity is that of the criminal awaiting his death-sentence. Bitter and fearful curiosity, as you see! Will you take this oath, Madame?"

"Say you the words, and I will say them after you, Monsieur."

And Diane said, after Gabriel, the following words:

"By my salvation, in this life and the next, I swear to reveal to no one on earth the secret which you are about to impart to me, and never to make any use of it to injure you, and to act in all ways just as if I had never known it, and never should know it."

"Very well," said Gabriel, "and I thank you for this first proof of your condescension. Now, in two words, you shall know all: my name is Gabriel de Montgommery, and Jacques de Montgommery was my father!"

"Your father!" cried Diane, springing to her feet in a state of stupefied excitement.

"So that if Diane de Castro is the count's daughter," said Gabriel, "Diane de Castro, whom I love, or whom I thought that I loved to distraction, is my sister!"

"Ah, I see," replied Diane de Poitiers, recovering herself a bit.—"This will be the constable's salvation," she thought to herself.

"Now, Madame," continued Gabriel, pale but firm, "are you willing to do me the further favor of swearing, as before, upon this crucifix, that Madame de Castro is King Henri II.'s daughter? You do not reply? Oh, why do you not reply. Madame?"

"Because I cannot take that oath, Monsieur."

"Ah, *mon Dieu, mon Dieu*! Diane is my father's child, then?" cried Gabriel, tottering.

"I did not say that! I will never assent to that!" cried Madame de Valentinois; "Diane de Castro is the king's daughter."

"Oh, really, Madame? Oh, how kind you are!" said Gabriel. "But, pardon me! Your own interest may induce you to say so. So swear it, Madame, swear it! In the name of your child, who will bless you for it, oh, swear it!"

"I will not swear," said the duchess. "Why should I?"

"But, Madame," said Gabriel, "this very moment you took the same oath simply to gratify your vulgar curiosity, as you told me yourself; and now, when a man's very life is at stake, when by saying these few words, you might rescue two souls from the bottomless pit, you ask, 'Why should I say these words?'"

"But I will not swear, Monsieur," said Diane, coldly and decidedly.

"And if I should marry Madame de Castro notwithstanding, Madame, and if Madame de Castro is my sister, don't you think that the crime will rebound upon you?"

"No," replied Diane, "not when I have not taken my oath to it."

"Oh, horrible! horrible!" cried Gabriel. "But consider, Madame, that I can tell everywhere that you loved the Comte de Montgommery, and were false to the king, and that I, the count's son, am certain of it."

"Mere moral certainty, without proofs," said Diane, with a wicked smile, having resumed her air of impertinent and haughty indifference. "I will say that you lie, Monsieur; and you told me yourself that when you affirm and I deny, you will not be the one to be believed. Consider, too, that I can say to the king that you have presumed to make love to me, threatening to circulate slanders about me if I didn't yield to you. And then you will be lost, Monsieur Gabriel de Montgommery. But pardon me," said she, rising; "I must leave you, Monsieur. You have really entertained me exceedingly, and your story is a very singular one."

She struck a bell, to summon a servant.

"Oh, this is infamous!" cried Gabriel, beating his brow with his clinched fists. "Oh, why are you a woman, or why am I a man? But, nevertheless, take care, Madame! for you shall not play with my heart and my life with impunity; and God will punish you, and avenge me for what you have done,—for this infamy, I say it again!"

"Do you think so?" said Diane. And she accompanied her words with a dry, mocking little laugh which was peculiar to her.

At this moment, the page whom she had called raised the tapestry curtain. She gave Gabriel a mocking salute and left the room.

"Well, well!" said she to herself, "my good constable is decidedly in luck. Dame Fortune is like me,—she loves him. Why the devil do we love him?"

Gabriel followed her out, mad with rage and grief.

CHAPTER XV
CATHERINE DE MÉDICIS

But Gabriel was strong and brave of heart, and filled with steadfast resolution. After the consternation of the first moments had abated, he shook off his despondency, held his head aloft once more, and requested an audience of the queen.

Catherine de Médicis had no doubt heard of this mysterious tragedy of her husband and the Comte de Montgommery; in fact, who knows that she did not herself play a part in it. At that time she was hardly more than twenty years old. Was it not likely that the jealousy of a beautiful but abandoned young wife would cause her to keep her eyes constantly open to every act and every misstep of her rival? Gabriel relied upon her memory to throw light upon the darkness of the path along which he was groping his way, but where he was so much interested in having his course made clear to him both as lover and as son, for his happiness' sake or for his revenge.

Catherine received Vicomte d'Exmès with that marked kindness which she had not failed to show him on every occasion.

"Is it you, my handsome king of the lists?" said she. "To what happy chance do I owe this welcome visit? You very seldom honor us, Monsieur d'Exmès; and I think this is the very first time that you have sought an audience of us in our apartments. But you are and always will be a welcome guest, remember that."

"Madame," said Gabriel. "I do not know how to thank you for such kindness; rest assured that my devotion—"

"Oh, never mind your devotion!" interposed the queen; "but let us come to the object which brings you here. Can I serve you in any way?"

"Yes, Madame, I think that you can."

"So much the better, Monsieur d'Exmès," replied Catherine, with a most engaging smile; "and if what you ask of me lies in my power, I promise beforehand to grant it. That may be rather a compromising agreement, perhaps, but I know you will not make an unfair use of it, my good friend."

"God forbid, Madame! I have no such intention."

"Go on, then, and tell me," said the queen, sighing.

"It is information, Madame, that I have ventured to seek from you,—nothing more. But to me this nothing is everything; so you will excuse me, I know, for recalling memories which may be painful to your Majesty. They relate to something which happened as long ago as the year 1539."

"Oh, dear, I was very young then,—almost a child," said the queen.

"But already very lovely, and most surely worthy of being loved," replied Gabriel.

"Some people used to say so," said the queen, delighted at the turn the conversation was taking.

"And yet," Gabriel went on, "another woman dared to encroach upon the right which was yours by the gift of God, and by your birth and beauty; and not content with drawing away from you, by witchery and enchantment, no doubt, the eyes and the heart of a husband who was too young to see clearly, this woman betrayed him who had betrayed you, and loved the Comte de Montgommery. But in your righteous contempt you may have forgotten all this, Madame?"

"By no means," said the queen; "and this incident, with all the intrigues dating from it, is very clear still in my mind. Yes, she loved the Comte de Montgommery; and then, seeing that her passion was discovered, she basely pretended that it was a mere feint to put the dauphin's affection for her to the proof; and when Montgommery disappeared, poor fellow,—made away with, perhaps, by her own order,—she never shed a tear for him, but appeared at a ball the next day, laughing and gay. Oh, yes, I shall always remember the first schemes by means of which this woman undermined my new-born power; for I was annoyed by them then, and I passed my days and my nights weeping. But since then my pride has come to my aid. I have always fulfilled my duty, and more too: I have compelled, by my dignified conduct, consistent and constant respect for myself as wife, as mother, and as queen. I have given seven children to the King of France; but now I love my husband only with a tranquil sort of affection, as a friend and the father of my sons, and I no longer recognize in him any right to demand any tenderer emotion. My life has been devoted to the public good long enough; and may I not now live a little for myself? Have I not bought my happiness sufficiently dear? If the devotion of some young and passionate heart should be laid at my feet, would it be a crime in me if I did not spurn it, Gabriel?"

Catherine's glances were quite in keeping with her words; but Gabriel's thoughts were elsewhere. As soon as the queen had ceased to speak of his father, he had ceased to listen, and had lost himself in thought. This revery, which Catherine interpreted as being in accord with her own wishes, by no means displeased her. But Gabriel soon broke the silence.

"One last explanation, and the most serious of all," said he. "You are so kind to me! I was sure that in coming to you I should be entirely satisfied. You have spoken of devotion; you may count absolutely on mine, Madame. But complete your work, for Heaven's sake! Since you knew the details of this tragic incident in the life of the Comte de Montgommery, do you know whether there was any doubt at the time that Madame de Castro, who was born some months after the count's disappearance, was really the king's daughter? Did not the tongue of scandal, of calumny, I may say, set afloat suspicion in that direction and ascribe to Monsieur de Montgommery the paternity of Diane?"

Catherine de Médicis looked at Gabriel for some time without a word, as if to satisfy herself of the feeling which had dictated his words. She thought she had discovered it, and began to smile.

"I have noticed," she said, "that you have been attracted by Madame de Castro, and have been assiduously paying court to her. Now I see your motive. Only, before you commit yourself, you wish to be sure, do you not, that you are following no false scent, and that it is really a daughter of the king to whom you are offering your homage? You don't wish, after you have married the legitimatized daughter of Henri II., to discover some fine day unexpectedly that your wife is the Comte de Montgommery's illegitimate child? In a word, you are ambitious, Monsieur d'Exmès. Don't protest, for it only makes me esteem you the more; and more than that, it may be of advantage to my plans for you, rather than detrimental to them. You are ambitious, are you not?"

"But, Madame," replied Gabriel, in great embarrassment, "perhaps it amounts to that—"

"Very good; I see that I have guessed your secret, young gentleman," said the queen. "Well, then! Are you willing to believe a friend? In the interest of these plans of yours, lay aside your views touching this Diane. Give up this doll-faced chit. I don't know, to tell the truth, whose daughter she is, whether king's or count's, and the last supposition may very well be the true one; but if she were born of the king, she is not the woman or the support that you stand in need of. Madame d'Angoulême's is a weak and yielding nature, all feeling and grace, if you please, but without force or energy or courage. She has succeeded in winning the king's good graces, I agree; but she hasn't the tact to take advantage of them. What you need, Gabriel, to help you to the fulfilment of your noble dreams, is a virile and courageous heart, which will assist you as it loves you, which will serve you and be served by you, and which will fill both your heart and your life. Such a heart you have found without being aware of it. Vicomte d'Exmès."

He looked at her in utter amazement; but she continued, warming to her subject:—

"Listen: our lofty destiny makes us queens free from the observance of the proprieties enjoined upon the common herd; and from our supreme height if we wish to be the object of the affection of a subject, we must take some steps forward ourselves, and extend a welcoming hand. Gabriel, you are handsome, brave, ardent, and proud! Since the first moment that I saw you I have felt for you a strange sentiment, and—I am not in error, am I?— your words and your looks, and even this very proceeding to-day, which is perhaps only a well-planned détour,—everything combines to make me believe that I have not to do with an ingrate."

"Madame!" said Gabriel, whose surprise had changed to alarm.

"Oh, yes, you are touched and surprised, I see," continued Catherine, with her sweetest smile. "But you do not judge me harshly, do you, for my necessary frankness? I say again, the queen must make excuses for the woman. You are shy, with all your ambition, Monsieur d'Exmès; and if I had been withheld by scruples which would be beneath me, I might have been deprived of a devotion which is very precious to me. I much preferred to be the first to speak. Come, then! collect yourself once more. Am I such a very terrible object?"

"Oh, yes!" muttered Gabriel, pale and trembling.

But the queen entirely misinterpreted the meaning of his exclamation.

"Come, come!" said she, with a playful pretence of misgiving. "I have not deprived you of your good sense yet, so far as to make you lose sight of your own interests, as you proved by the questions you put to me on the subject of Madame d'Angoulême. But set your mind at ease, for I do not desire your abasement, I say again, but your elevation. Gabriel, up to this time I have kept myself out of sight in the second rank; but do you know, I shall soon shine in the first. Madame Diane de Poitiers is no longer young enough to preserve her beauty and her supremacy. On the day when that creature's prestige begins to wane, my reign will begin; and mark well that I shall know how to reign, Gabriel. The instincts of domination which I feel at work in me assure me of it; and then, too, it is in the very Médicis blood. The king will learn some day that he has no more clever adviser, none more skilful and more experienced, than myself. And then, Gabriel, when that time comes, to what heights may not that man aspire who linked his fortune with mine when mine was still in the shadow; who loved in me the woman, not the queen? Will not the mistress of the whole realm be able to recompense worthily the man who devoted himself to Catherine? Will not this man be her second self, her right arm, the real king, with a mere phantom of a king above him? Will he not hold in his hand all the dignity and all the might of France? A fair dream, is it not, Gabriel? Well, Gabriel, do you choose to be that man?"

She valiantly held out her hand to him.

Gabriel kneeled at her feet and kissed that lovely white hand; but his nature was too frank and loyal to allow him to involve himself in the tricks and falsehoods of a simulated passion. Between deceit and danger he was too honest and too bold to hesitate a moment, so raising his noble head, he said,—

"Madame, the humble gentleman who is at your feet begs you to look upon him as your most obedient servant and your most devoted subject; but—"

"But," said Catherine, smiling, "these are not the worshipful terms which I require of you, my noble cavalier."

"And yet, Madame," continued Gabriel, "I cannot make use of any more tender and affectionate words in addressing you, for—pardon me, I beg—she whom I loved dearly before I ever saw you is Madame Diane de Castro; and no love, even though it be the love of a queen, can ever find a resting-place in this heart, which is always filled with the image of another."

"Ah!" exclaimed Catherine, with colorless cheeks and tightly closed lips.

Gabriel, with head cast down, waited manfully for the storm of indignation and scorn which was impending over him. Scorn and indignation are not apt to be long in coming, and after a few moments of silence,—

"Do you know, Monsieur d'Exmès," said Catherine, struggling to keep down her voice and her anger,—"do you know that I consider you very bold, not to say impudent! Who spoke to you of love, Monsieur? Where did you get the idea that I wished to tempt your bashful virtue? You must have a most exalted and presumptuous opinion of your own deserts to dare to think of such things, and to put such a hasty construction upon a kindness of heart whose only mistake was in bestowing itself in an undeserving quarter. You have very deeply injured a woman and a queen, Monsieur!"

"Oh, Madame," replied Gabriel, "pray believe that my religious veneration—"

"Enough!" Catherine interposed; "I know that you have insulted me, and that you came here to insult me! Why are you here? What purpose directed your steps? Of what importance to me are your love and Madame de Castro, or any of your concerns? You came to seek information from me! Absurd pretext! You desired to make a queen of France the confidante of your passion! It is senseless, I tell you! worse than that, it is an outrage!"

"No, Madame," replied Gabriel, standing proudly erect, "it is no outrage to have met an honest man who chose to wound you rather than deceive you."

"Hold your peace, Monsieur!" replied Catherine; "I command you to hold your peace and to leave me. Consider yourself lucky if I do not yet think best to divulge to the king your audacious offence. But never let me see you again, and henceforth consider Catherine de Médicis your bitter enemy. Yes, I shall come across you again, be sure, Monsieur d'Exmès! And now leave me."

Gabriel saluted the queen, and withdrew without a word.

"Well," he reflected when he was alone again, "one hatred more! But what difference would that make to me if I had only learned something about my father and Diane? The king's favorite and the king's wife for enemies! Fate may be preparing perhaps to make the king himself my enemy. And now for Diane, for the hour has arrived; and God grant that I may not be more sad and despairing when I part from her who loves me than I have been on leaving those who hate me!"

CHAPTER XVI
LOVER OR BROTHER?

When Jacinthe ushered Gabriel into the apartment in the Louvre occupied by Diane de Castro as the king's legitimatized daughter, she, in the pure and honest outpouring of her heart, rushed to meet her well-beloved without undertaking to dissemble her joy. She would not have refused to offer her brow to be kissed; but he contented himself with pressing her hand.

"Here you are at last, Gabriel!" said she. "How impatiently I have been awaiting you, dear! Lately I have not seemed to know whither to turn the full stream of happiness that I feel within me. I talk and laugh when I am all alone, and I am crazy with joy! But here you are, Gabriel, and we may at least have a happy hour together! But what is the matter, my love? You seem cold and serious and almost sad. Is it with such a solemn face and such cool reserve that you show your love for me, and your gratitude to God and my father?"

"To your father? Yes, let us speak of your father, Diane. As for this seriousness at which you wonder, it is my way to receive good fortune with a grave face; for I distrust her gifts, in the first place, having been unused to them heretofore, and my experience has been that she only too often hides a sorrow under the mask of a favor.

"I didn't know that you were such a philosopher, nor so unlucky, Gabriel!" replied the maiden, half in fun and half in anger. "But, come! you were saying that you wished to talk about the king; and I am very glad. How kind and generous he is, Gabriel!"

"Yes, Diane; and he loves you dearly, doesn't he?"

"With an infinite tenderness and gentleness, Gabriel."

"No doubt," muttered Vicomte d'Exmès, "for he may very well believe, poor dupe, that she is his child! Only one thing surprises me," he continued aloud; "and that is, how the king, who must have felt in his heart that he should love you thus dearly, could have allowed twelve years to elapse without ever seeing you or knowing you, and have left you at Vimoutiers, lost, to all intents and purposes. Have you never asked him, Diane, for an explanation of such strange indifference? Such utter forgetfulness, do you know, seems hardly consistent with the kind feeling that he seems to have for you now."

"Oh," said Diane, "it was not he who forgot me,—poor Papa!"

"But who was it, then?"

"Who? Why, Madame Diane de Poitiers, to be sure! I don't know if I ought to say my mother."

"And why did she make up her mind to abandon you thus, Diane? Ought she not to have been glad and proud, and to have glorified herself in the king's sight for having given birth to you, and having thus acquired one claim the more to his affection? What had she to fear? Her husband was dead; and her father—"

"All that is very true, Gabriel," said Diane; "and it would be very hard, not to say impossible, for me to justify in your eyes this extraordinary feeling—is it of pride?—which has made Madame de Valentinois refuse to acknowledge me formally as her child. Don't you know, dear, that in the first place she induced the king to conceal the fact of my birth; that she consented to my being recalled to court only at his urgent request, which was almost a command; and that she didn't choose even to be mentioned in the decree by which I was legitimatized? I have no inclination to complain of her for it, Gabriel, because if it had not been for this inexplicable pride of hers, I should never have known you, and you would not have loved me. But, nevertheless, I have sometimes been pained to think of the sort of repugnance which my mother seems to feel for everything that relates to me."

"A repugnance which may be remorse only," thought Gabriel, with terror; "she was able to deceive the king, and it was not without hesitation and dread—"

"But what are you thinking about, dear Gabriel?" said Diane. "And why do you ask me all these questions?"

"Oh, for no reason at all! A misgiving of my anxious heart,—that's all; don't worry about it, Diane. But, at all events, if your mother does seem to feel only aversion and almost hatred for you, your father, Diane,—your father makes up for her coldness by his affection, doesn't he? And you, if you do feel shy and constrained with Madame de Valentinois, your heart expands in the king's presence, does it not, and recognizes in him a true parent?"

"Oh, yes, indeed!" said Diane; "and the very first day that I saw him, when he spoke to me so tenderly, I felt drawn to him at once. It is not from policy that I am affectionate and obliging with him, but from instinct. It was not the king, not my benefactor and my patron, that I loved so dearly,—it was my father!"

"One can never be mistaken about such matters!" cried Gabriel, beside himself with joy. "Dear, dear Diane, my dearest love, I am glad that you love your father so, and that in his presence you feel the tender emotions of gratitude and love! This lovely filial devotion does you honor, Diane!"

"And I am glad, too, that you understand it and approve of it," said Diane. "But now that we have spoken of my father, and of his love for me and mine for him, and of our obligation to him, Gabriel, suppose we talk a little about ourselves and our own love; why not? Come, what do you say? We are selfish creatures," added she, with the lovely ingenousness which was hers alone. "Besides, if the king were here, he would reprove me for not thinking at all of myself,—of ourselves; and do you know, Gabriel, what he keeps saying to me every minute? 'My dear child, be happy! Be happy; do you understand? And in that way you will make me happy.' And so, Monsieur, now that our debt of gratitude is paid, let us not be too forgetful of ourselves."

"Very true," said Gabriel, thoughtfully,—"very true. Let us now give ourselves up to this attachment which binds us to each other for life. Let us look into our hearts, and see what is going on there. Let us lay bare our very souls to each other."

"Well, we will," said Diane; "that will be delightful!"

"Yes, delightful!" responded Gabriel, in a melancholy tone. "And do you, first, Diane, tell me what you feel for me. Don't you love me less than your father?"

"Oh, you jealous boy!" said Diane. "Be sure that my love for you is very different, and it is not by any means easy to explain. When I am with the king, I am calm, and my heart beats no more quickly than usual; but when I see you, oh, then I feel a curious agitation, which pains and delights me at the same time, and spreads over my whole being. To my father I can say, even before the whole world, the sweet and loving words which come to my lips; but to you, it seems to me that I should never dare to say even the one word 'Gabriel' before another soul, not even when I am your wife. In a word, the happiness which your presence brings me is as restless and unquiet—I had almost said painful—as the joy which I feel with my father is calm and peaceful; but the pain of the one is more ecstatic than the tranquillity of the other."

"Say no more! oh, say no more!" cried Gabriel, in despair. "Yes, you do love me, indeed; and it terrifies me! And yet it encourages me, too, I must say; for surely God would not have implanted such a passion in your heart, if it had been wrong for you to love me!"

"What do you mean, Gabriel?" asked Diane, in amazement. "Why should my confession, which I have the best right in the world to make to you, since you are going to be my husband,—why should it put you thus beside yourself? What danger can be hidden in my love?"

"None, Diane, none. Pay no attention to me. It is joy which intoxicates me thus,—pure joy! Such supreme happiness makes me dizzy with delight. But you didn't always love me so restlessly and with such painful sensations. When we used to walk together under the trees at Vimoutiers, you had only friendship for me,—fraternal friendship."

"I was only a child then," said Diane. "I had not then been dreaming of you for six solitary homesick years; my love had not then grown as my body grew; I had not lived two months in the midst of a court where licentious language and corrupt morals had made me cherish more fondly still the thought of our pure and holy affection."

"True, true, Diane!" said Gabriel.

"And now, do you, dear Gabriel, in your turn tell me of your devotion and passionate love for me. Open your heart to me, as I have laid mine bare to your gaze. If my words have sounded pleasantly in your ears, do you let me hear your voice telling me how much you love me, and how dearly you love me."

"Oh, as for me, I don't know," said Gabriel. "I cannot tell you that! Don't ask me about it, don't press me to ask myself, for it is too terrible!"

"But, Gabriel," cried Diane, in deadly terror, "it is your words that are terrible; don't you see that they are? What! You don't choose even to tell me that you love me?"

"If I love you, Diane! She asks me if I love her! Truly, then, yes, I do love you, like a madman, perhaps like a criminal!"

"Like a criminal!" cried Madame de Castro, beside herself with terror and amazement. "What crime can there be in our love? Are we not both free? Will not my father consent to our union? God and the angels must delight in such a love."

"Grant, oh, Lord, that she blaspheme not," cried Gabriel, in his heart, "even as I perhaps blasphemed myself, in speaking to Aloyse!"

"What can be the matter?" repeated Diane. "My dear, you are not sick, are you? And you, generally so strong, whence come these fanciful fears? For I have no fear when near you. I know that with you I am as safe as with my father. See, to recall you to yourself, to life and happiness, I press close to your breast without fear, my dearly beloved husband! I press my brow against your lips without hesitation."

Smiling bewitchingly, she approached him, her glorious face turned up to his, and her angelic glance soliciting his pure embrace.

But Gabriel pushed her away in terror. "Away!" he cried; "no, no! leave me, flee from me!"

"Oh, *mon Dieu!*" moaned Diane, letting her arms fall by her side. "*Mon Dieu!* he repels me; he loves me not!"

"I love you too well!" said Gabriel.

"If you love me, why should my proffered caresses be so terrible to you?"

"Are they really terrible to me, then?" said Gabriel to himself. "Is it my instinct which repels them, and not my reason? Oh, come, Diane, let me see you and know you, and feel your presence! Come, and let me press my lips on your brow with a brother's kiss, in which a betrothed lover may indulge himself."

He strained Diane to his heart, and pressed a long burning kiss on her hair.

"Ah, I deceived myself!" cried he, in rapture at her very touch. "It is not the voice of blood which is crying to you from my heart; it is the voice of love! I know it! Oh, what bliss!"

"What did you say, dear?" replied Diane. "If you say that you love me, you say all that I care to hear or to know."

"Oh, indeed I love you, blessed angel; I love you passionately, madly! Yes, I love you, and to feel your heart beating against mine, like this, is very heaven to me; or is it hell?" cried he, suddenly, releasing himself from her embrace. "Away, away! let me fly, for I am accursed!"

And he fled wildly from the room, leaving Diane dumb with terror, and as if turned to stone by despair.

Mary Stuart and Gabriel.

And he, poor fellow, no longer knew where he was going or what he was doing. He descended the stairs mechanically, reeling like a drunken man. These three fearful experiences were too much for his reason. When he reached the grand gallery of the Louvre, his eyes closed in spite of him, his legs gave way, and he sank on his knees against the wall, murmuring, —

"I foresaw that the angel would cause me more bitter agony than the two devils."

He had fainted. Night had come on; and no one was passing through the gallery.

He was recalled to his senses by feeling a soft hand smoothing his forehead, and hearing a sweet voice speaking to his very soul. He opened his eyes. The little queen-dauphine, Mary Stuart, stood before him, with a lighted taper in her hand.

"Ah, how fortunate! Another angel!" said Gabriel.

"Is it you, Monsieur d'Exmès?" said Mary. "Oh, how you frightened me! I thought you were dead. What is the matter? How pale you are! Do you feel any better? I will call for help, if you wish."

"Useless, Madame," said Gabriel, trying to rise. "Your voice has restored me to life."

"Let me help you," said Mary. "Poor fellow! Are you ill? You had fainted, hadn't you? As I was passing, I spied you lying here, and I hadn't strength enough to cry out. And then reflection gave me courage, and I came nearer to you; and I was pretty brave, I think. I laid my hand on your forehead, which was like ice. I called you, and you came to yourself. Do you still feel better?"

"Yes, Madame; and may God bless you for your goodness! I remember now, I had a fearful pain in my temples as if they were being pressed by an iron vice; my knees shook under me; and I fell here by this drapery. But how did the pain come on? Ah, yes, I remember now, I remember it all. Alas, *mon Dieu! mon Dieu!* Too well I remember."

"It is some terrible sorrow that oppresses you so, is it not?" asked Mary. "It must be so, for, see, you are paler than ever again at the mere remembrance of it. Lean on my arm, for I am willing and strong; and I will call help, and find somebody to go home with you."

"Thanks, Madame," said Gabriel, struggling to recover his strength and his resolution. "I find I still have strength enough to go home alone. See, I can walk without help, and with a firm step. I am no less grateful to you; and while I live I shall never forget your simple and touching kindness, Madame. You came to me like an angel of comfort at a painful crisis in my life. Nothing but death, Madame, can ever efface it from my heart."

"Oh, *mon Dieu!* what I did was the most natural thing in the world to do, Monsieur d'Exmès; I would have done as much for any suffering creature, and so much the more gladly for you whom I know to be the devoted friend of my Uncle de Guise. Pray don't thank me for such a small matter."

"This small matter was everything, Madame, in the state of despair to which I was reduced. You don't wish that I should thank you; but I, Madame, wish to remember it. Adieu; I shall remember."

"Adieu, Monsieur d'Exmès; pray take care of yourself, and try to find comfort somewhere."

She gave him her hand, which Gabriel kissed with deep respect. Then she left the gallery by one door, and he by another.

When he was outside of the walls of the Louvre, he walked along the river-bank, and arrived at the Rue des Jardins in about half an hour. He had but one thought in his brain, and was suffering terribly.

Aloyse was anxiously awaiting him.

"Well?" said she.

Gabriel struggled manfully to overcome a feeling of faintness which dimmed his sight anew. He would have liked well to weep, but he could not. He replied in a faltering voice, —

"I know nothing, Aloyse! Everything has been dumb and speechless, — these women and my heart as well. I know nothing except that my brow is as cold as ice, and yet I am burning up. *Mon Dieu! mon Dieu!*"

"Courage, Monseigneur!" said Aloyse.

"I have had courage," said Gabriel; "but God be merciful to me, I am dying!"

And once more he fell backward on the floor, but this time he did not come to himself again.

CHAPTER XVII
THE HOROSCOPE

"The sick man will live, Dame Aloyse! The danger has been very great, and his convalescence will be very slow. All this blood-letting has weakened the poor fellow terribly; but he will live, never fear! And thank God that the extreme debilitation of the body has lessened the blow that his mind has received, for we cannot cure those wounds; and this one of his might have been fatal,—indeed, it may yet be!"

The physician who spoke thus was a man of great height, with a great bulging forehead and deep-set and piercing eyes. The common people called him Master Nostredame; but he signed his own name Nostradamus. He seemed to be not more than fifty years old.

"But, holy Jesus, look at him, Messire!" replied Dame Aloyse. "He has been lying there since the evening of June 7; and it is now the 2d of July, and during that whole time he has not spoken one word,—has not even seemed to see me or to know me, and has been like one dead, alas! Look, if you touch his hand, he doesn't appear to notice it!"

"So much the better, I tell you, Dame Aloyse! I pray that he may be as long as possible in awaking to the remembrance of his sorrows. If he can continue, as I trust he will, another month in this weak state, without knowing or thinking about anything, he will recover, beyond a doubt."

"He will recover!" said Aloyse, raising her eyes to heaven as if offering thanks to God.

"Yes, he will recover if there is no relapse. And you may say so to that pretty maid who comes twice a day to get news of him; for there is an affair with some great lady hidden under all this, is there not? Sometimes that sort of thing is very delightful, and sometimes fatal."

"Yes, indeed, it is fatal; you are quite right, Master Nostredame," said Aloyse; with a sigh.

"God grant that he recover from his passion as well as from his illness, Dame Aloyse! if indeed illness and passion haven't always the same cause and the same effect. But I will answer for the one, and not for the other."

Nostradamus opened the soft and apparently lifeless hand that he held in his, and looked very carefully and attentively at the palm; he even lifted the skin from the fore and middle fingers. He seemed to be racking his brain to remember something.

"It is strange!" he said in an undertone, as if he were talking to himself. "Several times I have examined this hand, and every time it has seemed to me as if I had already examined it long ago. But what are the marks which have struck me so? The mensal line is of favorable length; the medial is a little doubtful; but the line of life is perfect. There is nothing extraordinary about it. The predominating characteristic of this youth should be a steadfast will, firm and unswerving as the arrow aimed by a sure hand. That is not what has aroused my wonder heretofore. And then my memories are too confused not to refer to some long ago time; and your master is not more than twenty-five, is he, Dame Aloyse?"

"He is only twenty-four, Messire."

"He was born in 1533, then. Do you know the day?"

"It was the 6th of May."

"But you don't know whether it was in the morning or the evening?"

"Pardon me! I was with his mother when he was born. It was just on the stroke of half after six in the morning."

Nostradamus made a note of these facts.

"I will see what was the condition of the heavens on that day at that hour," said he. "But if Vicomte d'Exmès were twenty years older, I would swear that I had already held his hand in mine; but that's of little consequence, after all. It is not the sorcerer, as the people sometimes call me, but the physician, who has work to do here; and I tell you again, Dame Aloyse, the physician will answer now for the invalid's welfare."

"Pardon, Master!" said Aloyse, sadly; "you say that you will answer for the disease, but that you will not answer for the passion."

"The passion! Oh! But," Nostradamus replied, smiling significantly, "I should say that the attendance of the little maid twice a day tends to show that the passion is not altogether a hopeless one."

"Quite the contrary, Master,—quite the contrary!" cried Aloyse, in an accent of horror.

"Come, come, Dame Aloyse! wealthy, gallant, young, and handsome as Vicomte d'Exmès is, a man is in no danger of being held off for long by the ladies in a time like ours. A brief postponement is the utmost he has to fear."

"But suppose that this is not the case, Master. Suppose that when Monseigneur is restored to life and reason, the first and only thought which his restored reason will entertain should be this: 'The woman whom I love is irrevocably lost to me,' then what will happen to him?"

"Oh, we must hope that this supposition of yours has no foundation in fact, for that would be terrible! Such an overwhelming grief as that would be a terrible strain for his enfeebled brain. So far as one can judge of a man by his features and the look of his eyes, your master, Aloyse, is no mere superficial creature; and in such a case as you suppose, his energetic and forceful will would be only one danger more, and being shattered by trying to do what is impossible, might shatter his life with it."

"Holy Jesus! my boy will die!" cried Aloyse.

"He will at least be in danger of inflammation of the brain," said Nostradamus. "But why need it be so? There must be some way of showing him a mere glimmer of hope. The most remote or most elusive chance it may be, yet he will grasp it, and it will save him."

"He shall be saved, then," said Aloyse, gloomily. "I will perjure my soul, but he shall be saved. Messire Nostredame, I thank you."

A week passed, and Gabriel seemed to be trying to think, even though he did not succeed. His eyes, still wandering and expressionless, seemed to be asking questions, nevertheless, of the faces and objects about him. Then he began to assist himself in the changes which they had to make in his position, to raise himself in bed alone, and to take of his own volition the potions that Nostradamus handed him.

Aloyse, standing unwearied at his pillow, waited.

At the end of another week, Gabriel could speak. Light had not yet fully evolved order out of the chaos of his mind. He could only say a few words, incoherent and unconnected, but which had reference to the events of his past. Aloyse fairly quaked with terror when the physician was there, lest he should reveal some of his secrets.

Her apprehensions were justified by the event; and one day, Gabriel, in a feverish sleep, cried aloud before Nostradamus, —

"They think that my true name is Vicomte d'Exmès. No, no, don't think it! I am the Comte de Montgommery."

"The Comte de Montgommery!" said Nostradamus, in whose brain the name had awakened some memory.

"Silence!" said Aloyse, her finger on her lip.

However, Nostradamus went away without Gabriel's having said anything further; and as he did not mention the words that had fallen from the invalid on the next or any following day, Aloyse, thinking it over, feared to attract his attention to something which it might be her master's interest to conceal. So the incident appeared to have been forgotten by both of them.

Gabriel continued to improve. He recognized Aloyse and Martin-Guerre; he asked for whatever he needed; and he spoke with a gentle sadness which made it possible to hope that his reason had returned.

One morning, it was the first day that he had left his bed, he said to Aloyse, —

"Well, nurse, and the war?"

"What war, Monseigneur?"

"Why, the war against Spain and England."

"Oh, Monseigneur, I hear sad news of that. The Spaniards, reinforced by twelve thousand English, have entered Picardy, they say, and there is fighting going on all along the frontier."

"So much the better," said Gabriel.

Aloyse attributed this reply to the remains of his delirium. But the next morning, with perfect coolness, Gabriel said to her, —

"I did not ask you yesterday if Monsieur de Guise had returned from Italy."

"He is on the way, Monseigneur," said Aloyse, in amazement.

"That is well! What day of the month is it, nurse?"

"Tuesday, August 4, Monseigneur."

"It will be two months on the 7th since I have been lying on this bed of anguish," was Gabriel's comment.

"Oh," cried Aloyse, trembling, "how well Monseigneur remembers!"

"Yes, I remember, Aloyse, — I remember; but," he added sadly, "though I have not forgotten, it seems that I have been forgotten. Has no one been to inquire for me, Aloyse?"

"Yes, indeed!" said Aloyse, in an uncertain voice, and anxiously watching the effect of her words on the young man's face, —"yes, indeed, Monseigneur! a maid named Jacinthe came twice a day to learn how you were. But for the last fortnight, since you have been perceptibly and surely improving, she has come no more."

"She comes no more! And do you know why, nurse?"

"Yes, Monseigneur. Because her mistress, according to what Jacinthe said the last time she came, has obtained the king's leave to withdraw to a convent till the end of the war at least."

"Really!" said Gabriel, with a sweet and melancholy smile.

And as a tear, the first he had shed for two months, rolled slowly down his cheek, he added, —

"Dear Diane!"

"Oh, Monseigneur," cried Aloyse, beside herself with delight, "Monseigneur has uttered that name! and without a shock, and without swooning. Master Nostredame was mistaken. Monseigneur is saved! Monseigneur will live, and I shall not need to be false to my oath."

We can see that the poor nurse's delight had almost made her mad; but Gabriel, luckily, did not notice her last words. He replied simply, with a smile full of bitterness, —

"Yes, I am saved; but still, dear Aloyse, I shall not live."

"How so, Monseigneur?" said Aloyse, trembling again in every limb.

"My body has held out manfully," Gabriel replied; "but my soul, Aloyse, my soul, do you think that it has not been stricken to death? I am going to recover from this long sickness, it is true; and I am allowing myself to be cured, as you see. But, luckily, there is fighting on the frontier; and I am captain of the Guards, and my place is where they are fighting. As soon as I am strong enough to mount my horse, I shall go where my place is. And at the very first battle in which I have a hand, Aloyse, I shall take good care so to arrange matters that I shall never have to return."

"You will kill yourself! Holy Virgin! And why, Monseigneur, — why, I pray you?"

"Why? Because Madame de Poitiers refused to speak, Aloyse; because Diane may be my sister; and because I love Diane; because it may be that the king was responsible for my father's murder; and because I cannot wreak my vengeance on him unless I am sure of it. And so, since I can neither avenge my father nor marry my sister, I don't see what more there is for me to do in this world. That is why I choose to leave it."

"No, Monseigneur, you shall not leave it," said Aloyse, gloomy and cast down, and in a spiritless voice. "You shall not leave it, because you have much to do, and a terrible task, I promise you. But I shall not speak to you of it until the day when you are entirely well again; and Master Nostredame tells me that you may hear what I have to say, and that you have sufficient strength to bear it."

That day arrived on the Tuesday of the week following. Gabriel had been out for the three days preceding, getting ready his equipments, and preparing for his departure; and Nostradamus had said he would come once more during the day to see his convalescent, but that it would be for the last time.

When Aloyse was alone with Gabriel, she said to him, —

"Monseigneur, have you considered well the extreme resolution you have taken, and do you persist in it?"

"I do indeed," said Gabriel.

"And you mean to kill yourself?"

"I mean to kill myself."

"And is it because you have no means of ascertaining whether Madame de Castro is or is not your sister that you mean to die?"

"For that very reason."

"What did I say to you, Monseigneur, to put you on the track of this fearful secret? Do you remember what I said!"

"To be sure! That God in the other world and two persons only in this had ever known this secret. The two human beings were Diane de Poitiers and the Comte de Montgommery, my father. I have begged and implored and threatened Madame de Valentinois; but when I left her, I was more uncertain and despairing than ever."

"But when I told you, Monseigneur," said Aloyse, "you declared that if it were necessary for you to descend into your father's tomb to wrest this secret from him, you would not shrink from the task."

"But," said Gabriel, "I have no idea where that tomb is situated."

"Nor I, but you must seek for it, Monseigneur."

"And even if I should find it," cried Gabriel, "God would have to work a miracle for me. The dead do not speak, Aloyse."

"No, the dead do not; but the living do."

"Great God! what do you mean?" said Gabriel, pale as a ghost.

"That you are not, as you kept calling yourself in your delirium, the Comte de Montgommery, Monseigneur, but only Vicomte de Montgommery, because your father, the Comte de Montgommery, is still living."

"Heaven and earth! Do you know that he is alive, my dear father?"

"I don't know it, Monseigneur, but I believe and hope so; for his was a strong and sturdy nature like yours, and should have resisted suffering and misfortune as valiantly. Now, if he is alive, he is not the one to refuse, as Madame Diane did, to reveal the secret on which your happiness depends!"

"But where shall we find him; of whom demand him? In Heaven's name, Aloyse, tell me!"

"It is a terrible story, Monseigneur! And I swore to my husband, by your father's command, never to reveal it to you; for as soon as you know it, you will plunge into the midst of fearful dangers, Monseigneur, and will declare war against foes a hundred times stronger than yourself. But the most desperate peril is preferable to certain death. You had made up your mind to die; and I knew that you would not grow weak in that determination. After all, I prefer to expose you to the doubtful chances of the bitter conflict which your hither dreaded in your behalf. At all events, your death will be less certain, and will be delayed a little. So I am going to tell you everything, Monseigneur; and it may be that God will pardon me for proving false to my oath."

"Yes, of course, dear Aloyse. My father! my father living! Oh, quickly! speak!"

But at this moment there was a soft knock at the door, and Nostradamus appeared.

"Aha, Monsieur d'Exmès," said he, "how bright and lively you are! I'm glad to see it! You were not like this a month ago. You seem to be all ready to take the field."

"Yes, indeed,—to take the field," said Gabriel, with sparkling eye, looking meaningly at Aloyse.

"So I see that the physician has no further business here," said Nostradamus.

"Nothing, save to receive my grateful thanks, Master, and I dare not say the value of your services, for under certain circumstances one's life is not valuable."

And Gabriel, pressing the doctor's hand, left in it a roll of gold-pieces.

"Thanks, Monsieur Vicomte d'Exmès," said Nostradamus. "But give me leave to make you a present which I think will prove of value to you."

"What is it, pray, Master?"

"You know, Monseigneur," Nostradamus began, "that I do not occupy myself entirely with men's illnesses. I have presumed to look farther and higher. I have tried to read their destinies,—a task full of uncertainty and obscurity; but in default of light, I have sometimes, I think, caught glimpses of the truth. God, I am convinced, has written twice over, in advance of his birth, the vast and mighty scheme of each man's destiny; in the stars of heaven, his native land, to which he raises his eyes so often, and in the lines of his hand,—an intricate conjuring book which he carries always with him, but which he cannot even begin to spell except at the cost of unwearying study. During many days and nights, Monseigneur, I have dug and delved away at these two sciences, as fathomless as the cask of the Danaïdes,— chiromancy and astrology. I have summoned before me all future ages; and a thousand years from now, those who are then alive may be sometimes amazed at my prophecies. But I know that the truth only shines in streaks, for although I sometimes see clearly, often, alas! I am in doubt. Nevertheless I am certain that I have now and then hours of clairvoyance which almost frighten me, Monseigneur. In one of these infrequent hours, I saw, twenty-five years ago, the destiny of a gentleman attached to the court of King François clearly written in the stars which watched over his birth and in the complicated lines of his hand. This extraordinary, curious, and perilous destiny made a strong impression on me. Fancy my astonishment, then, when in your hand and in the stars which presided over your birth, I seemed to read a horoscope like that which had so surprised me long ago; but I could not distinguish it so clearly as before and the lapse of twenty-five years had confused my memory. Last of all, Monseigneur, last month, in the height of your fever, you pronounced a name; I heard only the name, but it caught my attention at once. It was the name of the Comte de Montgommery."

"Of the Comte de Montgommery?" Gabriel cried in alarm.

"I tell you again, Monseigneur, that I heard nothing but the name; and the rest is of little importance, for that name was the name of the man whose destiny had been made as clear to me as the noonday sun. I hastened home and hunted among my old papers until I found the Comte de Montgommery's horoscope. But a most singular circumstance, Monseigneur, and one which I have never met with before in more than thirty years of study, is that there must be some mysterious connection, some strange affinity, between you and the Comte de Montgommery; and God, who never ordained the same destiny for two men, must have reserved both of you for the same fate. For I was not mistaken; the lines of the hand and the constellations had the same aspect for both. I should not dare to say that there was to be no difference in the details of your two lives; but the predominating feature of both horoscopes is the same. I long ago lost sight of the Comte de Montgommery; but I ascertained that one of my predictions in his regard was fulfilled. He wounded François I. in the face with a red-hot brand. Has the remainder of his destiny been fulfilled? That is what I cannot say. I can only be sure that the same misfortune and the same violent death which threatened him are impending over you."

"Can it be?" said Gabriel.

"Here, Monseigneur," said Nostradamus, handing to Vicomte d'Exmès a roll of parchment, "here is the horoscope which I drew off at the time for the Comte de Montgommery. I should make no changes in it were I to write yours to-day."

"Give it me, Master, give it me!" said Gabriel. "This is indeed an inestimable gift; and you cannot imagine how precious it is to me."

"One word more, Monsieur d'Exmès," said Nostradamus; "one last word to put you on your guard, though God be supreme, and one can hardly turn aside His plans. The nativity of Henri II. presaged that he would die in a duel or in single combat."

"But," asked Gabriel, "what connection?"

"When you read this scroll, you will understand me, Monseigneur. Meanwhile it remains only for me to take my leave of you, and to hope that the catastrophe with which God menaces your life may at least be not sought by you."

And having saluted Gabriel, who pressed his hand warmly and escorted him to the door, he took his leave.

As soon as he was with Aloyse once more, Gabriel unrolled the parchment; and having made sure that no one could interrupt him or spy upon him, he read aloud the following lines:—

"En joûte, en amour, cettuy touchera
Le front du roy,
Et cornes ou bien trou sanglant mettra
Au front du roy.
Mais le veuille ou non, toujours blessera
Le front du roy.
Enfin, l'aimera, puis, las! le tuera
Dame du roy."[2]

"It is well!" cried Gabriel, with beaming eye and a look of triumph. "Now, dear Aloyse, you may tell me how my father, the Comte de Montgommery, was entombed alive by King Henri II."

"By King Henri II.!" cried Aloyse; "how do you know, Monseigneur?"

"I guess it! But you can tell me of the crime, since God has pointed out to me my revenge."

[2] "In tilting and in love-making this youth shall ever
Be matched against the king,
And shall in winning hearts and breaking heads
E'en triumph o'er the king.
Yea, though he wish it not, still shall his brand
Wound in the face the king.
And then, alas! shall love him and destroy him
The lady of the king."

CHAPTER XVIII
THE LAST RESORT OF A COQUETTE

Elaborated and perfected by the aid of contemporary memoirs and chronicles, the narrative of Aloyse, who had been informed by her husband, Perrot Travigny, squire and confidential servant of the Comte de Montgommery, of all the incidents of his master's life, so far as he knew them,—the narrative of Aloyse, we say, thus perfected, gave the following sad story of Jacques de Montgommery, Gabriel's father. His son knew the leading details of it; but the sinister *dénouement*, which brought it to a close, was a sealed book to him, as to everybody else.

Jacques de Montgommery, Seigneur de Lorges, was, as all his ancestors had been, daring and brave; and during the stormy reign of François I. he was always to be found in the front rank when fighting was going on. And so he became a colonel in the French infantry very early in life.

But among his many brilliant exploits there was one untoward incident to which Nostradamus had had reference.

It was in 1521, when the Comte de Montgommery was barely twenty years old, and only a captain. It was a severe winter; and the young men, young King François at their head, were indulging in a snowball fight,—a sport not unattended with danger, and much in vogue at the time. They were divided into two parties, one defending a certain house which the other assaulted with bullets of snow, Comte d'Enghien, Seigneur de Cérisoles, was killed in just such a game. Jacques de Montgommery was very near killing the king on this occasion. The battle over, they set about warming themselves; the fire had been allowed to go out, and the whole crowd of young madcaps rushed about to rekindle it. Jacques came running in, first of all, with a blazing stick in a pair of tongs; but on the war he encountered François, who had no chance to protect himself, and received a violent blow on the face from the red-hot brand. Fortunately nothing came of it but a wound, although a very severe one; and the ugly scar left by it was the cause of the fashion of wearing the beard long and the hair short, which was ordained by François at that time.

As the Comte de Montgommery atoned for this unfortunate casualty by a thousand brilliant exploits, the king bore him no ill-will for it, and interposed no obstacle to his rising to the first rank at court and in the army. In 1530 Jacques married Claudine de Boissière. It was a mere marriage de convenance; but he long mourned for his wife, who died in 1533, when Gabriel was born. Melancholy, moreover, was the most marked trait of his character, as is the case with all those who are predestined to some fatality. When he was left a widower and alone, he found relief only on the battlefield, and was driven into danger by sheer ennui. But in 1538, after the truce of Nice, when this man of war and of action had to conform to the etiquette of the court, and to walk up and down in the galleries of the Tournelles or the Louvre, with his parade-sword at his side, he was near dying of disgust.

A mad passion saved him, and was his ruin.

The regal Circe involved this overgrown boy, sturdy and ingenuous, in her toils. He fell in love with Diane de Poitiers.

Three months he revolved about her, gloomy and lowering, without ever addressing a single word to her; nor was there any need of a word for the grande sénéchale to understand that his heart belonged to her. She made a note of that passion in a corner of her memory as something that might possibly be of use to her on occasion.

The occasion came. François I. began to neglect his beautiful mistress for Madame d'Étampes, who was less beautiful in face, but had the great advantage of being attractive in other respects.

When the signs that she was being superseded were unmistakable, Diane, for the first time in her life, spoke to Jacques de Montgommery.

This took place at the Tournelles, at a fête given by the king to the new favorite.

"Monsieur de Montgommery," said Diane, calling him by name.

He drew near her, with heaving chest, and made an awkward salutation.

"How very sad you are, Monsieur de Montgommery!" she said.

"To the point of death, Madame."

"And why, in Heaven's name!"

"Madame, because I should like to kill myself."

"For some one, no doubt?"

"To kill myself for some one would be very sweet; but, *ma foi*, to do it for nothing would be sweeter yet."

"What a fearful state of melancholy!" said Diane; "and whence comes this black despair, pray?"

"Ah! can I say, Madame?"

"Well, then, I know, Monsieur de Montgommery. You are in love with me."

Jacques turned white as a sheet; and then, with a more tremendous struggle than it would have cost him to cast himself headlong and alone into the midst of a whole battalion of the enemy, he replied in a harsh and uncertain voice, —

"Well, then, Madame, you are right. I do love you. So much the worse for me!"

"So much the better, rather," replied Diane, laughing.

"What did you say, Madame?" Montgommery cried, with his heart thumping against his ribs. "Ah, Madame, take heed! this is no joke, but a deep and sincere passion, whether it be a possible or an impossible one to gratify."

"And why should it be impossible?" asked Diane.

"Madame," was Jacques's reply, "pardon my frankness, but I never learned to envelop facts with many words. Does not the king love you, Madame?"

"Yes," sighed Diane; "he loves me."

"And don't you see, then, that it is not for me to declare my unworthy love, though I cannot help loving you?"

"Unworthy of you, it is true," said the duchess.

"Oh, no, not of me!" cried the count; "and if the day should ever come —
"

But Diane interrupted him with an air of grave melancholy and well assumed dignity, —

"Enough, Monsieur de Montgommery; let us put an end to this interview, I beg."

She bowed coldly, and turned away, leaving the poor count a prey to a whirl of conflicting emotions,—jealousy, love, hatred, grief, and joy. So Diane saw the adoration which made him bow down before her. But perhaps he had wounded her! He must have seemed unjust, ungrateful, cruel to her! He repeated to himself over and over again all the sublime nonsense of love.

The next day Diane de Poitiers said to François I., "You didn't know, did you, Sire, that Monsieur de Montgommery was in love with me?"

"What's that?" said François, laughing. "The Montgommerys are of an ancient family, and almost as nobly born, upon my word, as I; and what's more they are almost as brave, and now it seems that they are almost as good at love-making."

"And is that all the reply that your Majesty has to make to me?" Diane asked him.

"And what do you want me to say, my dear?" replied the king. "Do you really think that I ought to take it ill of the Comte de Montgommery that he has as good taste and as good eyes as I have?"

"If Madame d'Étampes were in question," muttered Diane, wounded to the quick, "you would not say so."

She pursued the conversation no further, but resolved to go on with the experiment. When she next saw Jacques some days later, she began to question him again,—

"How is this, Monsieur de Montgommery? Still more melancholy than usual?"

"I am indeed, Madame," said the count, humbly; "for I shudder to think that I have offended you."

"Not offended, Monsieur," said the duchess, "but grieved sorely."

"Oh, Madame," cried Montgomery, "I, who would give all my blood to spare you a tear,—how can it be that I have caused you the least grief?"

"Did you not tell me that because I was the king's favorite I had no right to aspire to the affection of a simple gentleman?"

"Ah, I had no such idea as that, Madame," said the count; "indeed, I could have no such idea, for I, a simple gentleman, love you with a passion as sincere as it is profound. I only meant to say to you that you could not love me, since the king loves you and you love him."

"The king does not love me, nor do I love the king," replied Diane.

"God in heaven! Then you may come to love me!" cried Montgommery.

"I may love you," replied Diane, calmly; "but I can never tell you that I love you."

"And why not, Madame?"

"To save my father's life," said Diane, "I consented to become the mistress of the King of France; but the way to restore my honor is not to become the mistress of the Comte de Montgommery."

She accompanied this half-refusal with so passionate and so languishing a glance that the count could not restrain himself.

"Ah, Madame," said he to the coquettish duchess, "if you love me as I love you—"

"Well, what then?"

"What then! Why, what matters the world, or the prejudices of family or of honor? For me you are the universe. For three months I have seen nothing but your face. I love you with all the blind devotion and all the ardor of a first passion. Your sovereign beauty intoxicates me and distracts me. If you love me as I love you, be Comtesse de Montgommery,—be my wife."

"Thanks, Count," said Diane, triumphantly. "I will remember these noble and generous words. Meanwhile you know that green and white are my colors."

Jacques in a transport of delight kissed Diane's hand, prouder and happier than if the crown of the whole world had been on his head.

And when François I., the following day, called Diane's attention to the fact that her new adorer had begun to wear her colors in public,—

"Has he not a right to, Sire?" said she, fixing her keen glance upon the king. "And may I not allow him to wear my colors when he offers to let me wear his name?"

"Is it possible?" the king asked.

"There is no doubt about it, Sire," the duchess replied, with confidence, thinking for a moment that her plan had succeeded, and that the jealousy of her unfaithful lord would reawaken his love.

But after a moment of silence, the king, rising to put an end to the interview, said to Diane, gayly,—

"If that is so, Madame, we will give the office of grand sénéchal—which has been vacant since the death of Monsieur de Brézé, your first husband—to Monsieur de Montgommery as a wedding present."

"And Monsieur de Montgommery will accept it," was Diane's proud reply; "for I will be a faithful and loyal wife to him, and I would not be false to my troth to him for all the kings in Christendom."

The king bowed and smiled, without making any reply, and left the room.

Unquestionably Madame d'Étampes's star was in the ascendant.

The same day Diane the ambitious, with bitter anger at her heart, said to the enraptured Jacques,—

"My gallant Count, my noble Montgommery, I love you with all my heart."

CHAPTER XIX
HOW HENRI II. BEGAN TO ENJOY HIS INHERITANCE DURING HIS FATHER'S LIFE

The marriage of Diane and the Comte de Montgommery was appointed to take place in three months; and it was currently rumored in that scandal-mongering and licentious court that Diane de Poitiers, in her eager desire for revenge, had given earnest-money to her future husband.

The three months passed. The Comte de Montgommery was more infatuated than ever; but Diane postponed the performance of her promise from day to day, on one pretext or another.

A very short time after she had given this promise, she had noticed that the young Dauphin Henri was in the habit of feasting his eyes upon her when no one was by. Thereupon a new ambition awoke in the heart of the imperious Diane. The title of Comtesse de Montgommery was only of use to conceal a defeat, while the title of favorite of the dauphin would be almost a triumph. What! Madame d'Étampes, who was always prating contemptuously about Diane's age, was loved by the father only; that was nothing. She, Diane, would be loved by the son! For her a youthful passion; for her hope; for her the future! Madame d'Étampes had succeeded her; but she would succeed Madame d'Étampes. She would keep always before her, waiting patiently and calmly for her time to come, a constant, living menace. For Henri would some day be king; and Diane, always beautiful, would be queen once more. It would be in truth a notable triumph.

Henri's character made her still more certain of her game. He was only nineteen at this time, but had taken part in more than one war; for four years he had been married to Catherine de Médicis, but remained none the less an uncouth and muddle-headed boy. He was as awkward and embarrassed at the fêtes at the Louvre, and in the presence of the other sex, as he was accomplished and daring in horsemanship, in feats of arms, or at tilting,—in all directions, in short, where skill and address were requisite. Being dull intellectually, and slow-witted, he was an easy prey to anybody who cared to take him up. Anne de Montmorency, who was not on good terms with the king, devoted his attention to the dauphin, and had no difficulty in enforcing his views upon him, and bringing his tastes to conform to his own, which were those of a man of mature years. He led him hither and thither according to his will and caprice. Ultimately he succeeded in planting in that weak and yielding mind the wide-spreading roots of an all-powerful influence, and obtained such control over Henri that thenceforth seemingly nothing but the ascendency of some woman could disturb his power.

But he was horrified before long to see that his pupil was on the verge of falling in love. Henri abandoned the friends with whom the constable had shrewdly surrounded him. Henri became melancholy and dreamy where he had been shy before. Montmorency looked around, and thought that he could see that it was Diane de Poitiers who was enthroned in his fancy. This rough gendarme preferred that it should be Diane rather than another, for in his vulgar fashion he estimated the royal courtesan much more nearly at her true worth than did the chivalrous Montgommery. He based his plans upon the low motives which he attributed to her, judging her by himself; and with his mind once more at ease, he left the dauphin to hover sighing about the grande sénéchale.

It was indeed her beauty which aroused Henri's sluggish heart. She was roguish and provoking and lively; her finely-shaped head moved very prettily and quickly hither and thither; her glance shone with promise; and her whole person had a sort of magnetic attraction (they called it magic in those days) which easily led poor Henri astray. It seemed to him that this fair creature would unveil to him the secret of a new life. The siren was to him, strange and innocent savage that he was, as fascinating and dangerous as the hidden mysteries of a cavern.

Diane saw all this; but she still hesitated to incur the risk of this new future, through fear of the past in the shape of François I., and of Comte de Montgommery in the present.

But one day when the king, always courteous and attentive to the other sex, even to those with whom he was not in love, and to those whom he had ceased to love, was talking with Diane de Poitiers in the embrasure of a window, he noticed the dauphin watching them with a sly and jealous look.

François called him.

"Aha, Monsieur my son, what are you doing there? Come this way," he said.

But Henri, pale and ashamed, after hesitating a moment between his duty and his fear, instead of replying to his father's invitation, adopted the expedient of running away as if he had not heard him.

"Well, well, what a boorish, shy dog!" said the king. "Can you understand such bashfulness, Madame Diane? Have you, goddess of the forests, ever seen a fallow deer more terrified? Ah, what a wretched failing?"

"Is it your Majesty's pleasure that I should undertake to amend Monseigneur le Dauphin's ways?" asked Diane, smiling.

"Surely," said the king, "it would be hard to imagine a prettier teacher or a more delightful apprenticeship."

"Consider his education completed, then, Sire," replied Diane; "I will take charge of it."

She soon hunted up the fugitive.

The Comte de Montgommery, being on duty that day, was not at the Louvre.

"I frighten you terribly, Monseigneur, do I not?"

Diane began the conversation thus; and the conversation thus begun was continued.

How she concluded it; how she seemed not to notice the prince's blunders, but hung upon his lightest word; how he left her with the conviction that he should soon be clever and fascinating; and how he did gradually become clever and fascinating with her; how, in short, she became his mistress in every sense of the word, ordering him about, giving him lessons, and humoring him all at the same time,—it was the same old, untranslatable comedy over again, which will always be played, but never has been and never will be written.

And Montgommery? Oh, Montgommery loved Diane too well to suspect her, and had devoted himself to her too blindly to have any clearness of vision left. Everybody at court was already gossiping about Madame de Poitiers's latest love-affair, as to which the noble count was in a state of blissful ignorance which Diane took good care not to dispel. The structure she was building was too fragile as yet for her not to dread the least shock, or any outburst; so while her ambition led her to maintain her hold on the dauphin, prudence kept her from breaking with the count.

CHAPTER XX
OF THE USEFULNESS OF FRIENDS

Now let us allow Aloyse to go on and finish her tale, having narrated these preliminary facts by way of explanation of what is to come.

"My husband, brave Perrot," she said to Gabriel, who was all rapt attention, "had not failed to hear the reports which were on everybody's lips about Madame Diane, and all the sport that was made of Monsieur de Montgommery; but he did not know whether it was his duty to warn his master, who he saw continued trustful and happy, or whether he should hold his peace about the shameful plot in which this ambitious woman had involved him. He told me of his hesitation, for I used to give him very good advice, and he had put my discretion and my loyalty to the proof; but in this matter I was as undecided as he as to what course we should take.

"One evening we were sitting in this very room, Monseigneur and Perrot and I; for the count never treated us as servants, but as friends, and had chosen to retain, even here in Paris, the patriarchal custom of passing winter evenings current in Normandy, where the master and his retainers used to warm themselves at the same fire after working together through the day. The count, buried in thought, his head resting on his hand, was sitting before the fire. He used commonly to pass the evening with Madame de Poitiers; but for some time she had very frequently sent word to him that she was ill and could not receive him. He was thinking about her, no doubt, while Perrot was fitting the straps of a cuirass, and I was spinning.

"It was the 7th of January, 1539, a cold and rainy evening, and the day after the Epiphany. Remember that ill-omened date, Monseigneur."

Gabriel nodded to show that no word escaped him, and Aloyse continued, —

"All at once Monsieur de Langeais, Monsieur de Boutières, and the Comte de Sancerre were announced, — three gentlemen of the court, friends of Monseigneur, but much closer friends of Madame d'Étampes. All three were wrapped in great dark cloaks; and although they came in laughing, I seemed to feel that they brought disaster with them; and my instinct, alas! was not far out of the way.

"The Comte de Montgommery rose and advanced to greet the new-comers with the hospitable and courtly manner which became him so well.

"'Welcome, my friends!' said he to the three, as he shook hands with them.

"At a sign from him I came forward to take their cloaks, and all of them sat down.

"'What good fortune brings you to my poor quarters?' the count asked.

"'A threefold bet,' replied Monsieur de Boutières; 'and your presence here, my dear Count, wins mine for me on the spot.'

"'As for mine,' said Monsieur de Langeais, 'it was won before we came here.'

"'And mine,' said the Comte de Sancerre, 'I shall win in a moment, as you will see.'

"'What were your bets, pray, gentlemen?' said Montgommery.

"'Well,' said Monsieur de Boutières, 'Langeais here made a bet with D'Enghien that the Dauphin would not be at the Louvre this evening. We have been there, and have duly decided that D'Enghien has lost.'

"'As for De Boutières,' said the Comte de Sancerre, 'he bet with Monsieur de Montejan that you would be at home this evening, my dear Count; and you see that he has won.'

"'And you have won, too, Sancerre, I'll warrant,' said Monsieur de Langeais; 'for in fact the three bets were really but one, and we must win or lose together. Sancerre, Monsieur de Montgommery, bet one hundred pistoles with D'Aussun that Madame de Poitiers was ill this evening.'

"Your father, Gabriel, turned fearfully pale.

"'You have won, too, Monsieur de Sancerre,' said he, with a trembling voice; 'for Madame la Grande Sénéchale just now sent word to me that she could receive no one this evening on account of a sudden indisposition.'

"'There,' cried Monsieur de Sancerre, 'just as I said! You will bear witness for me to D'Aussun, gentlemen, that he owes me a hundred pistoles.'

"Then they all fell to laughing like madmen; but the Comte de Montgommery remained very grave.

"'Now, my good friends,' said he, with an accent not free from bitterness, 'will you kindly explain this riddle for me?'

"'With all my heart, upon my word!' said Monsieur de Boutières; 'but first send these good people away.'

"We were already at the door, Perrot and I; but Monseigneur motioned for us to remain.

"'These are devoted friends of mine,' he said to the young gentlemen; 'and as I have nothing to blush for, I have nothing to conceal.'

"'As you choose!' said Monsieur de Langeais; 'it seems rather provincial, but the matter concerns you more than us, Count. And I am sure, too, that they must know the great secret, for it has made the circuit of the whole town; and you will be the last one to hear it, as is generally the case.'

"'Tell me, I beg you!' exclaimed Monsieur de Montgommery.

"'My dear Count,' resumed Monsieur de Langeais, 'we are going to tell you, because it pains us deeply to see a brave and courteous gentleman like yourself so deceived; but if we do tell you, it is only on condition that you accept the revelation philosophically,—that is to say, with a laugh,—for the whole matter is not worth your anger, I assure you; and then, too, any outburst of wrath would be disarmed beforehand.'

"'We shall see! I am waiting,' replied Monseigneur, coldly.

"'Dear Count,'—Monsieur de Boutières it was who spoke now, the youngest and most heedless of the three,—'you are acquainted with mythology, are you not? No doubt you know the story of Endymion? But what do you think was Endymion's age at the time of his liaison with Diane Phœbé? If you imagine that he was in the neighborhood of forty, you are mistaken, my dear fellow, for he was less than twenty, and hadn't a sign of a beard even. I know that from my governor, who has the whole story at his tongue's end. And that is how it happens that Endymion on this particular evening is not at the Louvre; and that Dame Luna is in bed and not to be seen, probably on account of the storm; and lastly, that you are at home, Monsieur de Montgommery,—whence it follows that my governor is a great man, and that we have won our three bets. *Vive la joie!*'

"'Your proofs?' asked the count, coldly.

"'Proofs!' replied Monsieur de Langeais, 'why, you can go and seek those for yourself. Don't you live within two steps of La Luna?'

"'Very true. Thanks!' was the count's only reply.

"He rose from his chair; and the three friends had to rise too, chilled and rather alarmed by Monsieur de Montgommery's stern and forbidding demeanor.

"'Come, come, Count,' said Monsieur de Sancerre, 'don't go and do anything foolish or imprudent! And remember that it is as dangerous to rub against the lion's whelp as against the lion himself.'

"'Don't be alarmed,' replied the count.

"'At least you don't intend to do yourself any harm?'

"'That's as it may be,' said he.

"He showed them to the door, or rather almost pushed them out, and then, coming back, said to Perrot,—

"'My cloak and my sword.'

"Perrot brought them to him.

"'Is it true that you knew this thing, you two?' asked the count, adjusting his sword.

"'Yes, Monseigneur,' replied Perrot, looking at the floor.

"'Why didn't you give me some warning of it, Perrot?'

"'But, Monseigneur—' my husband began falteringly.

"'Oh, it's all right; you are not my friends, you two, but just good people, that's all.'

"He tapped his squire on the shoulder good-naturedly. He was very pale, but spoke with a sort of solemn calmness. Again he said to Perrot,—

"'Is it a long while that these reports have been circulating?'

"'Monseigneur,' said Perrot, 'it is five months that you have been in love with Madame de Poitiers; and your marriage was arranged to take place in November. I am assured that Monseigneur le Dauphin has been in love with Madame Diane since about a month after she welcomed your addresses. However, it is hardly more than two months since it has been talked about, and personally I have known of it for only a fortnight. The rumors did not take definite shape until the postponement of the wedding, and the talk has been mostly under the rose, for fear of Monseigneur le Dauphin. Only yesterday I whipped one of Monsieur de la Garde's people for having the face to laugh about it in my hearing; and Monsieur de la Garde didn't dare to say a word.'

"'They shall not laugh any more about it,' said Monseigneur, in a tone that made me fairly shudder.

"When he was ready to depart, he passed his hand across his forehead, and said,—

"'Aloyse, bring Gabriel to me; I want to kiss him.'

"You were sleeping, Monseigneur Gabriel,—sleeping calmly like a little cherub; and you began to cry when I woke you and took you from your bed. I wrapped you in a blanket, and thus carried you to your father. He took you in his arms, gazed at you for some time without a word, as if to take his fill of the sight of you, then pressed a kiss upon your half-closed eyes. At the same time a tear fell on your rosy cheek,—the first tear which he, the strong proud man, had ever shed before me. He gave you back to my arms, saying,—

"'I commend my child to you, Aloyse.'

"Alas! they were the last words he ever said to me. They have remained where they fell, and I seem to hear them always.

"'I am going with you, Monseigneur,' said my good Perrot then.

"'No, Perrot. I must go alone. Do you stay here.'

"'But, Monseigneur—'

"'I wish it so,' said he.

"It was useless to protest further, when he spoke thus, and Perrot therefore remained silent. The count took our hands.

"'Adieu, my dear friends,' said he; 'no, not adieu! *au revoir*'

"And then he went away, calmly and with a firm step, as if he were going to return in a quarter of an hour.

"Perrot said not a word; but as soon as his master was out of the house, he too took down his cloak and his sword. We didn't exchange a word, and I made no attempt to prevent his going; he did but his duty in following the count, though it were to his death. He held out his arms to me, and I threw myself weeping into them; then having kissed me most tenderly, he followed Monsieur de Montgommery's footsteps. All this had not taken a minute, and we had not exchanged one word.

"Left alone, I fell upon a chair, sobbing and praying. The rain outside was falling with redoubled violence, and the wind was howling dismally. But you, Monseigneur Gabriel, you had fallen off again into a peaceful sleep, from which you were to awake an orphan."

CHAPTER XXI
WHEREIN IT IS SHOWN THAT JEALOUSY SOMETIMES ABOLISHED TITLES EVEN BEFORE THE FRENCH REVOLUTION

"As Monsieur de Langeais had said, the Hôtel de Brézé, where Madame Diane then lived, was in the Rue du Figuier St. Paul, only two steps from us, and there it still stands,—this abode of disaster.

"Perrot followed his master at a distance, saw him stop at Madame Diane's door, knock, and then go in. He drew near to the house. Monsieur de Montgommery was speaking haughtily and with much confidence to the valets, who were trying to prevent his entrance, declaring that their mistress was ill in her chamber; but the count forced his way in, and Perrot took advantage of the confusion to creep softly in behind him, as the door remained half open. He knew his way about the house very well, having carried more than one message to Madame Diane. He went upstairs in the darkness behind Monsieur de Montgommery, unopposed, either because nobody saw him, or because the squire's presence was of trifling consequence when the master had broken through all rules.

"At the top of the staircase the count found two of the duchess's women, terrified and weeping, who asked him what he wanted at such an unseasonable hour. Ten o'clock was just striking on all the clocks in the neighborhood. Monsieur de Montgommery replied firmly that he must see Madame Diane at once; that he had something of importance to tell her without delay, and that if she could not receive him, he would wait.

"He spoke loud enough to be heard in the duchess's bedroom, which was close at hand. One of the women went in, and came back at once to say that Madame de Poitiers had retired; but that she would come and speak with the count, who was to wait for her in the oratory.

"The dauphin was not there then, or else he was acting very timorously for a son of France. Monsieur de Montgommery followed the two women without objection as they lighted him into the oratory.

"Perrot then who had been crouching in the darkness of the stairway, went on to the floor above, and hid behind a high curtain in a corridor which separated Madame de Poitiers's bedroom from the oratory where Monsieur de Montgommery was awaiting her. At the ends of this wide passage-way were two disused doors, one of which had formerly led into the oratory, and the other into the bedroom. Perrot found to his great delight that by slipping behind the hangings of one or the other of these doors, which had been allowed to remain for symmetry's sake, though no longer in use, and by listening attentively, he could hear almost every word that was said in either apartment. Not that my brave husband was influenced by mere idle curiosity, Monseigneur; but the count's last words as he parted from us, and an undefinable instinct, warned him that his master was running some risk, and that at this very moment they were setting a trap for him perhaps; so he determined to remain at hand to assist him in case of need.

"Unfortunately, as you will see, Monseigneur, not one of the words that he heard and afterward repeated to me threw the least ray of light upon the obscure and fatal question which is in our minds to-day.

"Monsieur de Montgommery had not waited two minutes when Madame de Poitiers entered the oratory rather hurriedly.

"'What is the trouble, Monsieur?' said she; 'and why this nocturnal invasion after my request that you would not come to-day?'

"'I will tell you frankly in a word, Madame; but send these women away first. Now listen to me. I will be very brief. I have been told that I have a rival in your affection; that my rival is the dauphin, and that he is with you here this very evening.'

"'And you must have believed it, since you came running here to make sure?' said Madame Diane, haughtily.

"'I was in agony, Diane, and I came here hoping to find a cure for my suffering.'

"'Very well; and now you have seen me,' replied Madame de Poitiers, 'you know that your informants lied to you; so leave me to get some rest. In Heaven's name, go, Jacques!'

"'No, Diane,' said the count made suspicious, no doubt, by her haste to get rid of him; 'for if they did lie in claiming that the dauphin was here now, they may not have lied in assuring me that he will be here before the evening is over; and I shall be very glad to prove them slanderers at every point.'

"'And so you will remain, Monsieur?'

"'I will remain, Madame. Do you go and lie down if you are ill, Diane. I will keep watch over your slumber, if you are willing.'

"'But by what right will you do this, Monsieur?' cried Madame de Poitiers. 'What title have you? Am I not free still?'

"'No, Madame,' replied the count, steadily, 'you are no longer free to make a loyal gentleman whose attentions you have accepted the laughing-stock of the whole court.'

"'At all events, I will not accept this last attention,' said Madame Diane. 'You have no more right to remain here than other people have to laugh at you. You are not my husband, are you? And I don't bear your name, so far as I am aware.'

"'Oh, Madame,' cried the count, in despair, 'what does it matter to me how much they laugh at me? That is not the question? *Mon Dieu*, no! and you know it, Diane; and it is not my honor that lies bleeding and crying to you for pity, but my love. If I had been offended by the gibes of those three idiots, I would have drawn my sword on them, and that would have been the end of it. But my heart was torn, Diane, and I came flying to you. My dignity! my reputation! it is not about those that I am troubled, not in the least; it is because I love you, and am raving mad with jealousy; because you have told me and proved to me that you love me; and because I will kill any one who dares to interfere with this love which is my all, whether he be dauphin or the king himself, Madame! I don't worry about the shape my vengeance shall take, I assure you. But as God lives, I will be revenged!'

"'And revenged for what, pray? and why?' demanded an imperious voice behind Monsieur de Montgommery.

"Perrot shivered with fear of what was to come; for across the dimly lighted corridor he saw Monsieur le Dauphin, who is to-day king, and in his wake the harsh and mocking features of Monsieur de Montmorency.

"'Heaven help me!' cried Madame Diane, falling upon a couch and wringing her hands; 'this is just what I feared.'

"Monsieur de Montgommery at first gave only a short sharp cry of dismay. Then Perrot heard him say with a marvellously calm voice, —

"'Monseigneur le Dauphin, just one word, by your leave! Tell me that you have not come here because you love Madame de Poitiers, and because Madame de Poitiers loves you.'

"'Monsieur de Montgommery,' replied the dauphin, restraining his rising anger, 'just one word, by my command! Tell me that I do not find you here because Madame Diane loves you, and because you love Madame Diane.'

"Matters having reached this stage, the actors were no longer the heir of the mightiest throne in the world and a simple gentleman, his subject, but two men, angered and jealous rivals, two suffering hearts, two distraught minds.

"'I was Madame Diane's chosen and accepted husband, as everybody knew, and as you knew,' replied Monsieur de Montgommery, altogether omitting the title by which the prince had a claim to be addressed.

"'A mere promise in the air, a forgotten promise,' cried Henri; 'and although perhaps of more recent date than yours, the rights of my love are no less sure, and I will maintain them.'

"'Ah, the villain! he speaks of his rights!' cried the count, already drunk with rage and jealousy. 'Do you dare to say, then, that this woman belongs to you?'

"I say that she doesn't belong to you, at all events,' replied Henri; 'I say that I am at Madame's house with Madame's approbation, and I fancy that you can hardly say the same. So I am impatiently awaiting your departure, Monsieur.'

"'If you are so impatient, well and good! let us go together; that's very simple.'

"'A challenge!' cried Montmorency, coming forward at this. 'Do you dare, Monsieur, to offer a challenge to the Dauphin of France?'

"'There is no Dauphin of France in the case at all,' replied the count; 'there is only a man who claims to be beloved by the woman whom I love, that's all.'

"He must have made a pass at Henri at this juncture, for Perrot heard Diane cry out,—

"'He means to insult the prince! he will murder the prince! Help!'

"Embarrassed, no doubt, by the strange part she was playing, she rushed out of the room, notwithstanding Monsieur de Montmorency's efforts to detain her by assuring her that she need not be afraid, for they were two against one, and had a strong escort below. Perrot saw Madame Diane cross the corridor and burst into her own room, weeping violently and calling aloud for her women and the dauphin's people.

"But her flight had no tendency to allay the heat of the two adversaries, far from it; and Monsieur de Montgommery repeated with bitter meaning the word 'escort' which had just been uttered.

"'It is with the swords of his retainers, doubtless,' said he, 'that Monseigneur le Dauphin intends to avenge these insults?'

"'No, Monsieur,' replied Henri, proudly, 'my sword alone will suffice to punish an insolent villain.'

"Each already had his hand upon his sword-hilt, when Monsieur de Montmorency interposed.

"'Pardon, Monseigneur,' said he; 'but he who may be king to-morrow has no right to put his life in jeopardy to-day. You are not a man, Monseigneur; you are a whole nation. A dauphin of France draws his sword only for France herself.'

"'But in that case,' cried Monsieur de Montgommery, 'a dauphin of France, who has everything at command, should not filch from me the one on whom my whole life depends, who is in my eyes dearer than my honor, than my native country, than my child in its cradle, even than my immortal soul itself; for she had made me forget all these,—this woman who has perhaps been false to me. But no, she is not false to me; it cannot be, for I love her too dearly! Monseigneur, pardon my violence and my madness, I beg, and condescend to tell me that you do not love Diane. Of course you would not come to the house of one you loved accompanied by Monsieur de Montmorency and a mounted escort of eight or ten! I ought to have thought of that.'

"'I chose,' said Monsieur de Montmorency, 'to attend Monseigneur with an escort this evening, despite his objections, because I had been secretly warned that a trap would be laid for him to-day. However, I meant to go no farther than the door of the house; but your loud voice, Monsieur, reached my ears, and was the cause of my coming farther than I intended, and thus becoming convinced of the accuracy of the intelligence afforded by the unknown friends who put me upon my guard so opportunely.'

"'Ah, I know who they are, these unknown friends!' said the count, laughing bitterly. 'They are the same ones, no doubt, who notified me also that the dauphin would be here this evening; and their plans have succeeded to admiration, to their delight no doubt, and to hers who set them about it. For Madame d'Étampes, I presume, had no object except to compromise Madame de Poitiers by a public scandal. So Monsieur le Dauphin, in coming to pay his visit with an army in attendance, has marvellously helped on this marvellous scheme! Aha! so you have no longer to show the least discretion,

Henri de Valois, in your relations with Madame de Brézé? So you label her publicly as your declared favorite, do you? She is really yours by a certified and authenticated title; and I can no longer doubt or hope? You have surely stolen her from me beyond recall, and with her my happiness and my life? Well, then, by heaven and earth! I have no more occasion to be discreet either'. Because you are the son of France, Henri de Valois, is no reason why I should cease to be a gentleman; and you shall give me satisfaction for this insult, or you are nothing but a coward!"

"'Scoundrel!' cried the dauphin, drawing his sword and springing at the count.

"But Monsieur de Montmorency again threw himself between them.

"'Monseigneur, once more I say that in my presence the heir to the throne shall not cross swords about a woman with a —'

"'With a gentleman of more ancient race than you, foremost baron in Christendom though you be!' the count burst in, fairly beside himself. 'Besides, every noble is as good as the king; and kings have not always been so discreet, as you undertake to claim, and for very good reasons. Charles of Naples challenged Alphonse of Arragon, and François I., not so very long ago, challenged Charles V. "That was king against king," you say. 'Very well! Monsieur de Nemours, the king's nephew, called out an humble Spanish captain. The Montgommerys are every whit as good as the Valois; and as they have many times intermarried with the royal children of France and England, there is no reason why they should not fight with them. The Montgommerys of old bore the arms of France pure in the second and third quarterings. After their return from England, whither they followed William the Conqueror, their arms were azure, a lion, or, armed, and *lampassé* argent, with the motto *Garde lieu*! and three *fleurs-de-lis* on a field gules. Come, then, Monseigneur, our arms are like our swords, a fitting guarantee of our knightly prowess. Ah, if you loved this woman as I do, and if you hated me as I hate you! But no, you are a mere timid boy, happy in being able to hide behind your preceptor.'

"'Monsieur de Montmorency, let me go!' cried the dauphin, struggling fiercely with Montmorency, who was holding him back.

"'No, by Heaven!' said Montmorency, 'I will not let you fight with this madman! Below there! Help! help!' he shouted at the top of his voice.

"And Diane, too, leaning over the stairway, could be distinctly heard crying with all her might, —

"'Help! Come up, you fellows! Are you going to let your masters be murdered?'

"This Delilah-like perfidy—for, after all, they were two to one against Monsieur de Montgommery—undoubtedly excited the count's blind fury to the highest pitch. Perrot, paralyzed with terror, heard him say,—

"'Does it need, then, the last insult of all to convince you,—you and your go-between,—Henri de Valois, that you *must* give me satisfaction?'

"Perrot supposed that he then approached the dauphin and threatened to strike him with his hand, for Henri roared like a tiger. But Monsieur de Montmorency had evidently caught the count's arm, for while he was shrieking louder than ever, 'Help! help!' Perrot, who could see nothing, heard the prince cry out,—

"'His glove touched my face! He must die by no other hand than mine, now, Montmorency!'

"All this took place with the rapidity of lightning. Just at that moment the escort came in; then ensued a savage combat, and a tremendous noise of trampling, and clashing steel. Monsieur de Montmorency cried, 'Bind the madman!' And the dauphin, 'Don't kill him! In Heaven's name, don't kill him!'

"This one-sided battle didn't last a moment. Perrot hadn't time even to rush to his master's assistance. He got as far as the threshold; and there he saw one of the escort lying on the floor, and two or three others covered with blood. But the count was disarmed, and already bound and tightly held by five or six armed men who had attacked him at once. Perrot, who was not noticed in the confusion, thought he could be of more use to Monsieur de Montgommery by remaining free, and in condition to let his friends know, or to rescue him on some more favorable occasion. So he returned noiselessly to his post, and there, on the alert and with his hand on his sword, he waited—since his master was not killed, or even wounded—until it was time to show himself, and perhaps save him; for you will soon see, Monseigneur, that neither resolution nor daring was lacking in my good husband; But he was as prudent as he was valiant, and knew how to make skilful use of his opportunities. For the moment his cue was to watch; and that is what he did, carefully and with perfect self-possession.

"Meanwhile Monsieur de Montgommery, tightly pinioned, was still crying out,—

"'Didn't I tell you, Henri de Valois, that you would have to fight with ten swords against my one, and meet my insult with the obedient courage of your soldiers?'

"'You hear, Monsieur de Montmorency!' said the trembling dauphin.

"'Let him be gagged!' was Monsieur de Montmorency's only reply. 'I will soon give you your instructions,' said he to the men, 'as to what is to be done with him. Meanwhile keep careful watch on him; you shall answer for him to me with your heads.'

"And he left the oratory, taking the dauphin with him. They passed through the corridor, where Perrot was hiding behind the hangings, and went into Madame Diane's apartment.

"Perrot thereupon went over to the other wall, and applied his ear to the other disused door.

"The scene of which he had already been an auditor was on the whole less terrible than that to which he was now to listen."

CHAPTER XXII
DESCRIBES THE MOST CONVINCING PROOF THAT A WOMAN CAN GIVE THAT A MAN IS NOT HER LOVER

"'MONSIEUR de MONTMORENCY,' said the dauphin, as he entered the room, angry and cast down, 'if you had not held me back, I should be better content with myself and you than I am at present.'

"'Permit me to say, Monseigneur,' Montmorency replied, 'that you talk like a hot-headed youth, and not like the king's son. Your days do not belong to you; they belong to your people, Monseigneur, and crowned heads have different duties from other men.'

"'Why, then, should I be so angry with myself, and so ashamed?' said the prince. 'Ah! there you are, Madame,' he added, addressing Diane, whom he had just espied.

"And for the moment his wounded self-esteem got the better of his jealous passion.

"'It is at your house and through your connivance,' said he, 'that I have been insulted for the first time in my life.'

"'Alas! at my house, yes; but do not say through my connivance, Monseigneur,' replied Diane. 'Haven't I suffered quite as much as you,— yes, more than you? Am I not innocent of all this? Do you suppose that I care for that man, pray? Or that I have ever cared for him?'

"Having betrayed him, she now disowned him; it was very simple.

"'I love you and only you, Monseigneur, she went on; 'my heart and soul are yours only and absolutely; and my existence dates only from the day when you accepted this heart which is devoted to you. But before that it may be—yes, I remember vaguely that I did allow this Montgommery to entertain some hope. Never anything positive, and no definite engagement. But you came; and all else was forgotten. Since that time I swear to you— and you may believe my words rather than the jealous slanders of Madame d'Étampes and her friends—since that blessed time I have not had a single thought or a single heart-beat that has not been for you, Monseigneur. That man lies; that man is acting in concert with my enemies; that man has no right over her who belongs so completely to you, Henri. I hardly know the man; and not only do I not love him, but, Great Heaven, I hate and despise him! See, I don't even ask you if he be dead or alive. I think only of you. And as for him, I hate him!'

"'Is this true, Madame?' said the dauphin, still with something of gloomy distrust in his tone.

"'It will be very easy and a very short matter to prove it,' replied Monsieur de Montmorency. 'Monsieur de Montgommery is living, Madame; but he is securely bound and in no condition to do any harm. He has put a shameful outrage upon the prince. But to accuse him before the ordinary tribunals is not to be thought of; to punish him for such a crime would be more dangerous than the crime itself. On the other hand, it is still more utterly out of the question that Monseigneur le Dauphin should engage in single combat with this insolent scoundrel. Now what do you suggest, Madame? What shall we do with this man?'

"There was a moment of painful silence. Perrot held his breath so that he might not lose a syllable of the words which were so slow in coming. But it was evident that Madame Diane was in fear for herself as well as for what she was going to say. She hesitated about uttering her own sentence.

"But at last she had to speak; and with a voice that was still reasonably firm, she said,—

"'Monsieur de Montgommery has been guilty of the crime of lèse-majesté. Monsieur de Montmorency, to what penalty are they liable who commit that crime?'

"'Death,' the constable replied.

"'Then,' said Madame Diane, coldly, 'my opinion is that this man should die.'

"Both the others stood aghast at these words; and there was another pause before Monsieur de Montmorency replied,—

"'You mean by that, Madame, that you do not love Monsieur de Montgommery, and never have loved him.'

"'For my part,' said the dauphin, 'I am less desirous than ever now that he should die.'

"'I hold the same views,' said Montmorency, 'but on different grounds from yours, I take it, Monseigneur. The opinion which generosity moves you to express, I hold for prudential reasons. Monsieur de Montgommery has many friends and powerful allies in France and England; it is known at court that he was likely to meet us here to-night. If they come to us and ask us boldly and clamorously for news of him to-morrow, it must not be that we are able to produce only a dead body. Nobles cannot be treated like serfs and put to death without ceremony. We must be able to reply,—"Monsieur de Montgommery has absconded;" or, "Monsieur de Montgommery is wounded and ill;" but in any event, "Monsieur de Montgommery is alive!" 'And if we are pushed to the last extremity, and if they persist in clamoring for him to the end, well, then we must be in a position where if worst comes to worst, we can take him from his prison or his bed and produce him to the slanderers. But I hope that this precaution, necessary though it be, will nevertheless be useless. Monsieur de Montgommery will be sought for and inquired for to-morrow and the day after; but in a week's time the matter will begin to die out, and in a month he will not be mentioned at all. Nothing is forgotten so speedily as a friend; and we must help to change the subject of common gossip. My conclusion is, then, that the culprit must neither die nor live; he must disappear.'

"'So be it!' said the dauphin. 'Let him go; let him leave France! He has property and connections in England; let him take refuge there.'

"'Not by any means, Monseigneur,' Montmorency replied. 'Death is too much; but banishment is not enough. Would you like,' he added in a lower tone, 'to have this fellow tell in England rather than in France how he threatened you with an insulting gesture?'

"'Oh, don't remind me of that!' cried the dauphin, grinding his teeth.

"'Yet I must remind you of it, Monseigneur, to fortify you against a perilous decision. It is essential, I say again, that the count should tell no tales, living or dead. The men of our escort can be depended upon; and, besides, they have no idea with whom they are dealing. The governor of the Châtelet is a friend of mine; more than that, he is as deaf and dumb as his prison, and devoted to his Majesty's service. Let Monsieur de Montgommery be carried to the Châtelet this very night. A good strong dungeon will keep him for us, or give him back to us, as we choose. To-morrow he will have disappeared; and we will take pains to spread most contradictory and inconsistent reports as to his disappearance. If these rumors do not die out of themselves, and if the count's friends are too persistent in making search for him, which is hardly probable; and if they institute a rigorous and thorough inquiry, which would greatly surprise me,—why, then we can justify ourselves in one word by producing the register of the Châtelet, which will prove that Monsieur de Montgommery, accused of the crime of *lèse-majesté*, is held in prison pending the regular decree of the courts. Then, when this fact is once established, will it be our fault if the prison is unhealthy; and if grief and remorse have taken too strong a hold on Monsieur de Montgommery, and if he dies before he has had time to appear to answer to the charge?'

"'Oh, Monsieur!' cried the dauphin, in horror.

"'Never fear, Monseigneur,' replied the prince's adviser; 'we shall have no need to go to such lengths. The rumors caused by the count's disappearance will die away. His friends will be consoled, and will soon forget; and Monsieur de Montgommery will live, if he chooses, the life of a prisoner from the moment that he dies to the world.'

"'But has he not a son?' asked Madame Diane.

"'Yes, a very young boy, who will be told that no one knows what has become of his father, and who will, when he has grown up, if he lives to grow up, poor little orphan, have interests and passions of his own, and will not trouble himself to unearth a story fifteen or twenty years old.'

"'That is all very true, and well thought of,' said Madame de Poitiers. 'Come, I am inclined to accept it; nay, more, I approve of it, and marvel at it.'

"'You are really too kind, Madame,' replied Montmorency, much flattered, 'and I am very glad to see that we are suited to appreciate each other.'

"'But I neither approve of it nor marvel at it, for my part,' cried the dauphin; 'on the contrary, I oppose it and disclaim it.'

"'Disclaim it, Monseigneur, and you will do quite right,' said Monsieur de Montmorency. 'Disclaim it; but do not oppose it. Find fault with it; but let it go on. All this doesn't concern you at all; and I take the whole responsibility of the affair upon my shoulders, before God and man.'

"'But henceforth we shall be bound together by fellowship in crime, shall we not,' said the dauphin, 'and you will no longer be my friend simply, but my accomplice?'

"'Oh, Monseigneur, perish the thought!' cried the crafty minister. 'You ought not to compromise yourself by punishing the culprit any more than by fighting him. Is it your pleasure that we refer the whole matter to the king your father?'

"'No, no; let my father know nothing of all this,' said the dauphin, quickly.'

"'But my duty,' said Monsieur de Montmorency, 'will compel me to inform him, nevertheless, Monseigneur, if you persist in thinking that the time for chivalrous deeds is to last forever. Come, let us not hasten the affair, if you prefer not, and let us wait for time to ripen our judgment. Only let us make sure of the count's person, as an essential part of our final plans, whatever they may be; and then we will postpone for a time any final conclusion on the subject.'

"'Very well,' said the dauphin, whose feeble will was quick to grasp at this pretended adjournment of the painful subject. 'Monsieur de Montgommery will thus have time to reconsider his first unreflecting impulse, and I also may reflect at my leisure on what my conscience and my dignity demand that I should do.'

"'Let us go back to the Louvre, then, Monseigneur,' said Monsieur de Montmorency, 'and leave no doubt of our presence there. I will send him back to you to-morrow, Madame,' he continued, turning to Madame de Poitiers with a smile; 'for I can see that you love him with a real, heartfelt passion.'

"'But is Monseigneur le Dauphin convinced of it?' said Diane; 'and have I his forgiveness for this unfortunate meeting, so entirely unforeseen by me?'

"'Yes, indeed you must love me,—in truth, with a mighty love, Diane,' replied the dauphin, thoughtfully; 'and I am in too great need of believing it to doubt it. And as the count very truly said, I felt too keenly the pang which cut my heart when I fancied I had lost you, so that your love is henceforth necessary to my existence; and when I loved you once, it was for life.'

"'Ah, God grant that you speak the truth!' cried Diane, passionately, covering with kisses the hand that the dauphin held out to her in token of forgiveness.

"'And now let us be off without more delay,' said Monsieur de Montmorency.

"'*Au revoir*, Diane.'

"'*Au revoir*, my dear Lord,' said the duchess, with a most captivating accent upon the last words.

"She went with him to the door of the room. While the dauphin was descending the stairs, Monsieur de Montmorency opened the door of the oratory where Monsieur de Montgommery was still lying, guarded and bound, and said to the leader of the men-at-arms, —

"'I will send hither at once one of my people, who will instruct you what to do with your prisoner. Until then watch his every movement, and don't lose sight of him for one moment. You shall answer to me, all of you, with your lives.'

"'Very well, Monseigneur,' replied the soldier.

"'Besides, I shall be on the watch too,' said Madame de Poitiers, from the door where she was still standing.

"They all disappeared, and Perrot from his hiding-place could hear nothing but the regular tread of the sentinel stationed just within the oratory to guard the door, while his comrades guarded the prisoner."

CHAPTER XXIII
USELESS DEVOTION

Aloyse, having rested a few moments, for she could hardly breathe as she recalled this mournful story, collected herself once more, and at Gabriel's earnest entreaty finished her narrative in these words:—

"One o'clock in the morning was striking when the dauphin and his unscrupulous mentor took their leave. Perrot saw that his master was lost beyond all hope of rescue if he gave Monsieur de Montmorency's messenger time to arrive. The moment for him to act was at hand. He had noticed that Monsieur de Montmorency had not mentioned any countersign or any signal by which his envoy could be recognized; so after waiting about half an hour, to give Monsieur time to have given him his instructions, Perrot crept carefully out of his hiding-place, went down a few stairs on his toes, and then ascended them again, making his tread distinctly audible, and knocked at the door of the oratory.

"The scheme that he had formed on the spur of the moment was an audacious one; but its very audacity gave it some chance of success.

"'Who's there?' asked the sentinel.

"'A messenger from Monseigneur le Baron de Montmorency.'

"'Open,' said the leader of the party to the sentinel.

"The door opened, and Perrot entered boldly and confidently.

"'I am,' said he, 'the squire of Monsieur Charles de Manffol, who is attached to Monsieur de Montmorency's service, as you know. We were just going off guard at the Louvre, my master and I, when we met on the Grève Monsieur de Montmorency with a tall young man wrapped in a cloak. Monsieur de Montmorency recognized Monsieur de Manffol, and called him. After talking together a few moments, they both ordered me to come here to Madame Diane de Poitiers's house, Rue du Figuier. I should find here, they said, a prisoner, as to whom Monsieur de Montmorency has given me certain directions which I am about to carry out. I asked him for a small escort; but he told me that there was already a sufficient force here, and I see that there are more of you than I need to assist me in executing the conciliatory mission with which I am intrusted. Where is the prisoner? Ah, there he is! Remove the gag, for it is necessary that I should speak to him, and that he should be able to reply to me.'

"The conscientious leader of the men-at-arms still hesitated, despite Perrot's deliberate speech.

"'Have you no written order to give me?' he asked.

"'Does one write orders on the Place de Grève at two in the morning?' replied Perrot, shrugging his shoulders. 'Monsieur de Montmorency told me that you would expect me.'

"'Very true.'

"'Well, then, what game are you trying to play on me, my good fellow? Come, leave the room, you and your people; for what I have to say to this gentleman must be kept secret between ourselves. What! don't you hear me? Leave us, I say!'

"They did finally leave; and Perrot walked coolly up to Monsieur de Montgommery, who had been relieved of his gag.

"'My brave Perrot!' said the count, who had recognized his squire at once, 'how do you happen to be here?'

"'You shall know, Monseigneur; but we have not a moment to lose now. Listen.'

"In a few words he told him of the scene which had transpired in Madame Diane's apartment, and of the determination which Monsieur de Montmorency seemed to have taken of burying forever the terrible secret of the insult with the insulter. Thus it was necessary to escape this fatal captivity by a bold and desperate stroke.

"'And what do you mean to do, Perrot?' asked Monsieur de Montgommery. 'See, there are eight of them against us two, and here we are not in the house of our friends,' he added bitterly.

"'Never mind that!' said Perrot; 'do you just let me do all the acting and the talking, and you are saved, you are free.'

"'What's the use, Perrot?' said the count, gloomily. 'What more have I to do with life or liberty? Diane does not love me! Diane hates me and betrays me!'

"'Put by all remembrance of that woman, and think of your child, Monseigneur.'

"'You are right, Perrot; I have already neglected him too much, poor little Gabriel, and God is just to punish me for it. For his sake, then, I ought and I will try to avail myself of this last chance of safety which you hold out to me, my friend. But, in the first place, listen to me: if this chance fails me, if this undertaking, audacious to the point of madness, which you are about to venture on, fails, I do not wish to bequeath to the orphan for his inheritance, Perrot, the results of my unhappy fate; I do not wish to subject him after my disappearance from among the living to the powerful hatred to which I have been forced to yield. Swear to me, then, that if the prison or the tomb opens its doors to me, and you survive me, Gabriel shall never know from you the circumstances of his father's disappearance from the world. If he should come to know this terrible secret, he would try some day either to avenge me or to rescue me, and would ruin himself. I shall have a bitter enough reckoning to settle with his mother, without adding that burden to it. Let my son live in happiness, free from anxiety about his father's past! Swear this for me, Perrot, and do not consider yourself relieved from the obligation of this oath unless the three actors in the scene you have described to me die before I do, and the dauphin (who will be king then, no doubt), Madame Diane, and Monsieur de Montmorency carry their potent hatred with them to the grave, and can no longer harm my child. Then, in that very improbable concurrence of events, let him try, if he will, to learn of my whereabouts and to find me. But until then, let him know as little as everybody else—yes, less than anybody else—of his father's end. Do you promise me this, Perrot! Do you swear it? I will not give myself up to your rash and, I greatly fear, fruitless devotion, except on that one condition, Perrot.'

"'Do you wish it so, Monseigneur? Then I swear it.'

"'Upon the cross of your sword-hilt, Perrot, Gabriel shall never know from you of this perilous mystery?'

"'Upon the cross of my sword-hilt, Monseigneur!' said Perrot, his right hand held aloft.

"'Thanks, my dear friend. Now do with me as you will, my faithful servant. I place my reliance on your courage and the favor of God.'

"'Be self-possessed and confident, Monseigneur,' replied Perrot. 'You will soon see.'

"Recalling the leader of the men-at-arms, he said,—

"'What the prisoner has said to me is satisfactory, and you may unbind him and let him go.'

"'Unbind him! Let him go!' rejoined the astounded leader. "'To be sure! Such are Monsieur de Montmorency's orders.'

"'Monsieur de Montmorency,' replied the man-at-arms, shaking his head, 'ordered us to keep this prisoner in sight, and said as he went away that we should answer for it with our lives. How can it be that Monsieur de Montmorency now wishes us to set the gentleman at liberty?'

"'So that you refuse to obey me, who speak in his name, do you?' said Perrot, abating nothing of his assurance.

"'I hesitate. See here, if you were to order me to kill the man, or to throw him into the river, or to take him to the Bastille, we would obey, but to let him go!—that, you see, is not the sort of thing we're accustomed to.'

"'So be it!' replied Perrot, in no whit disconcerted. 'I have given you the orders that I received, and I wash my hands of the rest of it. You will answer to Monsieur de Montmorency for the consequences of your disobedience. As for me, there's nothing more for me to do here. Good-evening!'

"And he opened the door, as if to take his leave.

"'Ho, there, one moment!' said the leader; 'how quick you are! So you mean to declare that it is Monsieur de Montmorency's will that we should let this prisoner go? You are quite sure that it was Monsieur de Montmorency who sent you?'

"'You idiot!' replied Perrot; 'how else should I know that he had a prisoner under guard here? Has any other person gone out to tell of it, if it was not Monsieur de Montmorency himself?'

"'Well, your man shall be unbound!' said the soldier, as surly as a tiger whose prey has been torn from his grasp. 'How changeable these great lords are, *corps Dieu*!'

"'Good! I will await you,' said Perrot.

"He remained outside, nevertheless, on the topmost step of the staircase, with his face turned toward the stairs, and his drawn sword in his hand. If he saw the real messenger from Montmorency coming up, he must see to it that he came no farther.

"But he neither saw nor heard behind him Madame de Poitiers, who, aroused by the sound of voices, had come out of her chamber, and gone along to the open door of the oratory. She saw that they were releasing Monsieur de Montgommery, who was transfixed with horror as he saw her there.

"'Wretches!' she cried, 'what are you doing there?'

"'We are obeying the orders of Monsieur de Montmorency, Madame,' said the leader, 'and releasing the prisoner.'

"'It cannot be possible!' replied Madame de Poitiers. 'Monsieur de Montmorency can never have given such orders. Who brought you this order?'

"The men pointed out Perrot, who had turned about, stupefied with terror, on hearing Madame Diane's voice. A ray of light from the lamp fell full upon poor Perrot's pale face, and Madame Diane recognized him at once.

"'That man?' said she; 'that man is the prisoner's squire! Just see what you were about to do!'

"'That's a lie!' replied Perrot, still trying to deny his identity. 'I am Monsieur de Manffol's squire, and am sent here by Monsieur de Montmorency.'

"'Who says that he was sent by Monsieur de Montmorency?' chimed in the voice of a new arrival, who was the real envoy himself. 'My good fellows, this man lies! Here are the Montmorency ring and seal; and you ought to know me too. I am the Comte de Montausier.[3] What! you dared to take away the prisoner's gag, and were in the very act of releasing him? Wretches! Gag him again, and bind him tighter still!'

"'As you please!' said the chief of the guards; 'but the orders he gave us sounded all right, and were easy to understand.'

"'Poor Perrot!' was all the count said.

"He did not stoop to utter a word of reproach to Madame de Poitiers, though he would have had time enough before the handkerchief they put between his teeth was in place. It may be, too, that he feared to compromise his true-hearted squire any further; but Perrot, unluckily, wasn't as discreet as he, and said to Madame Diane indignantly,—

"'Well, Madame, you don't stop halfway in a felony, at least! Saint Peter denied his Lord three times, but Judas only betrayed him once. You have betrayed your lover three times within an hour. To be sure, Judas was only a man, while you are a woman and a duchess.'

"'Seize that man!' cried Madame Diane, in a perfect fury of rage.

"'Seize that man!' the Comte de Montausier echoed.

"'Ah, but I am not taken yet!' cried Perrot.

"And in so desperate a plight he took a desperate step; with one leap he was at Monsieur de Montgommery's side, and began to cut his bonds with his poniard, crying,—

"'Help yourself, Monseigneur, and let us sell our lives as dearly as we can!'

"But he had only time to free his left arm; for he could defend himself only partially while trying to cut the count's cords at the same time. Ten swords clashed with his. Surrounded, and struck at on all sides at once, a powerful blow that he received between the shoulders laid him at his master's feet, and he fell unconscious, and like a dead man."

[3] This exploit of the young Comte de Montausier, the apprehension of Montgommery, was a fitting prelude to the assassination of Lignerolles. It is well-known that Monsieur de Lignerolles having informed Charles IX. that the Duc d'Anjou, his master, had confided to him his secret scheme for getting rid of the leading Huguenots, the king induced his brother (D'Anjou) to have Lignerolles put out of the way as a precaution against any possible indiscretion on his part. The Comte de Montausier took charge of the execution, with four or five other gentlemen-executioners, all of whom eventually came to a wretched end. "Wherefore," says Brantôme, "we ought to take great care that we slay no man unjustly; for one scarcely ever hears of such a murder which has not been avenged with the sanction of God, who has put a sword at our side for use, and not to be abused."

CHAPTER XXIV
SHOWS THAT BLOOD-STAINS CAN NEVER BE COMPLETELY WASHED OUT

"Perrot knew nothing of what happened after that.

"When he came to himself, his first sensation was of bitter cold. Then he collected his thoughts, opened his eyes, and looked about him; it was still profoundly dark. He was lying on the moist earth, and a dead body lay beside him. By the light of the little lamp which is always burning in the recess of the image of the Virgin, he saw that he was in the Cemetery of the Innocents. The body that had been thrown down by his side was that of the guard who had been killed by Monsieur de Montgommery. They had undoubtedly supposed that my husband was dead.

"He tried to rise, but the terrible pain from his wounds prevented him. However, putting all his strength into an almost superhuman effort, he succeeded in standing up and taking a few steps. Just then the black darkness was relieved by the light of a lantern; and Perrot saw two evil-looking men approaching with spades and mattocks.

"'They told us we should find them at the foot of the image of the Virgin,' said one of them.

"'Here are the sparks,' said the other, spying the soldier. 'But, no, there's only one.'

"'Well, we must find the other, then.'

"The two grave-diggers turned the light of their lantern upon the ground near them; but Perrot had made shift to drag himself behind a tomb at some distance from the place where they were looking for him.

"'The Devil must have carried one man off,' remarked one of the men, who seemed to be in a joking mood.

"'In God's name, don't say such things,' cried the other, shuddering, 'at such an hour, and in such a place!'

"And he crossed himself, with every indication of terror.

"'Well, at all events, there's only one here,' said the first who had spoken. 'What's the odds? Bah! we will bury the one that is here, and then say that his friend had escaped; or it may be that they didn't count right.'

"They set about digging a grave; and Perrot, who was tottering away little by little, was glad to hear the jovial digger say to his companion, —

"'It has just occurred to me that if we admit that we found only one body, and dig only one grave, the man will give us only five pistoles, perhaps, instead of ten. Wouldn't it be better for our pockets to say nothing about this extraordinary escape of the second corpse?'

"'Yes, faith!' replied his devout companion. 'Let us content ourselves with saying that we have accomplished our task; and then we shall have told no lie.'

"Meanwhile, Perrot, faint as death, had got as far as Rue Aubry-le-Boucher. There he hailed a market gardener's wagon, returning from market, and asked the driver where he was going.

"'To Montreuil,' was the reply.

"'Then will you be kind enough to give me a lift as far as the corner of Rue Geoffroy L'Asnier and Rue St. Antoine, where I live?'

"'Get in,' said the gardener.

"In this way Perrot made the greater part of the journey to our lodgings without much fatigue; and yet ten times on the way he thought that he was dying. At last the wagon stopped at Rue Geoffroy L'Asnier.

"'Well, here you are at home, my friend,' said the gardener.

"'Thank you, my kind fellow!' said Perrot.

"He got down with much stumbling, and was obliged to lean against the first wall that he came to.

"'My comrade has had a little too much to drink,' remarked the peasant, starting up his horse.

"And away he went, singing the new *chanson* just written by Master François Rabelais, the jolly curé of Meudon: —

"'O Dieu, père Paterne,
Qui muas l'eau en vin,
Fais de mon cul lantern
Pour luire à mon voisin!'[4]

"It took Perrot an hour to get from Rue St. Antoine to Rue des Jardins. Luckily the January nights are long. He didn't meet a soul, and arrived home about six o'clock.

"My anxiety had kept me all night at the open window, Monseigneur, notwithstanding the cold. At Perrot's first call I rushed to the door and opened it.

"'Not a sound, on your life!' were his first words to me. 'Help me up to my room, but not a cry, not a word!'

"He went upstairs, leaning on my arm; while I, seeing that he was wounded and bleeding, didn't dare to speak, because he had forbidden me, but wept silently. When we finally got to our room, and I had taken off his coat and relieved him of his weapons, the poor soul's blood covered my hands, and I saw the great gaping wounds. He forbade my cry of horror by a stern gesture, and assumed the easiest position possible on the bed.

"'At least, let me call a surgeon, for God's sake!' I sobbed.

"'Useless!' was his answer. 'You know that I have a little skill in surgery. One of my wounds at least—the one just below the neck—is mortal; and I should not be alive now, I think, if something stronger than pain had not sustained me, and if God, who punishes assassins and traitors, had not prolonged my life for a few hours to serve His future plans. Soon the fever will seize me, and all will be over. No physician in the world can prevent that.'

"He spoke with such painful effort that I begged him to rest a little.

"'I must do so,' said he, 'and carefully husband what strength I have. But give me writing materials.'

"I brought what he asked for; but he had not then discovered that a sword-cut had mangled his right hand. At his best it was a hard matter for him to write, so he threw pen and paper aside.

"'Well, then, I must speak,' said he; 'and God will let me live long enough to finish what I have to say. For if it should ever come to pass that He, the just and merciful God, should aim a blow at my master's three enemies, in their omnipotence or in their life, which are the perishable goods of the wicked, then Monsieur de Montgommery may be saved by his son.'

"Then, Monseigneur," continued Aloyse, "Perrot began and told me the whole mournful story which I have fully detailed to you. There were long and frequent interruptions; and when he felt too exhausted to continue, he told me to leave him, and go down and show myself to the people in the house. I pretended, and without much pretence either, to be very anxious about the count and my husband. I sent everybody to make inquiries at the Louvre, and among Monsieur le Comte de Montgommery's friends one by one, and then among his acquaintances. Madame de Poitiers sent word that she had not seen him, and Monsieur de Montmorency that he didn't understand why they came to bother him.

"So all suspicion was diverted from me, as Perrot wished; and his murderers might well believe that their secret was hidden in the master's dungeon and the squire's grave.

"When I had thus put the servants off the scent for some time, and had intrusted you to one of them, Monseigneur Gabriel, I went back to my poor Perrot, who bravely resumed his narrative.

"About midday the fearful agony which had racked him up to that time seemed to abate somewhat. He spoke with less difficulty and with some animation. But as I was taking heart over this improvement, he said to me, smiling mournfully,—

"'This apparent change for the better means simply that the fever is coming on, as I told you it would. But, God be praised! I have finished describing this frightful plot. Now you know what no other but God and these three assassins know; and your loyal heart, always steadfast and strong, will enable you, I am sure, to keep this secret of death and blood until the day when, as I hope and pray, you may reveal it to him who has the right to know it. You have heard the oath that Monsieur de Montgommery required of me; and you must repeat the same oath to me, Aloyse.

"'So long as it is dangerous for Gabriel to know that his father is living,—so long as the three all-powerful enemies who have slain my master shall be left in this world by God's wrath,—do you keep silent, Aloyse. Swear it to your dying husband.'

"Weeping, I swore it; and it is that sacred oath which I am now proving false to, Monseigneur, for your three foes, more powerful and more to be dreaded than ever, are still living. But you were about to die yourself; and if you make a wise and discreet use of my revelation, that which threatens to destroy you may be your father's salvation and yours. But tell me again, Monseigneur, that I have not committed an unpardonable sin, and that because of my good intentions, God and my dear Perrot will forgive my perjury."

"There is no perjury in all this, blessed creature," replied Gabriel; "and there has been throughout your conduct naught but heroic devotion. But tell me the rest! tell me the rest!"

"Perrot," continued Aloyse, "went on to say,—

"'When I shall be no more, dear wife, you will do wisely to close this house, dismiss the servants, and betake yourself to Montgommery with Gabriel and our child. And even at Montgommery don't live in the château, but in our little house; and bring up the heir of the noble counts, if not in absolute secrecy, still without any luxury or display, so that his friends may know him, and his enemies forget him. All our good people down yonder, both the intendant and the chaplain, will assist you in fulfilling the important duty which the Lord has put upon you. It would be much better that Gabriel himself until he is eighteen at least should be ignorant of the name he bears, but should know only that he is of gentle birth. You will see. Our worthy chaplain and Monsieur de Vimoutiers, the child's guardian, will assist you with their advice; but even from these loyal friends you must conceal the tale that I have told you. Confine yourself to saying that you fear that Gabriel may be in danger from his father's powerful enemies.'

"Perrot also gave me all manner of cautions, which he repeated in a thousand different forms until his suffering began again, accompanied by weakness which was no less grievous to look upon; and yet he employed every moment of comparative ease to cheer me up and comfort me.

"He also mentioned to me and made me promise one thing which required by no means the least display of energy on my part, I confess, and was not the least potent cause of suffering to me.

"'In Monsieur de Montmorency's mind,' said he, 'I am buried in the Cemetery of the Innocents; so I must have disappeared with the count. If any sign of my return here should be discovered, you would be lost, Aloyse, and Gabriel too, perhaps! But your arm is strong and your heart is brave. When you have closed my eyes, collect all the strength of your soul and body, wait till the middle of the night when everybody here is sound asleep after the labors of the day, and then take my body down into the old burial-vault of the lords of Brissac, to whom this hotel formerly belonged. No one ever enters that abandoned tomb; and you will find the key to it, all rusty, in the great clothes-press in the count's room. Thus I shall have consecrated burial; and although a simple squire may be unworthy to lie among so many great nobles, still after death we are all nothing but Christians, are we?'

"As my poor Perrot seemed to be growing weaken and insisted on having my word, I promised all that he asked. Toward evening he became delirious, and to that, frightful agony succeeded. I beat my breast in despair at my inability to relieve him; but he made a motion that it was of no avail.

"At last, burning up with fever, and racked by terrible agony, he said, —

"'Aloyse, give me some water, —just a drop.'

"I had already offered, in my ignorance, to give him something to quench the burning thirst from which he said he was suffering, but he had persistently declined it; so I hastened to find a glass, which I handed to him.

"Before he took it, he said, —

"'Aloyse, one last kiss and one last adieu! and remember; remember!'

"I covered his face with kisses and tears. Then he asked me for the crucifix, and placed his dying lips upon the nails of the cross of Jesus, saying only, 'Oh, *mon Dieu!* oh, *mon Dieu!*' He pressed my hand with a last trembling grasp, and took the glass which I offered him. He took but one swallow, trembled violently all over, and fell back upon the pillow.

"He was dead.

"I passed the rest of the evening praying and weeping. However, I went, as I usually did, to superintend your retiring, Monseigneur. You can well believe that no one wondered at my grief. Terror reigned in the house; and all the faithful servants were grieving over the probable fate of their master and their good comrade Perrot.

"However, about two in the morning, everything was quiet, and I alone was awake. I washed away the blood with which my husband's body was covered, wrapped it in a cloth, and putting myself in God's hands, I set about taking down the dear burden, which weighed still heavier at my heart than in my arms. When my strength gave out, I knelt by the body and prayed.

"At last, after what seemed an interminable half-hour, I reached the door of the vault. When I opened it, not without considerable difficulty, an icy blast came rushing out and extinguished the lamp which I carried, and almost suffocated me. But I revived speedily, and laid my husband's body in a tomb which was open and empty, and which seemed as if it were waiting to receive him; then having kissed his cold lips once more and for the last time, I let down the heavy marble slab, which separated me forever from the beloved husband of my bosom. The noise of the stone falling upon stone frightened me so that, scarcely taking time to close the door of the vault, I fled like a mad woman, and never stopped until I reached my own room, where I fell upon a chair, completely exhausted. However, it was necessary that I should burn up the bloody cloths and bandages before daybreak, so that they might not betray me. When the first ray of light appeared, my weary task was done, and not a single trace remained of the events of the preceding day and night. I had put everything out of sight with the great care displayed by a criminal who means to leave nothing to bear witness to or to recall his crime.

"But such long and wearisome toil prostrated me completely, and I fell ill. However, it was my duty to live for the sake of the two orphans whom Providence had intrusted to my sole protection; and I did live, Monseigneur."

"Poor woman! poor martyr!" said Gabriel, taking her hand in his.

"A month later," continued the nurse, "I carried you to Montgommery, in obedience to my husband's dying instructions.

"In the sequel it turned out as Monsieur de Montmorency had predicted. The inexplicable disappearance of the Comte de Montgommery and his squire made a noise at court for about a week; then the talk began to die out; and finally, the expected arrival of the Emperor Charles V., who was on his way through France to chastise the people of Ghent, became the universal subject of conversation.

"It was in May of the same year, five months after your father's disappearance, that Diane de Castro was born."

"Yes," rejoined Gabriel, thoughtfully; "and did Madame de Poitiers belong to my father? Did she love the dauphin after him or simultaneously?— sombre questions these, which cannot be answered satisfactorily by the slanderous gossip of an idle court. But my father is alive! He must be alive! And Aloyse, I will find him. There are two men living in me now,—a son and a lover, who will find a way to discover his living tomb."

"God grant it!" said Aloyse.

"And have you learned nothing since, nurse," said Gabriel, "as to the prison where these wretches may have buried my father?"

"Nothing, Monseigneur; and the only clew that we have on that point is the remark of Monsieur de Montmorency as reported by Perrot,—that the governor of the Châtelet was a devoted friend of his, and could be depended upon."

"The Châtelet!" cried Gabriel; "the Châtelet!"

For like a flash of lightning his memory brought before him all at once the gloomy, desolate old man, who might never utter a word, and whom he had seen with such a strange agitation of the heart, in one of the deepest dungeons of the royal prison.

Bursting into tears, Gabriel threw himself into the arms of his faithful and true-hearted nurse.

> [4] "Oh, God, our Heavenly Father,
> Who changedst water to wine,
> Make of my breech a lantern
> To light this friend of mine!"

"To seek the king, Monseigneur."

"Hm! The king has other business on hand than receiving you, my young friend. But wait a moment! I am going to his Majesty also, for he just sent for me. Let us go up together; I will be your sponsor, and you shall lend me the support of your strong arm. One good turn for another. In fact, that is just what I was going to say to his Majesty; for you have heard the sad news, I suppose?"

"No, indeed," Gabriel replied; "for I have just come from home; and I only noticed that there seemed to be something exciting in the air."

"I should say as much!" said the cardinal. "Monsieur de Montmorency has been up to his old tricks down yonder with the army. He undertook to fly to the relief of St. Quentin, which was in a state of siege, did the gallant constable! Don't go so fast, I beg you, Monsieur d'Exmès, for I no longer have the sprightly legs of twenty years. I was saying that he offered battle to the enemy, the intrepid general! It was day before yesterday, August 10, St. Laurent's Day. He had almost as many troops as the Spaniards, a superb body of cavalry,—the very pick and flower of the French nobility. Oh, well! he had so skilfully arranged matters, experienced commander that he is, that he sustained a most overwhelming defeat in the plains of Gibercourt and Lizerolles; that he was himself wounded and made prisoner, and with him all the leading officers and generals who did not remain on the field. Monsieur d'Enghien is among the latter; and of the whole infantry not a hundred men have come back. And that explains why everybody is so absorbed, Monsieur d'Exmès, and why his Majesty needs me, no doubt."

"Great God!" cried Gabriel, appalled, even in the depths of his own sorrow, by this great public calamity; "Great God! are the days of Poitiers and Agincourt returning upon poor France? But St. Quentin, Monseigneur?"

"St. Quentin," the cardinal replied, "was still holding out when the courier left; and the constable's nephew, Monsieur l'Amiral Gaspard de Coligny, who is defending the town, has sworn to lessen the result of his uncle's defeat by allowing himself to be buried in the ruins of the place rather than surrender it. But I am much afraid that he may be buried already, and the last rampart which kept the enemy out carried."

"In that case the kingdom is lost!" said Gabriel.

"May God protect France!" rejoined the cardinal. "But here we are at the king's apartments; and we will see what steps he proposes to take to protect himself."

The guards, as well they might, allowed the cardinal to pass with a bow, for they saw in him the man necessary for the emergency, and whose write to my brother, and you need not to be told that whatever man can do, Monsieur de Guise will do."

And the cardinal, saluting the king and Madame Diane, entered the closet to write the letter which Henri desired.

Gabriel had remained apart, thinking deeply and unnoticed. His generous young heart was deeply moved by contemplation of the terrible extremity to which France was reduced. He forgot that it was Monsieur de Montmorency, his bitterest enemy, who had been beaten, wounded, and captured. For the moment he saw in him only the commander of the French forces. In fact, he thought almost as much of his country's danger as of his father's suffering. The noble youth had a sympathetic heart, which was easily aroused by deep feeling, and he pitied all who were in distress; and when the king, after the cardinal had left the room, sank back despairingly upon his couch, with his head in his hands, crying aloud, —

"Oh, St. Quentin! on thee now hangs the destiny of France! St. Quentin, my noble city! If thou canst still resist but for one short week, Monsieur de Guise will have time to return, and the defence of thy faithful walls be organized anew! Whereas if they fall, the foe will march upon Paris, and all will be lost. St. Quentin, oh, I would give thee a new privilege for each hour of resistance, and a diamond for each of thy crumbling stones, if thou couldst hold out only one week more!"

"Sire, it shall hold out, and more than a week!" said Gabriel, coming forward.

He had made his resolution; and a sublime resolution it was!

"Monsieur d'Exmès!" cried Henri and Diane, in the same breath, — the king in wonder, and Diane with contempt.

"How did you come here, Monsieur?" asked the king, sternly.

"Sire, I entered with his Eminence."

"That's a different matter," said Henri; "but what were you saying, pray, Monsieur d'Exmès? — that St. Quentin might hold out, I think."

"Yes, Sire; and you said, did you not, that if it did hold out, you would endow it with freedom and wealth?"

"I say it again," said the king.

"Very well, Sire; and would you refuse to the man who should make its holding out possible what you would accord to the town which held out? To the man whose energetic will should infect the whole city, and who would not surrender it until the last piece of the wall crumbles under the enemy's cannon? The favor which this man shall ask at your hands, this man who shall have given you this week's respite, and thus preserved your kingdom, shall he ask it in vain, Sire, and will you chaffer about an act of mercy with, him who has given you back an empire?"

"No, by Heaven!" cried the king; "and whatever a king has to give that man shall have."

"A bargain, Sire; for not only can a king give, but he can forgive as well. And it is a pardon, and not titles or gold which this man will ask at your hands."

"But who is he? Where is this deliverer?" said the king.

"He stands before you, Sire. It is I, the humble captain of your Guards, but who feel in my heart and my arm a superhuman strength, which shall help me to prove that I make no vain boast in undertaking to save at one and the same time my country and my father."

"Your father, Monsieur d'Exmès!" said the astonished king.

"I am not Monsieur d'Exmès," said Gabriel. "I am Gabriel de Montgommery, son of Comte Jacques de Montgommery, whom you ought to remember, Sire."

"The son of the Comte de Montgommery!" cried the king, rising and turning pale.

Madame Diane too fell back upon her couch with a gesture of terror.

"Yes, Sire," replied Gabriel, calmly; "I am the Vicomte de Montgommery, who, in exchange for the service which he will render you by maintaining the defence of St. Quentin for a week, asks you for nothing but his father's liberty."

"Your father, Monsieur!" said the king. "Your father is dead, has disappeared. What do I know about him? I don't know, I'm sure, where your father is."

"But I do, Sire; I know," replied Gabriel, choking down a terrible dread. "My father has been in the Châtelet for eighteen years past, awaiting the divine gift of death; or the royal gift of mercy. My father is alive; I am certain of it. As to his crime, of that I know nothing."

"You know nothing of it?" the king asked, frowning darkly.

"I know nothing of it, Sire; but surely it should have been a serious offence to have deserved so long an imprisonment. But it could not have been an unpardonable one, since it did not merit death. Sire, listen. In eighteen years justice has had time to slumber and clemency to awake. Human passions, whether evil or good, do not resist so long as that. My father, who was a vigorous man when he entered his prison, will come out of it old and feeble. However guilty he may have been, has not his expiation been ample? And even if it should happen that his punishment was too severe, is he not too weak to remember? Restore to liberty, Sire, a poor prisoner, who will henceforth be of no consequence in the world. Remember, O Christian king, the words of the Christian creed, and forgive the sins of another that your own sins may be forgiven!"

These last words were uttered in a meaning tone which caused the king and Madame de Valentinois to look at each other in anxious and terrified inquiry.

But Gabriel chose only to touch delicately upon this sore spot in their consciences, and made haste to continue, —

"Please take notice, Sire, that I address you as an obedient and devoted subject. I have not said to you, 'My father was not tried; my father was secretly condemned without an opportunity to be heard in his own defence; and such injustice seems much like revenge. So I, his son, am about to appeal boldly to the nobility of France from this secret judgment which has been pronounced upon him. I am about to declare from the house-tops to every one who wears a sword the insult which has been offered to us all in the person of one gentleman—'"

Henri moved uneasily in his seat.

"I have not said this, Sire," Gabriel went on. "I know that there are emergencies stronger than law and right, and where an arbitrary act is the least perilous. I respect, as my father undoubtedly would respect, the secrets of a past which lies so far behind us. I ask you simply to allow me to commute the balance of my father's punishment by a glorious exploit of deliverance. I offer you by way of ransom for him to hold St. Quentin for a week against the enemy; and if that is not enough, why, to make up for the eventual loss of St. Quentin by capturing some other town from the Spaniards or the English! Surely that will be worth the gift of freedom to an old gray-headed man. Well, I will do all this and more too! for the cause which strengthens my arm is a pure and holy one. My will is strong and daring: and I know that God will be with me."

Madame Diane could not restrain a smile of incredulity at this heroic exhibition of youthful enthusiasm and confidence such as she had never seen and could not appreciate.

"I understand your smile, Madame," rejoined Gabriel, with a sad glance at her; "you think that I shall fall under this great task, do you not? *Mon*

Dieu! it may be so. It may be that my presentiments mislead me. But what then? Why, then I shall die. Yes, Madame, yes, Sire, if the enemy enters St. Quentin before the end of the eighth day, I shall die in the breach for the town which I have failed to defend. Neither God nor my father nor you can ask more of me than that. My destiny will then have been fulfilled as the Lord has seen fit: my father will die in his dungeon, and I upon the field of battle; and you,—you will be relieved by natural means of the debt and of your creditor at the same time. Then you can be easy in your mind."

"That last remark of his is very true, at all events," whispered Diane, in the ear of the king, who was absorbed in thought.

However, she said aloud to Gabriel, while Henri maintained a dreamy silence,—

"Even supposing that you fall, Monsieur, leaving your work half done, it is easy to imagine that you will leave some inheritor of your name behind you, or some confidant of your secret."

"I swear to you by my father's safety," said Gabriel, "that when I die everything shall die with me, and that no one will then have the right to importune his Majesty on this subject. I put myself in God's hands in advance, I say again; and you ought, in like manner, Sire, to recognize His intervention, if He shall endow me with the strength to fulfil my vast design. But here and now, if I die, I relieve you from all obligation and from all responsibility, Sire,—at least before men; but the rights of the Most High are not lost by prescription."

Henri shuddered. His naturally irresolute mind did not know what course to decide upon; and the vacillating prince turned to Madame de Poitiers as if to ask for aid and advice.

She, understanding fully his hesitation, to which she was well used, responded to his glance with a peculiar smile.

"Is it not your opinion, Sire, that we ought to rely upon the word of Monsieur d'Exmès, who is a loyal gentleman, and, I believe, of a chivalrous and knightly character? I know not whether his request is or is not well founded; and your Majesty's silence in that regard affords no ground upon which I or any one can allege anything, and leaves the whole question in uncertainty. But in my humble opinion, Sire, you should not reject so generous a proffer; and if I were in your place, I would gladly pledge my royal word to Monsieur d'Exmès to grant him, if he fulfil his heroic and daring promise, whatever favor he might choose to ask at my hands on his return."

"Ah, Madame, I ask no more than that," said Gabriel.

"Just one word more," resumed Diane. "How," she added, fixing a piercing glance upon the young man,—"how and why did you make up your mind to speak of a mysterious affair, which seems to be of some consequence, before me,—before a woman who may be anything but discreet for aught you know of her, and an entire stranger to this whole matter?"

"I had two reasons, Madame," replied Gabriel, with perfect sang-froid. "In the first place, I imagined that there neither could be nor should be any secret in his Majesty's heart so far as you are concerned. In that case, it was only disclosing to you what you were sure to know sooner or later, or what you already knew. In the second place, I hoped, as indeed has come to pass, that you would deign to support my request to the king; that you would urge him to put me to this proof; and that you, a woman, would be found, as you always have been, on the side of clemency."

It would have been impossible for the closest scrutiny to detect in Gabriel's tone the least inflection of irony, or upon his calm and unmoved features the slightest symptom of a disdainful smile; and Madame Diane's penetrating gaze was thrown away.

She responded to a speech which might after all have been meant to be complimentary by a slight inclination of the head.

"Allow me one more question," she said, "just as to one circumstance which has aroused my curiosity, that is all. How is it that you who are so young happen to be in possession of a secret that is eighteen years old?"

"I reply so much the more willingly, Madame," said Gabriel, gravely and sombrely, "because my reply may serve to convince you of God's intervention in the matter. My father's squire, one Perrot Travigny, who was killed in the transactions which preceded the disappearance of the count, has risen from the tomb, by the grace of God, and has revealed to me what I have told you."

At this reply, delivered in a tone of the utmost solemnity, the king arose, pale and breathless, and even Madame de Poitiers, despite her nerves of steel, could not repress a shudder of terror. At that superstitious epoch, when apparitions and ghosts were freely believed in, Gabriel's words, uttered with the conviction of truth personified, might well have had a terrifying effect upon two tormented consciences.

"Enough, enough, Monsieur!" said the king, hastily, with trembling voice; "and everything that you ask is granted. Leave us! leave us!"

"And I may set out for St. Quentin, then, within the hour, relying upon your Majesty's word?"

"Yes, yes, Monsieur, set out at once!" said the king, who, notwithstanding Diane's warning glances, had great difficulty in mastering his distress; "set out at once! Do what you have promised; and I give you my word as king and gentleman that I will do what you wish."

Gabriel, with joy at his heart, bent low before the king and duchess, and took his leave without another word, as if, having obtained his desire, he had not a moment more to lose.

"At last! He is not here now!" said the king, breathing deeply, as if relieved of a heavy burden.

"Sire," said Madame de Poitiers, "be calm, and try to regain your self-command. You came very near betraying yourself before that man."

"That is no man, Madame," said the king, as one dreaming; "that is my ever-living remorse: it is my reproachful conscience."

"Well, Sire," said Diane, who was herself again, "you have done very well to accede to this Gabriel's request, and to send him where he is now going; for I am very much mistaken, or your remorse will soon die before St. Quentin, and you will then be rid of your conscience."

The Cardinal de Lorraine returned at this moment with the letter he had been writing to his brother, and the king had no time to reply.

Meanwhile Gabriel, leaving the king with a light heart, had only one thought and one wish in the world: it was to see once more, with hope beating high in his breast, her whom he had left with death in his soul; to say to Diane de Castro all that he hoped from the future, and to draw from her loved glances the courage of which he should stand so much in need.

He knew that she had gone into a convent; but into what convent? It might be that her women had not gone with her; and he turned his steps in the direction of her former apartment at the Louvre, to question Jacinthe.

Jacinthe was with her mistress; but Denise, the second waiting-maid, had stayed behind; and it was she who received Gabriel.

"Ah, Monsieur d'Exmès!" she cried. "You are such a welcome visitor; for it may perhaps be that you have come to give me some news of my dear mistress."

"On the contrary, Denise, I have come to learn of her from you," said Gabriel.

"Ah, Holy Virgin! I know nothing at all, and I am terribly frightened about her."

"But why so anxious, Denise?" asked Gabriel, who began to be anxious himself.

"Why!" replied the maid; "why, you must know where Madame de Castro is now!

"Indeed, no! I know nothing about it, Denise; and it is just what I hoped to learn from you."

"Holy Virgin! and didn't you know, Monseigneur, that she asked leave of the king to enter a convent a month ago?"

"I know that; and then?"

"And then! Ah, that is the terrible part of it. For do you know what convent she chose? That of the Benedictines, of which her old friend, Sister Monique, is superior, at St. Quentin, Monseigneur,—at St. Quentin, at this very moment besieged and perhaps taken by these English and Spanish heathens. She had not been there a fortnight, Monseigneur, when the siege began."

"Oh," cried Gabriel, "the hand of God is in all this! He awakens the son in me to new life, by arousing the lover anew, and thus doubles my courage and my strength. Thanks, Denise. This for your good news," he added, placing a purse in her hand. "Pray to Heaven for your mistress and for me."

In hot haste he went down once more into the courtyard of the Louvre, where Martin-Guerre was awaiting him.

"Where do we go now, Monseigneur?" asked the squire.

"Where the cannon is echoing, Martin,—to St. Quentin! to St. Quentin! We must be there day after to-morrow, so we start within the hour, my fine fellow."

"Ah, so much the better!" cried Martin. "Oh, mighty Saint Martin, my patron saint," he added, "I am content now to be a drunkard and a gambler and a rake; but I give you fair warning that I would throw myself into the midst of the enemy's battalions if ever I were a coward!"

CHAPTER XXVI
JEAN PEUQUOY THE WEAVER

A general council of the military leaders and prominent citizens was being held in the St. Quentin town-hall. It was the 15th of August already, and the town had not yet capitulated; but there was much talk about capitulation. The suffering and destitution of the inhabitants were at their height; and since there was no hope of saving the place, and since the enemy, some day, sooner or later, were sure to gain possession, would it not be better to put an end to so much misery?

Gaspard de Coligny, the gallant admiral, whom the Constable de Montmorency, his uncle, had intrusted with the defence of the place, had determined not to admit the Spaniard until the last extremity. He knew that each day's delay, terrible though it was to the suffering people, might be the salvation of the kingdom. But what could he do against the discouragement and mutterings of the whole population? The war outside the walls gave no time for fighting within; and if the people of St. Quentin should refuse some day to perform the labor which was required of them as well as of the troops, further resistance would be useless, and it would remain but to deliver the keys of the town, and with them the key of France, to Philip II. and his general, Philibert Emmanuel of Savoy.

However, he had resolved, before contemplating such a disastrous step, to make one last supreme effort; and with that in view he had convoked this assembly of the principal men of the town, whom we will now allow to complete our information as to the desperate condition of the fortifications, and, above all, as to the condition of the brave hearts of their defenders;— the most important fortifications of all.

The speech with which the admiral opened the sitting appealing eloquently to the patriotism of his hearers, was received with depressing silence. Then Gaspard de Coligny directly questioned Captain Oger, one of the valiant gentlemen who served under him. He hoped by beginning with the officers to urge the citizens on to further resistance. But Captain Oger's advice unluckily was not what the admiral anticipated.

"Since you have done me the honor to ask my opinion, Monsieur l'Amiral," said he, "I will say what I have to say frankly, but with much sorrow: St. Quentin can hold out no longer. If we had any hope of maintaining ourselves for a week even, or for four days, or for two days, I would say, 'These two days may afford time for the army to be reorganized; these two days may save our country, — therefore let us not surrender until the last stone in the walls has crumbled, and the last man has fallen.' But I am convinced that the next assault, which may be made within an hour, will be the last. Is it not, then, better, while there is still time, to save what can be saved of the town by capitulation, and escape pillage at least, if we cannot escape defeat?"

"Yes, yes, that is true! Well said! that is the only reasonable course to take," muttered those who heard him.

"No, gentlemen, no!" cried the admiral; "we are not dealing with reason now, but with sentiment. Besides, I do not believe that one single assault will let the Spaniards into the town, when we have already repelled five. Come, Lauxford, you know the present condition of the works and the countermines: are not the fortifications sufficiently strong to hold out for a long time to come? Speak frankly, and don't represent matters any more or less favorable than they really are. We have come together to learn the truth; and it is the truth I ask of you."

"I will tell it to you," replied the engineer Lauxford, "or rather I will let the facts speak for themselves; they will tell you the truth better than I, and without flattery. For this purpose, all you need to do is to go over with me in your mind the vulnerable points of these fortifications. Monsieur l'Amiral, at the present moment there are four practicable openings for the enemy; and I must confess that I am much surprised that he has not already made use of them. In the first place, there is a breach in the wall at the Boulevard St. Martin wide enough for twenty men to pass through abreast. We have lost there more than two hundred men, — living walls, who cannot, however, supply the lack of walls of stone. At the Porte St. Jean, the great tower alone is still standing, and the best curtain is battered to pieces. There is a countermine at that point, all closed and ready; but I fear that if we fire it, we shall cause the destruction of the great tower; which alone holds the assailants in check, and the ruins of which would serve them as ladders. At the hamlet of Remicourt, the Spanish trenches have cut through the outer wall of the moat, and they have taken up a position there under cover of a mantlet, behind which they are battering away at the walls without intermission. Finally, on the Faubourg d'Isle side, you know, Monsieur l'Amiral, that the enemy is in possession not only of the moats, but of the boulevard and the abbey; and they are so firmly lodged there that it is no longer possible to inflict any damage on them at that point, while, step by step, they are scaling the parapet,—which is only five or six feet thick,— attacking in flank with their batteries the men at work on the Boulevard de la Reine, and worrying them so that it has been impracticable to keep them at work. The remainder of the fortifications will perhaps stand out; but there are the four mortal wounds, and they will soon sap the life of the city, Monseigneur. You have asked me for the truth, and I have given it to you in all its melancholy details, leaving to your wisdom and foresight to say what use shall be made of it."

Thereupon the mutterings of the throng began again, and although no one dared to say it aloud, every one was saying under his breath,—

"The best thing to do is to capitulate, and not risk the disastrous chances of an assault."

But the admiral rejoined, undismayed,—

"Hold, gentlemen, another word! As you say, Monsieur Lauxford, if our walls are wreak, we have, to supplement their weakness, our gallant soldiers,—living ramparts. With them, and with the earnest concurrence of the citizens, is it not possible to postpone the taking of the town for a few days? (And what would be a shameful act to-day will cover us with glory then.) Yes, the fortifications are too weak, I agree; but we have troops in sufficient numbers, have we not, Monsieur de Rambouillet?"

"Monsieur l'Amiral," said the captain who was addressed, "if we were down in the square, in the midst of the crowd, who are awaiting the result of our deliberations, I would say yes; for we should do our utmost to inspire hope and confidence in every breast. But here, in council, before those whose courage needs no proof or stimulus, I do not hesitate to tell you that we have not men enough for the difficult and dangerous work to be done. We have given arms to every one who was able to carry them. The rest are employed in the defensive works, and children and old men are doing their share there. Even the women are assisting in the good work by saving and nursing the wounded. In short, not one arm is idle, and yet arms are sadly needed. There is not a spot on the ramparts where there is one man too many, and there are frequently not enough. Multiply as we will, it is impossible to arrange our forces so that fifty more men are not absolutely necessary at the Porte St. Jean, and at least fifty others at the Boulevard St. Martin. The disaster of St. Laurent has deprived us of reinforcements that we had reason to anticipate; and unless you expect succor from Paris, Monseigneur, it is for you to consider if, in such dire extremity, you ought to risk the lives of the small number of men we have left, and of this remnant of our gallant gendarmerie, who may still do much good service in helping to defend other places, and perhaps to save our country."

The whole assembly murmured approval of these words; and the distant shouting of the people who were crowding around the building on the outside was a still more eloquent commentary upon them.

But at this moment a voice of thunder cried,—

"Silence!"

Every voice was hushed; for he who spoke in such a commanding and steady voice was Jean Peuquoy, the syndic of the guild of weavers,—a citizen who was held in the highest esteem and consideration, and was a little feared by the people.

Jean Peuquoy was a type of the sturdy bourgeoisie, who loved their city as a mother and as a child, worshipped her and grumbled at her, lived always for her, and would die for her if need were. For the honest weaver there was no world but France, and in all France naught but St. Quentin. No one was so well versed as he in the history and traditions of the town, its ancient customs, and old-time legends. There was not a quarter, not a street, not a house, which in its present or its past had any secrets from Jean Peuquoy. He was in himself the municipality personified. His shop was a second Grand'place, and his wooden house in the Rue St. Martin another town-hall. This venerable mansion was made noticeable by a very peculiar coat-of-arms,—a shuttle crowned between the antlers of a full-grown stag. One of Jean Peuquoy's ancestors (for Jean Peuquoy reckoned up his ancestors like any gentleman)—a weaver like himself, it need not be said, and in addition an archer of renown—had put out the two eyes of this fine stag with two shafts at more than a hundred paces. These superb antlers are still to be seen at St. Quentin in the Rue St. Martin. Every one for ten leagues around knew the antlers and the weaver. Jean Peuquoy was thus the city itself; and every dweller in St. Quentin listened to the voice of his country speaking through him.

And so no one stirred when the weaver's voice, rising above the grumbling and the muttering, shouted, "Silence!"

"Yes, be silent!" he continued, "and lend me your ears for one moment, my fellow-citizens and good friends, I beseech you. Let us look over together, with your leave, what we have already done, and we may perhaps learn from that what we have still to do. When the enemy sat down before our walls; when we saw this swarm of Spaniards, English, Germans, and Walloons, under the redoubtable Philibert Emmanuel of Savoy, swooping down like locusts around our town,—we bravely accepted our lot, did we not? We did not murmur, nor did we accuse Providence of having cruelly selected St. Quentin as the expiatory sacrifice of France. Far from it; and Monsieur l'Amiral will do us the justice to say that from the very hour of his arrival, bringing us the mighty succor of his experience and valor, we did our best to forward his plans with our persons and our property. We have furnished supplies and money, and have ourselves shouldered the cross-bow and wielded the pick and shovel. Those of us who have not acted as sentinels on the walls have been digging in the town. We have helped to discipline and restore order among the rebellious peasants in the suburbs, who refused to work in payment for the protection we had afforded them. In short, we have done, I honestly believe, everything that could possibly be asked of men whose trade is not war. So we hoped that our lord the king would speedily remember his loyal subjects in St. Quentin, and would send us without delay the succor that we needed; and so it happened. Monsieur de Montmorency came hurrying hither to drive the forces of Philip II. from our gates, and we thanked God and the king; but the fatal day of St. Laurent dashed our hopes to the ground in a few short hours. The constable was taken, his army cut to pieces, and we were left in a more hopeless state than ever. Five days have passed since then, and the enemy have made good use of them. Three fierce assaults have cost us more than two hundred men and whole sections of the walls. The cannon thunders unceasingly. Listen! it echoes my very words. But we do not wish to hear it, and listen only on the side where Paris lies, to hear if we cannot distinguish some sound to announce the arrival of further reinforcement. But no; and our last resources are, so far as we can see, exhausted. The king abandons us, and has many other things to do than to think of us. He must collect around him at Paris all that remains of his forces, and must save the kingdom rather than one poor town; and if he does turn his eyes and his thoughts toward St. Quentin now and then, it is only to ask if its death-agony will last long enough to give France time to recover. But as to hope or chance of relief, there is no more now for us, dear countrymen and friends. Monsieur de Rambouillet and Monsieur de Lauxford have spoken the truth. We lack fortifications and troops; our city is dying; we are abandoned, despairing, and lost!"

"Yes, yes!" cried the whole assembly, with one accord; "we must surrender! we must surrender!"

"Not so," rejoined Jean Peuquoy; "we must die!"

An amazed silence followed this unexpected conclusion. The weaver profited by it to proceed with increased animation.

"We must die. What we have already done points out to us what remains for us to do. Messieurs Lauxford and de Rambouillet say that we cannot hold out; but Monsieur de Coligny says that we must hold out! And let us do it! You know whether I am devoted to our good town of St. Quentin, my dear brothers. I love her as I loved my old mother, in very truth. Every bullet that strikes her venerable walls seems to pierce my heart; and yet now that the general has spoken, I feel that he must be obeyed. Let not the arm rebel against the head, and St. Quentin perish! Monsieur l'Amiral knows what he is doing and what he means to do. He has weighed, in his wisdom, the fate of one city against the fate of France. He has decided that St. Quentin must die, like a sentinel at his post; so be it. The man who murmurs is a coward; and he who disobeys, a traitor. The walls are crumbling: let us make new walls with our dead bodies; let us gain a week, let us gain two days, or an hour even, at the price of all our blood and all our property. Monsieur l'Amiral knows the worth of all this; and since he asks it of us, we must do it. He will have to answer for it to God and to the king; but that doesn't concern us. As for us, our business is to die when he says, 'Die!' Let Monsieur de Coligny's conscience look out for the rest. He is responsible, and we must submit."

After these solemn, mournful words, every tongue was still, every head lowered, Gaspard de Coligny's like the others, and even to a greater degree than the others. It was in truth a heavy burden which the syndic of weavers put upon him; and he could not forbear a shudder as he thought of all these lives with which he was thus made chargeable.

"I see by your silence, my friends and brothers," continued Jean Peuquoy, "that you understand and approve what I have said; but one cannot expect husbands and fathers to pronounce sentence aloud upon their wives and children. To say nothing is to make a favorable reply. You will allow Monsieur l'Amiral to make orphans of your children and widows of your wives; but you cannot pronounce their sentence yourselves, is it not so? It is quite right too. Say nothing and die. No one would be so brutal as to require you to cry: 'Meure St. Quentin!' But if your patriotic hearts beat, as I believe they do, in unison with mine, you can at least cry, 'Vive la France!'"

"Vive la France!" echoed a few voices, as feeble as the wailing of children, and as mournful as sobs.

Then Gaspard de Coligny, deeply moved, and in a state of intense agitation, rose hastily from his seat.

"Listen to me; listen!" he cried: "I will not accept such a fearful responsibility alone. I was able to resist you when you wished to yield to the enemy, but when you do yield to me, I can no longer discuss the question; and since every soul in this assembly is of a contrary opinion to that which I hold, and since you all deem the sacrifice useless—"

"I believe, may God forgive me," broke in a loud voice from the crowd, "that even you are about to speak of giving up the town, Monsieur l'Amiral."

CHAPTER XXVII
GABRIEL AT WORK

"Who dares thus to interrupt me?" demanded Gaspard de Coligny, with a gathering frown.

"I!" said a man, attired in the costume of a peasant of the suburbs of St. Quentin, making his way forward through the crowd.

"A peasant!" exclaimed the admiral.

"No, not a peasant," rejoined the stranger, "but Vicomte d'Exmès, captain of the king's Guards, who comes in his Majesty's name."

"In the king's name!" exclaimed the throng of astonished citizens.

"In the king's name," repeated Gabriel; "and you see that he has not abandoned his noble people of St. Quentin; on the contrary, he is still anxious about them. I came in, disguised as a peasant, three hours since; and during these three hours I have examined the walls and listened to your deliberations. But let me say that what I have heard hardly agrees with what I saw. Whence this discouragement, suitable for none but women, which seems to have stricken with panic the stoutest hearts? How comes it that you thus suddenly lose all hope, and leave yourselves a prey to imaginary fears? What! have you sunk so low that you can only rebel against the will of Monsieur l'Amiral, or bend your necks to the yoke in resignation? Show your face, by the living God, not to your leaders, but to the enemy; and if you cannot overcome them, at least let your defeat be more glorious than a triumph. I come from the ramparts; and I tell you that you can hold them two weeks yet, and the king only asks you to keep the enemy at bay one week to insure the salvation of France. To all that you have listened to in this hall I will make answer in two words, and will point out to you a remedy for your ills and a ray of hope to calm your fears."

The officers and notables crowded around Gabriel, already under the magic spell of his powerful and sympathetic will.

"Hear him! hear him!" they cried.

It was amid a breathless stillness that Gabriel continued,—

"In the first place, Monsieur Engineer Lauxford, what did you say,— that four weak spots in the fortifications were like open gates for the enemy to come in? Well, let us see. The Faubourg d'Isle side is in the greatest danger; the Spaniards are masters of the abbey, and from that point they are keeping up such a well-directed fire that our workmen don't dare to show themselves. Allow me, Monsieur Lauxford, to point out to you a very simple and very excellent way to protect them, which I saw put in practice by the besieged at Civitella this very year. It consists simply in screening our workmen from the Spanish batteries by placing old flatboats across the boulevard, piled upon one another, and filled with bags of earth. The cannon-balls waste their force in the soft soil; and behind that shelter our workmen will be as safe as if they were out of range of the cannon. At the hamlet of Remicourt, the enemy, under cover of a mantlet, are calmly undermining the wall, you say? I have with my own eyes verified the fact. But that is the place, Monsieur Engineer, where we must locate a countermine, and not at the Porte St. Jean, where the great tower makes your countermine not only useless but dangerous. So remove your sappers and miners from the western to the southern side, Monsieur Lauxford, and you will find great advantage in so doing. But the Porte St. Jean, you will ask, and the Boulevard St. Martin, are they to be left undefended? Fifty men at the first, and fifty at the second point will be enough; so Monsieur de Rambouillet himself has told us. But," he added, "these hundred men are not forthcoming. Very well! I will furnish them."

A murmur of glad surprise was heard all over the room.

"Yes," resumed Gabriel, in a steadier tone, as he saw that their hearts were somewhat encouraged by his words, "I left Baron de Vaulpergues with his company of three hundred lancers three leagues from here. We understand each other. I agreed to come here, risking all the perils of passing through the enemy's camp, in order to satisfy myself as to the most favorable points for him to make his way into the town with his men. I am here, as you see; and my plans are made. I shall now return to Vaulpergues. We shall divide his company into three. I shall take command in person of one of these detachments; and at nightfall, there being no moon, we propose to march from three different directions, each toward a postern designated beforehand. Surely we shall be very unfortunate if only one of our three detachments eludes the enemy, when their attention is called off by the other two. In any event, there will surely be one; and a hundred determined men will be thrown into the town, where, fortunately, there is no lack of provisions. These hundred men will be posted, as I said, at the Porte St.

Jean and the Boulevard St. Michel; and now tell me, Monsieur Lauxford and Monsieur de Rambouillet,—tell me, I beg, what spot in the walls will then offer an easy entrance to the enemy."

With universal acclamation the assembly received these stirring words, which so powerfully awakened new hope in their despondent hearts.

"Oh," cried Jean Peuquoy, "now we can fight, and we can conquer."

"Fight, yes; but as for victory, I dare not hope it," rejoined Gabriel, with an air of authority. "I have no desire to make matters appear better than they really are, but only that they should not be made to appear worse. I wished to prove to every one of you, and first of all, to you, Master Jean Peuquoy, who have given utterance to such noble but gloomy words,—I wished to prove to you, in the first place, that the king does not abandon you, and in the second place, that your fall might be glorious, but obstinate resistance must be of the greatest service. You said a moment since, 'Let us offer ourselves as a sacrifice;' and now you say, 'Let us fight.' It is a great step forward. Yes, it is possible, nay, it may be probable that the sixty thousand men who are now besieging your frail ramparts will end by carrying them. But in the first place, do not imagine that the noble struggle you will have maintained will expose you to cruel reprisals. Philibert Emmanuel is a brave soldier, who loves and honors bravery in others, and will never punish you for your valor. And last of all, think that if you can hold out ten or twelve days more, you will perhaps have lost your town, but you will surely have saved your country. A sublime and noble end! Towns, like men, have their patents of nobility; and the mighty deeds that they accomplish are their titles and their ancestors. Your little children, men of St. Quentin, will some day be proud of their fathers. Your walls may be destroyed; but who can ever destroy the glorious memory of this siege? Courage, then, heroic sentinels of a kingdom! Save the king, and save your country. But a moment ago, with heads bowed down, you seemed to have resolved to die, the willing victims of stern necessity. Lift up your heads! If you perish, let it be as willing heroes, and your memory shall never perish! Thus you can heartily join me in the cry: 'Vive la France!' and 'Vive St. Quentin!'"

"Vive la France! Vive St. Quentin! Vive le roi!" burst enthusiastically from a hundred throats.

"And now," said Gabriel, "to the ramparts and to work! and encourage by your example your fellow-citizens, who await you. To-morrow a hundred pairs of arms more, I swear, shall be here to aid you in your work of salvation and of glory."

"To the ramparts!" cried the throng.

And out they rushed, carried away with joy and hope and pride, and inspiring with their words and their enthusiasm those who had not heard the words of the unhoped-for liberator, who had been sent by God and the king to the disheartened town.

Gaspard de Coligny, the worthy and high-minded commander, had listened to Gabriel in silence born of wonder and admiration. When the whole assemblage had dispersed with triumphant shouts, he left the seat he had occupied, went up to the young man, and pressed his hand with an air of amazement.

"Thanks, Monsieur," said he; "you have saved St. Quentin and myself from disgrace, and it may be France and the king from destruction."

"Alas! I have done nothing as yet, Monsieur l'Amiral," said Gabriel. "I must now go back to Vaulpergues; and God alone can enable me to go out as I came in, and to introduce the hundred men I have promised into the town. It is God and not I to whom thanks must be rendered, ten days from now."

CHAPTER XXVIII
WHEREIN MARTIN-GUERRE IS NOT CLEVER

Gabriel de Montgommery remained in conversation with the admiral more than an hour.

Coligny could but marvel at the firmness and boldness and knowledge displayed by this youth, who talked of strategy like a commanding general, of defensive works like an engineer, and of moral influence like a gray-headed sage. Gabriel, on his side, admired the upright and noble character of Gaspard, and the kind-heartedness and honesty of conscience which made him perhaps the purest and most loyal gentleman of the age. Certainly the nephew bore but little resemblance to the uncle! At the end of an hour the two men, one with hair that was already turning gray, while the locks of the other were still of the hue of the raven, understood and appreciated each other as if their acquaintance were of twenty years' standing.

When they had fully agreed upon the measures to be taken to facilitate the entrance of Vaulpergues's troops on the following night, Gabriel took leave of the admiral, saying to him confidently: "Au revoir!" He carried with him the countersigns and necessary signals.

Martin-Guerre, disguised as a peasant, like his master, awaited him at the foot of the staircase in the town-hall.

"Ah, there you are, Monseigneur!" cried the worthy squire. "I am very glad indeed to see you again; for a whole hour I have heard nothing from every passer-by but the name of Vicomte d'Exmès, accompanied with exclamations of wonder and extravagant praise! You have upset the whole town. What talisman did you bring, Monseigneur, to make such a revolution in the hearts of the whole population?"

"The word of a resolute man, Martin,—nothing more. But talking is not enough, and now we must act."

"Let us act, then, Monseigneur,—for my part, actions suit me better than words. We are going, I see, to take a walk in the fields under the noses of the enemies' sentinels. Well, Monseigneur, I am ready."

"Don't be in too great haste, Martin," rejoined Gabriel; "it is too light, and I must wait for the dusk before leaving the town, by agreement with the admiral. We have therefore almost three hours before us. Then too I have something to do meanwhile," he added, with some embarrassment. "Yes, a very important matter to look after,—some information to seek."

"I understand," said Martin-Guerre, "something about the strength of the garrison, is it not, or about the weak spots in the fortifications? What untiring zeal!"

"You don't understand anything at all about it," said Gabriel, smiling. "No, I know all that I want to know about the ramparts and the troops; and it is with a matter more—more personal that I am occupied just now."

"Speak, Monseigneur; and if I can help you in any way—"

"Yes, Martin, you are, I know, a faithful servant and a devoted friend, so I have no secrets from you except those which do not belong to me. If you don't know whom I am seeking for anxiously and fondly in this town, after my duties are done, Martin, it must be because you have forgotten."

"Oh, pardon, Monseigneur, I know now!" cried Martin. "It is, is it not, a—a Benedictine?"

"It is, Martin. What can have become of her in this panic-stricken town. In truth, I didn't dare to ask Monsieur l'Amiral for fear of betraying myself by my distress. And then, too, would he have been able to answer? Diane changed her name, no doubt, when she entered the convent."

"Yes," rejoined Martin; "for I must say that which she bore, and which is a lovely name in my opinion, has a slightly heathenish sound, because of Madame de Poitiers, I suppose. Sister Diane! The fact is that that name is as offensive as my other self when he is tipsy."

"What shall I do, then?" said Gabriel. "The best way would be perhaps to inquire, in the first place, about the Benedictine convent in a general way."

"Yes," said Martin-Guerre; "and then we will go from the general to the particular, as my old curé used to say when he was suspected of being a Lutheran. Well, Monseigneur, I am at your orders to make these inquiries, as for every other purpose."

"We must go about it separately, Martin; and then we shall have two chances instead of one. Be careful and reserved, and try above all things not to drink, you incorrigible tippler! We need all our self-possession."

"Oh, Monseigneur knows that since we left Paris I have regained my former sobriety, and drink nothing but pure water. I have only seen double once."

"I am glad to hear it," said Gabriel. "Well, then, Martin, in two hours meet me at this spot."

"I will be here, Monseigneur."

And they separated.

Two hours later they met as they had agreed. Gabriel was radiant, but Martin-Guerre very sheepish. All that the latter had learned was that the Benedictines had chosen to share with the other women of the town the labor and honor of nursing and watching the wounded; that every day they were scattered about among the ambulances, and did not return to the convent till evening; and that soldiers and citizens alike were unsparing of their admiration and veneration for them.

Gabriel, by good luck, had learned something more. When the first person he met had told him all that Martin-Guerre had learned, Gabriel asked the name of the superior of the convent. It was, if his memory served him, Mother Monique, Diane de Castro's friend. Gabriel then inquired where the saintly woman was to be found.

"In the place where the danger is greatest," was the reply.

Gabriel made his way to the Faubourg d'Isle, and actually found the superior there. She knew already by the public reports who the Vicomte d'Exmès was, what he had said at the town-hall, and what part he was going to play at St. Quentin. She received him as the envoy of the king and the savior of the city.

"You will not be surprised, Mother," said Gabriel, "that coming in the king's name, I ask you for news of his Majesty's daughter, Madame Diane de Castro. I have sought her in vain among the nuns whom I have met on my way. She is not ill, I trust?"

"No, Monsieur le Vicomte," replied the superior; "but I required her to remain at the convent to-day, and take a little rest, for not one of us has equalled her in devotion and courage. She has been everywhere, and always ready, practising at all times and in all places, and with a sort of joy and eagerness, her sublime charity, which is our gallantry. Ah, she is the worthy daughter of the blood of France! And yet she is unwilling that her title and her rank should become known; and she will take it very kindly of you, Monsieur le Vicomte, to respect her noble incognito. But no matter! if she does hide her noble birth, she shows her kind heart; and all those who are suffering rejoice to see her angel's face pass like a ray of celestial hope in the midst of their pain. She is called, from the name of the order, Sister Benedicta; but our poor wounded fellows, who do not know Latin, call her the Sister Bénie."

"And well the name fits Madame la Duchesse!" cried Gabriel, who felt tears of joy gathering in his eyes. "And may I see her to-morrow, Mother,— that is, if I return?"

"You will return, brother," replied the superior; "and in that spot where you hear the most pitiful groans and shrieks of pain, there you will find Sister Bénie."

Thus it was that Gabriel rejoined Martin-Guerre, with his heart full to overflowing with renewed courage, and certain now, as the superior was, that he would come safe and unscathed through the perils of the night.

CHAPTER XXIX
WHEREIN MARTIN-GUERRE IS A BUNGLER

Gabriel had acquired sufficiently accurate information about the suburbs of St. Quentin to avoid going astray in a region where he was an utter stranger. Under cover of nightfall he and Martin-Guerre left the town by the least carefully guarded postern without hindrance. Wrapped in long dark cloaks, they glided into the moat-like shadows, and thence by the breach in the wall into the fields.

But they were not beyond the greatest danger. Small bodies of the enemy patrolled the suburbs day and night; encampments were scattered here and there about the besieged town, and any encounter might be fatal to our peasant-soldiers. The least risk that they ran was to be delayed a day; that is to say, to make the projected expedition entirely useless.

And so when after a half-hour of travelling they arrived at a cross-roads, Gabriel stopped and seemed to reflect. Martin-Guerre also stopped, but he did not reflect. That task he ordinarily left to his master. Martin-Guerre was a brave and loyal squire, but he had no desire or ability to be anything more than the hand; Gabriel was the head.

"Martin," Gabriel began, after a moment's thought, "here are two roads, both of which lead to the forest of Angimont, where Baron de Vaulpergues is waiting for us. If we keep together, Martin, we may be taken together; while if we separate, we have a double chance of carrying out our plans and of finding Madame de Castro. Let us each take a different road. Do you take this one; it is the longest, but the safest, according to Monsieur l'Amiral. You will, however, have to go near the Walloon encampment, where Monsieur de Montmorency is probably a prisoner. You must avoid it by making a detour, as we did last night. Use all your assurance and self-possession. If you fall in with any troops, you must pass yourself off for a peasant of Angimont, and say that you have been carrying provisions to the Spanish camp at St. Quentin, and were delayed on your return. Do your best to imitate the Picardy patois, which will not be very difficult with foreigners. But, above all things, err rather on the side of audacity than timidity. Assume an air of confidence, for if you hesitate, you are lost."

"Oh, be quite easy, Monseigneur," said Martin-Guerre, with a very self-satisfied mien. "I am not so simple as I seem, and I will give a good account of myself."

"Well said, Martin. I will take this other road; it is shorter, but more dangerous, for it is the main highway from Paris, which is watched more carefully than all the others. I shall run across more than one hostile party, I fear, and I shall have to drown myself in the ditches, or flay myself in the thickets, more than once; and when all is said and done, it is very possible that I may not accomplish my purpose. But no matter, Martin! Wait for me just half an hour; if I do not join you in that time, let Monsieur de Vaulpergues set out without delay. It will then be about midnight, and the danger will not be so great as in the evening. Nevertheless, Martin, advise him from me to adopt every possible precaution. You know what is to be done,—to divide his company into three detachments, and approach the town as quietly as possible from three opposite directions. It is too much to hope that all three detachments should succeed in getting into the place; but the failure of one may very well be the salvation of the others. But it's all the same! It is quite possible that we shall meet no more, my good Martin; but we must think only of the welfare of the country. Your hand! And may God keep you!"

"Oh, I pray only for you, Monseigneur!" rejoined Martin. "If He will only preserve you, He may do what He pleases with me; for I am good for nothing except to worship you and serve you. So I hope to have some fine sport with these infernal Spaniards to-night."

"I like to see you in this frame of mind, Martin. Well, adieu! Good luck to you, and keep cool, above all things!"

"Good luck, Monseigneur, and don't be too rash!"

The master and squire then separated. Everything went well at first with Martin; and although it was scarcely possible for him to lose his way, he nevertheless showed considerable skill in avoiding some suspicious-looking armed men from whom the darkness hid him. But as he drew near the Walloon encampment, the sentinels became much more numerous.

At the fork of two roads, Martin-Guerre suddenly found himself between two parties of soldiers, one on foot, and the other mounted; and a sharp *Qui vive?* told the unlucky squire that he was discovered.

"Well," said he, "now the time has come to show the impudence which my master recommended to me so forcibly."

And struck with an almost providentially bright idea, he began to sing at the top of his voice, and very opportunely, the following ballad of the siege of Metz:—

> "Le vendredi de la Toussaint,
> Est arrivé la Germanie
> À la belle croix de Messain
> Pour faire grande boucherie."[5]

"Hola! qui va la?" cried a harsh voice with an accent and pronunciation almost unintelligible, but which we will not undertake to describe lest we become unintelligible ourselves.

"A peasant from Angimont," replied Martin-Guerre, in a no less nondescript patois.

And he kept on his way and his song with increasing vigor and spirit,—

> "Se campant au haut des vignes
> Le duc d'Albe et sa compagnie,
> À Saint-Arnou, près nos fossés,
> C'était pour faire l'entreprise
> De reconnaître nos fossés—"[6]

"Ho, there! Will you hold your noise and stop, wretched peasant, with your cursed song?" shouted the same harsh voice.

Martin-Guerre reflected that these importunate fellows who hailed him were ten against one; that, thanks to their horses, they could overtake him with ease, and that he might do an immense amount of harm by running away. So he stopped short. After all, he was not altogether disappointed at having an opportunity to display his self-possession and his cleverness. His master, who seemed sometimes to doubt the existence of those qualities in him, would have no excuse for it henceforth, if he should succeed in extricating himself with address from such a perilous position.

At first he assumed an air of most perfect self-confidence.

"By Saint Quentin the martyr!" he muttered, approaching his captors, "this is a fine business for you, keeping a poor belated peasant away from his wife and little ones at Angimont. Come, tell me, pray, what you want of me."

He meant to say this in Picardy patois; but he really said it in the dialect of Auvergne with the accent of a Provençal.

The man who had hailed him had a similar intention of replying in French, but the best he could do was Walloon with a German accent.

"What do we want of you? To question you and search you, night-prowler; for how do we know that there isn't a spy hidden under your peasant's smock?"

"Go on, then; question me and search me," was Martin-Guerre's response, accompanied with a hoarse and most unnatural laugh.

"We will take you to camp with us."

"To camp!" exclaimed Martin. "Oh, well, that's all right. I will speak to the general. Ah, you choose to arrest an unfortunate peasant on his way back from carrying supplies to your comrades down yonder at St. Quentin! May I be damned if I ever do it again! I will let your whole army die of hunger first. I was going to Angimont after more supplies; but you stop me on the way. Ah, you don't know me yet. I'll be even with you for this! 'Saint Quentin, tête de kien,' says the Picardy proverb. Take me for a spy indeed! I propose to complain to your chief. Let us go to your camp!"

"*Mordieu*! What gibberish!" retorted the commander of the scouting party. "I am the chief, my friend; and it is with me that you will have to reckon when we can see you plainly, if you please. Do you suppose we are going to rouse the generals for a blackguard like you?"

"Yes, I do; and it is to the generals that I propose to be taken!" cried Martin-Guerre, volubly. "I have something to say to the generals and the marshals. I propose to say to them that a man who is supplying you and your people with food is not to be arrested thus without once crying, 'Look out!' I have done nothing wrong. I am an honest inhabitant of Angimont. I mean to demand an indemnity for my trouble; and you shall be hung for yours, you wretches!"

"Comrade, he seems sure of his ground, do you know!" said one of the soldiers to his chief.

"Yes," replied the other; "and I would let him go if it didn't seem to me every little while that I recognize his figure and his voice. Come forward; everything will be explained in camp."

Martin-Guerre, placed between two of the horsemen for safe-keeping, never ceased to swear and grumble during the whole journey. As he entered the tent to which they escorted him in the first place, he swore and grumbled still more.

"So this is the way you treat your allies, is it? Oh, well, just wait till we furnish any more oats for your horses, or meal for you! I give you up. As soon as you have recognized me and let me go, I will go back to Angimont, and not leave the place again; or better still, I will leave it, and enter a complaint against you to Monseigneur Philibert Emmanuel in person, the first thing to-morrow morning. He is not the man to allow such an affront to be put upon me."

At this moment the ensign who was in command of the party held a torch to Martin-Guerre's face. He fell back three steps in wonder and horror.

"By the devil!" he cried, "I was not mistaken. It is he, the miserable villain! Don't you recognize him now, you fellows?"

"Yes, indeed we do!" repeated each of the troops in turn, as he examined Martin-Guerre's features with a curiosity which in every case changed at once to rage.

"Ah, you do recognize me at last, then?" rejoined the poor squire, who began to be seriously alarmed. "You know who I am? Martin Cornouiller of Angimont. And you are going to release me, are you not!"

"We release you, you villain, you rake, you gallows-bird!" cried the ensign, with flaming eyes and threatening fists.

"Well, well, what the deuce is the matter, my friend?" said Martin. "Perhaps I am no longer Martin Cornouiller?"

"No, you are not Martin Cornouiller," replied the ensign; "and to unmask you and prove you a liar, here are ten men standing around you, who know you well. My friends, tell this impostor his name, to convict him of deceit and infernal falsehood."

"It's Arnauld du Thill! it's that scoundrel, Arnauld du Thill!" the ten voices shouted in chorus with terrifying unanimity.

"Arnauld du Thill! What do you mean?" asked Martin, turning pale.

"Oh, yes, deny yourself now, you villain!" cried the ensign. "But luckily here are ten witnesses to contradict you. Before them, notwithstanding your peasant's dress, have you the face to declare that I didn't take you prisoner at the battle of St. Laurent in attendance upon the constable?"

"No, no, I am Martin Cornouiller," stammered Martin, who was beginning to lose his head.

"You are Martin Cornouiller?" said the ensign, with a contemptuous laugh; "you are not that coward Arnauld du Thill, who promised me a ransom, whom I treated with every consideration, and who only last night made his escape, carrying with him not only the little money that I possessed, but my dearly-loved Gudule, the lovely *vivandière*? Villain! what have you done with Gudule?"

"What have you done with Gudule?" echoed his companions, in ominous chorus.

"What have I done with Gudule?" said Martin-Guerre, completely crushed. "How can I tell, miserable wretch that I am! Ah, well, do you really all recognize me? Are you perfectly sure that you are not mistaken? Can you swear that my name is—Arnauld du Thill; that this fine fellow took me prisoner at the battle of St. Laurent; and that I have treacherously carried off his Gudule? Can you swear to all this?"

"Yes, yes, yes!" cried the ten voices, vigorously. "Very well. I am not surprised," said Martin-Guerre, piteously (he was apt to wander a little, we remember, when this matter of his twofold existence was touched upon). "No, indeed, I am not surprised. I would have insisted until to-morrow that my name is Martin Cornouiller; but you know me as Arnauld du Thill. I was here yesterday, it seems; so I say no more. Expect no more resistance from me, for I submit. From the moment that this turns out to be so, my feet and hands are tied. I did not foresee this. It has been such a long time since my alibis ceased to trouble me. Come on! it's all right. Do with me as you will; carry me off; imprison me; strangle me; what you tell me of Gudule puts the finishing touch to my conviction that you are right. Yes, I recognize my own hand in that! But I am very glad to know that my name is Arnauld du Thill."

Poor Martin-Guerre thenceforth confessed everything that they chose, allowed himself to be overwhelmed with insults and reproaches, and offered his all to God by way of penance for the new offences that they charged him with. As he could not tell what had become of Gudule, they loaded him with chains, and subjected him to all varieties of ill-treatment, but without wearing out his angelic patience. All that he regretted was that he had not had time to fulfil his commission to Baron de Vaulpergues; but who could have imagined that new crimes would rise to confront him, and reduce to nothing his splendid schemes for exhibiting his address and presence of mind?

"One thing that consoles me, however," he reflected, in the damp corner where they had flung him down upon the ground, "is that perhaps

Arnauld du Thill may enter St. Quentin triumphantly with a detachment of Vaulpergues's company. But no, no! that is a delusive hope too; and what I know of the blackguard would lead me rather to guess that the monster is at some inn on the road to Paris with the fair Gudule. Alas, alas! I can't help thinking that I could put more heart into my penance if I had at least some little knowledge of the sin."

[5] "On Friday after All Saints
All Germany came down
With fire and sword and rapine
To sack our well-loved town."

[6] "Encamped above the vineyards,
Bold Alva and his band
Came spying round St. Arnou,
Our trenches to—"

CHAPTER XXX
THE STRATEGY OF WAR

Fanciful as it appeared to him, Martin-Guerre's hope was realized nevertheless. When Gabriel after a thousand narrow escapes reached the forest where Baron de Vaulpergues was awaiting him, the first face that he saw was that of his squire, and the first words he uttered were, "Martin-Guerre!"

"Here I am, Monseigneur," was the squire's reply, in a steady voice.

This Martin-Guerre needed nobody to advise or urge him to be impudent.

"Were you much ahead of me, Martin?" asked Gabriel.

"I have been here an hour, Monseigneur."

"Have you really? But it seems to me that you have changed your dress, for surely you hadn't on that doublet when you left me three hours ago."

"No, Monseigneur; I obtained this one of a peasant who was more appropriately dressed than I, as I thought, and gave him mine in exchange."

"Very well! and you had no unfortunate encounter?"

"Not one, Monseigneur."

"Quite the contrary," said the Baron de Vaulpergues, coming up to them, "for the blackguard, when he arrived here, was accompanied by a very charming little maiden, upon my word,—a Flemish *vivandière*, so far as we could judge from her speech. She seemed to be very sad, poor creature; but he very roughly though with much discretion dismissed her at the edge of the forest before coming to this spot, despite her tears.

"Now, Monsieur d'Exmès," he continued, "if your idea and the admiral's agree with mine, we shall not start for half an hour. It is not yet midnight; and in my judgment we ought not to reach St. Quentin till toward three o'clock. That is the time when sentinels get weary and relax their vigilance somewhat. Don't you think with me, Monsieur le Vicomte?"

"Most decidedly I do; and Monsieur de Coligny's instructions are in perfect accord with your opinion. At three in the morning he will expect us; and we ought to arrive then if we are ever to arrive."

"Oh, we shall get there, Monseigneur, allow me to assure you!" said Arnauld-Martin. "I made good use of my opportunity to examine the surroundings of the Walloon camp when I came by; and I can guide you by that road as safely as if I had been in the neighborhood for a fortnight."

"This is most marvellous, Martin!" cried Gabriel,—"such wonders accomplished in so short a time! Why, I shall have as much confidence henceforth in your intelligence as in your loyalty!"

"Oh, Monseigneur, if you will rely on my zeal and my discretion, I ask for nothing more!"

The crafty fellow's plot was so well contrived, and so favored by luck and his audacity, that since Gabriel's arrival the impostor had spoken nothing but the truth.

While Gabriel and Vaulpergues were deliberating aside as to what road they should take, he, for his part, was completing the details of his plan, so as not to interfere with the miraculous chances which had served him so well thus far.

This is what actually occurred. Arnauld, having escaped with Gudule's assistance from the camp where he was held a prisoner, had prowled about in the neighboring woods for eighteen hours, not daring to leave their shelter for fear of falling into the hands of the enemy. Toward evening he thought that he saw in the forest of Angimont the tracks of horsemen who must, he judged, be anxious to keep out of sight, or they would not have resorted to such impracticable paths. Therefore they must be Frenchmen lying in ambush, so Arnauld tried to overtake them, and succeeded. It was then that he dismissed Gudule with all possible speed; and the poor child returned, weeping, to the tents, expecting, no doubt, to find another lover there to take the place of the one she had lost. The first one of Vaulpergues's soldiers whom Arnauld fell in with called him Martin-Guerre; and for very good reasons he did not undeceive him. Listening with all his ears, and saying very little himself, he soon learned everything. Vicomte d'Exmès was expected to return that very night, after having notified the admiral at St. Quentin of Vaulpergues's approach, and bringing with him the necessary plans and instructions to facilitate throwing the detachment into the place. Martin-Guerre was with him, they said; so they naturally took Arnauld to be Martin, and questioned him about his master.

"He will soon be here," was his reply. "We came by different roads."

In his own mind he was considering what a fine thing it would be for him if he could attach himself to Gabriel. In the first place, his means of subsistence in these hard times would be assured; then he knew that his master, the constable, at present Philibert Emmanuel's prisoner, was suffering less, possibly, from the disgrace of his defeat and captivity than from the thought that his detested rival, the Duc de Guise, would soon be omnipotent at court, and would exercise unbounded influence over the king's mind. To dog the steps of a friend of Guise, then, would be to establish himself at the very fountain-head of information, which he could sell at a high price to the constable. Last of all, was not Gabriel personally an enemy of the Montmorencys, and the principal obstacle in the way of the marriage of Duc François with Madame de Castro?

Arnauld remembered all this, but could not avoid the reflection at the same time that the return of the true Martin-Guerre to his master's side might well upset all his fine plans. In order to avoid being convicted of imposture, he lay in wait for Gabriel's coming, hoping to be able to keep the credulous Martin-Guerre out of the way, or to get rid of him altogether. Imagine his delight, then, when Gabriel came up to him alone, and at once recognized him as his squire. Arnauld had spoken the truth without knowing it. After that he left everything to chance, and relying upon his patron the devil having led poor Martin into the toils of the Spaniards, he boldly assumed the rôle of the absentee, in which he succeeded admirably, as we have seen.

Meanwhile the conference between Gabriel and Vaulpergues came to an end; and when the three detachments were under arms, and ready to start on their respective routes, Arnauld insisted on accompanying Gabriel on the road which led by the Walloon camp. It was the road which the real Martin-Guerre was to have taken; and if they should happen to meet him, Arnauld wanted to be on the spot, so that he might make him disappear, or disappear himself, as need required.

But they passed the camp without seeing anything of Martin; and the thought of that trifling danger was soon lost sight of in the more serious peril which awaited him, as well as Gabriel and the little band of whom they made part, before the closely invested walls of St. Quentin.

Within the town the anxiety was no less acute, as may well be imagined; for the salvation or destruction of all depended almost entirely on the bold *coup-de-main* to be undertaken by Gabriel and Vaulpergues. So at two o'clock in the morning the admiral in person made the round of the points agreed upon between himself and Gabriel, enjoining upon the picked men, who were posted as sentinels at these important spots, the most watchful attention. Then he mounted to the belfry tower, whence he could overlook the whole town and all the neighborhood; and there, dumb and motionless, scarcely breathing, he listened in the silence, and looked out upon the night. But he heard only the deadened, far-off sound of the Spanish miners and the French counterminers; he saw naught but the tents of the enemy, and, farther away, the gloomy forest of Origny standing darkly out in the black night.

Unable to overcome his restlessness, the admiral determined to go to the spot where the fate of St. Quentin was to be decided. He came down from the tower, and on horseback, attended by several officers, rode to the Boulevard de la Reine, and up to one of the posterns at which Vaulpergues might be expected, and waited, standing on an angle of the ramparts.

Just as three o'clock was striking from La Collégiale, the hoot of an owl was heard from the heart of the marshes of the Somme.

"God be praised! there they are!" cried the admiral.

Monsieur du Breuil, at a sign from Coligny, using his hands as a speaking-trumpet, imitated distinctly the cry of the osprey.

Then a deathly silence followed. The admiral and his companions stood as if made of stone, their ears on the alert, and their hearts heating fast.

Suddenly a musket-shot was heard in the direction from which the cry had come; and almost at the same moment there was a general discharge, accompanied by sharp cries and a terrible uproar.

The first detachment was discovered.

"A hundred brave men gone already!" cried the admiral.

He came rapidly down from the boulevard, remounted his horse, and without another word rode in the direction of the Boulevard St. Martin, where he expected another part of Vaulpergues's company.

There he was seized again with the same anguish of soul. Gaspard de Coligny at this moment resembled a gambler who has staked his fortune upon three casts of the dice: the first cast was lost; what luck awaited him in the second?

Alas! the same cry was heard outside the ramparts, and the same answer made from the town; then, as if this second scene were merely a fatal repetition of the first, a sentinel gave the alarm again, and the rattle of musketry and the heart-rending shrieks told the terrified people of St. Quentin that a second combat—say rather, a second butchery had occurred.

"Two hundred martyrs!" said Coligny, in a grief-stricken voice.

And again throwing himself upon his horse, in two minutes he was at the postern of the faubourg, which was the third of the posts agreed upon between Gabriel and himself. He rode so quickly that he was the first man on the rampart; and his officers joined him there one by one. But listen as eagerly as they might, they could hear nothing but the groans of the dying in the distance and the shouts of the victors.

The admiral thought that all was lost. The enemy's camp was aroused. There could not be a Spanish soldier who was not awake now. He who was in command of the third party might well have thought best not to march right upon such deadly peril, and had probably withdrawn without hazarding a blow. Thus the third and last throw had failed the ruined gambler. Coligny kept saying to himself that very probably the last detachment had been surprised with the second, and that the noise of the two massacres had been combined.

A tear—a burning tear of despair and rage—rolled down the admiral's swarthy cheek. In a few hours the people, discouraged anew by this last calamity, would demand in loud tones that the place be surrendered; and even were they not to make such a demand, Gaspard de Coligny no longer deceived himself with the hope that with troops so exhausted and demoralized as his, the first assault would not open the gates of St. Quentin and of France to the Spaniards. And surely the assault would not be long in coming, and the signal for it would probably be given as soon as day broke, if not even at once during the darkness, while these thirty thousand men, bursting with pride over the slaughter of three hundred, were still drunk with their magnificent exploit.

As if to confirm Coligny's apprehensions, Du Breuil, the governor of the town, uttered the word *alerte* in his ear in a stifled voice; and as he turned toward him, he pointed out a body of men in the moat, dark and noiseless, who seemed to be marching out of the darkness toward the postern.

"Are they friends or foes?" asked Du Breuil, in a low voice.

"Silence!" whispered the admiral; "let us be on our guard in any event."

"How can they make so little noise?" said the governor. "I seem to see horses, and yet there is not a sound, and the very earth seems deadened beneath their steps! Really, they seem like phantoms!"

The superstitious Du Breuil crossed himself as a precautionary measure; but Coligny, grave and thoughtful, carefully watched the dumb black mass without fear and without sign of emotion.

When the new-comers were hardly fifty paces away, Coligny himself mimicked the cry of the osprey.

The hoot of the owl replied.

Thereupon the admiral, beside himself with joy, rushing to the guard at the postern, ordered it to be opened immediately; and a hundred horsemen, enveloped, men and beasts, in ample black cloaks, rode into the town without a sound. Then it could be seen that the hoofs of the horses, which beat so softly upon the ground, were wrapped in pieces of cloth filled with sand. It was due to their adoption of this expedient, which was suggested to them only when the two other detachments had been betrayed by the noise they made, that the third party had succeeded in making their way in unobstructed; and the man who had thought of this expedient, and who was in command of the party, was no other than Gabriel.

It was a small matter, no doubt, this reinforcement of a hundred men; but it would suffice to keep the two threatened positions defended for a few days, and, above all, it was the first happy circumstance of this siege, which had been so fruitful in disasters. The news of such good augury went through the town like the wind. Doors were thrown open, windows illuminated, and universal acclamations welcomed Gabriel and his men as they passed.

"No, no!—no rejoicing," said Gabriel, gravely and sadly. "Remember the two hundred poor fellows who fell down there."

He raised his hat as if to salute the heroic dead, among whom was the noble Vaulpergues.

"Yes," responded Coligny, "we pity them and honor them. But, Monsieur d'Exmès, what shall we say to you? How shall we thank you? At least, my friend, let me fold you in my arms, for you have already twice saved St. Quentin."

But Gabriel, pressing his hand warmly, again rejoined,—

"Monsieur l'Amiral, tell me that in ten days' time."

CHAPTER XXXI
ARNAULD DU THILL'S MEMORY

It was full time that the successful stroke should be accomplished, and the welcome succor be thrown into the town. Day was beginning to break; and Gabriel, completely worn out from having hardly closed his eyes for four days, was taken to the town-hall by the admiral, who gave him the next room to the one he himself occupied. There Gabriel threw himself upon the bed, and slept as if he would never wake.

It was four o'clock in the afternoon before his refreshing slumber, of which the poor youth, with all his anxiety, stood so much in need, was broken by Coligny's entrance. An assault had been made by the enemy during the day and gallantly repulsed, but another was threatened for the next day; and the admiral, who had had every reason thus far to. think well of Gabriel's advice, had come to ask it once more. Gabriel was soon out of bed and ready to receive Coligny.

"Just a word to my squire, Monsieur l'Amiral," said he, "and I am at your service."

"At your convenience, Vicomte d'Exmès," rejoined Coligny. "As the Spanish flag would be flying over this building at this moment but for you, I may well say to you, 'You are at home.'"

Gabriel went to the door, and called Martin-Guerre. He came at once, and Gabriel led him aside.

"My good Martin," said he, "I told you yesterday that I should have hereafter as much confidence in your intelligence as in your loyalty, and I will prove it to you. You must go at once to the ambulance at the Faubourg d'Isle. There you will inquire, not for Madame de Castro, but for the superior of the Benedictines, good Mother Monique; and it is she alone whom you must ask to say to Sister Bénie—you understand, to Sister Bénie—that Vicomte d'Exmès, on a mission at St. Quentin from the king, will call upon her within an hour, and that he entreats her to await him there. You see, Monsieur de Coligny is likely to keep me here some time; and in a matter of life and death, you know, one must always put duty before pleasure. So go, and let her know at least that my heart is with her."

"She shall know it, Monseigneur," said Martin, eagerly; and he was off on the moment, leaving his master somewhat less impatient, as well as easier in his mind.

He made the best of his way to the ambulance at the Faubourg d'Isle, and asked for Sister Monique on all sides with much earnestness of manner.

The superior was pointed out to him.

"Ah, Mother!" said the cunning scamp, approaching her. "I am very glad to find you at last; my poor master would have been so cast down if I had not been able to execute my commission to you and Madame de Castro."

"Who are you, pray, my friend, and whence do you come?" asked the superior, surprised as well as grieved to find that Gabriel had kept so ill the secret she had confided to him.

"I come on behalf of Vicomte d'Exmès," rejoined the false Martin-Guerre, affecting a sort of simple-minded artlessness. "You must know Vicomte d'Exmès, I should think! The whole town is talking of nothing but him."

"To be sure!" said the superior; "I know our deliverer. We have prayed heartily for him. I had the honor of seeing him here yesterday; and I counted on seeing him again to-day after what he said."

"He is coming; yes, his Lordship is coming," continued Arnauld-Martin. "But Monsieur de Coligny delays him; and in his impatience he sent me on in advance to you and to Madame de Castro. Don't be astonished, Mother, that I know that name and pronounce it. Long time loyalty, put to the proof over and over again, justifies my master in trusting as implicitly in me as in himself; and he has no secrets from his trusty and devoted servant. I have only wit and intellect enough, so people say, to love him and protect him; but I have that instinct in good measure, at least, and no one can deny it me, by the relics of Saint Quentin! Oh, pardon me, Mother, for swearing so before you. I didn't realize what I was doing; and habit, you know, and the impulse of the heart—"

"It's all right!" said Mother Monique, smiling; "so Monsieur d'Exmès is coming, is he? He will be very welcome. Sister Bénie is very anxious to see him, to have news of the king, who sent him hither."

"Ha, ha!" Martin laughed in an idiotic way, and said, "The king, who sent him to St. Quentin, but not to Madame Diane, I suppose."

"What do you mean?" asked the superior.

"I say, Madame, that I, who love Vicomte d'Exmès as a master and as a brother, am truly glad that you, a woman so worthy of respect and endowed with such abundant authority, should interest yourself a little in the love-affairs of Monseigneur and Madame de Castro."

"The love-affairs of Madame de Castro!" cried the horrified superior.

"Yes, to be sure," responded the treacherous scoundrel. "Madame Diane must surely have confided everything to you, her real mother and her only friend?"

"She has spoken to me in a vague way of suffering in which her heart was involved," said the nun; "but of an unhallowed love, and of the viscount's name, I know nothing, absolutely nothing."

"Oh, yes, you deny it from modesty, no doubt," rejoined Arnauld, shaking his head very knowingly. "In truth, for my part, I think your conduct is very estimable; and I am very grateful to you for it. You are acting very bravely too! 'Ah!' you said to yourself, 'the king is opposed to the love of these children. Diane's father would be furiously angry if he should suspect that they ever saw each other! Oh, well! I, holy and upright woman that I am, will defy his royal Majesty and his paternal authority, and will lend the poor lovers the sanction of my approval and my character; I will arrange interviews for them, and will give new life to their hope and bid their remorse be still.' Indeed, the assistance you are rendering them is superb, is magnificent, do you understand?"

"Holy Virgin!" was all the superior could say, clasping her hands in terror and amazement, for her heart was timid and her conscience easily alarmed. "Holy Virgin! a father and a king defied, and my name and my life entangled in these intrigues!"

"Hold!" said Arnauld; "I see my master down there now, hurrying to thank you in person for your kind offices, and to ask you, the impatient youth, when and how he can, thanks to you, see his adored mistress once more."

Gabriel did come up at this moment, breathless and eager; but before he reached her side, the superior stopped him with a motion of her hand, and said, drawing herself up to her full height, —

"Not a step farther, and not a word, Monsieur le Vicomte! I know now by what title, and with what intentions, you desire to see Madame de Castro. Do not imagine that hereafter I shall lend a hand to forward your schemes, which are, I fear, unworthy of a gentleman. Besides, not only ought I to decline, but I do not choose, to listen to you any more; furthermore, I intend to use my authority to deprive Diane of every opportunity and every excuse for meeting you, whether in the parlor of the convent or in the ambulances. She is her own mistress, I know, and has not taken the vows which bind her to us; but so long as she thinks fit to remain in the convent, her chosen asylum, she may rely upon my protection to keep her honor safe, and not her love."

With a frigid bow the superior saluted Gabriel, who stood transfixed with astonishment; and then she withdrew without waiting for his reply, and without once turning toward him.

"What does all this mean?" asked the young man of his pretended squire, after a moment of speechless stupefaction.

"I know no more about it than you do, Monseigneur," replied Arnauld, who imposed a mask of consternation upon the delight he really felt. "Madame la Supérieure received me very ill, if I must say so, and declared that she was thoroughly acquainted with your designs, but that it was her duty to oppose them, and to do her best to advance the views of the king, and that Madame Diane no longer loved you, even if she had ever done so."

"Diane loves me no longer!" cried Gabriel, turning pale. "Alas! alas!" he continued, "so much the better perhaps! Meanwhile I wish to see her again, and to prove to her that I am neither indifferent to her nor guilty in her regard. This last interview, which I need to encourage me in my task, it is absolutely necessary that you should help me to obtain, Martin-Guerre."

"Monseigneur knows," replied Arnauld, with humility, "that I am the devoted instrument of his will, and that I obey him in all things, as the hand obeys the head. I will use every effort, as I have done up to this very moment, to procure for Monseigneur the interview which he craves with Madame de Castro."

Thereupon, laughing behind his cape, the crafty scamp followed Gabriel, as he returned in deep dejection to the town-hall.

In the evening, when the false Martin-Guerre, after making a circuit of the fortifications, found himself alone in his room, he drew from his breast a paper which he perused with an appearance of the liveliest satisfaction.

Arnauld du Thill's account with Monsieur le Connétable de Montmorency, from the day when he was forcibly separated from Monseigneur. (This account comprises public as well as private services.)

For having (while held a prisoner after the battle of St. Laurent, and being taken before Philibert Emmanuel) advised that general to release the constable without ransom, upon the specious pretext that Monseigneur would do less harm to the Spaniards with his sword than good by his advice to the king. . . . fifty crowns.

For having escaped by a clever trick from the camp where he was held, and having thus saved Monsieur le Connétable the expense of his ransom, which in his generosity he would not have hesitated to pay in order to recover so faithful and valuable a servant . . . one hundred crowns.

For having skilfully guided by little-known paths the detachment which Vicomte d'Exmès was leading to the relief of St. Quentin and of Monsieur l'Amiral de Coligny, the well-loved nephew of Monsieur le Connétable . . . . twenty livres.

There was more than one other item in Master Arnauld's list quite as impertinently greedy as these. When he had read them all through, he took his pen, and added the following:—

For having, under the name of Martin-Guerre, entered the service of Vicomte d'Exmès, and while in such service denounced said viscount to the superior of the Benedictines as the lover of Madame de Castro, and thus insured the separation of these two young people, according to the best interests of Monsieur le Connétable . . . two hundred crowns.

"That is not very dear," said Arnauld; "and this last item quite outdoes all the others. The sum total is very satisfactory. It amounts nearly to a thousand livres, and with a little imagination we can put it up to two thousand; and when I have my hand on them, *ma foi*! I will go out of business, take a wife, and be a good father to my children, and church-warden of my parish somewhere in the provinces, and thus fulfil the dream of my whole life, and the honorable end of all my wicked deeds."

Arnauld went to bed and slept on these virtuous reflections.

The next day he was commissioned by Gabriel to go in search of Diane once more; and we can guess how he acquitted himself of the commission. Leaving Monsieur de Coligny, Gabriel himself began to investigate and make inquiries. But about ten in the morning the enemy made a furious assault; and he had to hasten to the boulevards. As usual, Gabriel performed prodigies of valor, and acted as if he had two lives to lose.

He did have two to save; besides, if he made himself conspicuous by his gallantry, doubtless Diane would hear his name talked of.

CHAPTER XXXII
THEOLOGY

Gabriel was returning in a state of utter exhaustion from the point where the assault had taken place, with Gaspard de Coligny, when two men, passing very near him, mentioned the name of Sister Bénie. He left the admiral, and running after the men, asked them eagerly if they knew anything of her whose name they had mentioned.

"Oh, *mon Dieu*! no, Captain, no more than yourself," replied one of them, who was no other than Jean Peuquoy. "In fact, I was just expressing some anxiety about her to my companion here; for no one has seen the lovely brave girl all day long, and I was just saying that after such a brisk engagement as we have just had, there are many poor wounded fellows who are much in need of her nursing and her heavenly smile. But we shall soon know if she is seriously ill; for it will be her turn to do night duty with the ambulance to-morrow. She has never missed her turn yet; and there are too few of the nuns, and they relieve one another too frequently, to be willing or able to get along without her except in case of absolute necessity. We shall see her to-morrow evening, then, no doubt; and I shall thank God for one poor invalid's sake, for she knows how to comfort and encourage them like a real Notre Dame."

"Thanks, my friend, thanks!" said Gabriel, pressing Jean Peuquoy's hand warmly, and leaving the good man much surprised at being so honored.

Gaspard de Coligny had heard Jean Peuquoy, and noticed Gabriel's delight. When they were walking together again, he said nothing to him on the subject at first; but when they were once in the house and by themselves in the room where the admiral kept his papers and issued his orders, he said to Gabriel with his pleasant smile, —

"You take a very lively interest, I see, my friend, in this nun, Sister Bénie."

"The same interest that Jean Peuquoy takes," replied Gabriel, blushing; "the same interest that you take yourself, no doubt, Monsieur l'Amiral, for you must have noticed, as I have, how sorely our wounded need her, and what a beneficial influence her words and her very presence exert upon them and upon all the combatants."

"Why do you try to deceive me, my friend?" said the admiral. "You must have very little confidence in me that you try thus to lie to me."

"What, Monsieur l'Amiral!" responded Gabriel, more and more embarrassed; "who has been able to make you believe—"

"That Sister Bénie is no other than Madame Diane de Castro, and that you are deeply in love with her?"

"You know that?" cried Gabriel, amazed beyond measure.

"Why should I not know it?" rejoined the admiral. "Is not Monsieur le Connétable my uncle! Is there anything at court that he doesn't know all about? Has not Madame de Poitiers the king's ear, and has not Monsieur de Montmorency Diane de Poitiers's heart? As very weighty interests of our family are apparently involved in all this, I was naturally informed of the whole business, so that I might be on my guard, and render every aid to forward the schemes of my noble relative. I had not been a day at my post in St. Quentin, to defend the place or to die here, when I received an express from my uncle. It was not, as I supposed at first, to inform me of the movements of the enemy and the constable's proposed operations. By no means! The messenger had risked a thousand dangers to notify me that Madame Diane de Castro, the king's daughter, was at the convent of the Benedictines at St. Quentin under an assumed name, and that I must keep a strict watch over her movements. Then again, yesterday a Flemish messenger, bribed by Monsieur de Montmorency in his captivity, inquired for me at the southern gate. I fancied that he had come from my uncle to tell me to take courage; that it was for me to re-establish the glory of the Montmorencys, sullied by the defeat of St. Laurent; and that the king would infallibly add other reinforcements to those brought hither by you, Gabriel; and that I must in any event die in the breach rather than deliver St. Quentin. But no, no! the purchased messenger came not to bring me any such stirring words to encourage and sustain me; and I was grievously mistaken. The man was only instructed to notify me that Vicomte d'Exmès, who had come in the night before upon the pretence of fighting and dying here, was in love with Madame de Castro, who is betrothed to my cousin, François de

Montmorency, and that the meeting of the lovers might have a bad effect upon the vast plans being matured by my uncle; but that luckily I was governor of St. Quentin, and it was my duty to devote all my energies to the task of keeping Madame Diane and Gabriel d'Exmès apart; and, above all, to prevent their having any conversation together, and thus to contribute to the elevation and power of my house!"

All this was said with a bitterness and melancholy that were very perceptible; but Gabriel thought of nothing but the blow aimed at his hopes.

"And so, Monsieur," he said to the admiral, with bitter anger at his heart, "it was you who denounced me to the superior of the Benedictines, and who, faithful to your uncle's instructions, count, no doubt, upon taking from me, one by one, all the chances which I may still have of finding Diane and seeing her again."

"Hold your peace, young man!" cried the admiral, with an unspeakably proud expression. "But I forgive you," he added more gently; "for your passion blinds you, and you have not yet had time to know Gaspard de Coligny."

There was so much noble and dignified kindness in the tone in which these words were uttered that all Gabriel's suspicions vanished like mist, and he was deeply ashamed that he had entertained them for one moment.

"Pardon me!" he said, stretching out his hand to Gaspard. "How could I ever have thought that you would allow yourself to be led into such intrigues? A thousand pardons, Monsieur l'Amiral!"

"Oh, it's all right, Gabriel!" rejoined Coligny; "and I know that your impulses are youthful and pure. No, indeed, I do not mingle in such underhand practices; on the contrary, I despise them and those who have conceived them. In such performances I can see no glory, but only shame for my family; and far from wishing to profit by them, I blush at them. If these men, who build up their fortune by such means, scandalous or not; who, in their haste to gratify their ambition and their greed, never heed the sorrow and the desolation of those who are as good as they; who would even, to arrive a little sooner at their goal, pass over the dead body of their mother-land,—if these men are my kinsmen, it must be the punishment which God inflicts upon me for my pride, and with which He recalls me to humility; it is an encouragement to me to show myself harsh toward myself and just to my neighbors, as a means of redeeming the sins of my relatives."

"Yes," rejoined Gabriel, "I know that the honor and virtue of the days of the apostles dwell in your breast, Monsieur l'Amiral; and I beg your pardon once more for having for one moment spoken to you as to one of the fine gentlemen without faith or law whom I have learned too well to despise and detest."

"Alas!" said Coligny, "we should rather pity them,—these poor fools who are ambitious of nothing, these wretched, blinded Papists. But," he continued, "I forget that I am not speaking to one of my brothers in religious matters. Never mind, Gabriel; you are worthy of being one of us, and you will come to us sooner or later. Yes; God, in whose hands all means are holy, will lead you to the right, I foresee, through this very passion; and this unequal conflict in which your love will cause you to hurl yourself against a corrupt court will end in bringing you into our ranks some day. I shall be happy to sow in your breast, my friend, the first seeds of the divine harvest."

"I knew, Monsieur l'Amiral," said Gabriel, "that you were of the Reformed religion; and that very fact has led me to esteem the persecuted sect. Nevertheless, you see, I am weak in mind, being feeble in heart; and I am sure that I shall always profess the same religion that Diane does."

"Oh, well!" said Gaspard, in whom, as in most of his sect, the fever of proselytism was at its height,—"oh, well! if Madame de Castro is of the religion of virtue and truth, she is of our faith, and so will you be, Gabriel. So will you be, I say again, because that dissolute court, rash youth, against which you are taking up arms, will overcome you; and you will burn to be revenged. Do you believe that Monsieur de Montmorency, who has set his heart upon the king's daughter for his son, will consent to give up that rich prize to you?"

"Alas! perhaps I shall not dispute it with him," said Gabriel. "Only let the king remain true to his sworn promise to me—"

"Sworn promise!" exclaimed the admiral. "Do you talk of sworn promises in connection with the man who, after he had commanded the parliament to discuss the question of liberty of conscience freely before him, had Anne Dubourg and Dufaur burned at the stake for having pleaded the cause of the reform, relying upon the royal word?"

"Oh, don't say so, Monsieur l'Amiral!" cried Gabriel. "Don't tell me that King Henri will not keep the solemn promise that he has given me; for in that event not my faith alone would rise in rebellion, but my sword too, I fear: I would not become a Huguenot, but a murderer."

"Not if you become a Huguenot," rejoined Gaspard. "We may be martyrs, but shall never be assassins. But your vengeance, though it be not a bloody one, may be none the less terrible, my friend. You will assist us with your youthful ardor and your zealous devotion in a work of renovation which is likely to be more depressing to the king than a thrust of the sword. Remember, Gabriel, that it is our purpose to wrest from him his iniquitous and monstrous privileges; remember that it is not in the Church alone, but in the government that we are striving to introduce reforms which will be helpful to the worthy, but a menace to the wicked. You have seen whether I love France and serve her. Well, then, I am for these reforms partly because I see in them the true greatness of my country. Oh, Gabriel, Gabriel, if you had but read once the convincing arguments of our Luther, you would see how soon the spirit of investigation and liberty which breathes in them would put a new soul in your body, and open a new life before you."

"My life is my love for Diane," was Gabriel's response; "and my soul is in the sacred task which God has imposed upon me, and which I trust to accomplish."

"The love and the task of a man," said Gaspard, "which may surely be reconciled with the love and the task of a Christian. You are young, and do not see clearly, my friend; but I foresee only too plainly, and my heart bleeds to say it to you, that your eyes will be opened by misfortune. Your generosity and your purity of soul will sooner or later bring grief upon you in that licentious and scandalous court, just as tall trees attract the lightning in a storm. Then you will call to mind what I have said to you to-day. You will learn to know our books,—this one, for instance;" and the admiral took up a volume that was lying open on the table. "You will understand these outspoken and stern, but just and noble words, which are spoken to us by one as young as yourself, a councillor of the Bordeaux parliament, named Étienne de la Boétie. And then you will say, Gabriel, in the words of this vigorous work, 'La Servitude Volontaire': 'What a misfortune, or what a crime it is to see an infinite number of men not obeying, but servilely following,—not being governed, but tyrannized over by one individual, and not by a Hercules or a Samson, but by one little man, generally the most faint-hearted and effeminate in the whole land.'"

"Those are indeed not only dangerous, but bold words, and stimulating to the intellect," said Gabriel. "You are quite right, too, Monsieur l'Amiral; it may be that rage will some day drive me into your ranks, and that oppression will lead me to espouse the cause of the oppressed. But until that time comes, you see, my life is too full to admit these new ideas which you have laid before me; and I have too much to do to leave me time to read books."

Nevertheless, Gaspard de Coligny continued to urge upon him warmly the doctrines and ideas which were then fermenting in his mind like new wine, and the conversation was prolonged to great length between the passionate young man and his earnest elder,—the one as determined and impetuous as action, the other grave and serious as thought.

Moreover, the admiral was hardly at fault in his gloomy forebodings; and misfortune was preparing to fertilize the seeds which this interview had sown in Gabriel's ardent soul.

CHAPTER XXXIII
SISTER BÉNIE

It was a calm and beautiful August evening. In the sky, which was of a deep blue studded with stars, the moon had not yet risen; but the night was so much the more full of mystery, more dreamy, and more enchanting.

This mild tranquillity was in striking contrast with the commotion and uproar which had lasted through the day. The Spaniards had made two assaults in quick succession, and had been twice beaten back; but not before they had killed and wounded a larger number than the few defenders of the town could afford to lose. The enemy, on the other hand, had a strong reserve of fresh troops to replace those who were wearied in the contests of the day. So that Gabriel, always on his guard, feared that the two assaults were intended simply to exhaust the strength of the garrison and relax their vigilance, and that a third assault or a nocturnal surprise might have more chance of success. Meanwhile ten o'clock struck from La Collégiale, and nothing took place to confirm his suspicions. Not a light was to be seen among the Spanish tents. In the camp, as in the town, nothing could be heard but the monotonous cry of the sentinels; and the camp itself, like the town, seemed to be reposing after the severe labors of the day.

Consequently Gabriel, after making one last tour of the fortifications, thought that he might for a moment relax the unintermitted watch which he had kept over the town, like a son over his dying mother. St. Quentin had already held out four days since the young man's arrival. Four days more, and he will have kept the promise he made the king; and it will remain only for the king to be true to his.

Gabriel had ordered his squire to attend him, but without saying where he was going. Since his ill-luck of a day or two before with the superior, he had begun to have some suspicions of Martin-Guerre's intelligence, if not of his loyalty. So he had forborne to tell him of the precious information he had procured from Jean Peuquoy; and the false Martin-Guerre, who supposed he was accompanying his master merely on a circuit of the walls, was surprised to see him turn his steps toward the Boulevard de la Reine, where the principal ambulance had been established.

"Are you going to see some wounded man, Monseigneur?" said he.

"Silence!" was Gabriel's only reply, placing his finger to his lips.

The principal ambulance, which Gabriel and Arnauld reached at this moment, was quite near the ramparts, and not far from the Faubourg d'Isle, which was the most dangerous point, and the one consequently where relief was most essential. It was a large building which had been used before the siege as a storehouse for provisions, but had been placed at the disposal of the surgeons when the need became urgent. The mild summer night made it possible to leave the door in the centre open, to renew and freshen the air. From the foot of the steps, which led up to an outside gallery, Gabriel was able to look into this abode of suffering, where lamps were always kept burning.

It was a heart-rending spectacle. Here and there were a few blood-stained beds prepared in great haste; but such luxuries were reserved for the privileged few. The greater part were stretched on the floor, on mattresses or coverlets, or in some cases on straw simply. Sharp or plaintive moans were continually calling the surgeons or their assistants from all sides; but they, in spite of their zeal, could not hear them all. They attended to dressing those wounds which were most in need of it, and performed the most pressing amputations; the others had to wait. The trembling of fever or the convulsions of agony made the poor wretches twist and turn on their pallets; and where in some corner one of them lay at full length, motionless and without a sound, the winding-sheet laid upon his face told only too plainly that he would nevermore move or complain.

Before this sad and heart-rending picture the strongest and hardest hearts would have lost their courage and their callousness. Even Arnauld du Thill could not repress a shudder; and Gabriel's face became as pale as death.

But all at once a sad smile appeared upon the young man's pallid countenance. In the midst of this Inferno overflowing with suffering, like that described by Dante, a calm and radiant angel, a sweet and lovely Beatrix, burst upon his sight. Diane, Sister Bénie rather, passed tranquilly and sadly in and out among these poor sufferers.

Never had she seemed more beautiful to the dazzled Gabriel. Indeed, at the fêtes of the court, gold and diamonds and velvet did not so well become her as did the coarse woollen dress and white nun's stomacher in that dismal ambulance. With her lovely profile, her modest demeanor, and her look of consolation and encouragement, she might have been taken for the very incarnation of Pity, descending to this home of suffering. The most vivid imagination of a Christian soul could not picture her in more admirable guise; and nothing could be so affecting as to see this peerless beauty lean over the emaciated faces disfigured by anguish, and this king's child holding out her lovely hand to these nameless, dying soldiers.

Gabriel involuntarily thought of Madame Diane de Poitiers, engrossed at that moment, no doubt, with extravagant trifling and shameless amours; and marvelling at the marked contrast between the two Dianes, he said to himself that God had surely endowed the daughter with such virtues to redeem the faults of the mother.

While Gabriel, who was not ordinarily addicted to the habit of dreaming, thus lost himself in his reflections and his comparisons without taking heed of the flight of time, within the ambulance quiet gradually succeeded to the former confusion. The evening was already well advanced; the surgeons completed their rounds; and the bustle and the noise ceased. Silence and repose were enjoined upon the wounded men; and soothing draughts made it easier for them to obey the injunction. Here and there a pitiful moan would be heard, but no more of the almost incessant, heart-rending shrieks of pain. Before another quarter of an hour had elapsed, everything became as calm and quiet as such suffering can be.

Diane had said her last words of comfort and hope to her patients, and had urged rest and patience upon them after the physicians, and more effectively than they. All did their best to obey her voice, so sweet in its imperiousness. When she saw that the prescriptions ordered for each one were at hand, and that for the moment there was no further need of her, she drew a long breath, as if to relieve her breast from its oppressive burden, and drew near the exterior gallery, meaning, no doubt, to take a breath or two of fresh air at the door, and to obtain a little surcease of the wretchedness and weakness of man by gazing upon the stars in God's heaven.

She leaned upon a sort of stone balustrade; and her look, bent upward to the sky, failed to perceive at the foot of the steps, and within ten feet of her, Gabriel in a perfect ecstasy of delight at the sight of her, as if he were standing before some heavenly apparition.

A sharp movement on the part of Martin-Guerre, who did not seem to share in his ecstasy, brought our lover back to earth again.

"Martin," said he, in a low voice to his squire, "you see what a marvellous chance is within my grasp. I must and will take advantage of it, and speak—alas! perhaps for the last time—to Madame Diane. Do you meanwhile see that no one interrupts us, and keep watch a little apart, remaining nevertheless within call. Go, my faithful fellow; go."

"But, Monseigneur," Martin began to object, "are you not afraid that Madame la Supérieure—"

"She is in another room probably," said Gabriel. "At all events, I must not hesitate, in view of the necessity which may hereafter separate us forever."

Martin seemed to yield, and moved away, swearing to himself.

Gabriel drew a little nearer Diane; and restraining his voice so as to arouse the attention of no one else, he called her name softly,—

"Diane! Diane!"

Diane was startled; and her eyes, which had hardly got used to the darkness, did not detect Gabriel at first.

"Did some one call me?" she said. "Who is it?"

"I," Gabriel replied, as if Medea's monosyllable were enough to reveal his identity to her.

In good sooth it was; for Diane, without pursuing her inquiries any further, rejoined in a voice trembling with feeling and surprise:—

"You, Monsieur d'Exmès! Is it really you? And what do you want of me in this place and at this hour? If, as I have been told, you bring me news of the king my father, you have delayed it long, and you have chosen place and time very ill; if not, you know that there is nothing I can listen to from you, and nothing I want to hear. Well, Monsieur d'Exmès, you do not reply. Do you not understand me? You say nothing? What does this silence mean, Gabriel?"

"'Gabriel!' It is well with us, then!" cried the youth. "I made no reply, Diane, because your cold words froze my blood, and because I hadn't the strength to call you 'Madame,' as you called me 'Monsieur.'"

"Do not call me 'Madame,' and call me 'Diane' no more. Madame de Castro is no longer here. It is Sister Bénie who stands before you. Call me 'sister,' and I will call you my brother."

"What! What do you say?" cried Gabriel, recoiling in terror. "I call you my sister! Why in God's name do you ask me to call you my sister?"

"Why, it is the name by which every one knows me now," said Diane. "Is it such a terrible name, pray?"

"Yes, yes, indeed it is! Or rather, no! Forgive me; I am mad. It is a lovely and dear name. I will accustom myself to it, Diane; I will accustom myself to it—my sister."

"You must," Diane responded with a sad smile. "Besides, it is the real Christian title which will be suitable for me henceforth; for although I have not yet taken the vows, I am even now a nun at heart, and I soon shall be one in fact, I hope, when I shall have obtained the king's consent. Do you bring me that consent, my brother?"

"Oh!" exclaimed Gabriel, in a tone wherein reproach and grief were mingled.

"*Mon Dieu!*" said Diane, "there is not the least bitterness in my words, I assure you. I have suffered so much recently among men that I have naturally sought shelter with God. It is not anger which rules my actions and my words, but sorrow."

Indeed, there was in Diane's speech an accent that told of sadness and suffering; and yet in her heart that sadness was mingled with an involuntary joy which she could not conceal at the sight of Gabriel, whom she had long ago believed to be lost to her love and to the world, and whom she found to-day vigorous and manly, and, it might be, still fond of her.

And so, without wishing, almost without knowing it, she had descended two or three steps, and drawn on by an invincible power, had come so much nearer to Gabriel.

"Listen," said he. "This cruel misunderstanding which is rending our hearts must come to an end. I can no longer bear the thought that you do not understand me, that you believe in my indifference to you or (who knows?) in my hatred for you. That terrible suspicion worries me even in the midst of the sacred and difficult task which it is for me to accomplish. But come a little apart, my sister. You still trust in me, do you not? Let us move away from this spot, I beg you. Even if we cannot be seen, we may be overheard; and I have reason to fear that some one may desire to interrupt our interview,—this interview which, I tell you, my sister, is essential to my reason and my peace of mind."

Diane reflected no longer. Such words from such lips were omnipotent with her. She ascended two steps to look into the hall and see if she was needed; and finding everything quiet, she at once went back to Gabriel, resting her hand confidingly in the loyal one of her faithful knight.

"Thanks," said Gabriel. "Moments are precious; for what I fear, do you know, is that the superior, who knows of my love now, would object to our having this explanation, deep and pure though my love for you is, my sister."

"That explains, then," said Diane, "why, after having told me of your arrival and of your wish to see me, good Mother Monique, informed by some one, no doubt, of the past, which I confess I had partly concealed from her, has kept me from leaving the convent for three days, and would have kept me in this evening too if my turn to do night duty in the ambulance had not arrived, and I had not insisted upon fulfilling my sad duty. Oh, Gabriel, is it not wrong in me to deceive her,—my sweet and venerable friend?"

"Must I then tell you again that with me it is as if you were with your brother, alas! that I ought to and will hush the impulses of my heart, and speak to you only as a friend should speak, but a friend who is ever devoted to you, and would gladly die for you, but who will listen to his melancholy rather than his love, never fear?"

"Speak, then, my brother!" said Diane.

"My brother!"—that horrible and yet delightful name always reminded Gabriel of the strange and mysterious alternative which his destiny had laid before him, and like a magic word drove away the burning thoughts which the silent night and the ravishing beauty of his beloved might well have awakened in the young man's heart.

"My sister," said he, in a steady voice, "it was absolutely necessary that I should see you and speak with you, so that I might address two prayers to you. One relates to the past, the other to the future. You are kind and obliging, Diane; and I know you will grant them both to a dear friend who may perhaps never meet you more on his path through life, and whom a fatal and perilous mission exposes to the risk of death at every moment."

"Oh, don't say that! don't say that!" cried Madame de Castro, almost fainting, and proving the extent of her love in her distraction and horror at the thought.

"I say it to you, my sister," Gabriel responded, "not to alarm you, but that you may not refuse me a pardon and a favor. The pardon is for the terror and grief which my delirious utterances must have caused you the day when I saw you last at Paris. I cast terror and desolation into your poor heart. Alas, my sister, it was not I who spoke to you; it was the fever in my blood. I did not know what I said, upon my word! And a terrible revelation, which had been made to me that very day, and which I could scarcely keep to myself, filled my soul with madness and despair. Perhaps you remember, my sister, that it was just after leaving you that I was stricken with that long and painful illness which almost cost me my life or my reason?"

"Do I remember it, Gabriel!" cried Diane.

"Do not call me Gabriel, if you please! Call me always your brother, as you did just now,—call me your brother! That name, which terrified me at first, I find it necessary to hear now."

"As you choose, my brother," said Diane, with amazement.

At that moment, fifty paces from them, the regular tramp of a body of men on the march was heard, and Sister Bénie, full of terror, pressed close to Gabriel.

"Who is that? *Mon Dieu*! they will see us!" she exclaimed.

"It is one of our patrols," answered Gabriel, much disturbed.

"But they will pass very near us, and will recognize me or hail us. Oh, let me go in, quick, before they come any nearer! Let me go, I pray!"

"No; it is too late!" said Gabriel, detaining her. "To attempt to fly now would be to expose yourself. Come this way, rather,—come up here, my sister!"

And followed by the trembling Diane, he hastily mounted a stairway, hidden by a stone buttress, which led to the very walls. There he ensconced Diane and himself between an untenanted sentry-box and the battlements.

The patrol passed within twenty paces without seeing them.

"Well, this certainly is a poorly guarded point!" said Gabriel, in whom his dominant thought was always on the alert.

But his mind at once reverted to Diane, who was hardly at her ease yet.

"You may feel safe now, my sister," said he; "the danger is over. But now listen to me, for time passes, and my two burdens are still heavy on my heart. In the first place, you have not told me that you forgive my madness, and so I am still carrying this weary load of the past."

"Does one forgive the madness of fever and the ravings of despair?" said Diane. "No, my brother, we must pity and comfort them rather. I bore you no ill-will; no, I wept for you. And now that I see that you are restored to life and reason, I am resigned to the will of God."

"Ah, my sister, it is not resignation alone that you should feel!" cried Gabriel; "you must be hopeful too. That is why I was anxious to see you. You have lifted my burden of remorse for the past, and I thank you; but you must also remove the weight of anguish which weighs upon my heart for your future. You are, as you well know, one of the principal objects for which I live. It is necessary that my mind should be tranquillized as to that object, so that I may only have to concern myself, as I go my way, with the perils of the road; it must be that I may count upon finding you waiting for me at the end of my journey with a welcoming smile, sad if I fail, and joyous if I succeed, but in any event with the welcoming smile of a friend. With that object in view, there should be no misunderstanding between us. Meanwhile, my sister, it will be necessary that you should trust my word, and have a little confidence in me; for the secret which lies at the root of all my actions does not belong to me. I have sworn not to reveal it; and if I wish that the promises made to me should be kept, I must in my turn keep the promises that I have made to others."

"Explain yourself," said Diane.

"Ah," rejoined Gabriel, "you see how I hesitate and beat around the bush, because I am thinking of the garb that you wear, and of the name of sister, by which I am calling you, and, more than all else, of the profound respect for you that dominates my heart; and I do not wish to say one word to awake distressing memories or elusive hopes. And yet I must say to you that your beloved image has never been effaced, has never even faded in my soul, and that no person and no event can ever weaken it."

"My brother!" Diane interrupted, confused and delighted at the same time.

"Oh, hear me to the end, my sister!" said Gabriel. "I say again, nothing has changed, and nothing will ever change, this ardent—devotion which I have consecrated to you; and more than that, I am only too happy to think and to say that whatever happens to me, it will always be not only my blessed privilege, but my bounden duty, to love you. But what is the nature of this sentiment? God only knows, alas! but we shall soon know too, I hope. Meanwhile, this is what I have to ask of you, my sister: trusting in the Lord and your father, do you leave everything to Providence and my friendship, hoping nothing, but not despairing either. Understand me, pray! You told me long ago that you loved me; and pardon my presumption, but I seem to feel in my heart that you can love me still if our fate so wills. Now, my wish is to lessen the too distressing effect of my mad words when I parted from you at the Louvre. We must not deceive ourselves with vain imaginings, nor, on the other hand, believe that everything is over for us in this world. We must wait. In a short time I shall come to you and say one of two things. Either this: 'Diane, I love you; remember our childhood and your promises. You must be mine, Diane; and we must resort to every possible means to obtain the king's consent.' Or else I shall say to you: 'My sister, an irresistible fatality stands in the way of our love, and opposes our happiness; we are in no way to blame for it, and it is something more than human—yes, almost divine—which stands between us, my sister. I give you back your promise; you are free. Give your life to another; you cannot be blamed for it, nor even, alas! are you to be pitied. No; our tears, even, would be out of place. Let us bow our heads without a word, and accept with resignation our inevitable destiny. You will always be dear and holy in my eyes; but our two lives, which may still, thank God! be lived side by side, can never be united.'"

"What a strange and fearful enigma!" Madame de Castro, lost in terrified thought, could not refrain from saying.

"An enigma," responded Gabriel, "of which I can give you the key-word at that time, no doubt. Until then it will be in vain that you seek to discover the secret, my sister; so be patient, and pray. Promise me, at least, that you believe in my loyalty to you, and that you will no longer cherish the purpose of renouncing the world to bury yourself in a cloister. Promise me that you will have faith and hope, even as you have already had charity."

"Faith in you and hope in God; yes, I can readily promise that now, my brother. But why do you wish me to promise to return to the world if I am not to go thither in your company? Is not my heart enough? And why do you wish that I should give my life to you as well, when, after all, it may not be to you that I devote it? Within and without, everything is dark, O God!"

"Sister," said Gabriel, in his deep, solemn tones, "I ask this promise of you that I may go forward in peace of mind and resolution upon my perilous and perhaps fatal path, and that I may be sure of finding you free and waiting for me at the rendezvous which I have appointed for you."

"Very well, my brother; and I will obey you," said Diane.

"Oh, thanks, thanks!" cried Gabriel. "Now the future belongs to me. Will you place your hand in mine as a pledge of your promise, my sister?"

"Here it is, my brother."

"Ah, now I am sure of being victorious!" cried the impetuous youth. "Henceforth it seems to me as if nothing could contravene my wishes and my plans."

At this moment, as if to give the lie twice over to this hopeful dream, voices were heard from the direction of the town calling Sister Bénie; and at the same time Gabriel thought that he heard a slight noise in the moat behind him. But at first he concerned himself only with Diane's terror.

"They are looking for me and calling me. Holy Virgin! if they should find us together! Adieu, my brother! Adieu, Gabriel!"

"*Au revoir*, my sister; *au revoir*, Diane! And now go! I will stay here. You wandered out by yourself to take the air. We shall meet soon again; and once more I thank you."

Diane hastily descended the steps and ran to meet the people, who with torches in their hands were calling her name everywhere with all their might, Mother Monique at their head.

Who, by seemingly foolish hints, had aroused the superior? Who, if not Master Arnauld, who with the most grief-stricken air was among those who were hunting for Sister Bénie? No one had such an ingenuous air as this rascal could assume, wherein he resembled the true Martin-Guerre so much the more.

Gabriel, reassured as to Diane's safety when he saw her join Mother Monique and her search-party unharmed, was making ready to leave the fortifications himself, when suddenly a dark form rose from the ground behind him.

A man, an enemy, armed from head to foot, was just bestriding the wall.

To rush at this man and prostrate him with one blow of his sword, crying in a sonorous voice, "Alarm! alarm!" to spring to the top of the ladder, covered with Spaniards, which was placed against the wall,—was the work of but an instant for Gabriel.

It was an attempted night surprise, and Gabriel had not erred: the enemy had made the two day assaults in quick succession to enable them to make this bold attempt at night with better chance of success.

But Providence or, to speak more accurately, if perhaps with less religious feeling, love had led Gabriel to the spot. Before another man had time to follow upon the platform the one he had already killed, he seized with his strong hands the two uprights of the ladder and overturned it, with the ten men who were upon it.

Their cries as they struck the ground were confused with Gabriel's unceasing shouts, "To arms!" But at a distance of twenty paces another ladder was already against the wall; and at that point there was no footing for Gabriel. Luckily he spied in the shadow a large rock; and the imminent peril increasing his strength, he succeeded in raising it upon the parapet, whence he had only to push it over upon the second ladder. The great weight broke it in two at a blow; and the poor wretches who were swarming up fell into the moat, bruised or dying, their agonizing shrieks causing their companions to hesitate.

Meanwhile Gabriel's shouts had given the alarm; the sentinels had taken it up; the drums were beating to arms; the alarm-bell on La Collégiale was ringing lustily. Five minutes had not elapsed ere more than a hundred men had joined Vicomte d'Exmès, and were ready to assist him in repulsing any assailants who might still dare to show their heads, and likewise firing upon those who were in the moat, and unable to respond to the volleys from their arquebuses.

Thus this bold *coup de main* of the Spaniards failed. Its only chance of success, in truth, was to find that the point of attack was undefended, as they supposed that it was; but Gabriel, happening to be on the spot, had baffled their scheme. The assaulting party had no choice but to withdraw, which they did as quickly as possible, leaving, however, a number of dead behind them, and carrying away a number of injured men.

Again the town had been saved, and again by Gabriel's hand.

But it was necessary that it should still hold out for four long and weary days, before the promise he had made to the king would be fulfilled.

CHAPTER XXXIV
A VICTORIOUS DEFEAT

The first effect of the unexpected check they had received was to discourage the besiegers; and they seemed to realize that they could never gain possession of the town except by dealing with the remaining resources of resistance one by one, and thus making each of them unavailable. For three days they made no fresh assault; but all their batteries were kept in play, and all their mines were working without rest or intermission. The men who defended the place, seemingly endowed with more than human energy and courage, appeared to be invincible; the Spaniards assailed the walls, and found them less solid than the breasts of those who manned them. The towers crumbled; the trenches were filled with the debris; and the fortifications were levelled, bit by bit.

At last, four days after the abortive night attack, the Spaniards once more hazarded an assault. It was the eighth and last day of the allotted time. If the attack of the enemy was unsuccessful once more, Gabriel would have saved his father as well as the town; if not, all his trouble and all his labor had been thrown away, and the old man, Diane, and himself would be all lost.

Therefore it can well be imagined that it would be more than impossible to describe the superhuman, god-like valor and courage displayed by him on that day of days. One would hardly have believed that so much strength and untiring vigor could exist in the soul and body of one man. He saw not danger or death, but thought only of his father and his betrothed; and he hurled himself against the pikes, and moved hither and thither amid the thickly flying cannon-balls and bullets as if he were invulnerable. A piece of stone struck him in the side, and a lance-head in the face; but he felt not the wounds. He seemed intoxicated with daring; he ran to and fro, waving his sword, and encouraging his men not only with his words, but by his example. He was to be seen wherever the peril was most imminent. As the soul gives life to the whole body, so did he to the whole town. He was in himself ten men, twenty, —yes, a hundred; and yet in his superb exaltation his coolness and clear-headedness never failed him. With a glance swifter than light he saw where danger threatened, and was on the spot in the twinkling of an eye; and when the assailants fell back, and our brave fellows, electrified by his contagious gallantry, had clearly regained the advantage, like a flash Gabriel was off to some other threatened point, and began again his heroic work, an utter stranger to weariness or weakness.

This lasted six hours, from one o'clock to seven.

At seven it grew dark; and the Spaniards fell back on all sides. Behind a few crumbling pieces of stone-work, with a few fragments of towers and a handful of exhausted and wounded soldiers, St. Quentin had again added one day more, several days, it might be, to the record of her glorious resistance.

When the last man of the enemy had left the last of the points of assault, Gabriel fell back into the arms of those who were near him, utterly worn out with fatigue and with joy.

They bore him in triumph to the town-hall.

His wounds were but slight, and his swoon could not be of long duration. When he regained his senses, Admiral de Coligny was at his side, his face radiant with pleasure.

"Monsieur l'Amiral," were Gabriel's first words, "it's not a dream, is it? There has been a fierce assault to-day, which we succeeded in repelling?"

"Yes, my friend, and thanks to you in great measure," replied Gaspard.

"And the week that the king allotted me has passed!" cried Gabriel. "Oh, thank God! thank God!"

"And to complete your satisfaction, my dear fellow," rejoined the admiral, "I bring you some glorious news. Under cover of our obstinate defence of St. Quentin, the preparations for the defence of the whole kingdom have apparently been perfected; one of my spies, who succeeded in seeing the constable and entering the town again during the confusion to-day, has given me every reason to hope for the best in that regard. Monsieur de Guise has arrived at Paris with the Italian army, and in concert with the Cardinal de Lorraine, is engaged in raising men, and putting towns in a posture of defence. St. Quentin, in her dismantled and depopulated condition, could not beat back another assault; but her work and ours is done, and France is saved, my friend. Yes, behind our faithful ramparts every one is under arms: the nobility and all the orders of the State have arisen; recruits abound; the free gifts from the clergy are pouring in; and two troops of German auxiliaries have been retained. When the enemy shall have made an end of us, and that cannot now be long delayed unfortunately, he will at least find others ready to challenge him. France is saved, Gabriel!"

"Ah, Monsieur l'Amiral, you cannot imagine how much good you have done me," Gabriel responded. "But allow me to ask one question; it is from no vain feeling of conceit that I ask it; you know me too well now to believe that. No, there is beneath my question a very serious and very deep meaning, believe me. Monsieur l'Amiral, in two words, do you think that my presence here during the last week has counted for anything in the fortunate result of the siege of St. Quentin?"

"For everything, my friend, for everything!" the admiral replied with generous frankness. "The day of your arrival you saw yourself that except for your unexpected intervention I should have yielded; that my courage was giving way under the terrible weight of responsibility with which my conscience was burdened; and that I should then have delivered to the Spaniard the keys of this city with which the king had intrusted me. The next day did you not succeed in carrying out your undertaking of throwing reinforcements into the town,—weak reinforcements, to be sure, but sufficient nevertheless to rekindle the courage of the besieged? I say nothing of the sagacious advice which you gave to our miners and engineers. I say nothing of the superb gallantry which you have displayed all the time and at all points during every assault. But who almost miraculously saved the town from being surprised by a night attack four days since? And this very day, who, with unheard-of temerity and success, succeeded in prolonging still farther a resistance which I confess I believed to be impossible? You, always you, my friend, who, being everywhere present and unfailingly ready at every corner of the fortifications, seemed in very truth to have acquired the angels' gift of ubiquity; so that our soldiers know no other name for you than Captain *Five-Hundred*, Gabriel, I say to you with sincere delight and profound gratitude that you are the first and sole deliverer of this town, and consequently of France."

"Oh, many, many thanks, Monsieur l'Amiral, for your too kind and flattering words! But pardon me! are you willing to repeat them in his Majesty's presence?"

"It is not my wish simply, my friend," the admiral replied; "it is my duty; and you know that Gaspard de Coligny never proves recreant to his duty."

"What good fortune!" said Gabriel; "and what do I not owe you for it, Monsieur l'Amiral? But are you willing to make my obligation still greater? Say nothing to any one, I beseech you, not even to Monsieur le Connétable, in fact, to any one rather than to him, of what I have been able to do to assist you in your glorious task. Let the king alone know it. His Majesty will see from that I was influenced by no thirst for glory or for reputation, but only by my wish to keep a promise I made to him; and it lies in his power to give me, if he chooses, a reward a thousand times more precious in my sight than all the honors and dignities of his realm. Yes, Monsieur l'Amiral, let this reward but be bestowed upon me, and Henri's debt to me, if debt there be, will be paid a hundred times over."

"It should be a magnificent recompense, then," rejoined the admiral. "God grant that the king's gratitude may not disappoint you! However, I will do as you wish, Gabriel; and although it costs me a pang to keep silent as to your deserts, since you ask me, I will say nothing."

"Ah!" cried Gabriel, "what a long and weary time it has been since I have felt such peace as reigns in my heart at this moment! How pleasant it is to be able to hope and believe, even though it be but a little, in the future! Now I will go upon the walls and fight with a light heart, and it seems as if I should be unconquerable. Can it be that iron or lead will dare to wound a man in whose heart hope is born?"

"Do not rely too much upon that, my friend, I pray you!" said Coligny, smiling. "For I can already say to you without hesitation that you are deceived by your conviction of victory. The town is almost entirely open on all sides; a few cannon-balls will soon level the last fragments of her walls and her towers. More than that, we have scarcely one able-bodied man left; and the troops who have so gallantly supplied the place of fortifications hitherto are now in their turn lacking. The next assault will make the enemy masters of the place; and we must cherish no delusions in that direction."

"But may it not be that Monsieur de Guise will send us reinforcements from Paris?" asked Gabriel.

"Monsieur de Guise," Gaspard answered, "will not expose his precious forces for the sake of a town three quarters taken; and he will be quite right. Let him keep his men in the heart of France, for there they are most needed. St. Quentin is sacrificed. The expiatory victim has struggled long enough, thank God! and it only remains for her to fall nobly; and in that we will try still to help her, will we not, Gabriel? We must make the triumph of the

Spaniard before St. Quentin cost him more than a defeat. We will fight no longer for our own salvation, but for the sake of fighting."

"Yes, yes, for pleasure, for sport!" said Gabriel, joyfully,—"a hero's pleasure, Monsieur l'Amiral, and sport worthy of you! Well, then, so be it! let us amuse ourselves by holding the town two or three or four days more, if we can. Let us hold Philip II., Philibert Emmanuel, Spain, England, and Flanders all in check before a few pieces of crumbling stone. It will be a little more time gained for Monsieur de Guise, and an entertaining spectacle for us. What do you say?"

"I say, my friend, that your pleasantry is sublime, and that there is glory hidden in your jokes."

The event justified the hope of Gabriel and Coligny. In fact, Philip II. and his general, Philibert Emmanuel, being furiously indignant at being delayed so long before one town, and at having already made ten fruitless assaults, determined not to hazard an eleventh without being assured of success. As they had done before, they allowed three days to pass without an assault, and made use of their batteries instead of their soldiers, since it had been abundantly proved that in that heroic town the walls were not so enduring and steadfast as the hearts of its defenders. The admiral and Vicomte d'Exmès spent the three days in having the damage inflicted by the batteries and mines repaired as fast as possible by their workmen; but unfortunately arms were wanting. On the 26th of August, at noon, not a single section of the walls remained standing. The houses were left without protection, as in an open town, and the soldiers were so few that they could not even form a single line at the principal posts.

Gabriel himself had to admit this; and before the signal for the assault was given,—the town was apparently at the besiegers' mercy.

At all events it was not taken at the breach defended by Gabriel. With him there were Monsieur du Breuil and Jean Peuquoy; and all three fought so well, and showed such marvellous prowess, that they drove back the assailants three times. Gabriel, above all, gave himself up to the work with a joyous heart; and Jean Peuquoy was so astounded at the mighty blows of the sword which he saw him dealing to right and left that he came very near being killed himself in his openmouthed admiration, and Gabriel was compelled on two different occasions to save his admirer's life.

So the worthy bourgeois swore upon the spot an everlasting worship and devotion for the viscount. He even exclaimed in his enthusiasm that he regretted his native town a little less because he should have another attachment to cherish; and that although it was true that St. Quentin had given him his life, Vicomte d'Exmès had preserved it for him!

Nevertheless, despite his noble efforts, the town absolutely could hold out no longer; the ramparts were no more than one unbroken breach; and Gabriel, Du Breuil, and Jean Peuquoy were still fighting away, while the streets behind them were filled with the enemy, who had gained possession of the town.

But the gallant little city had nobly held out for seventeen days, and had successfully resisted eleven assaults.

Twelve days had passed since Gabriel's arrival; and he had surpassed the terms of his promise to the king by twice forty-eight hours!

CHAPTER XXXV
ARNAULD DU THILL IS STILL
UP TO HIS LITTLE TRICKS

At first, pillage and slaughter were the order of the day; but Philibert issued a very strict prohibition, and put a speedy end to the confusion; and Admiral de Coligny having been taken before him, Philibert complimented him in the highest terms.

"I cannot punish gallantry; and the town of St. Quentin will be treated no more harshly than if she had capitulated the day that we sat down before the walls."

And the victor, as high-minded as the vanquished, allowed the admiral to discuss with him the conditions which should be imposed.

St. Quentin was naturally declared a Spanish town; but those of the people who preferred not to accept the domination of the stranger were at liberty to withdraw, giving, up all claim to their houses, however. Moreover, everybody, soldiers and citizens, were free from that moment; and Philibert retained only fifty prisoners of all ages and conditions and both sexes, selected by him or his captains, for the purpose of holding them to ransom, and thus procuring means wherewith to pay the arrears due to the troops. The property and persons of all others were to be respected; and Philibert gave his personal attention to the prevention of disorder. However, as Coligny had exhausted all his personal fortune in maintaining the siege, he was courteous enough to ask no ransom for him. The admiral would be free the next day to join his uncle, the Constable de Montmorency, at Paris, who had not found his conquerors so disinterested after the battle of St. Laurent, but had furnished ransom in a round sum, which France would eventually pay in one way or another, no doubt; but Philibert Emmanuel considered it an honor to become the friend of Gaspard, and did not choose to put a price upon his freedom. His principal officers and the wealthiest citizens would suffice to pay the expenses of the siege.

These terms, which were certainly more favorable than he had any right to expect, were accepted submissively by Coligny, and by the citizens with mingled sentiments of joy and fear. The important question to be solved was, upon whom would the dreaded choice of Philibert Emmanuel and his officers fall? That was what the next day would bring forth; and when that day came, the proudest became very lowly, and the wealthiest made a great deal of talk about their poverty.

Arnauld du Thill, who was a very expert and ingenious haggler, passed the night thinking over matters, and finally hit upon a combination which might, he thought, turn out very profitably for him. He arrayed himself as handsomely as possible, and from an early hour in the morning walked proudly up and down the streets, which were filled to overflowing with the victorious besiegers of all nations,—German, English, Spaniards, etc.

"What a Tower of Babel!" said Arnauld, anxiously, hearing nothing but foreign jargon. "With the few English words that I know I shall never be able to enter into negotiations with any of these jabberers. Some say, 'Carajo'!' others, 'Goddam!' and others still, 'Tausend saperment!' and not one —"

"*Tripes et boyaux*! Will you halt, you villain?" shouted a harsh voice behind Arnauld at this moment.

Arnauld turned hurriedly about toward the man, who, despite his very marked English accent, seemed thus familiar with the niceties of the French tongue.

He was a great fellow, with a pale face and sandy hair, who had the appearance of being a sharp trader and a stupid man. Arnauld du Thill recognized an Englishman at the first glance.

"What can I do for you?" he asked.

"I make you my prisoner; that's what you can do for me," replied the man, who embellished his discourse with English slang, which Arnauld tried hard to imitate, so as to make himself more intelligible to his interlocutor.

"Why do you make me your prisoner rather than another?" he continued?—"rather than that weaver over there, for instance?"

"Because you are fitted out better than the weaver," was the Englishman's reply.

"Oh, yes!" Arnauld retorted. "And by what right, please, do you arrest me?—you who are only a simple archer, I think."

"Oh, I am not acting on my own account, but in the name of my master, Lord Grey, who commands the English archers, and to whom Duke Philibert Emmanuel has allotted, as his share in the prize, three prisoners,— two noblemen and one bourgeois,—with whatever ransom he may be able to get for them. Now, my master, who knows that I have two hands and a pair of eyes, instructed me to follow the chase and ferret out three prisoners of value for him. You are the best game I have fallen in with yet; so I take you by the collar, Messire Bourgeois."

"It is a great honor for a poor squire," retorted Arnauld, modestly. "Will your master feed me well, do you think?"

"Blackguard! Do you suppose he proposes to feed you for long?" said the archer.

"Until it pleases him to set me at liberty, I imagine that he surely will not let me die of hunger."

"Hm!" said the archer. "Can it be that I have taken a poor old naked wolf for a fox with a magnificent pelt?"

"I am afraid so, my lord archer," said Arnauld; "and if Lord Grey, your master, has promised you a commission according to the value of the prizes you obtain for him, I fear that twenty or thirty blows with a club will be the only benefit you will derive from me. What I say is not for the purpose of deceiving you, and I advise you to try it."

"You rascal! It may well be that you are right!" rejoined the Englishman, examining the sly fellow more closely; "and I may lose with you what Lord Grey promised to give me,—one livre in every hundred that he realizes from his prisoners."

"This is the man for me," thought Arnauld. "Hallo, then," said he, aloud, "my hostile friend, if I put you in a way to lay your hand on a very rich prize,—on a prisoner worth ten thousand Tours livres, for instance,— would you be the man to show some little gratitude to me?"

"Ten thousand Tours livres!" cried the Englishman. "Prisoners of that sort are pretty scarce. Why, I should get a hundred livres then,—not a bad nest-egg."

"Yes; but you would have to give fifty to the friend who put it in your way. That's fair, is it not?"

"Oh, well, I'll do it," said Lord Grey's archer, after a momentary hesitation. "But take me to the man at once, and give me his name."

"We need not go far to find him," Arnauld responded. "Just a few steps this way! See, I don't wish to show myself with you on the square; let me hide behind the corner of this house. There; now you go on. Do you see on the balcony of that house a gentleman talking with a citizen?"

"I do," said the Briton. "Is that my man?"

"That is our man."

"His name?"

"Vicomte d'Exmès."

"Oh, indeed!" rejoined the archer. "So that is Vicomte d'Exmès. He is very handsomely spoken of at the camp. Is he as wealthy as he is gallant?"

"I will answer to you for that."

"Do you know him very well, then, Master?"

"*Pardieu*! I am his squire."

"Ah, Judas!" The archer could not restrain the exclamation.

"No," was Arnauld's unmoved comment; "for Judas was hanged, and I shall not be."

"It may be that you will find it difficult to escape," said the archer, who had his jocose moments.

"Well, we shall see," retorted Arnauld; "but no more talk. Do you hold to our bargain,—yes or no?"

"It's done!" the Englishman replied; "and I will escort your master to my lord. Afterward you shall point out to me another nobleman and some substantial citizen, if you know any such."

"I know the right ones at the same price,—half of your commission."

"You shall have it, you emissary of the devil!"

"I am yours rather," said Arnauld. "But, come, no trickery! Between two rascals each must be careful of his footing. Besides, I should find you again sure. Will your master pay cash?"

"Cash in advance; you shall come with us to my lord upon the pretext of accompanying your viscount; I shall get my pay, and will give you your share at once. But you in return, being very grateful, as you should be, will help me to find my second and third prizes, won't you?"

"We'll see about that," said Arnauld. "Let us attend to the first one now."

"That's a very short matter," said the archer. "Your master is too rough in time of war not to be mild and gentle in time of peace; we know that. Take two minutes' start of me, and take up your station behind him; you will see that I know my business."

Arnauld left his worthy pupil, entered the town-hall, and with a smile on his false face went into the room where Gabriel was talking with Jean Peuquoy, and asked him if he had need of him. He was still speaking when the archer came in with an apologetic air. He went straight up to the viscount, who looked at him with much amazement, and bowing low,—

"Have I the honor of speaking to Monseigneur le Vicomte d'Exmès?" he asked with such a look as every merchant has for his merchandise.

"I am Vicomte d'Exmès," Gabriel replied with increasing wonder; "what do you want with me?"

"Your sword, Monseigneur," said the archer, bowing almost to the floor.

"You!" exclaimed Gabriel, recoiling from him with a motion of inexpressible contempt.

"In the name of my master, Lord Grey, Monseigneur," replied the modest archer, "you are named as one of the fifty prisoners whom Monseigneur l'Amiral is to put in the hands of the victors. Don't blame poor me for being forced to be the bearer of this unpleasant information."

"Blame you for it!" said Gabriel, "no! But Lord Grey, a gentleman, forsooth! might have taken the trouble to ask me for my sword himself. It is to him that I desire to hand it; do you understand?"

"As Monseigneur pleases."

"And I am glad to believe that he will accept a ransom for me?"

"Oh, never fear, never fear, Monseigneur!" said the archer, eagerly.

"I am at your service, then," said Gabriel.

"But this is an indignity," cried Jean Peuquoy. "You do wrong to submit thus, Monseigneur. Refuse to go; for you are not of St. Quentin,—you are not of the town!"

"Master Jean Peuquoy is right," Arnauld du Thill earnestly interposed, stealthily making a sign to the archer to denounce the citizen to him. "Yes, Master Jean Peuquoy has put his finger upon the truth: Monseigneur is not of St. Quentin; and Master Jean Peuquoy knows it. Yes, indeed, he knows the whole town! He has been burgher for forty years, and syndic of his guild, and captain of the bowmen! What have you to say to that, Englishman?"

"I have just this to say," replied the Briton, who had taken his cue,—"that if this is Master Jean Peuquoy, I have an order to arrest him too, for his name is on my list."

"Me!" ejaculated the worthy burgher.

"Even you, Master," was the response.

Peuquoy looked inquiringly at Gabriel.

"Alas, Messire Jean," said Vicomte d'Exmès, sighing in spite of himself, "I think that our best plan, after having done our duty as soldiers during the battle, will be to bow to the rights of the victors, now that the battle is done. Let us submit, Master Jean Peuquoy."

"And go with this fellow?" asked Peuquoy.

"To be sure, my good friend; and glad am I in this latest trial not to be separated from you."

"That is very true, Monseigneur," said Peuquoy, with emotion; "and you are very kind to say it. Besides, when such a noble and gallant captain as yourself accepts his lot with equanimity, ought an unfortunate burgher like myself to complain? Let us go. Varlet," he went on, addressing the archer, "it is done; and I am your prisoner or your master's."

"Remember that you are going with me to Lord Grey's quarters," rejoined the archer, "where you will remain, if you please, until you have furnished a handsome ransom."

"Where I will remain forever, son of the evil one!" cried Jean Peuquoy. "Your English master shall never know the color of my crowns; I will die first. If he is a Christian, he will have to support me until my last hour; and I forewarn you that I am a very hearty eater."

The archer cast a terrified glance in the direction of Arnauld du Thill; but the latter reassured him with a nod, and pointed to Gabriel, who was laughing at his friend's outburst. The Englishman knew how to take a joke, and began to laugh heartily.

"As to that, Monseigneur," said he, "and you, Messire, I am going to take—"

"You are going to precede us to Lord Grey's quarters," Gabriel interrupted haughtily; "and we will arrange details with your master."

"As Monseigneur pleases," said the archer, with humility.

Walking in front of them, but taking good care to keep an eye on them, he escorted the gentleman and the burgher to Lord Grey's quarters, while Arnauld du Thill followed at some distance.

Lord Grey was a dull-witted, phlegmatic soldier, bored to death, and himself a bore, for whom war was mere trafficking, and who was in a very bad humor at receiving no pay for himself and his troops except such as he might get from the ransom of three unfortunate prisoners. He received Gabriel and Jean Peuquoy with cold dignity.

"So it is Vicomte d'Exmès whom I have the honor to have for my prisoner," said he, looking at Gabriel with curiosity. "You have given us a good deal of trouble, Monsieur; and if I were to demand for your ransom all that you have cost King Philip II., I fancy that King Henri's France could hardly pay it."

"I did my best," said Gabriel, simply.

"Your best is very good; and I congratulate you!" retorted Lord Grey. "But that is not the question now. The chances of war, although you did wonders to prevent it, have put you in my power, you and your mighty sword. Oh, keep it, Monsieur, keep it," he added, as he saw that Gabriel made a movement as if to hand it to him. "But what can you offer to redeem my right to your service? Let us arrange that matter. I am well aware that gallantry and wealth do not always go together, unluckily. However, I cannot afford to forego my right entirely. Would five thousand crowns seem a fitting price for you to pay for your liberty?"

"No, my Lord," said Gabriel.

"No? You think it too much?" rejoined Lord Grey. "Ah, but this accursed war! And such a poor country! Come, four thousand crowns is not too much, by Heaven!"

"It is not enough, my Lord," replied Gabriel, coolly.

"What, Monsieur! what did you say?" cried the Englishman.

"I say," Gabriel replied, "that you misunderstood my words, my Lord. You asked me if five thousand crowns seemed to me a reasonable ransom, and I said no; for in my own opinion I am worth twice that, my Lord."

"Very well!" rejoined Lord Grey; "and in truth, your king may very well spare that amount to retain such a gallant soldier as you."

"I trust I shall not be obliged to call upon the king," said Gabriel; "for my private fortune, I am sure, will enable me to meet this unforeseen expenditure, and to deal directly with you in this matter."

"So much the better!" said Lord Grey, somewhat surprised. "That makes ten thousand crowns that you are to account to me for, then; and I beg your pardon, but when may I expect the payment?"

"You will readily understand," said Gabriel, "that I brought no such sum with me to a besieged town; on the other hand, the resources of Monsieur de Coligny and his friends, I believe, like my own, have run pretty low, therefore I do not wish to trouble them by requesting a loan. But if you will allow me a little time, I can send for it from Paris—"

"Very well!" said Lord Grey; "meanwhile I will content myself with your word, which is as good as gold. But as business is business, and as a certain misunderstanding that exists between my soldiers and the Spaniards may oblige me to return to England, you will not take it ill if I keep you in custody until the full quittance of the sum agreed upon,—not in this Spanish town of St. Quentin, which I am on the point of leaving, but at Calais, which is in English hands, and of which my brother-in-law, Lord Wentworth, is governor. Does that arrangement meet your views?"

"To admiration!" said Gabriel, on whose pale lips a bitter smile appeared. "I only ask your leave to send my squire to Paris to procure the gold, so that neither my captivity nor your confidence may be protracted any further than is necessary."

"Nothing could be more reasonable," Lord Grey replied; "and pending the return of your emissary, be assured that you will be treated by my brother-in-law with all the consideration that is due you. You will have all possible freedom at Calais, the more so because it is a strong fortified town; and Lord Wentworth will take good care of you, for he is more addicted to feasting and debauchery than he ought to be. But that is his own affair; fortunately his wife, who was my sister, is dead. I only wished to tell you that you would not be likely to be bored."

Gabriel bowed without replying.

"And now, Master," resumed Lord Grey, turning to Jean Peuquoy, who had shrugged his shoulders in wonder more than once during the foregoing scene,—"now for you. You are, I see, the burgher who has been allotted to me with two gentlemen."

"I am Jean Peuquoy, my Lord."

"Well, Jean Peuquoy, what ransom may we ask for you?"

"Oh, I am going to dicker with you, Monseigneur! Trader against trader, as they say. Oh, you may knit your brows! I am not proud, my Lord, and in my own opinion I am not worth ten livres."

"Nonsense!" said Lord Grey, scornfully. "You shall pay a hundred livres; that is hardly as much as I promised the archer who brought you here."

"A hundred livres! So be it, my Lord, if you value me so high," retorted the shrewd captain of the bowmen. "But you don't want a hundred livres cash, do you?"

"What! Haven't you that petty sum, even?"

"I had it, my Lord," said Peuquoy, "but I gave it all to the poor and the wounded during the siege."

"But you have friends, surely, or kinsmen?"

"Friends? Ah, we mustn't rely too much upon friends, my Lord. And kinsmen? No, I have none: my wife died childless, and I have no brother; only a cousin—"

"Well, and this cousin?" asked Lord Grey, with some signs of losing patience.

"This cousin, my Lord, who will undoubtedly pay the sum you ask of me, happens to live at Calais."

"Ah, indeed!" said Lord Grey, suspiciously.

"*Mon Dieu*! yes, my Lord," added Jean Peuquoy, with every appearance of absolute sincerity; "my cousin's name is Pierre Peuquoy, and he has been for more than thirty years a gunsmith at the sign of the God Mars, Rue du Martroi."

"And he is devoted to you, is he?" asked Lord Grey.

"I believe him to be, my Lord! I am the last of the Peuquoys of my branch; so that it goes without saying that his feeling for me amounts to veneration. More than two centuries ago, one of our ancestral Peuquoys had two sons, one of whom became a weaver and settled at St. Quentin, while the other adopted the armorer's trade, and took up his abode at Calais. Ever since that time the St. Quentin Peuquoys have been weavers, and the Calais Peuquoys have continued to forge arms and armor. But although separated, distance has never cooled their mutual affection; and they have always assisted each other, as occasion arose, and as befits those bound together by ties of blood, and descendants of the same ancestor. I am sure that Pierre will loan me the sum necessary to redeem my freedom; nevertheless, I have not seen this good cousin of mine for ten years,—for you English are by no means free with your permission to us Frenchmen to enter your strong towns."

"Yes, yes," said Lord Grey, pleasantly, "for more than two hundred and ten years the Calais Peuquoys have been Englishmen."

"Oh!" cried Jean, warmly, "the Peuquoys—"

Then he suddenly interrupted himself.

"Well, well," Lord Grey rejoined in surprise, "the Peuquoys—"

"The Peuquoys, my Lord," said Jean, twirling his cap about in an embarrassed way,—"the Peuquoys do not concern themselves with politics, that is what I was about to say. Whether they are English or French, so long as they possess an anvil with which to earn their daily bread at Calais, and a shuttle here in St. Quentin, the Peuquoys have no fault to find."

"Well, who knows?" said Lord Grey, jocosely; "perhaps you will set up for yourself as a weaver in Calais, and thus become a subject of Queen Mary. Then the Peuquoys will be united at last after so many years."

"Upon my word! that may very well be," said Jean, artlessly.

Gabriel could not conceal his surprise at hearing the gallant burgher, who had taken such an heroic part in the defence of his town, talk as calmly about becoming an Englishman as of changing his helmet; but a wink which Jean Peuquoy bestowed upon him while Lord Grey was looking the other way reassured Gabriel as to his friend's loyalty, and convinced him that some mystery lay hidden under his joking.

Lord Grey soon dismissed them both.

"To-morrow we will leave St. Quentin for Calais together," he said. "Meanwhile you are at liberty to make such preparations as you choose, and to take your leave of your friends. I allow you to go on your parole so much the more readily," said he, with his peculiar delicacy, "because you will be challenged at the gates, and no one is allowed to leave the town without a permit from the governor."

Gabriel saluted Lord Grey without a word, and left the house with Jean Peuquoy, without noticing that his squire, Martin-Guerre, remained behind instead of following him.

"What is your intention, my friend?" he said to Peuquoy, when they were in the street. "Is it possible that you haven't a hundred crowns to pay your ransom with at once? Why do you persist in making this journey to Calais? Does this armorer cousin really exist? What strange object have you in all this?"

"Hush!" replied Jean Peuquoy, mysteriously. "In this Spanish atmosphere I hardly dare to risk a word. You can rely upon your squire, Martin-Guerre, can you not?"

"I will answer for him," Gabriel answered; "notwithstanding some lapses of memory and occasional backsliding, his is the most faithful heart in the world."

"Good!" said Peuquoy. "We must not send him at once from here, to obtain the money for your ransom at Paris, but take him to Calais with us, and let him start from there. We cannot have too many pairs of eyes."

"But what do these precautions mean, pray?" asked Gabriel. "I see: you have no relative at all in Calais?"

"Indeed I have," replied Peuquoy, eagerly. "Pierre Peuquoy really exists, and just as really has he been brought up to love and sigh for his former country, France; and like me, he stands ready to strike a blow in case of need, if you should chance to conceive while in that city some such heroic plan as you have put in execution here so many times."

"My noble friend," Gabriel responded, pressing the burgher's hand, "I divine your meaning; but you estimate my abilities too high, and judge me by your own measure. You know not how much selfishness there is in what you call my heroism; nor do you know that in the future, a sacred duty— even more sacred, if that can be, than my country's glory—has the first and only claim upon me."

"Well, then," said Jean Peuquoy, "you will fulfil that duty as you have all your other duties! And among the others," he added, lowering his voice, "there may be an opportunity afforded which will call upon you to take your revenge at Calais for St. Quentin."

CHAPTER XXXVI
CONTINUATION OF MASTER ARNAULD
DU THILL'S HONORABLE NEGOTIATIONS

Let us now leave the young captain and the old burgher to their dreams of conquest, and return to the squire and the archer settling their accounts in Lord Grey's house.

The archer, after the two prisoners had taken their leave, asked for his promised commission from his master, who gave it to him without much demur, being well-satisfied with the skilful selection his emissary had made.

Arnauld du Thill, in turn, waited for his share, which, we must do the Englishman the justice to say, he brought him in good faith. He found Arnauld in a corner scrawling some fresh lines on the Constable de Montmorency's endless account, and muttering to himself,—

"For having cleverly arranged to have Vicomte d'Exmès included among the prisoners of war, and having thus relieved Monseigneur le Connétable from said viscount for a time—"

"What are you doing there, my friend?" said the archer, seizing him by the shoulder.

"What am I doing? Making out an account," replied the false Martin-Guerre. "How does ours stand?"

"Here is what I owe you," said the archer, putting the crowns in Arnauld's hands, which he proceeded to count very carefully. "You see that I have kept my promise, and don't regret parting with the money. You have put me on the track of two unexceptional prisoners.—especially your master, who never chaffered or haggled, but did just the opposite. Old Graybeard made some trouble, to be sure; but he was not very bad for a citizen, and without your help I have no doubt I should have fared worse."

"I believe you," said Arnauld, pocketing the coins.

"But come now," said the archer, "our work isn't all done yet. You see that I am good pay; and you must stir yourself to point out my third prize now,—the second noble prisoner to whom we are entitled."

"By the mass!" Arnauld replied, "I have nothing more to say, and you have only to choose."

"I know that very well; and what I want you to do is to help me choose among all the men and women, old men and children of noble birth, whom we may lay our hands upon in this good town."

"What!" asked Arnauld, "do women count too?"

"Indeed they do," said the Englishman, "and better than all; and if you know one who is young and beautiful as well as noble and rich, we shall have a pretty plum to divide, for Lord Grey will dispose of her at a large advance to his brother-in-law, Lord Wentworth, who likes female prisoners much better than male, so far as one can judge."

"Unfortunately I know of none," said Arnauld du Thill. "And yet! but no, no, it isn't possible."

"Why so, comrade? Are we not masters and victors here! And besides, nobody but the admiral was exempted by the terms of the capitulation."

"Very true," said Arnauld; "but the fair damsel whom I have in mind must not come near my master or even see him again; and to keep them in captivity in the same town would be but a poor way to keep them apart."

"Bah! do you suppose that my Lord Wentworth won't know enough to keep his pretty bird out of sight, and for himself alone?" asked the archer.

"Yes, at Calais," said Arnauld, meditating; "but on the way? My master will have ample opportunity to see her and speak with her."

"Not if I order otherwise," was the response. "We shall travel in two sections, one of which will be in advance of the other at least two hours, consequently there will be ample distance between the knight and his lady, if that will please you."

"Yes, but what will the old constable say?" asked Arnauld, aloud. "If he knows that I have had a hand in this transaction, he will hang me up at short notice!"

"Why should he know? Why need any one know?" was the suggestion of the tempter. "You surely will not be the one to talk about it; and as surely your money will not tell whence it came—"

"And the money would be forthcoming, eh?" asked Arnauld.

"There will be half of it for you."

"What a pity!" rejoined the squire; "for it would be a handsome sum, I fancy, and I don't imagine the father would haggle about it."

"Is he a duke or a prince?" asked the archer.

"He is a king, comrade, and is called Henri, the second of that name."

"A daughter of the king here!" cried the Englishman. "Upon my soul, if you don't tell me at once where I can find the gentle dove, I shall feel obliged to strangle you, my good fellow! A daughter of the king!"

"And a pearl of beauty too," said Arnauld.

"Oho! My Lord Wentworth will lose his head over her," the archer replied. "Comrade," he added in a solemn tone, drawing forth his purse, and opening it before Arnauld's fascinated eyes, "this and its contents are yours in exchange for the name and abode of the fair one."

"Done!" said Arnauld, unable to resist, and seizing the purse.

"Her name?" asked the archer.

"Diane de Castro, called Sister Bénie."

"And her abode?"

"The Benedictine convent."

"I fly," cried the Englishman, disappearing.

"That's all right," said Arnauld to himself, turning about to seek his master,—"that's all right; I shall not put this down on the constable's account."

CHAPTER XXXVII
LORD WENTWORTH

Three days later, on the 1st of September, Lord Wentworth, governor of Calais, having received final instructions from his brother-in-law, Lord Grey, and having seen him off for England, mounted his horse and rode back to his hotel, where Gabriel and Jean Peuquoy were then quartered, as well as Diane, who was in another part of the house.

Madame de Castro had no idea that her lover was so near; and in conformity with the promise given to Arnauld by Lord Grey's minion, she had not had the least opportunity of communicating with him after leaving St. Quentin.

Lord Wentworth offered a most striking contrast to his brother-in-law; for the former was as affable and approachable and open-handed as the latter was arrogant and cold and covetous. He was a tall, fine-looking man, with most refined manners. He was apparently about forty; a few white hairs were already scattered here and there among his profuse black locks, which were naturally curly. But his youthful air and the eager fire in his gray eyes showed that the impetuous passion of a young man was still dominant within him; and he led as joyous and active a life as if he were still only twenty.

He went first into the hall where Vicomte d'Exmès and Jean Peuquoy were awaiting him, and saluted them affably and smilingly as his guests and not his prisoners.

"Welcome to my house, Monsieur, and you too, Master," said he. "I am very much indebted to my dear brother-in-law for having brought you here, Monsieur le Vicomte; and I have double cause to rejoice in the taking of St. Quentin. Pardon me; but in this gloomy abode of war, where I am confined, agreeable distractions are of such rare occurrence, and society is so limited, that I am very happy to find some one from time to time whom it is a pleasure to converse with; and I fear that my own selfishness will lead me to wish that your ransom may be delayed as long as possible."

"It is likely to be delayed longer than I supposed, my Lord," Gabriel replied. "Lord Grey may have told you that my squire, whom I intended to send to Paris to bring the money, fell into a dispute *en route*, being drunk at the time, with one of the escort, and received a wound in the head, slight, it is true, but which I fear will detain him at Calais longer than I hoped."

"So much the worse for the poor fellow, and so much the better for me," said Lord Wentworth.

"You are too kind, my Lord," said Gabriel, with a sad smile.

"No, indeed; upon my word, there's no kindness about it. True kindness, no doubt, would move me to allow you to start for Paris yourself at once, on parole. But I tell you again, I am too selfish and too bored to think of that; and I have no difficulty, although from different motives, in entering into the suspicious intentions of my brother-in-law, who made me solemnly promise not to give you your liberty except in exchange for a bag of crowns. What do you say? Shall we be prisoners together, and do our best to sweeten the tedium of captivity for each other?"

Gabriel bowed without saying a word. He would have liked much better that Lord Wentworth should have accepted his parole and left him free to go about his task. But could he, a perfect stranger, expect such confidence?

He comforted himself a little with the thought that Coligny was probably with Henri II. at that moment. He had enjoined upon him to report to the king what he had been able to do toward prolonging the resistance of St. Quentin. Surely his noble friend could not have failed him! And Henri, true to his royal word, was perhaps waiting but-for the son's return to fulfil his promise with regard to the father.

It was not surprising that Gabriel was not altogether able to master his uneasiness, because of its twofold character; he had not even succeeded in catching a glimpse of another person equally dear to him before leaving St. Quentin. So he heartily cursed the mishap that had befallen that incorrigible drunkard, Martin-Guerre, and was far from sharing Jean Peuquoy's satisfaction on that point; for the worthy burgher was secretly delighted to find his mysterious schemes forwarded by this very delay which caused Gabriel so much sorrow.

Meanwhile Lord Wentworth, not choosing to notice his prisoner's gloomy distraction, continued,—

"Moreover, Monsieur d'Exmès, I shall do my best not to be too harsh a jailer; and to prove to you at once that my actions are directed by no insulting suspicion, I will cheerfully give you permission to go in and out at your will, and to go wherever you please in the town, if you will give me your parole that you will not attempt to escape."

At this, Jean Peuquoy could not restrain a movement of unequivocal satisfaction; and to communicate it to Gabriel, he gave a sharp twitch at the young man's coat-tail, and thereby considerably surprised him.

"I accept gratefully, my Lord," Gabriel replied to the governor's courteous offer; "and you have my word of honor that I will not think of any such attempt."

"That is quite satisfactory, Monsieur," said Lord Wentworth; "and if the hospitality which it is in my power, and which duty and pleasure prompt me, to offer you (although my temporary quarters are but ill adapted to your proper entertainment) seems burdensome and perchance tiresome, why, you must not feel at all constrained to accept it; rest assured I shall not take it ill of you in the least if you prefer more free and more convenient quarters, such as you can easily find in Calais, to the poor accommodations which I can place at your disposal."

"Oh, Monsieur le Vicomte," said Jean Peuquoy, in a tone of entreaty, "if you would only condescend to accept the best chamber in the house of my cousin, Pierre Peuquoy the armorer, you would make him very proud, and you would fill my cup of happiness, I swear to you!"

And the worthy man accompanied these words with a meaning gesture; for good Peuquoy was all mystery and reticence now, and had become so obscure as almost to inspire fear.

"Thanks, my friend," said Gabriel; "but really, to take advantage of such permission would be perhaps to abuse it."

"No, I assure you," said Lord Wentworth, warmly, "you are entirely at liberty to accept this lodging at Pierre Peuquoy's. He is a rich bourgeois, energetic and skilful at his trade, and the honestest fellow imaginable. I know him well, for I have often bought arms of him; and he has a very pretty creature at his house too,—his daughter or his wife, I am not very clear which."

"His sister, my Lord," said Jean Peuquoy,—"my cousin Babette. Oh, yes, she is very comely; and if only I were not so old! But the Peuquoys won't die out after all; Pierre has lost his wife, but she left him two sturdy boys, who will amuse you, Monsieur le Vicomte, if you choose to accept my cousin's very cordial hospitality."

"I not only authorize you to accept it, but engage that you will do so," added Lord Wentworth.

Indeed, Gabriel began to think, and not unreasonably, that the handsome and courtly governor of Calais was very willing to disencumber himself, for private reasons, of a companion who would be always in his house, and who, by virtue of the very freedom that he allowed him, might interfere with his own. In fact, Lord Wentworth did reason thus; for as Lord Grey had expressed it elegantly to Arnauld, he preferred female prisoners to male.

Gabriel no longer had any scruples, and said, turning to Jean Peuquoy with a smile, —

"Since Lord Wentworth permits me, my friend, I will stay at your cousin's."

Jean Peuquoy almost leaped for joy.

"Upon my word, I really think that you do very wisely," said Lord Wentworth. "Not that I should not have been delighted to entertain you as best I could; but in a house guarded night and day by soldiers, and where my tedious authority requires me to maintain strict rules, you might not have found yourself always at your ease, as you will with the brave armorer. And a young man has need to be at his ease, we all know."

"You seem to know it, at all events," said Gabriel, laughing; "and I can see that you know the full value of independence."

"Yes, indeed I do!" rejoined Lord Wentworth, in the same playful tone; "I am not yet old enough to despise liberty."

Then, turning to Jean Peuquoy, —

"Do you rely upon your cousin's purse, Master Peuquoy," said he, "in your own behalf, as you rely upon his house when Monsieur d'Exmès's welfare is in question? Lord Grey told me that you expected to borrow the hundred crowns agreed upon for your ransom."

"Whatever Pierre owns belongs to Jean," was the burgher's sententious reply; "it is always so with the Peuquoys. I was so sure beforehand that my cousin's house was mine that I have already sent Monsieur d'Exmès's wounded squire there; and I am so sure too that his purse is as open to me as his door that I beg you to send one of your people with me to bring back the sum agreed upon."

"Useless, Master Peuquoy," said Lord Wentworth; "and you also are free to go on parole. I will come and call upon Vicomte d'Exmès at Pierre Peuquoy's to-morrow or the next day; and I will select, as an equivalent of the sum due my brother-in-law, one of the beautiful suits of armor which your cousin makes so well."

"As you please, my Lord," said Jean.

"Meanwhile, Monsieur d'Exmès," said the governor, "need I say to you that as often as you choose to knock at my door you will be as welcome as you are at liberty not to do it at all? I repeat, life is rather dull at Calais, as you will soon discover, no doubt; and you will enter into an alliance with me, I trust, against our common enemy, ennui. Your presence is a very great boon, by which I desire to profit as much as possible. If you keep away from me, I shall importune you, I give you fair warning; and remember too, that I only give you a sort of half liberty, and that the friend ought to bring the prisoner here with him often."

"Thanks, my Lord," said Gabriel; "I accept with gratitude all your kindness. By way of revenge," he added, smiling; "for war has its sudden changes, and the friend of to-day may become the enemy of to-morrow."

"Oh," said Lord Wentworth, "I am safe, too safe, alas! behind these impregnable walls. If the French were fated to recapture Calais, they would not have waited two hundred years for it. I am quite tranquil about it; and if it ever falls to your lot to do the honors of Paris to me, it will be in time of peace, I fancy."

"Let us leave it in God's hands, my Lord," said Gabriel. "Monsieur de Coligny, whom I have just left, used to say that man's wisest course was to wait."

"Very true; and meanwhile to live as happily as possible. Apropos, Monsieur, it has occurred to me that you must be badly off for funds; you know that my purse is at your disposal."

"Thanks again, my Lord; my own, though not sufficiently well lined to allow me to pay my ransom on the spot, is at least amply furnished to defray the cost of my stay here. My only real anxiety, I confess, is lest your cousin's house, Master Peuquoy, cannot open its doors thus unexpectedly to three new guests without inconvenience; and in that case I should much prefer to go in search of another lodging, where for a few crowns—"

"You are joking," interrupted Jean, eagerly; "for Pierre's house is large enough, thank God, to hold three whole families, if necessary. In the provinces they don't build so stingily and in such narrow places as in Paris."

"Very true," said Lord Wentworth; "and I promise you, Monsieur d'Exmès, that the armorer's dwelling is not unworthy of a captain. A more numerous suite than yours could easily be accommodated there; and two trades might be carried oil under its roof without inconvenience. Was it not your intention, Master Peuquoy, to settle there and carry on your occupation of weaving? Lord Grey said something of such a plan, which I shall be very glad to see carried out."

"And which very possibly will be carried out," said Jean. "If Calais and St. Quentin are to belong to the same masters, I should prefer to be near my family."

"Yes," rejoined Lord Wentworth, who misunderstood the meaning of the cunning burgher's words; "yes, it may be that St. Quentin will be an English town before long. But I am keeping you," he added; "and after the fatigues of the journey, you must be in need of rest, Monsieur d'Exmès. Once more I tell you both you are free. *Au revoir*; we shall soon meet again, shall we not?"

He escorted the captain and the burgher to the door, shaking the hand of one and nodding amicably to the other, and left them to make the best of their way to the Rue du Martroi. On that street, if our readers remember, Pierre Peuquoy lived, at the sign of the God Mars, and there we shall soon find Gabriel and Jean again, if God so wills it.

"Upon my word!" said Lord Wentworth, when he had seen the last of them, "I believe that I was very shrewd in thus getting rid of having to entertain Vicomte d'Exmès in my house. He is a gentleman, and has lived at court; and if he has ever seen the fair prisoner who is in my grasp, he surely would never cease to remember her. Yes, indeed; for even I, who have not yet talked with her, was dazzled by her when she merely passed before me two hours since. How fair she is! I love her! I love her! Poor heart, so long dumb in this gloomy solitude, how you are beating now! But this youth, who seems to me so gallant and brave, might well have interfered unpleasantly, on recognizing his king's daughter, in the relations which I calculate upon establishing with Madame Diane. The presence of a fellow-countryman, perhaps a friend, would no doubt have delayed Madame de Castro's avowals, or encouraged her in her refusal. Let us have no third party in our affairs. Even if I have no disposition to have recourse in all this to means unworthy of myself, it is unnecessary for me to create obstacles."

He struck a peculiar stroke upon a bell. In a moment a lady's maid appeared.

"Jane," said Lord Wentworth, in English, "have you offered your services to this lady, as I told you?"

"Yes, my Lord."

"How is she now, Jane?"

"She appears sad, my Lord, but not overwhelmed. She has a proud look, and speaks firmly, and gives her orders mildly, but as if she were used to being obeyed."

"Very well," said the governor. "Has she partaken of the refreshment which you put before her?"

"She has scarcely touched a piece of fruit, my Lord; under the confident air that she affects, it is not difficult to detect a good deal of anxiety and suffering."

"That will do, Jane," said Lord Wentworth. "Go you back to the lady, and ask her in my name—in the name of Lord Wentworth, governor of Calais, on whom Lord Grey's rights have devolved—if she is willing to receive me. Go, and come back at once."

In a few minutes, which seemed ages to Lord Wentworth, the maid reappeared.

"Well?" he asked.

"Well, my Lord," Jane replied, "the lady not only consents, but desires to see you at once."

"Indeed! everything goes as well as possible," said Lord Wentworth to himself.

"But she has kept old Mary with her," added Jane, "and told me to come right back again."

"Very well, Jane, go. She must be obeyed in everything, you understand. Go, and say that I am but a moment behind you."

Jane went out; and Lord Wentworth, with his heart beating like a lover of twenty, began to mount the stairs which led to Diane de Castro's apartments.

"Oh, what bliss!" he said. "I love her! And she whom I love, a king's daughter too, is in my power!"

CHAPTER XXXVIII
THE AMOROUS JAILER

Diane de Castro received Lord Wentworth with the calm and modest dignity which lent an irresistible potency and charm to her angelic expression and her lovely features. Beneath her apparent calmness there was, however, much anguish of mind; and the poor girl trembled inwardly as she acknowledged the governor's salutation, and with a queenly gesture motioned him to take his seat on a couch a few paces away from her.

Then she signed to the two maids, who were apparently preparing to withdraw, to remain in the room; and as Lord Wentworth, lost in admiration, said nothing, she determined to break the silence herself.

"It is to Lord Wentworth, governor of Calais, that I am speaking, I believe?" said she.

"Lord Wentworth, Madame, your obedient servant, awaits your commands."

"My commands!" She repeated his words bitterly. "Oh, my Lord, do not say so, or I must think that you mock me! If my prayers and my supplications, in no sense commands, had been listened to, I should not be here. You know who I am, my Lord, and of what family?"

"I know, Madame, that you are Madame de Castro, the beloved daughter of King Henri II."

"Why, then, have I been made a prisoner?" asked Diane, whose voice faltered rather than became stronger as she put the question.

"For the very reason that you were a king's daughter, Madame," Wentworth replied; "because by the terms of the capitulation agreed to by Admiral de Coligny, it was stipulated that fifty prisoners should be placed in the hands of the victors, to be selected by them from all ranks, and of any age or either sex, and because they very naturally chose the most illustrious, the most dangerous, and if you will permit me to say so, those who could afford to pay the heaviest ransom."

"But how was it known," Diane rejoined, "that I was in hiding at St. Quentin under the name and in the garb of a Benedictine nun? Besides the superior of the convent, only one person in the whole town knew my secret."

"Very well! then it must have been that person who betrayed you,— that's all," said Lord Wentworth.

"Oh, no, indeed; I am sure it was not!" cried Diane, with such earnest conviction that Lord Wentworth felt stung to the heart by jealousy, and could find nothing to say in reply.

"It was the day after the capitulation of St. Quentin," continued Diane, with renewed animation. "I had fled for refuge, trembling and afraid, to the inmost corner of my cell. Some one in the parlor asked for Sister Bénie, which was my name as a novice, my Lord. It was an English soldier who inquired for me. I dreaded some misfortune, some terrible news. Nevertheless, I went down to the parlor, a prey to that dreadful curiosity which makes us even in our suffering so anxious to ascertain what causes our tears to flow. The archer, whom I had never seen before, announced that I was his prisoner. I was indignant and resisted; but what could I do against force? There were three of them; yes, my Lord, three soldiers to arrest one poor woman. I ask your pardon if this hurts you; but I am simply telling you what happened. These men seized me, and called upon me to confess that I was Diane de Castro, daughter of the King of France. I denied it at first; but as they were dragging me away, despite my denials, I asked to be taken to Monsieur l'Amiral de Coligny; and as the admiral did not know Sister Bénie, I avowed that I was she whom they named. Perhaps you believe, my Lord, that upon my avowal they yielded to my prayer and granted me the very simple favor of being taken to Monsieur l'Amiral, who would have recognized me and demanded my freedom! By no means! They simply exulted over their capture, pushed and dragged me along more quickly, and put me, or rather threw me, weeping and in despair, into a closed litter; and when, almost suffocated with sobs, and utterly overcome with grief, I nevertheless made an effort to learn whither I was being taken, I had already left St. Quentin and was on the road to Calais. Then Lord Grey, who, I was told, was in command of the escort, refused to listen to me; and I learned from a common soldier that I was his master's prisoner, and was being taken to Calais pending the payment of my ransom. Without any further information than that, I was brought here, my Lord."

"Unfortunately I can add nothing more, Madame," responded Lord Wentworth, thoughtfully.

"Nothing, my Lord!" continued Diane. "You cannot tell me why I was not allowed to speak to the superior of the Benedictines, nor to Monsieur l'Amiral! You cannot tell me for what purpose I am wanted, pray, when I was not allowed to go near those who might have announced my captivity to the king, and have sent the amount of the ransom you demand from Paris! Why this sort of secret abduction! Why was I not allowed even to see Lord Grey, who gave orders for all this, as I was informed?"

"You did see Lord Grey, Madame, a short time ago, when you passed us. It was he with whom I was talking, and who saluted you when I did."

"Pardon me, my Lord; I knew not in whose presence I was," said Diane. "But since you have talked with Lord Grey, who is your kinsman, so this maid informs me, he must have informed you of his intentions toward me."

"In fact, Madame, before taking ship for England, he did explain them to me,—indeed, he was just doing so when you were being escorted to this house. He informed me that you had been mentioned to him at St. Quentin as being the king's daughter; and that having three prisoners allotted to him for his share, he had eagerly seized upon so valuable a prize without notifying a soul, thus avoiding all dispute. His simple object was to get the largest possible ransom for you, Madame; and I was jokingly applauding my covetous brother-in-law when you passed through the room where we were talking. I saw you, Madame; and I at once realized that if you were the king's daughter by right of birth, you were a very queen by right of loveliness. From that moment, to my shame be it said, I entirely changed my opinion as to Lord Grey's plans for the future at least, if not as to what he had already done. Yes; and I no longer approved his design of holding you to ransom. I urged upon him that we might hope for much greater things,—that England and France being at war, you might be very useful as an exchange for some important prisoner, and that you might even be worth a town. In short, I at last persuaded him not to abandon so rich a prize for a few paltry crowns. You are at Calais,—a town that belongs to us, and is impregnable; we must therefore keep you in our hands and wait."

"What!" exclaimed Diane. "You gave Lord Grey such advice as that, and boast about it to my face! Oh, my Lord, why did you thus set yourself against my being set at liberty? What had I ever done to you? You had seen me only for a moment. Did you hate me, pray?"

"I had seen you for but one moment, and I loved you, Madame," said Lord Wentworth, desperately.

Diane recoiled, shuddering and turning pale.

"Jane! Mary!" she cried, calling the two attendants, who were standing apart in the embrasure of a window.

But Wentworth made an imperious sign to them, and they did not stir. Then he continued, sighing sadly,—

"Be not alarmed, Madame. I am a gentleman; and it is not you, but I, who should fear and tremble. Yes, I love you, and could no longer refrain from telling you so; yes, when I saw you pass, so sweet and lovely, and so like a goddess, my whole heart went out to you. Yes, besides, you are in my power here; and I have but to raise my hand to be obeyed. But never mind; fear nothing, for I am more in your power, alas! than you are in mine; and of the two, you are not the real prisoner. You are the queen, Madame, and I your faithful slave. Command, and I obey."

"Then, Monsieur," said Diane, with palpitating heart, "send me back to Paris, whence I will send you such sum by way of ransom as you choose to name."

Lord Wentworth hesitated a moment before he replied,—

"Anything but that, Madame: for I feel that sacrifice is beyond my strength. I tell you that one glance from your eyes has bound my life to yours forever! Here, in this place of banishment where I am caged up, it is long since my ardent heart has entertained a passion worthy of itself. As soon as I saw you, so beautiful and noble and proud, I felt that all the stored-up energy of ray soul had henceforth an object and an end. I have loved you for but two hours; but if you knew me, you would know that it is as if I had loved you ten years."

"But in Heaven's name, what is your wish, my Lord?" said Diane. "What do you hope for? What do you expect? What is your purpose?"

"I wish to see you, Madame, and to revel in your lovely and fascinating presence,—that is all. Do not for a moment suspect me of designs unworthy a gentleman. But it is my right, my blessed right, to keep you near me; and I profit by it."

"And do you suppose, my Lord," said Madame de Castro, "that such violence will drive my heart into responding to yours?"

"I do not suppose so," said Lord Wentworth, gently; "but when you see from day to day how submissive I am, and how respectful, and how eagerly I come to learn of your welfare, and to be able to feast my eyes upon you for a moment, perhaps you will be touched by the resignation of one who begs where he might command."

"And then the daughter of France, moved to pity, would become the mistress of Lord Wentworth?" was Diane's rejoinder, with a contemptuous smile.

"Then," responded the governor, "Lord Wentworth, the last scion of one of the wealthiest and most illustrious families in England, on his knees will offer his name and his life to Madame de Castro. My passion, you see, is as honorable as it is sincere."

"Is he ambitious, I wonder?" thought Diane.

"Listen, my Lord," she rejoined aloud, trying to force a smile. "I advise you to let me go, and send me to my father the king; and I will not consider myself out of your debt by the mere payment of a ransom. When the war between the two countries is at an end, as it must be sooner or later, if I cannot give you myself, I will at least obtain for you,—I give you my word,—as many, yes, more and greater, honors and dignities than you could hope for if you were my husband. Be generous, my Lord, and my gratitude shall be yours."

"I divine your thoughts, Madame," said Wentworth, bitterly; "but I am more disinterested than you think, and more ambitious as well. Of all the treasures in the whole universe, I hope only for you."

"One word more, then, my Lord, which you will perhaps understand better," said Diane, embarrassed but proud at the same time. "I am beloved by another, my Lord."

"And do you suppose I am going to deliver you to this rival by letting you go?" cried Wentworth, fairly beside himself. "No! he shall at least be as wretched as I,—more wretched, indeed, for he cannot see you, Madame. From this day only three events can deliver you: either my death,—and I am still young and vigorous; or peace between France and England,—but wars between those countries usually last a hundred years, as you know; or the taking of Calais,—but Calais is impregnable. In default of the occurrence of one of these three almost hopeless events, I fancy you will be my prisoner for a long time; for I have purchased all Lord Grey's rights over you, and I would not receive a ransom for you, even though it were an empire! As for flight, it will be better for you not to think of it; for I shall watch you, and you will see what a careful and cautious jailer a man makes who is in love."

With these words Lord Wentworth bowed low and withdrew, leaving Diane a prey to bitter despair.

Her only consolation, and that but a slight one, lay in the reflection that death was a sure refuge, which was always open for the unfortunate when danger was at its height.

CHAPTER XXXIX
THE ARMORER'S HOUSE

Pierre Peuquoy's house was located at the corner of the Rue du Martroi and the market-place. On both sides it stood upon broad wooden pillars, such as are still to be seen in the Central Market at Paris. It had two stories, besides one in the roof. On its front wood and brick and stone were arranged in curious arabesques which were symmetrical, though they seemed to have been formed at hazard. In addition the supports of the windows and the great beams showed extraordinary figures of animals twisted into all sorts of amusing shapes. The whole was homely and unpretentious, but not devoid of invention and taste. The broad, high roof projected sufficiently to afford a covering for an outside gallery with a railing, which extended around the whole second floor as in Swiss châlets.

Above the glass door of the shop hung the sign, a sort of wooden banner, so to speak, upon which was a warrior, painted in all the panoply of war, to represent the God Mars, in which undertaking he was assisted no doubt by the following inscription: "Au Dieu Mars. Pierre Peuquoy, Armurier."

On the doorstep stood a complete suit of armor, helmet, breastplate, armlets, and leggings, which served as a realistic sign to such customers as were unable to read.

Moreover, through the leaded panes of the shop-front, other outfits and arms of all sorts, offensive and defensive, could be distinguished, notwithstanding the darkness of the interior. The display of swords, above all, was remarkable for the number and variety and magnificence of the specimens.

Two apprentices, seated under the pillars, were hailing the passers-by, and making most enticing offers of their wares.

Pierre Peuquoy himself was commonly to be found in all his majesty either in his back shop, which looked out on the courtyard, or at his forge, which was set up in a shed at the end of the courtyard. He only appeared when some customer of importance, attracted by the cries of the apprentices, or it may be by Peuquoy's reputation, asked to see the master.

The back shop, which was better lighted than the one in front, served as parlor and dining-room in one. It was wainscoted in oak throughout, and had for furniture a square table with twisted feet, chairs covered with tapestry, and a superb chest of drawers on which was Pierre Peuquoy's chef d'œuvre, executed by himself under his father's eye, when he had served his apprenticeship; it was a beautiful miniature suit of armor, all inlaid with gold, and of the finest and most delicate workmanship. No one could imagine the amount of skill and patience necessary to perfect such a work of art.

Opposite the chest, in a niche in the wainscot, stood a plaster image of the Virgin with a consecrated box. Thus the thought of God was always on guard in the family's living-room.

Another room at right angles to this was almost wholly occupied by a straight wooden stairway which led to the floors above.

Pierre Peuquoy, delighted beyond measure to receive Vicomte d'Exmès and Jean beneath his roof, had actually given up the whole first floor to Gabriel and his cousin; so that there were the guest-chambers. He himself occupied the second floor with his young sister Babette and his children. The wounded squire, Arnauld du Thill, was also accommodated on the second floor; while the apprentices lodged in the attic. In all the rooms, which were convenient and snug, there was an air, if not of wealth, at least of comfort and modest abundance suited to the old-fashioned citizen of every age.

It is at table that we renew our acquaintance with Gabriel and Jean Peuquoy, just as their worthy host has finished doing the honors of a bountiful supper. Babette was waiting upon the guests; and the children were seated at a respectful distance from their elders.

"Great Heaven, Monseigneur," said the armorer, "how little you eat, if you will allow me to say so! You are all anxiety, and Jean is lost in thought; but if the repast is but modest, the heart that offers it is in the right place. At least, have a few of these grapes, for they are very scarce in our country. I learned from my grand-father, who had it from his, that in old days, when the French were masters here, the vineyards of Calais yielded bountifully, and the grapes were golden; but alas! since the town has been English, the grape deceives itself by fancying that it is in England, where it isn't accustomed to grow ripe."

Gabriel could but smile at the strange reasoning in which brave Pierre's patriotism found vent.

"Come," said he, raising his glass, "I drink to the ripening of the grapes of Calais!"

We may readily believe that the Peuquoys responded warmly to such a toast! Supper at an end, Pierre offered thanks while his guests listened, standing bareheaded. Then the children were sent to bed.

"Now you may retire, Babette," said the armorer to his sister. "See that the apprentices don't make too much noise; and before you go to your room, go with Gertrude and inquire if Monsieur le Vicomte's squire is in need of aught."

Pretty Babette blushed, and left the room with a courtesy.

"Now, my dear friend and cousin," said Pierre to Jean, "here we are alone, we three; and if you have any private communication to make to me, I am ready to hear it."

Gabriel looked at Jean in amazement, but he replied with his most serious expression,—

"I did tell you, Pierre, that I had some matters of importance to talk over with you."

"I will withdraw," said Gabriel.

"Pardon me, Monsieur le Vicomte," said Jean, "your presence at our interview is not only useful, but necessary; for without your concurrence the projects which I am about to confide to Pierre will have no chance of success."

"I will listen to you in that case, my friend," said Gabriel, relapsing into his dreamy melancholy.

"Yes, Monseigneur," said the bourgeois, "yes, listen to us; and as you listen, you will raise your head once more with hope, and perhaps (who knows?) with joy."

Gabriel smiled mournfully at the thought that joy would be an unknown friend to him while he remained powerless to do aught to obtain his father's liberty or to make clear his right to Diane's love. Nevertheless, the brave youth turned toward Jean, and motioned to him to proceed.

Then Jean looked gravely at Pierre.

"Cousin," said he, "and more than cousin,—brother,—it is for you to speak first, in order to show Monsieur d'Exmès what reliance may be placed upon your patriotism. So tell us, Pierre, in what sentiments toward France your father brought you up, and was himself reared by his father. Tell us whether you have ever become English at heart, even though you have been English by force of events for above two hundred years. Tell us, last of all, whether if the emergency should arise, you would consider that you owed your blood and your assistance to the old country of your ancestors, or to the new allegiance which has been forced upon you."

"Jean," replied the other bourgeois, with as solemn a mien as his cousin, "I do not know what I should think or how I should feel if I bore an English name, and came of English stock; but I do know by experience that when a family has once been French, whether for a moment only or for more than two centuries, every other domination becomes insupportable to the members of that family, and seems to them as hard and bitter as slavery or banishment; furthermore, that one of my forefathers, Jean, who saw Calais fall into English hands, never spoke of France before his son without weeping, or of England without bitter hate. His son did the same with his own son; and this twofold sentiment of regret and detestation has been handed down from generation to generation without losing any of its strength or changing its form. The air of our old bourgeois houses is a great preservative. The Pierre Peuquoy of two centuries ago lives again in the Pierre Peuquoy of to-day; and with the same French name, I have the same French heart, Jean. The insult as well as the grief is as of yesterday. Say not that I have two countries, Jean; there is, and there can ever be, but one! And if the time comes when I must choose between the country to which men have made me submit and the country which God has given me, be sure that I shall not hesitate."

"You hear, Monseigneur!" cried Jean, turning to Vicomte d'Exmès.

"Yes, my friend, yes, I hear; and it is grand, it is noble!" was Gabriel's reply, albeit he seemed still a little distraught.

"One word, Pierre," said Jean; "unfortunately all our fellow-countrymen here do not think with you, do they? No doubt you are the only child of France to be found in Calais at the end of two hundred years, who has not turned his back upon his mother-country."

"You are wrong, Jean," replied the armorer; "I spoke in general, and not for myself alone. I do not say that every one who bears a French name, as I do, has not forgotten his origin; but many bourgeois families never have ceased to love France, and deeply regret their separation from her; and it is among these families that the Peuquoys like to select their wives. In the civic guard, of which I am a member against my will, there is many a citizen who would break his halberd in twain rather than turn it against a French soldier."

"That's a very good thing to know," muttered Jean Peuquoy, rubbing his hands; "and you must hold some rank in this same civic guard? So well thought of and respected as you are, that goes without saying."

"No, Jean; I have persistently refused all rank, so as to avoid all responsibility."

"So much the worse, and yet so much the better! Is the duty you have to perform a hard one, Pierre? And does your turn come often?"

"Well, yes," said Pierre, "the service is both frequent and hard, because in a place like Calais, the garrison is never large enough. My turn comes the 5th of every month."

"The 5th of every month regularly, Pierre? It seems to me that the English are not prudent to fix every man's day of service in advance."

"Oh," said the armorer, shaking his head, "there is not much danger after holding the place for two centuries. Besides, they can't help being a little suspicious at all times of the civic guard, and take care to station them only at points which are naturally impregnable; for instance, I always do sentry duty on the platform of the Octagonal Tower, which is much more efficiently protected by the sea than by me, and where none but sea-gulls can approach, I think."

"Aha! so you are always on sentry duty on the platform of the Octagonal Tower on the 5th of the month, Pierre?"

"Yes; from four to six in the morning. I was allowed to select my own time, and I prefer that because during three fourths of the year I can see the sun rise out of the ocean at that hour; and that is a divine spectacle even for a poor trader like myself."

"A spectacle so divine, in fact, Pierre," said Jean Peuquoy, lowering his voice, "that if, despite the strength of the position, some bold adventurer should try to scale the side of your Octagonal Tower, you would not see him, I'll wager, so deeply absorbed would you be in contemplating it."

Pierre looked wonderingly at his cousin.

"I should not see him, to be sure," he replied after a moment's hesitation, "for I should know that no one but a Frenchman could have any interest in getting into the city; and since I am under constraint, I have no duty toward those who constrain me,—in tact, rather than repulse the assailant, I might perhaps assist him to get in."

"Well said, Pierre!" cried Jean. "You see, Monseigneur, that Pierre is a devoted Frenchman," he added, addressing Gabriel.

"Yes, indeed I do, Master," replied the latter, still paying little heed in spite of himself to an interview which seemed to him of no use. "I see that he is; but alas! what is the good of his devotion?"

"What good? I am going to tell you," was Jean's response; "for I think it is my turn now to speak. Well, then, Monsieur le Vicomte, if you choose, we can take our revenge for St. Quentin here at Calais. The English, relying upon their two centuries of possession, are slumbering in false security; this sleepy confidence will be their ruin. Monseigneur can see that we have auxiliaries within the town always ready. Let us carefully mature plans; let your intervention with the powers that he come to our aid, and my reason, even more surely than my instinct, tells me that a bold stroke will make us masters of the town. You understand me, do you not, Monseigneur?"

"Yes, yes, to be sure!" Gabriel replied, having actually heard nothing, but being aroused by this direct appeal from his revery. "Yes, your cousin wishes to return, does he not, to our fair kingdom of France,—to be transferred to some French town, Amiens, for instance? Very well; I will speak to my Lord Wentworth about it, and to Monsieur de Guise as well. The thing may easily be arranged; and my assistance, which you request, shall not fail you. Go on, my friend; I am quite at your service. Certainly I am listening."

And again he relapsed into his omnipotent distraction. For the voice he was listening to at that moment was not, in truth, Jean Peuquoy's; no, it was the voice of King Henri in his own heart, giving the order, upon hearing the admiral's account of the siege of St. Quentin, to release the Comte de Montgommery on the spot. Again, it was the voice of his father, proving to him (for he was still gloomy and jealous) that Diane was indeed the daughter of his becrowned rival. Finally, it was the voice of Diane herself, which, after so many bitter trials, was able to say to him, and which he could hear give forth those divine words of sweetest meaning, "Truly I love you!"

It is easy to understand that while dreaming such delightful dreams as these, he could hardly listen to the daring and confident schemes of the worthy Jean.

The solemn burgher appeared somewhat hurt that Gabriel had vouchsafed so little attention to a scheme which certainly did not lack grandeur and courage, and it was with some chagrin that he rejoined.

"If Monseigneur had condescended to lend a somewhat less preoccupied ear to what I was saying, he would have noticed that our ideas, Pierre's and mine, were not so personal and less contemptible than he seems to think them."

Gabriel made no response.

"He does not hear us, Jean," said Pierre Peuquoy, calling his cousin's attention to the fresh absorption of his guest. "Perhaps he has some plan, some personal passion of his own."

"At all events, his cannot be less selfish than ours," retorted Jean, in a tone not free from bitterness. "I should even say that this gentleman was indeed selfish had I not seen him defying danger with a sort of fury, and actually exposing his life too, to save mine; still, he ought to have listened when I was earnestly looking for the glory and welfare of our common country. Without him, however, with all our zealous ardor, we shall be only helpless tools, Pierre. So far we possess the right feeling! We lack brain and power."

"Never mind! the sentiment is a good one, for I heard it and understood it, brother," said the armorer.

And the two cousins solemnly grasped each other's hands.

"Meanwhile, we must give up our idea, or at least postpone trying to carry it out," said Jean; "for what can the arm do without the head, or the people without the nobility?"

And then this burgher of the olden time added with a meaning smile, —

"Until the day when the people shall be the arm and the head at once!"